W9-CEL-645

DANGEROUS

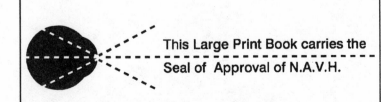

This Large Print Book carries the
Seal of Approval of N.A.V.H.

DANGEROUS

MINERVA SPENCER

THORNDIKE PRESS
A part of Gale, a Cengage Company

Farmington Hills, Mich • San Francisco • New York • Waterville, Maine
Meriden, Conn • Mason, Ohio • Chicago

GALE
A Cengage Company

Copyright © 2018 by Shantal M. LaViolette.
The Outcasts.
Thorndike Press, a part of Gale, a Cengage Company.

ALL RIGHTS RESERVED
Thorndike Press® Large Print Romance.
The text of this Large Print edition is unabridged.
Other aspects of the book may vary from the original edition.
Set in 16 pt. Plantin.

> **LIBRARY OF CONGRESS CIP DATA ON FILE.**
> **CATALOGUING IN PUBLICATION FOR THIS BOOK**
> **IS AVAILABLE FROM THE LIBRARY OF CONGRESS**
>
> ISBN-13: 978-1-4328-6288-6 (hardcover)

Published in 2019 by arrangement with Zebra Books, an imprint of Kensington Publishing Corp.

Printed in the United States of America
1 2 3 4 5 6 7 23 22 21 20 19

For Alicia Condon.
Thanks for loving my book.

ACKNOWLEDGMENTS

First and foremost I'm deeply grateful to Alicia Condon for picking my manuscript out of the pile that day in February. I am also grateful to the numerous people at Kensington who work like crazy to produce such a beautiful cover and tidy contents. Thanks to my agent, Jessica Alvarez, for gracefully putting up with my hundreds of questions. A HUGE thanks to Elizabeth Hoyt for agreeing to read a complete stranger's book and giving me such a lovely blurb!

To George McFetridge and Marla Murphy who both told me 2017 would be my year — and they were right! Thanks for the hours and hours of time you spent reading, discussing, and listening. Thanks for the type of friendship and support that helped me keep going through the rough patches. You guys are just too damned cool.

I'm also very grateful to Nancy Mayer, who knows so much about Regency England it is scary. Also a big thank-you to the wonderful Land of Enchantment Romance Authors. I am particularly grateful to my fellow historical author Louise Bergen, my carpool buddy/Yoda Jeffe Kennedy, and Tamra Baumann — all of whom are kind, knowledgeable, and all-around fabulous. Thanks to Mary Lane and Doug for listening so patiently. Thank you, Theresa Romain, for being generous to a stranger. A huge thanks to Bernard Cornwell for his invaluable help on the subject of eighteenth-century sailing times/distances — sorry my questions made your eyes cross. . . .

Love and gratitude to my mom, who really is The Best Mom in the World.

Last but not least, words cannot express my appreciation for my "hugsband" Brantly for his cheerful willingness to get in the car and buy me Pepsi and M&Ms, no matter the time of day or night.

CHAPTER ONE

London, 1811

Euphemia Marlington considered poisoning the Duke of Carlisle. After all, in the harem poison was a perfectly reasonable solution to one's problems.

Unfortunately, poison was not the answer to this particular problem.

First, she had no poison, or any idea how one acquired such a thing in this cold, confusing country.

Second, and far more important, poisoning one's father was considered bad *ton.*

The Duke of Carlisle could have no idea what was going through his daughter's mind as he paced a circuit around his massive mahogany desk, his voice droning on in a now familiar lecture. Mia ensured her father's ignorance by keeping her expression meek and mild, a skill she had perfected during the seventeen years she'd spent in Baba Hassan's palace. Appearing serene while entertaining murderous thoughts made up a large part of days spent among sixty or so women, at least fifty of whom would have liked to see her dead.

Mia realized the duke's cavernous study had gone silent. She looked up to find a pair of green eyes blazing down at her.

"Are you *listening* to me, Euphemia?" His bristly auburn eyebrows arched like angry red caterpillars.

Mia cursed her wandering attention. "I am sorry, Your Grace, but I did not fully comprehend." It was a small lie, and one that had worked well several times in the past six weeks. While it was true she still thought in Arabic, Mia understood English perfectly well.

Unless her attention had wandered.

The duke's suspicious glare told her claiming a language-related misunderstanding was no longer as compelling as it had been weeks before.

"*I said,* you must take care what you disclose to people. I have gone to great lengths to conceal the more lurid details of your past. Talk of beheadings, poisonings, and, er . . . eunuchs makes my task far more difficult." Her father's pale skin darkened at being forced to articulate the word *eunuch.*

Mia ducked her head to hide a smile.

The duke — apparently interpreting her bowed head as a sign of contrition — resumed pacing, the thick brown and gold Aubusson carpet muffling the sounds of his booted feet. He cleared his throat several times, as if to scour his mouth of the distasteful syllables he'd just been forced to utter, and continued.

"My efforts on your behalf have been promising, but that will change if you insist on disclosing every last sordid detail of your past."

Not *every* detail, Mia thought as she eyed her father from beneath lowered lashes. How would the duke react if she told him about the existence of her seventeen-year-old son, Jibril? Or if she described — in *sordid detail* — some of Sultan Babba Hassan's more exotic perversions? Was it better to appall him with the truth or to allow him to continue treating her as if she were a girl of fifteen, rather than a woman of almost three and thirty?

The answer to that question was obvious: the truth would serve nobody's interest, least of all Mia's.

"I am sorry, Your Grace," she murmured.

The duke grunted and resumed his journey around the room. "Your cousin assures me you've worked hard to conduct yourself

11

in a respectable manner. However, after this *latest* fiasco —" He shook his head, lines creasing his otherwise smooth brow.

Her father was referring to a dinner party at which she'd stated that beheading criminals was more humane than hanging them. How could Mia have known that such a simple statement would cause such consternation?

The duke stopped in front of her again. "I am concerned your cousin Rebecca is not firm enough with you. Perhaps you would benefit from a stricter hand — your aunt Philippa's, for instance?"

Mia winced. A single week under her aunt Philippa's gimlet eye had been more terrifying than seventeen years in a harem full of scheming women.

The duke nodded, an unpleasant expression taking possession of his handsome features. "Yes, I can see that in spite of the *language barrier* you understand how your life would change were I to send you to live at Burnewood Park with my sister."

The horrid suggestion made Mia's body twitch to prostrate itself — an action she'd employed with Babba Hassan whenever she'd faced his displeasure; displeasure that caused more than one woman to lose her head. Luckily, Mia restrained the impulse before she could act on it. The last time she'd employed the gesture of humble respect — the day she'd arrived in England — the duke had been mortified into speechlessness to find his daughter groveling at his well-shod feet.

She bowed her head, instead. "I should not care to live with Aunt Philippa, Your Grace."

The duke's sigh floated above her head like the distant rumble of thunder. "Look at me, Euphemia." Mia looked up. Her father's stern features were tinged with resignation. "I would have thought you would *wish* to forget your wretched past and begin a new life. You are no longer young, of course, but you are still attractive and within childbearing years. Your history is something of an . . . obstacle." He stopped, as if nonplussed by the inadequacy of the word. "But there are several respectable men who are quite willing to marry you. You must cultivate acceptance and learn to accept minor, er, shortcomings in your suitors."

Shortcomings. The word caused an almost hysterical bubble of mirth to rise in her throat. What the duke really meant was the only men willing to take an older woman with a dubious past were senile, hideous, brainless, diseased, or some combination thereof.

She said, "Yes, Your Grace."

"I know these are not the handsome princes of girlish fantasies, but you are no longer a girl, Euphemia." His tone was matter-of-fact, as if he were speaking about the state of Carlisle House's drains, rather than his only daughter's happiness. "If you do not mend your ways soon, even these few choices will disappear and the only course open to you will be a quiet life at Burnewood Park, and we both know you don't wish for that." He let those words sit for a moment before continuing. "The Season is almost over and it is time you made a decision about your future. Do you understand me?"

"Yes, Your Grace, I understand." *All too well.* Her father wished to have Mia off his hands before she did something so scandalous she would be unmarriageable.

"Very good, then." The duke's forehead reverted to its smooth, unlined state. "This ball tonight will be an excellent opportunity to further your acquaintance with several of the men who have expressed an interest in you. You need merely behave with decorum and enjoy yourself — ah, within reason, of course." He patted her on the shoulder, returned to his chair, and resumed examining his ledger.

The audience was at an end.

Outside the duke's study a pair of towering footmen stood sentry. One of them broke from his frozen state long enough to close the door behind her.

"Thank you," Mia said, even though she knew it was not done to thank servants.

The man's eyes remained fixed on some point over her left shoulder but a dull flush climbed up the muscular column of his throat.

Mia had been back in England for weeks but she was still distracted by the presence of attractive men who weren't eunuchs. That fascination often worked both ways and she could feel the weight of curious eyes on her back as she made her way toward the library.

It was the same no matter whether she went to a shop or a ball or her family's dining room; people were desperate to learn more about the Duke of Carlisle's mysterious daughter. Her father's servants, the crowds of strangers who waited for hours outside Carlisle House every day just to catch a glimpse of her, and, most especially, the men who wrote for the various scandal sheets available on every street corner in London.

Newspapermen couldn't generate stories about her fast enough to satisfy their hungry readers. The most intrepid men had tried to get those stories firsthand. They had climbed into Mia's carriage — once while it was still moving; hidden in the boot of the duke's town coach; and sneaked into the fitting room at her favorite *modiste*. One enterprising man had even masqueraded as a female and secured a scullery maid position at Carlisle House.

The entire *country* clamored to know more about Mia's mysterious past. Everyone, that was, except the members of her own family, who lived in a state of perpetual terror that she would do or say something horrific to push their family name beyond the pale.

Mia opened the library door and stopped. Her younger brother sat at the massive desk that dominated the far side of the book-lined room. Only the top of his head was visible above the teetering piles of books and papers. She stifled a groan. Was there nowhere in this enormous house she could be alone and think? She met her brother's startled green eyes.

"I'm sorry, Cian. I did not know you were working. I will leave you to your studies." She began backing out of the room but Cian leapt to his feet.

"Please, stay. I'd love your company." He gestured to the mountain of books. "I'm having a wretched time thinking today."

Mia sighed and closed the library door behind her.

"You think too much, Cian." She crossed the gleaming expanse of dark wood between them and lowered herself onto the oxblood leather sofa across from his desk.

"So Father says."

Mia grimaced. "Ah, Father." She pulled on the ribbons that held her thin kid slippers to her ankles and kicked them off before tucking her feet beneath her. She looked up to find Cian staring and held up a hand. "Please, Brother, I have just come from one scolding. Do not give me another."

Cian shook his head, the action causing a lock of auburn hair to fall over his brow. "I don't give a rap how you sit, Mia. But you know Father does. You'd better get used to rakings if you insist on sitting that way." He shifted a stack of books to one side to see her better. "But enough of that. Tell me, are you excited about tonight?"

"No."

Cian laughed.

"I am not jesting. Tonight is just another opportunity for me to do or say something mortifying and draw Father's censure."

"Oh come, Mia. I've read nothing about you in the betting book at my club." He grinned. "Not in the past week, at any rate."

"Ha. Very amusing. I should think my behavior at the Charrings' ball provided enough to fill several books." Mia propped an elbow on the back of the settee and dropped her chin into her palm.

Cian's smile faded. "You must forget about that, er, incident, Mia. I've not heard it mentioned in ages."

That *incident* was Mia's disastrous first ball. Mia thought her brother's reassurance was naïve and optimistic. Just because men were no longer putting wagers in betting books did not mean the matter had been forgotten.

"In any event," he continued. "I understand there will be numerous swains in attendance this evening."

Her brother appeared determined to put the best face on an event that was no better than a public auction.

Mia shrugged. "Yes, there will be no undesirables at tonight's dinner, only the finest pedigrees. After Father caught me talking to the scion of a coal magnate at the Powells' soiree, I now understand that wealth derived from coal or textiles is considered detrimental to the bloodline. Imbecility, decrepitude, and foppery are, however, quite acceptable."

Cian glanced at the door, as if somebody — the duke? — might be listening at the keyhole.

"My dear sister, you must curb your tongue if you are to catch even such men as fit those descriptions."

"So I've been told. Father also made it plain he would sequester me with Aunt Philippa for the remainder of my days if I did not marry by the end of the Season."

Cian opened his mouth, and then closed it again.

Something about her brother's forlorn expression pricked Mia's conscience. "Don't mind me, Cian, I'm still smarting from the scolding Father gave me."

"Do you know whom he has assembled for your perusal tonight?"

"Oh yes. I have seen the guest list." Mia struggled to keep her voice light, even though her blood hummed with fury at the men her father was offering for her consideration. "There will be placards on the table before each one: Lord Cranston — octogenarian, drools, mistakes me for one of his seven daughters and is in dire need of an heir and a new roof on his country house in

Devon. Viscount Maugham, who is two and twenty, has skin as fair as a young girl's and a decided partiality for young boys."

"Mia!"

Cian started so violently he dislodged a stack of books and fumbled to catch them before they slid to the floor. "Who told you such a thing?"

"I am two and thirty, Cian." She raised her brows. "Tell me, Brother, do I not speak the truth?" Cian remained mute but his bright red face made her smile. "Your countenance is most articulate." Indeed, Mia could not recall the last time *she'd* worn such roses on her cheeks. The sultan had used up her blushes years ago.

"You may know such a thing, Mia, but you cannot speak of it in company, and never around Father."

"I am not in company, Cian, I am with you. If I cannot speak openly with you, who else is there? Cousin Rebecca?"

"Good Lord, no!"

Mia heaved a sigh. "Oh, Cian, as if I would do such a foolish thing."

"No, no, I don't suppose you would." His green eyes were dazed and he stared at the cluttered surface of his desk before looking up. "If you must speak of such matters, you might as well do so with me — provided we are alone. I want you to give me your word you will never do so if anyone else might hear."

Mia gave him a look of disbelief, instead.

"I am serious, Mia — your word." Cian's stern mouth and piercing stare made his resemblance to their father more than a little marked, a comparison she doubted he would appreciate.

"Very well, Cian, I give you my *word*. Shall we spit on our palms and shake, as we used to do when we were young?"

Cian groaned and lowered his head into both hands.

"I was jesting," she said, laughing. "I vow I will not speak of such matters unless we are very much alone. Will that serve?"

Rather than a look of relief, two lines of worry grew between his eyes. "Surely not all your suitors are terrible?"

Mia wanted to comfort her brother almost as much as she wanted it for herself. It wasn't as if her marital requirements were stringent. She didn't expect love or companionship — far from it. All she wanted was indifference. The less interest her husband showed in her, the easier it would be for her to make plans to escape back to Oran.

Unfortunately, that wasn't the kind of thing she could share with Cian. Especially given the public embarrassment he'd suffer when she deserted whatever man she did marry. If only she could just disappear without all the bother and fuss of marriages and husbands. But her father had made that impossible by refusing to release anything but pin money until she was wedded. And even if she had enough money to purchase passage back to Oran, the strict watch the duke kept on her made organizing such an escape impossible. The sad truth was she had to marry.

"Mia?"

Mia looked up and gave Cian a reassuring smile, the best she could offer under the circumstances. "In spite of all my complaining, I'm looking forward to tonight's ball." The relieved expression that spread across his face at her small lie was gratifying. She slipped her feet into her shoes, tied the ribbons, and stood.

"I will leave you to your studies." She braved the mountain of books and papers to kiss him on the cheek before turning to leave.

"Save a dance for your little brother," he called after her.

Mia closed the door and leaned against it. Should she tell Cian her plans? Was it possible she'd misjudged him? After all, he was not happy here, either. He spent most of his days buried in books to avoid the crushing expectations the duke laid upon him. Would he help her?

Mia pushed away from the door, shaking her head at such wishful thoughts. Cian might sympathize with her on matrimonial matters, but he would never understand her desire to return to Oran. Nor would he be happy to learn about the existence of her son. To any member of the Upper Ten Thousand — her own family included — her precious Jibril would be nothing but the half-caste bastard of a heathen savage.

No, finding her way back to her son was a task she must face alone. She could trust no one, not even her brother. The sooner she did as her father ordered and selected a husband, the sooner she could escape this horrible country and return to Jibril.

Mia would make her choice tonight, no matter how poor the options.

CHAPTER TWO

Sayer held out two waistcoats for Adam's approval.

Adam was about to reject both and order something more suitable for an evening at his club when the Duke of Carlisle's face flickered through his mind. The aloof peer had acted so happy to see him at White's, Adam had been dazzled. After all, when was the last time anyone had been thrilled to see his face?

But if the duke's warm welcome had bemused him, their odd conversation had left Adam intrigued. He was still intrigued a full four days later.

"Damn," he muttered.

"I beg your pardon, my lord?"

Adam sighed. "The one on the right, Sayer."

His valet helped him into the white silk waistcoat while Adam engaged in the same internal argument he'd been having since his meeting with the duke on Tuesday. Should he, or should he not, go to the man's wretched dinner and ball?

The Duke of Carlisle — an older, well-respected peer with whom he'd exchanged fewer than a dozen words in his life — had accosted him with all the bonhomie of a long-lost friend. He'd hardly waited for Adam to remove his hat and gloves before dragging him to a table.

"Ah, Exley, I'd hoped to find you here today. A moment of your time, if you do not mind?"

"It would be a pleasure, Your Grace," Adam had replied after a second of stunned silence. His lips twitched even now as he recalled the faces of those who'd been lounging around the club that morning. Every eye in the place had been riveted on the fascinating sight of one of the *ton*'s proudest and most proper members supplicating one of its most notorious and disagreeable — two epithets Adam knew were often applied to him, although never to his face.

The duke had led him to a pair of chairs by the dormant fireplace and waved away a hovering waiter. "I say, Exley, did you receive an invitation to that affair we're having this Saturday?"

"Affair?"

"Yes, a ball for my daughter."

Adam blinked and shifted in his chair. "I did not."

The duke flicked his hand. "No matter. I daresay my scatty cousin, the one who organized the damn thing, didn't know you were in town." To his credit, the duke's pale skin tinted a pale pink at this blatant untruth. The older man would know, along with his "scatty cousin" and every other member of the *ton,* that Adam rarely left London, even after the Season's end.

"In any event," Carlisle had continued, undeterred, "I'm issuing you a personal invitation."

"I am honored, Your Grace." *And bloody curious,* he could have added. After all, few people, and none of them bearing the title "duke," had been eager to associate with Adam for almost ten years, not since he'd been dubbed the "Murderous Marquess." Yet another name used exclusively behind Adam's back.

Carlisle had then leaned closer to Adam, as if he were about to embark on a confidential topic. "You must know Lady Euphemia has been away for some time, eh?"

Adam had been unable to do more than gape at the older man's casual reference to his daughter's seventeen-year absence — a subject that had so mesmerized the people of Britain that dozens of savvy newspapermen had made their fortunes feeding the public's hunger on the subject. Euphemia Marlington had even pushed Boney from people's minds. For almost six weeks now, one question had dominated the scandal sheets: Just what had the duke's daughter been up to all these years?

Adam had looked across at one of the few men in England who surely knew the answer to that question and smiled. "I seem to recall hearing something about your daughter's return."

His irony had been too subtle for Carlisle. "You haven't met her yet, eh?"

"We have not crossed paths, Your Grace." Indeed, it would have been more than a little odd had they done so. Adam did not attend *ton* functions and he doubted Lady Euphemia frequented gaming hells, men's clubs, or Adam's mistress's *pied-à-terre,* the places he could usually be found.

"You must make her acquaintance, Exley. She's marriage-mad like all the rest of her sex, of course." He'd chuckled, his color deepening. "Now that she's returned home, she's keen to be setting up her nursery."

The duke could not have been more appallingly blatant had he provided Adam with a teasing chart. He'd half feared the older man would go on to offer details of his daughter's estrus and when her next heat cycle began.

When Adam had failed to comment, the duke had added, "She will make some fortunate man an excellent wife."

"I daresay the candidates for her hand are flatteringly numerous, Your Grace."

Carlisle's smile had faltered under Adam's cool mockery. "And how is your family, Exley? You have three girls, don't you?"

It hadn't been the most subtle way of reminding Adam he had no heir, but it must have been persuasive enough. After all, here he was, dressing for his first *ton* event in almost a decade.

Adam paused in his ruminations while Sayer helped him into his newest coat, a rather strenuous ordeal that took several minutes and left both men breathing hard by the time they'd finished. He pushed his hair off his forehead and fastened the coat's silver and onyx buttons while he considered the meaning behind the duke's invitation.

Carlisle could not have made his intentions any clearer had he shown up at White's with a stud book, auction block, and gavel. He wanted his daughter married and he wanted it to happen quickly. Adam could understand the man's urgency; the woman was no spring pullet. But what he could not understand was why the duke wished to marry his only daughter to a man with Adam's reputation.

Sayer approached him with a tray bearing fobs, pins, rings, watches, and quizzing glasses. Adam slipped on his rather gaudy signet ring — a large ruby in a heavy gold setting — selected the plainest of his silver quizzing glasses, and opted for a single fob bearing a sapphire cabochon. Once he was accoutered, he stood back and studied his reflection in the tri-fold dressing mirror. Three identical men in flawless evening attire looked back at him. All three appeared slightly puzzled and a little annoyed. He frowned. There was still time to change into something else and go to his club.

"Your carriage is ready, my lord," Sayer informed him, holding out his cloak and hat.

Adam would have sworn his valet, a man who could have taught the Sphinx a thing or two about discretion, was pleased. It didn't take a genius to imagine the talk flying around the servants' quarters just now. No doubt they all — even the impassive Sayer — were thrilled by the notion their master was emerging from self-imposed exile and reentering society. After all, how pleasant could it be to work for a man most of London considered a cold-blooded murderer?

They would view this ball as the first step toward rehabilitation. Next he would take a wife and soon he would have a nursery full of children. Children he wouldn't keep hidden away in the country, as he did his three daughters.

Adam took his hat and gloves from his valet's hands. "Don't wait up for me, Sayer."

He strode through the silent corridor and down a semicircular set of marble stairs, his lips twisting. Tonight would be the social equivalent of death by a thousand cuts. He would spend the entire evening tolerating the calumny of his peers just to make the acquaintance of a woman he had no desire to meet and no intention of marrying — a woman who resembled either an aging matron or an opera dancer, depending on which set of gossips one gave credence to.

Or perhaps she was something even worse? After all, what must be wrong with her if her own father would seek a man like Adam for a son-in-law?

Mia stared at her reflection as LaValle

fussed with her hair. The Frenchwoman was high in the instep, but she was skilled at her job. She'd tamed Mia's unruly red curls and dressed them in a way that made her appear taller, if only by an inch or two.

If Mia could change one thing about her appearance it would be her height. At just five feet, she had to look up to anyone over the age of ten. She knew her diminutive size was the reason men felt entitled to order her around. She was childlike in size, so men treated her like a child.

She was not, however, dressed like a child. Her gown was a clinging jade-green silk masterpiece, with a single, almost insubstantial, petticoat. The dress would most likely scandalize her father, but Mia had ordered it from the dressmaker of his choosing, so how could he take issue with it? The full-length garment was quite tame when compared to what she'd worn at the sultan's palace, where she'd spent a good deal of time either naked or near enough. The desert was hot, and cool stone walls only provided so much relief. Frequent dips in the bathing pools helped one stay sane during the sweltering summers.

LaValle fastened the famed Carlisle emeralds around her neck and stepped back. *"Voila!"*

Mia examined her reflection in the glass, tilting her head from side to side. She had endured endless taunting as a young woman in the sultan's harem. Even after she'd established her authority, her red hair, small frame, and freckled skin had been subjects of amusement for the dark-eyed, lush-bodied beauties who'd vied for Babba Hassan's attention. The attractive, polished woman who looked back at Mia in the mirror was a far different person from that terrified, gawky young girl; she looked . . . regal.

Just then her cousin Rebecca entered her dressing room. She stopped in the doorway and lifted a gloved hand to her mouth. "Oh Mia, you look perfect — just like a doll."

The older woman was dressed in a nondescript brownish gray, a color that did not suit any woman alive. Mia sighed. Her cousin was not beautiful, but she had a pretty face and soft gray eyes. In a gown of blue or lavender she would look quite attractive.

"Thank you, Cousin Rebecca. You look lovely, too," she lied, standing on tiptoe to give her a peck on the cheek.

Rebecca turned pink and patted Mia awkwardly on the arm.

It saddened Mia that her family seemed

unwilling — or unable — to express affection. Physical affection had helped her survive in the sultan's palace. She'd cuddled her son constantly when he was a baby. They'd remained close as Jibril grew up, although he'd drawn the line on public embraces when his half brother Assad had teased him that hugs were for children.

Mia pushed away her longing for her son and offered Rebecca her arm. She smiled up at her tall cousin. "Are you ready?"

The large drawing room was crowded with auburn-haired relatives and a conspicuous number of single men. Mia was engaged in conversation with the buck-toothed son of a northern earl — a middle-aged man who could not keep his eyes from the bodice of her gown long enough to complete a sentence — when an odd hush fell over the assemblage. She followed the stunned gazes of those around her to a slim, dark-haired man standing beside her father. Mia nudged her brother, who was engaged in a heated discussion with an older man from his philosophical society.

"Cian, who is that?"

"Who is whom?" he repeated, his mind still on the discussion she had interrupted.

"That man — the one talking with Father."

Cian's eyes followed hers and his entire body stiffened. "*Good God.* How could he?"

"How could who do what?" Mia asked, glancing from her brother's outraged face to the man everyone was staring at. Unlike the duke, who sported an embroidered green silk waistcoat, the stranger wore not a hint of color. His hair was dark enough to look black and contrasted sharply with his pale skin, adding a sense of the dramatic to his appearance. Mia was too far away to discern the color of his eyes, but could see they were set below shapely, well-defined dark brows. High, sharp cheekbones and a determined jaw framed unsmiling lips.

The duke leaned toward him and spoke. The man merely raised his quizzing glass and surveyed the room as a hawk might sweep a field for rodents. Even from a distance Mia could feel her father's anger at the other man's careless dismissal of whatever he'd said. A smile pulled at her lips. Who was this man who treated one of the most powerful peers in England like a nuisance?

She tapped Cian's arm with her fan. "Who is he?"

"He is Adam de Courtney, the Marquess

of Exley." Cian pushed the words through gritted teeth.

"Why are you staring daggers at him?"

"I am *not* staring daggers at him." He turned and stared daggers at Mia instead, his eyes narrowed and his mouth a compressed pink line.

Mia bit back a smile at his almost comical outrage. "Why is every person in this room trying to appear as if they were not staring at him?"

"They are staring because it is unheard of to see him in such an environment."

"In a house?"

Cian gave her such a withering look Mia couldn't help laughing.

"No, at a *respectable* event with *decent* people. He hasn't been to a *ton* function since . . ."

"Yes, since?" Mia prodded.

He gave an impatient shake of his head. "It doesn't matter. Not for a very long time." His eyes snapped back to the marquess, who was now saying something to their father. The duke, who had already been frowning, suddenly appeared thunderous.

"Goodness. What could he be saying to make Father look so cross?" Mia asked.

"Whatever it is, Father deserves it."

Before she could ask her brother to explain his cryptic comment, the marquess raised his glass and fixed it on her.

Cian swore. "What bloody cheek." He edged his body in front of her.

Mia took her brother's arm. "I do not require your protection, Cian."

He ignored her and inched even closer. *"Damnation,"* he hissed. "He's coming this way. Don't speak to him, Mia. Let me handle this."

Aunts, cousins, and prospective suitors vanished into the nearby furniture like quail into tall grass as the Marquess of Exley came toward them, moving with the languid grace of a predator on the prowl. He was no more than medium height, his body slim, but sleekly muscled. His austere black-and-white clothing looked as if it had been stitched to his graceful frame. His coat tapered from broad shoulders to narrow, compact hips and well-developed thighs and calves — the legs of an active man. By the time he reached their side of the room, only Mia and Cian remained to greet him.

Mia wrenched her gaze away from his snug black breeches and looked up into eyes that were a startling pale blue — an unusual color made even more striking by the thick, dark lashes that fringed his lids. He smiled slightly at her obvious scrutiny and turned his unnerving eyes on her brother. "Perhaps you would introduce us, Abermarle?" His voice was low, velvety, and precise — as attractive as his person.

Cian stood mute, his hands fisted at his sides. The marquess scrutinized the younger man the same way he might study a spot on his cravat. The longer his eyes lingered, the more Cian's face mottled.

Mia itched to cuff her brother. What was *wrong* with him?

Instead, she stepped around him and held out her hand, hoping to interrupt the hostile *tableau vivant* before Cian attacked the other man. "I am Euphemia Marlington."

The marquess bowed low over her proffered hand. "I am delighted to make your acquaintance, Lady Euphemia. I am Exley." His lips, which looked as hard and cold as stone, left a burning imprint on the cool satin of her glove.

Mia dropped into her lowest curtsy, the one she'd reserved for the sultan. When she rose, it was to find his icy eyes glinting with approval.

His lips flexed into something that almost passed for a smile. "Are you pleased to be back in the bosom of your family, my lady?" It was an innocuous question, but she sensed the irony behind it.

Mia glanced at her father; the duke was watching her with eyes every bit as stony as his bosom. Did every person in the room — every person in London — know how much her return had mortified her father?

If they did, there was no point in letting them all know how much it hurt her.

She beamed up at the marquess. "Very much so, my lord. I am especially thrilled to be reunited with my little brother." They both turned to Cian. Her brother was glaring at the marquess as if he were a dangerous and unpredictable reptile.

Mia's smile began to falter and she grasped at the first thought that came to mind. "My brother tells me your presence here tonight is something of a rarity, Lord Exley."

His dark brows arched, as if he was surprised to hear Cian could actually speak. "I do not care for this type of social occasion in general, but your father convinced me I would miss tonight at my peril."

In case she might misunderstand his meaning — that her father was conducting a public auction with Mia on the block — Exley began a deliberate examination of her person, the same way he might inspect bloodstock at Tattersall's. His eyes licked over her like blue fire, burning her skin through her clothing, scorching her from head to toe and leaving no part of her body unscathed. He dwelt longest on her chest, which was rising and falling as if she'd just run a footrace. His expression shifted subtly from cruel and calculating to . . . pleased, but still calculating.

The brazen appraisal was enough to bring Cian out of his trance, and he stepped toward the marquess. "Look here, Exley, just what the devil —"

"Dinner is served!" the duke's butler proclaimed in a stentorian voice.

Exley extended his arm. "May I claim the honor of escorting you to dinner, Lady Euphemia?"

Mia bowed her head and laid her hand on the cool, smooth fabric of his sleeve. She could not have resisted the quiet note of command in his voice even if she'd wanted to — and she did not want to.

CHAPTER THREE

They made the short journey from the drawing room to the dining room in silence. Exley was no more than average height, but even so, Mia's head barely reached his shoulder and he had to fit his longer stride to hers. They paused in the double doorway, staring along with several other couples at the magnificent sight before them.

The panels between three rooms had been opened to create a massive dining room. Gargantuan chandeliers lighted the vast expanse, each fixture blazing with enough candles to illuminate half of London for a week. Although the duke was conservative, tonight he'd set aside his personal preferences and embraced the newest dining fashion, *service à la russe.* To that end, a table draped in acres of white linen held forty covers, each comprised of dozens of pieces of silverware, china, and crystal along with numerous personal cruets and condiments.

The glittering exhibition was hard to look at directly and the guests — jaded and inured to opulence as they were — approached the display with hushed reverence.

The marquess led her to a chair near the head of the table. "You are here, my lady." He glanced at the placard beside her and his lips twitched. "Ah, what a surprise," he said in a tone the antithesis of that emotion. "I have the excellent fortune to be seated beside you."

Was it the appalling reception he'd received from her family and guests that made him so contemptuous or was he always that way? Mia mentally shrugged. Contempt was far more appealing than the insincere fawning of the other men pursuing her hand and money. In fact, Exley was the first of her father's suitors she'd not taken in immediate disgust; quite the opposite. The man was almost shockingly handsome.

The duke had paraded eligible men before her for months; why was she only meeting the marquess now? She nibbled her lower lip. Perhaps she'd misread matters and he wasn't a potential suitor at all. But why would he be seated beside her if he wasn't? Maybe he was —

"Good evening, Mia."

Mia winced at the loathsome voice and forced a smile onto her face before turning to greet its owner. "Good evening, Mr. Chambers."

The Honorable Horace Chambers — the Duke of Carlisle's current favorite for son-in-law — chuckled, causing his chins to jiggle. "Oh come now, we are great friends, Mia. You must call me Horry."

Mia made a noncommittal noise and smiled.

He beamed, his eyes moving over her skin like the sticky feet of a bluebottle fly. "You look ravishing, my dear." The sheen of sweat on Chambers's upper lip made it hard not to snatch her hand away when he placed his damp, spatulate fingers on her wrist. Chambers was perhaps a decade older than Mia but his heavy body and florid countenance made him appear older than her father. His avuncular manner was belied by his eyes, which held a look she had last seen in the sultan's when she'd been a very young girl.

Mia reached for her linen napkin, using the movement to free her arm from his soggy grasp. Chambers's protuberant orbs slid past her and landed on the marquess. His eyes narrowed and he grunted, as though he'd encountered something both unexpected and unpleasant.

When Mia turned to gauge the marquess's response, she saw the woman on his left had pushed her chair so far away she was in danger of sitting in her neighbor's lap. Heat crept up her neck at the woman's outrageous behavior. *What the devil is* wrong *with these people?*

"Do you come to London often, my lord?" Mia asked, hoping to distract the marquess from both Chambers's rude, unblinking stare and the woman's terrified retreat.

Exley took the roll of linen from the top plate on the tower of china, his movements unhurried and graceful. "My country seat is in Hampshire but I spend most of my time in Town."

Mia's brain scrambled to recall Hampshire's location on the map. Was it near the water? Was it in the south? She could hardly ask the man if there were any convenient ports where she might secure passage to Oran and escape.

Instead she said, "You prefer town living yet you shun society entertainments? Tell me, my lord, what is it you *do* enjoy?"

His gaze locked on her. "I am enjoying myself right now."

The inflection in his cool voice was so slight Mia thought she might have imagined it. Was the beautiful block of ice flirting with her? If so, he was very subtle about it. He behaved nothing like her other suitors, who'd gone after her generous dowry like a pack of baying, slavering hounds hunting a fox. Was the man a potential suitor, or not? She had no time to employ the usual delicacy.

"And your wife, does she join you in London, my lord?"

"My wife died several years ago."

Mia was disgusted by the way her heart capered at the news. What kind of beast was she? What if the man had loved his wife and was still brokenhearted? She searched his face for signs of emotion and found nothing. But at least she now knew he was a widower seeking a wife. Did he want Mia for her dowry or an heir or both?

"Do you have children, my lord?"

"I have three daughters." He spoke abruptly, as if female offspring were hardly worth mentioning.

"How old are your daughters, my lord?"

"My eldest is seventeen and the other two are still in the schoolroom." He turned to examine the individual menu beside his saltcellar, apparently more interested in the meal than his daughters — or her conversation.

Mia didn't mind. In fact, she was glad for a brief reprieve from his uncomfortable gaze. The man burned with an intensity that was both exciting and exhausting. He was also so perfect she itched to stroke his smooth, angular jaw and feel the tickle of his black, spiky eyelashes. And that mouth . . .

Her skin prickled with awareness and she looked up to meet her father's eyes.

The duke's hard green gaze flickered between Exley and Chambers before returning to Mia. The message was clear. He was done bringing her suitors, like a cat offering up dead mice. Mia would either make her choice from among these men, or he would make it for her.

She had known for months this day would come and she'd not spent her time idly. One by one she'd ferreted out information about the parade of impoverished peers who sought her hand. Not an easy task when she was both short of money and connections.

Mia wasn't overly fussy when it came to choosing a husband but she'd have to bed the man — at least until she escaped. As such, she preferred not to contract the pox from the impoverished but genial Lord Herringford, or nurse bruises and broken bones from Horace Chambers, who enjoyed beating his lovers.

The most recent suitor she'd investigated was Viscount Maugham. Unfortunately, the young peer's country estate was too far inland to be suitable for Mia's escape plans. On the positive side, the viscount was so effeminate Mia doubted he was capable of bedding her, an assumption that made Maugham her favorite candidate.

Until tonight.

Mia studied the marquess's austere profile from beneath lowered lashes. Bedding such a beautiful man did not look like it would be a chore, but what lurked below his attractive surface? If she judged him solely by the reception he'd received tonight, his past must be horrible indeed. But people treated her much the same way and she had done nothing to merit such behavior. As far as the *ton* was concerned, being different was enough reason to be an outcast.

Mia gave his handsome profile a thorough inspection, as if his secrets would reveal themselves if she examined him closely enough.

Exley chose that moment to look at her. His cold eyes blazed at her obvious scrutiny and his lips twisted.

Mia bristled. *How dare he look down his elegant nose at me in such a manner? And just when I'd begun to feel sorry for him.* She returned his scathing stare with interest, giving her napkin a savage snap before laying it across her lap. She'd allowed his pretty face to soften her judgment. He was just another odious fortune hunter who viewed her as low-hanging fruit. No doubt he expected her to tremble with gratitude at the chance to marry a marquess, even one who was some sort of vile social outcast.

Mia helped herself to oysters on the half shell from a hovering footman. If the marquess wanted her, or her money, he would have to earn it, just like the others. Because she had run out of time to investigate him with more subtle methods, he would have to endure a more direct, and brutal, approach.

"Tell me, my lord, is your eldest daughter out and enjoying the Season?"

His lips thinned at the resurgence of the vexatious subject of daughters. "No. She is in Hampshire with her sisters."

So, he was one of those horrid men who believed women and children should be left in the country while he cavorted in London? In other words, he was exactly the kind of man Mia was looking for.

He was also the kind of man who — inexplicably — brought out her devilish,

47

teasing side.

"Your children live alone in the country while you entertain yourself in London?"

The marquess snorted, a sound that was dangerously close to a laugh. "They are not being suckled by wolves, Lady Euphemia. My sister lives with them."

"How convenient for you, Lord Exley."

He lifted one elegant shoulder. "Many people would say I render my children a service with my absence."

"And your wife, did you render her a similar service?" Mia bit down on her lower lip so hard the tangy, metallic taste of blood flooded her mouth. What was she doing? She had begun this conversation to spare him from rudeness, not inflict more. Instead she'd lost sight of the point of her questions and had allowed his cool dismissal of his daughters to goad her into foolishness — and cruelty.

Twin slashes of color appeared high on his cheekbones and his eyes bored into her. "Unfortunately, the only person who could tell you what *services* I render in my capacity of husband is no longer available." His eyes dropped to her décolletage. "Perhaps that will soon change."

Mia's face heated. Was she actually blushing? The notion was so diverting she almost missed his next words.

He turned his entire body toward her and his smile made the hairs on the back of Mia's neck stand up. "But my life is such a tedious, well-trammeled subject, my lady. I would rather speak of *you.*"

"Oh?" Her mouth insisted on uttering the encouraging syllable in spite of the warning her brain was shrieking.

"Yes, I understand your skill on the dance floor is . . . entrancing." He watched her like a little boy who had just kicked over an anthill and was eager to witness the results. "Stories of your prowess are what lured me here tonight." His voice was almost caressing as he set the hook deeper.

Mia dropped her eyes, suddenly struggling to catch her breath. *How dare he?*

She stared at the table without seeing her plate. Her chest rose and fell like a cornered rabbit's as the horrid memory crawled from its hiding place and filled her mind. He was referring to Lord and Lady Charring's ball, the first society event she'd attended. It had been an intimate affair with only three hundred or so of the *ton*'s finest in attendance.

Rebecca had given careful thought to Mia's first dance partner, an older man who was one of the duke's cronies. A few minutes into the dance — a Scottish reel — the man's face had turned an alarming shade of red. Concerned for his health, Mia suggested they rest. The moment they stepped off the dance floor, the duke had descended like the winged hangman of death. He'd clutched her arm hard enough to leave bruises and hustled her from the ballroom under the eyes of half the *ton.*

Mia had been stunned. What had she done? She loved dancing and it was one of the few things she had always excelled at. Even when Babba Hassan had no longer wanted her in his bed, he'd still summoned her to dance for him.

Her father's ice-cold rage that night had been unlike anything she'd ever witnessed. Mia shuddered at the memory. It had also been the turning point for her, the moment she'd decided she could not live in this country.

Mia looked up at the man who'd just rubbed her nose in the humiliating memory. He stared back, his face unreadable. It occurred to her that perhaps she shouldn't have probed into his past quite so crudely. Mia crushed the unwelcome notion like an annoying insect.

Rather than stab Exley with her fork — her preferred response — she gave him a silky smile. "It is a shame you were not there, my lord, perhaps I could have taught you something."

His pupils flared and he leaned toward her. "Perhaps you can teach me something tonight. Do you have any dances remaining — maybe a reel?"

Hateful, odious wretch.

"If entertainment is what you seek, you shall have it, my lord. I will reserve no less than the opening set for you." She punctuated her words by turning her back on him.

CHAPTER FOUR

Adam stared at her stiff shoulders and rigid back and grimaced. She'd baited him and he had reacted without thinking, his response brutal and unsporting — something he never did.

She laughed at something Horace Chambers said and the older man grinned as though his horse had just won the Gold Cup at Ascot. The old roué had watched Carlisle's daughter with the eyes of a jealous lover from the moment they'd all sat down at the dinner table. The instant she turned away from Adam, Chambers had descended on her like a boar in rut.

The older man was a repellant deviant with an evil reputation, but was Adam any better? He'd behaved toward Euphemia Marlington like the cruel beast he was reputed to be. He was sitting at this table, a party to this farce. No, Adam wasn't any different from Chambers or any of the other degenerate horrors Carlisle had assembled.

A wave of self-loathing swept over him. Had it come to this? Would he compete with molesters, drunks, and diseased fortune hunters for a woman who'd no doubt had little say in the sordid auctioning of her person? Was he willing to mortgage what remained of his dignity for an heir?

A footman cleared away his untouched soup and three more servants appeared behind him, each bearing heaping platters of delicacies. Adam hadn't attended a large *ton* dinner since *service à la russe* had become fashionable. He decided the process was fatiguing. He signaled another footman to replenish his Madeira.

His eyes wandered over the other dinner guests — none of whom would meet his gaze — as he pondered the woman beside him and the unexpected effect she'd had on him. She was the last thing he'd thought to find tonight. Her beautiful face and delectable figure weren't all, or even most, of what he found fascinating. It was her sea-green eyes, which overflowed with curiosity, humor, and sheer *life.*

Adam realized his gaze had drifted back to her perfect profile. She moved with such grace that even the simple process of putting food into her shapely pink mouth looked like an act of Eastern deviance. With her looks and her father's money she should have no problem finding a decent spouse, and yet the duke had assembled the worst men society had to offer.

She must have done something truly heinous.

Adam's lips twisted bitterly; coming from him that was a richly ironic conclusion. What if the only thing she was guilty of was being an object of gossip? Who knew better than he how easily the *ton* judged, sentenced, and punished its members without any evidence?

She turned her green catlike eyes his way and caught him staring. She lifted one flame-colored eyebrow, a slight, mocking smile on her face.

Adam deliberately mirrored her action, amused as she tried — and failed — to suppress a smile. Once it started, it just kept growing, displaying white, even teeth and a tiny crescent-shaped dimple at the corner of her mouth.

"What are your plans after the Season is over?" he asked with careful politeness, determined to behave himself for the remainder of the meal.

"We are to retire to our family seat." She might have smiled at him, but the reserve in her voice told him she'd not forgiven him quite yet. She glanced at the platter the footman held beside her and her lips compressed in a moue of distaste before she helped herself to a portion.

"You do not care for *saumon en gelée*?" he asked, amused.

"It is not what I am accustomed to."

"Oh? What are you accustomed to?"

She wrinkled her nose and gave the gelatinous food a poke with her fork. "I am hungry for something that is not bland like infant food."

"Such as?"

Her eyes glazed and her lips curled into a sensual smile that sent his blood rushing south.

What is this? He took a deep drink of wine.

She sighed heavily and the action did distracting things to her bodice. Not to mention Adam's groin.

"I have been dreaming of dates."

"Dates?" he repeated, certain he'd misheard.

"Dates." Her eyes narrowed to sultry, emerald slits. "Sweet and plump and hot." The tip of her pink tongue darted out and Adam's heart stuttered. "They are firm and sticky and explode at the slightest pressure from my tongue, filling my mouth with their tangy heat."

Adam's fork clattered against his plate.

She raised a hand to her throat, her fingers lightly caressing and her lips parted. "I yearn for couscous, so drenched in oil it slides down my throat."

Good Lord. Adam swallowed audibly while an erection of alarming proportions strained against the placket of his breeches as if it were trying to thrust its way through the thick wooden tabletop. He shifted in his chair and winced before looking up.

Her eyes were open and her expression was no longer sultry, but amused. Whatever she saw on his face made her grin.

The treacherous little minx. She'd made him as hard as iron with nothing more than talk of food. Grudging admiration vied with his rampant arousal and almost made him smile — but he repressed it.

"Tell me, my lady, where did you learn to appreciate such things?" he asked, pleased to hear his voice gave no sign of the commotion beneath the table.

She speared a piece of the fish that had disgusted her only a moment earlier, popped it into her mouth, chewed, and swallowed, a wicked twist to her lips.

"Why, during my time in a Maltese convent, Lord Exley."

Adam's control slipped and his mouth curved into an answering smile. This dinner had been worth attending, after all.

Lord Exley's smile came and went more quickly than a shooting star. He raised a corner of snowy linen to his mouth. When it came away, his expression was once again impassive.

"How fascinating. Tell me, how did you come to find yourself in a convent — in Malta, of all places?"

Mia ate another bite, making a show of savoring her food — as if even gelatinous fish was more interesting than a conversation with him. "Were you aware my family is Catholic?"

"I was not."

"Do you know much about Catholicism, Lord Exley?"

"Have you returned to England to proselytize, my lady?"

Mia smiled at his arch look. "I'm afraid my proselytizing days are behind me, my lord."

"What a pity," he murmured. "You were saying?"

"My mother was a very devout Catholic and it was her dearest wish that I attend the same convent school that she had, a very old establishment just outside Rome." That much of her story, at least, was the truth.

"My parents put me and my old nurse — who was accompanying me in the capacity of companion — on a ship that never reached Rome. We were harried by corsairs almost immediately upon entering the Mediterranean." Here was where the true story ended and her father's carefully crafted tale began. "Our captain did the best he could for his passengers and took us to the island of Malta. There was a small convent on the island which offered safe port to those unwilling to venture off the island and risk the possibility of capture by corsairs. My nurse made arrangements for me to remain while she boarded the next vessel for England, to bring back help."

How Mia wished that were true.

The last time she'd seen her beloved nurse's face was when the corsairs had laughingly passed the older woman from man to man and then cut off her head when she wouldn't stop crying. The memory of that day was like a leering imp from a Bosch painting: it hovered at the edges of her mind, waiting to leap out at her when she least expected.

Mia looked away from the marquess's razor-sharp gaze. "I didn't learn until I returned home that her ship never reached England. As a result, nobody knew where I was — until recently."

They ate in silence for a while.

"How old were you?" he finally asked.

"I passed my fourteenth birthday onboard the ship."

"And you remained in the convent all these years?" For the first time, she heard skepticism in his voice. Mia couldn't blame him. Her father's tale was less than believable.

"Yes, until a few months ago."

He studied the blood-red liquid in the cut-crystal glass before asking his next question. "You faced no problems when the French seized control of the island?"

Mia paused, her own glass halfway to her mouth. The French had controlled Malta? She grimaced and drank deeply to hide her confusion. She had repeated the stupid story to dozens of people in the past weeks, none of whom could have located Malta on a map, much less recite its political history. None except the man beside her.

Mia gave a mental shrug. It was time to diverge from her father's fairy tale and script one of her own. "I am fluent in Italian and French, so it was not difficult to pass myself off as the daughter of a poor but devout family from Turin."

"I see. What about when *we* took control of the island in 1800? Why did you not seek help getting back to England at that time?"

Mia almost laughed. *Will it never end?*

"It was a turbulent time and only a very few of His Majesty's men remained behind. Most of the ones I saw were of the lower orders, men who were more likely to sell or ransom a duke's daughter than help her."

"So you hid in the convent for seventeen years?"

"I did not need to hide once I joined the sisters."

His eyes widened. "You became a nun." It was not a question.

"Yes."

"Isn't fourteen rather young for that type of thing?"

Nuns were, of course, yet another subject Mia knew nothing about.

"Oh, not at all. There were dozens younger than me." She took another drink before plunging deeper into the conversational quicksand. "Dear Sister Genevieve was only thirteen when she entered the convent. You could say we became closer than real sisters. How I miss her." She sighed heavily to add veracity.

A muscle twitched at the corner of his

unsmiling mouth. "It sounds . . . idyllic. How could you bear to leave such a rewarding situation?"

A footman appeared beside her with something that resembled boiled fowl in a pasty-looking cream sauce. Mia's mind raced while she served herself. The marquess was the only person to have probed past the surface of the ridiculous story. What else could she tell him?

She absently cut a small piece of food and put it in her mouth. It was not as wretched as it looked. She chewed, swallowed, and took a sip of wine. And then inspiration struck.

"Crocodiles," she said.

The marquess's fork and knife hovered above his plate. "I beg your pardon?"

"I ultimately left because of crocodiles. We went to the jungle in the interior of the island to tend to the lepers, as we did every year. This year, tragedy struck. Our barge capsized and many in our order were eaten by crocodiles before they could make it across the river to shore." She paused for dramatic effect. "Even dear Sister Genevieve."

He chewed for what seemed like a long time before swallowing. "I wasn't aware Malta had any jungles. Or crocodiles."

61

Drat, drat, drat. "I'm afraid you have been misinformed, Lord Exley. The island is infested with them. Crocodiles, that is, not jungles."

He raised his linen to his lips and coughed.

"Mia, my dear?" Chambers laid his soggy hand on her shoulder.

Mia gritted her teeth. "One moment."

The marquess was still dabbing his lips, his shoulders shaking slightly.

She leaned toward him. "Are you quite all right, my lord?"

He coughed one last time, his unusual eyes watering. "Just a piece of pepper," he said hoarsely.

"Mia?" Chambers's voice went up half an octave.

"Will you excuse me, my lord?"

"By all means," he said, lifting his napkin and covering his mouth just as another coughing spell struck.

Adam had begun to worry he might choke to death. He'd not been so amused in . . . well, not in a long time and certainly never at a tedious *ton* function.

He watched from the corner of his watering eye as she giggled and flirted with the self-important Chambers. The corpulent man preened and puffed up like the randy old rooster he was. Had Adam looked as fatuous as she'd spun her outrageous story to him?

He grimaced. Probably.

He ate his food, sipped his wine, and watched as she worked her magic on the other man. She was like a chameleon. She discerned what a man liked and then gave him exactly that. It was unnerving. What was the real woman like? And why did he even care?

He glanced down the table at Carlisle, the only peer in a decade to voluntarily consider Adam as a son-in-law. The Duke of Carlisle looked up just then and met his eyes, lifting his glass a fraction of an inch before taking a drink.

Adam ignored the gesture and turned back to Carlisle's daughter. She was nodding and simpering while Chambers, the ass, maundered on about a horse.

For the first time in a very long while, Adam was intrigued by another human being. He had come here tonight out of curiosity, rather than any serious search for his next wife. He'd stopped thinking about remarrying years ago, when it became apparent that not even the most desperate man would give his daughter to the Murderous Marquess.

And then Euphemia Marlington had looked at him openly and frankly — without judgment or fear — and his tight control had slipped a little. Adam stared at her beautiful profile, his mind seething with unfamiliar, uncomfortable, and unwanted feelings.

Just what had she done that her father was willing to barter her to a man everyone believed had killed not one, but two, wives?

More importantly, how far was Adam willing to go to find out?

CHAPTER FIVE

Chambers kept Mia trapped all the way through the dessert course, ensuring she did not get another chance to speak with Lord Exley. She had hoped to have a word with him after the men returned from their port, but Cian appeared and hurriedly whisked her off to the receiving line. Almost as if he wished to keep her away from the intriguing marquess.

Mia stood between her father and Cian and greeted hundreds of expensively garbed and elegantly coiffed strangers. In between smiling at guests and murmuring greetings, Mia watched the ever-growing crowd that filled the enormous ballroom. The Marquess of Exley was never difficult to find. Wherever he stood he was surrounded by several feet of empty space. She had never seen anything quite like it.

The only person who approached him was Viscount Danforth, an attractive man who was perhaps ten years Exley's junior. Each man was a perfect example of male beauty, one sunny and fair, the other dark and brooding. The young lord's presence appeared to have a humanizing effect on Exley, whose expression of contempt softened while the two chatted.

By the time their father released Mia and Cian from their duties, she was vibrating with excitement at the prospect of her first dance.

"Mia, I must speak to you for a moment," Cian murmured, taking her arm and pulling her into a small alcove before she reached the dance floor. He glanced around nervously. "I wanted to tell you about Exley."

"Yes?" she prodded when he paused.

"The thing is —" Again he stopped, his brow furrowed.

Amusement vied with exasperation as Mia waited for him to finish. "Yes? Tell me, what is the thing?"

His next words came out in a rush. "There is no reason you should endure the slight of a man like Exley offering for you."

His words surprised a laugh out of her. "He hasn't offered for me, Cian."

"He will."

Mia blinked. Just what did her brother

know that she didn't?

"Look." Cian frowned, as though he was agonizing over something and how to say it. "The truth is, you needn't take any of the horrors Father has thrown at you — Maugham, Chambers, none of them. I will not let him force you into an unhappy marriage. I give you my word on that." He swallowed, as if recalling whom he was speaking of defying.

Mia took his hand and squeezed it. "I am flattered by your concern for me, Cian. But I'm well able to take care of myself." She glanced toward the dance floor, where couples were beginning to assemble for the first set. "Come, we must take our places to open the ball."

"I think you should —" Cian stopped, his eyes on something outside the alcove.

The hum of voices died and Mia saw Exley walking toward them. The slim marquess split the crowd like a ship's prow parted water, leaving trails of gawking, whispering, pointing men and women in his wake.

He stopped in front of Mia and held out a hand, his expression bland. "I believe this set is mine, my lady."

The dance offered few opportunities to speak to one's partner, which turned out to be just as well. Mia focused her attention on the steps, an action made difficult by the oddly heated sensation the marquess's gloved hand provoked each time they touched.

"For a man who does not attend many balls, you certainly dance well," Mia said as they came together in formation.

A tiny smile softened his stern mouth. "You are too kind, my lady. Your own dancing is shockingly —"

The figure split just then. Mia shot him a dangerous glare, aware he'd timed his words to coincide with the long break.

His eyes were hooded when they next approached to interlace. He leaned toward her and spoke one soft word: "Proper."

Mia's laughter drew startled glances from those around them and a mocking look from her partner. She could almost forgive him for his wretched comment at dinner. Almost.

By the end of the set she was more than a little heated, both by the dance and his proximity.

"May I fetch you a glass of champagne?" he asked, leading her toward a small sofa near the French doors.

"That would be lovely."

She watched his fine shoulders cleave a path through the milling guests while she fanned her heated face. Mia had spent a good deal of time reading other people's faces. The harem had been more dangerous than shark-infested waters and her survival, and that of her son, had often depended on her ability to see beneath the surface. Tonight, her skills were failing her. The marquess was entirely unreadable — something she found both intriguing and arousing. Was the man looking for a wife, or wasn't he?

"Mia!" a voice hissed behind her, making her jump. She turned to find her brother, partly hidden by a giant potted palm.

"What the devil are you doing back there, Cian?"

His eyes fixed on something over her shoulder. "Hurry, Mia, before he returns." He held out his hand, as if she might take it and leap over the settee. "Come away with me now."

Mia scowled. "Cian —"

"Hurry, he is coming back."

Mia turned her back on his foolishness. The marquess was walking toward her with two glasses. She raised her fan to her face. "You should leave now, Cian."

"I am trying to protect you."

"I don't need protection. Now, please *go.*"

The palm fronds rustled. "Mia, dammit."

Exley stopped in front of her and held out a glass of champagne.

Mia lowered her fan and took the glass. "Thank you, my lord."

"My pleasure." He cast a lazy glance over her shoulder. "Are you comfortable behind the sofa, wedged beside that plant, Abermarle, or would you like to sit on the settee? Perhaps between me and your sister?"

Mia choked back a laugh.

Rustling and scraping noises emanated from behind her as Cian struggled free of the foliage and came around the side of the sofa.

The marquess held out his glass. "I wasn't aware you'd be joining us. Please, take mine."

Cian flinched away, as if the other man had offered him poison. He glared down at her. "Mia —"

Mia smiled at the marquess. "Please, have a seat, Lord Exley." She motioned to the space beside her. "My brother came to claim this dance but I assured him I could not move another step until the next set. He was just leaving."

Cian shot the marquess a dark look before pivoting on his heel and marching off.

Exley sat and the two of them watched Cian depart, his shoulders stiff with disapproval.

"Your brother is merely trying to protect you."

"Yes, he seems to believe you are very dangerous. He is not the only one." Mia nodded to the empty space around them. "Perhaps you could tell me why everyone is so terrified of you, my lord?"

"It is hardly a conversation for polite company."

She glared at him and *tsked* loudly.

His black brows arched.

"It is beyond irksome to be the only person in the room who is ignorant, my lord."

Exley took a sip of champagne while Mia struggled to regain her temper. The precious seconds were slipping past and she did not have time for this foolishness. Tonight was all she had before —

"The reason your guests are avoiding me, and your brother is desperate to spirit you away, is because almost everyone here believes I hurled my first wife from the roof of my house. They are not sure how I disposed of my second wife, as her body was never found." His eyes were no longer hooded, but wide open, avid to gauge the result of his shocking disclosure.

"Almost all of them? What do the rest of

71

them believe?"

Something flickered in his eyes. Surprise?

Mia waved her hand. "Never mind. I do not care what any of them think, to be perfectly honest. Most people are fools who will believe whatever they want to believe, regardless of the truth." She gave him a hard look. "I know this from personal experience. What *does* interest me is why you are here tonight. I will speak plainly, my lord. I am looking for a husband — although perhaps not with as much eagerness and diligence as my father. I have not been happy with the men my father has put before me — until tonight."

He took another sip of champagne.

Mia clenched the cut-crystal glass so tightly it hurt. The silence stretched and frustration mingled with despair in her breast. She told herself she didn't care. She told herself —

"I'm listening, my lady."

She took a deep breath. "My father has run out of patience, my lord, which means I have run out of time. I am not seeking a love match. I want a husband who will grant me a certain degree of personal liberty, a man who will be satisfied with separate lives." Mia stopped and watched him like a hawk. People's faces always disclosed the most immediately after they'd heard something interesting or surprising. The more time they had to think about it, the more time they had to mask their true feelings.

Exley finished the remainder of his drink, set the empty glass on the small table, and adjusted one of his cuffs before turning to her, his expression unchanged.

Mia snorted. She would have learned just as much, if not more, if she'd watched his foot.

"I find I cannot gauge your reaction. Tell me, Lord Exley, do you find my disclosure surprising, unappealing, intriguing?"

He stared at the dance floor. "Surprising? No, I would not say surprising. Who does not like to have their way, man or woman? Unappealing? Well, it depends on what you get up to while you are *going your own way.* If you have plans to turn my house into a distillery or brothel, I might have something to say to that. Intriguing?" He leaned back, stretched out his elegantly clad legs, and turned, giving her a direct look. "Very."

Mia's entire body tingled at the heat that flared in his cold eyes. Her carefully constructed sentences came apart in her head, and it was a struggle to gather them back together. "My plans do not include distilleries, bawdy houses, or anything unusual," she lied. "It is simple, really. I'm not a girl and I chafe under the harsh restrictions my father imposes on me. I merely wish to be my own mistress. I expect, of course, to defer to my husband's authority in important matters, but I would prefer to live a separate existence in the country as I do not care for London. In short, sir, I would like a marriage without emotional entanglement."

The marquess's eyebrows, his only expressive feature, crept up his forehead, as if he had a difficult time imagining something as foreign as an emotion — not to mention becoming entangled by one.

They took each other's measure before she broke the silence. "What of you, my lord? Why do you wish to marry? It does not sound as if your two experiences with marriage were felicitous." Mia did not mean to be cruel, but she needed to know what he wanted and why he was here tonight — a place he clearly wished not to be.

"I need an heir." His pupils flared until his eyes were almost black, as if he were imagining the process of getting an heir. With her.

Heat washed over her. He'd looked sinful with pale eyes. With dark eyes, he became almost satanic. She stared down at her clenched hands and nodded. "Your property is entailed."

"Yes."

She looked up at his clipped response and saw nothing of the heat that had scorched her only a moment before.

"My previous heir — a distant cousin — managed to get himself killed by Napoleon, leaving me with his younger brother, a man who is both a drunkard and a fool. He will beggar the House of de Courtney in his lifetime." He shrugged, as if that was all there was to say on the matter. He surveyed the dancers with the same lack of interest he seemed to show everything. But Mia knew it for what it was: a pose. He would not be at this ball enduring the snubs of hundreds if he wasn't interested.

Could he be counted on to leave her in the country after he bedded her a few times? How vigilant would he be ensuring she fulfilled her part of the bargain? It was a risk — a gamble. Viscount Maugham would be a more practical choice, but there was just something about the lone, enigmatic man beside her. . . .

Mia studied his starkly beautiful profile. Would she be able to use him to get what she wanted? Something fluttered in her at the thought of manipulating him so coldly

— her conscience? She shrugged it away. Men had no qualms about using women, sacrificing them for their own desires, like pieces on a chessboard. Based on the marquess's callous attitude toward his daughters, he was no different. Her eyes lingered on his unyielding features. No, he would not hesitate to use her for his purposes.

He turned to her and Mia lowered her eyes under his probing look. His piercing intelligence was yet another danger. Again she shrugged away the concern. He might be smart, but she was smarter. He could look and wonder, but she would make sure he found nothing. She would need to manage him carefully, but she had years of experience handling a dangerous man.

"I am past the prime age to bear children. Does that not concern you?" she finally asked.

"I am aware of your age."

"My father will not wait patiently for an extended courtship."

He did not smile or laugh, but, for some reason, Mia knew the comment amused him. She saw her brother's red head bobbing through the crowd toward them.

"My brother is approaching. I'm afraid our time is over."

He nodded and stood. "It has been a most

enlightening evening, my lady."

An almost crippling sense of despair ballooned inside her at his dismissive tone of voice. So, Viscount Maugham would be her choice after all.

She accepted his proffered hand and stood. "It has been a pleasure, my lord."

The marquess bowed low. "Indeed it has. Perhaps we shall see each other again before you leave town."

The vague words caused her hand to clench around his. What did he mean by that? Would he call on her?

"Are you ready, Mia?" Cian shouldered between them and Exley released her hand.

The marquess favored Cian with the merest of nods and strode away.

"He didn't do anything untoward, did he?" Cian demanded, turning to watch the other man leave.

"No."

He took her hand and placed it on his arm. "You look rather pale. Are you quite all right?"

Was she?

"Yes, I am fine," she lied.

He patted her hand. "Thank God that is over."

Mia couldn't help echoing his sentiment. The marquess was a clever, dangerous man and she'd begun their association with a lie, and not a small one. Part of her hoped she would never see him again. But another part of her mind — the larger, louder part — desperately hoped this was not the end between them. She had never been so attracted, so mentally and physically *stimulated,* by a man before. Not that she'd had many opportunities in the harem or the few weeks she'd lived in London. It might be foolish, but she would welcome the opportunity to engage in intimate caresses with such a man, not to mention pit her wits against his — just as long as she was far away when he finally discovered her lies.

As Mia danced she searched the noisy, glittering throng for one slim form.

She located him easily by the empty space in the otherwise crowded ballroom. He was approaching the duke, who still stood near the entrance. The two men exchanged a few words before Exley signaled to one of the hovering footmen and then strode from the room.

He was leaving. Mia had been his only dance partner.

Adam flung himself with uncharacteristic force onto the soft leather of the carriage seat and rapped on the roof. His brain was fogged and his nerves felt exposed and raw, as if he'd just been flayed. He dropped his head back against the squabs and closed his eyes. Nothing had gone as he'd expected tonight, nothing. At least not with Euphemia Marlington.

As for the rest of the evening — the disgusted stares of men like Cian Marlington and Horace Chambers, the utter terror of women he'd never even met — that had all been exactly what he'd expected.

Adam thought back to the final words he'd spoken to her. Why had he said them? Why had he said anything?

You said less than nothing, his conscience assured him.

That was not true, and he knew it. Saying nothing was the only thing that was saying nothing. Saying anything else was . . . well, it was saying something.

She would more than likely expect him to pay a call.

Who cares what she expects? The thought hurtled out of some dark recess in his mind with all the force of a charging bull. Adam told himself he *didn't* care what she expected, but he cared a great deal what he would do. After tonight, it scared the hell out of him that he had no idea what that might be.

She'd rattled him, and he hadn't been rattled in a very long time. He didn't like it.

Adam's mind was a chaotic mess and he couldn't pinpoint what had unnerved him most: The longing that had struck him like a brutal kick to the stomach as he'd watched her greet her guests beside her father and brother? Or the openness in her clear green eyes when she'd asked him why her brother and all the other guests were behaving like boors.

Could she really have been ignorant of his past? She'd appeared genuinely annoyed when she'd pressed him for the truth, yet her reaction to his grim disclosure had been dismissive, as if he'd confessed to nothing more serious than filching cookies. Rather than be daunted by his words, she'd all but offered herself to him. What kind of woman was eager to become the third wife of a man with two mysteriously dead wives? Either a stupid one, a fearless one, or a mad one.

Or perhaps an intelligent, dangerous one?

Adam snorted. Not that he'd found her unintelligent — far from it. Indeed, her approach to marriage appeared logical, unemotional, and . . . almost *male.* He frowned. So, not only was she much too attractive for a man's comfort, she was also far too clever.

As for being dangerous? Well, he'd almost heard the wheels turning in her scheming mind, both when she'd been spinning her ridiculous yarn and later when she'd spoken "frankly" about her spousal requirements. In spite of her avowedly frank behavior, Adam didn't believe she'd been entirely honest with him. He'd destroyed too many men at the card table to doubt his ability to accurately read faces: the woman was up to something.

Adam shrugged. He wasn't about to waste his time speculating what it was she had planned. No sane man could guess at the workings of the female mind, and there was little reward to be had trying. As the Bard said, "That way madness lies . . ."

If he decided to throw caution to the winds and marry her — not that he was entertaining the idea, mind — it would be on his terms, not hers. She could have all the secrets she wanted, but if she thought to make a fool of him, she had a hard lesson waiting for her. That didn't mean he wouldn't treat her with all the gentlemanly respect she deserved, but he would make damned sure she made a good-faith effort to deliver on her part of the bargain if they married.

Again, not that he was seriously considering marriage to Euphemia Marlington or any other woman, no matter how sultry her eyes, or wicked her lying pink lips —

Adam swore under his breath. You'd think he'd never seen a woman before tonight. But there was just something about her . . . something *knowing* in her eyes. A man would never be bored in her presence. Nor would bedding her be a chore. His cock, primed for action since her blasted description of dates and couscous, hardened the rest of the way as he imagined her lithe, naked body beneath his.

Adam allowed himself to enjoy the image of her naked beneath him for what it was — a male fantasy — and then he pushed it away. He wasn't in the market for a mistress. He needed an heir, not a companion or an interesting bed partner. Her ability to breed was the only thing he need be concerned about. And *that* interest, he told himself, would be far better served with a younger and more fecund woman. An image of his second wife drifted through his head, and Adam frowned.

The carriage door opened, startling him out of his thoughts.

"We're here, Your Lordship."

Adam hadn't even realized the carriage had stopped. He shoved away thoughts of wives and flashing green eyes and lying pink lips and hopped out of the carriage.

"Come back for me at the usual time," he told his coachman, taking the steps to his mistress's town house two at a time. Some energetic bed sport and a much-needed release would clear his muddled head. Indeed, an evening with the delectable Susannah St. Martin was just the thing to push thoughts of redheaded sirens and marriage from any man's mind.

CHAPTER SIX

Mia was positive every dipsomaniac, lecher, fop, and penniless peer in London had shown up to offer for her. Scarcely would one man leave the drawing room than another would file in. She'd received no fewer than five offers of marriage. The duke looked increasingly implacable each time she'd vacillated and begged for a little more time to consider the offers. She was on the verge of hiding in her room and locking the door when the Marquess of Exley was announced.

She shot to her feet, anger at his much delayed appearance warring with joy that he'd actually shown up: joy won.

"Show the marquess in," Mia said.

"Tell the marquess we are not at home," her cousin Rebecca said at the same time.

The young footman gaped.

Mia's eyes locked with her cousin's as she

carefully smoothed her mint-colored muslin.

"Show the marquess in," Mia repeated, employing the tone she'd used in the harem to command respect. The door shut behind the footman and Mia lowered herself onto the settee, her legs as shaky as a newborn foal's.

Rebecca fluttered beside her like a frantic moth. "My dear Mia, I do not think you should —"

Mia raised a hand to halt the flow. "I know you do not care for him, Rebecca, but your approval is not necessary." She threw back her shoulders and folded her trembling hands in her lap. She couldn't have said whether she shook with anticipation or dread, but she most certainly felt alive, more alive than she'd felt since the last time she spoke to him.

"But Mia, my dear, just —"

The door opened and Exley stepped into the room.

"Lady Euphemia." He graced her with an exquisite bow.

Mia could only stare. The wretched man was even more gorgeous in daylight than he'd been by candlelight. While sunlight exposed the small lines that radiated from the corner of his eyes and the grooves that bracketed his mouth, those subtle signs of age somehow added to his appeal. His coat was a dark blue that made his pale eyes even more striking. His lithe, muscular legs in fawn-colored pantaloons were more sinfully sculpted than they had been in black satin.

"What a pleasant surprise, my lord."

He looked amused by her waspish tone. "I did try to call yesterday but could scarcely see the front door for carriages, horses, and gentlemen callers."

Mia ignored his mocking comment. "Are you acquainted with my cousin, Miss Rebecca Devane?"

Rebecca dropped a shaky curtsy.

"A pleasure, Miss Devane." He gave the older woman a slight bow.

Mia gestured to the chair across from her. "Please, sit."

He ignored the available chairs, choosing to sit beside Mia on the small settee.

Oh, my.

Rebecca, who'd only just sat down, sprang to her feet again. "Oh . . . yes, er . . . quite. If you'll excuse me, my lady, I was just about to get my basket," she said, apparently unaware her basket was on the small table beside her chair. "I am in need of a particular color of silk. A shade of green," she dithered, inching sideways toward the door, her eyes the size of billiard balls. She searched blindly behind her back with one hand for the door handle, as if she didn't dare take her eyes from the marquess. She finally managed to open the door a crack and sidle through the opening.

Mia sighed. "She has not gone for embroidery silk, my lord. I would guess she's gone in search of my brother."

"Or perhaps the local constabulary," he suggested drily.

Mia chuckled at this welcome sign of humor. "In any event, I suspect we do not have much time. If you have anything of a private nature to say, I suggest you do so now."

He took her hand in both of his, a mocking smile playing on his lips. "I will follow your lead and speak frankly. Do you know of anything that would prevent you from conceiving a child? Also, notwithstanding my willingness to let you go your own way, I would require you to agree to my exclusive presence in your bed until you have provided me with an heir."

Mia knew she should be offended by his questions, as if she were a broodmare he was considering purchasing. But she was not.

"I know of no problems with conception

and I am prepared to accept your attentions in my bed, as regularly as you deem necessary. Nor will I lie with another."

His jaw tightened slightly at her words. Such a mild reaction would have meant nothing in another man, but in Exley, a man who restrained his emotions like tightly leashed beasts, it was as good as a declaration of desire.

"Lady Euphemia, will you do me the honor of becoming my wife?"

She hesitated. "You would marry me without knowing anything of my past? Anything beyond my time in the . . . convent?"

"I have asked the only questions I wish to ask. Have you any for me?"

Mia had none he was likely to answer. Besides, she'd taken care of the most important questions using the duke's library. The Marquess of Exley's seat was an ancient castle off the southern coast. Exham Castle was not far from Eastbourne, the same port where Mia had landed when she'd returned to England.

She'd found out very little about his prior wives. The first, Veronica Caton, had come from an impoverished family in the north, and the second, Lady Sarah Tewkes, was from an impoverished family in the south.

Both were dead. Neither Cian nor Rebecca knew anything about either of Exley's marriages other than vague gossip, although both had cautioned her repeatedly to stay away from the marquess.

Mia found the notion of such a cold man killing anyone in a fit of passion laughable. And he'd clearly married neither woman for financial gain. What did that leave? Was he some manner of deranged lunatic? Mia chewed her lip as she looked into his expressionless face. He certainly did not seem mad. It was a risk to marry him without searching deeper into his past, but she was out of time.

"Yes, I will marry you. I only ask that the ceremony take place soon."

His lids dropped to half-mast. "As soon as you wish, my lady." He leaned close and brushed his lips over hers. The heat in his eyes and the lightness of his touch made for a heady combination and her vision blurred, as though she'd consumed too much champagne. She inhaled deeply as he feathered kisses across her mouth. He smelled of soap, cologne, wool, coffee, horse, and the ineffable scent that made each human being unique.

Mia leaned into his kiss and he cupped her jaw with a cool, oddly calloused hand.

She slid one hand up the smooth fabric of his coat, reaching out to steady herself with her other hand. She encountered a sculpted thigh rather than the settee and a low noise emanated from his throat at her touch. His hand snaked behind her neck, drawing her closer. Mia melted against him. His body was warm and hard and real beneath his fine clothing and he stroked her neck with strong, sensitive fingers.

His skilled tongue and firm touch were as different from the sultan's moist, cloying kisses and clumsy groping as could be. It was a kiss that combined tenderness and strength; he was a man as intent on giving pleasure as taking it. His fingers brushed lightly up the side of her body, a phantom touch that tantalized and caressed before slipping back down to her waist. All the while, his deft tongue probed and explored, his mouth hot and insistent.

She looked up into eyes that were pale slits and his lips curved into a smile that was pure sensuality before he plunged deeply into her mouth.

Mia twined her body around his like a vine, drawing him closer while she savored his taste and texture. She slid her hand up past his cravat and into the surprisingly soft hair at the nape of his neck, moving from the taut cords of his neck to the hard lines of his jaw. His muscles lengthened and bunched beneath her fingers as he opened to explore her more deeply, as if he could not be inside her deeply enough.

The sitting room door flew open and banged against the wall.

Mia closed her eyes against the unwanted distraction and gripped the marquess's neck tighter.

"Dammit, Exley, take your hands off my sister!"

Mia moaned with disappointment as the marquess removed his beautiful hands and mouth from her body. His lips were no longer cruel and thin but swollen and bruised, and his movements were satisfyingly languorous. Her entire body pulsed at the hungry, possessive glint in his eyes.

"Mia, come away from him this instant," her brother ordered.

She wrenched her eyes from the object of her desire. Irritation became fury at the sight of her brother's angry, righteous face and she glared at him through a haze of red. "You are not my keeper, Cian."

The marquess laid a gentling hand on her shoulder and stood.

"I would speak with His Grace, Abermarle." He spoke softly, with his usual cool command.

"You're bloody well right we'll speak with my father, Exley. There is no time like the present." Cian stalked through the open doorway without another word, revealing that Rebecca had been cowering behind him.

Exley looked down at her, his eyes cold and hooded, as if their all-too-brief tussle on the sofa had been a figment of Mia's imagination. "I apologize for my unseemly haste, my lady, but if I dally much longer he will have quite the lead on me and I am not dressed for sprinting." He bowed and closed the door softly behind him.

"Oh Mia," Rebecca cried, almost breathless with hysteria. "Please tell me you cannot be considering the attentions of *that man.*"

Mia drew herself up. "I will thank you not to refer to my betrothed in that fashion."

"Betrothed! But you cannot sacrifice yourself, Mia. You cannot!" Rebecca collapsed into a heap on the settee beside her, taking the place Exley had just vacated.

"Calm yourself, Cousin. I know more than enough. He has had two wives and they have died. Neither you nor Cian have been able to tell me anything exceptional about either woman's death. There is nothing but rumor, conjecture, and gossip."

Rebecca cried even harder.

Mia sighed, unwillingly recalling the hundreds of crying episodes she'd been forced to tolerate during her time in the harem. At least there would be no danger of poison or knives this time. She put an arm around the weeping woman and uttered soothing words while patting her back.

Cian Marlington stood in front of the duke, his hands fisted at his sides. "Have you no shame, Father?"

The Duke of Carlisle shot to his feet, his proud, handsome features suffused with anger. "You forget yourself," he thundered, forgetting himself as well in his sudden rage. "If you cannot control yourself, you will leave the room."

Adam smiled at the rare spectacle of the distinguished Duke of Carlisle engaging in a common row with his rebellious heir. It occurred to Adam that this was something he could look forward to himself if he managed to get his own fiery, redheaded offspring off Euphemia Marlington.

The younger man whipped around as if Adam had spoken out loud.

"You find this amusing, Exley?" Abermarle demanded, and then lunged across the room, one arm thrust out as if to grab him. Adam seized the outstretched arm at the wrist, yanked it low to pull him off balance, and then twisted it sharply behind his back, until Abermarle arched and grunted with pain.

"I don't think so, my good man," Adam said, sliding an arm around his brother-in-law-to-be's neck and flexing, the action eliciting a choked squawk. "After all, it would be nothing to me to add another corpse to the pile, would it?" He gave a quick squeeze to punctuate his question before giving the younger man a sharp push that sent him stumbling toward his father's desk.

"Good God, Cian, what is wrong with you?" The duke came from behind the massive slab of mahogany and grabbed his son by the shoulders. "Gather your wits, boy. You are making a fool of yourself."

"It is you who should gather your wits, Father. *You* who are selling your daughter to a murdering villain who is so debased he can't even be bothered to defend himself against the claims leveled against him." He shot Adam a look of unbridled loathing.

Adam lowered himself into one of the fan-backed chairs across from the duke's impressive desk, placed his booted ankle on his opposite knee, and leaned back. He felt his face shift into its habitually bored lines, and this time it wasn't an act. He really *was* bored with the small drama unfolding before him.

Abermarle stood his ground and boiled with impotent rage as his hot green gaze flickered from his father to Adam and back. The younger man was as unpredictable and angry as his flaming hair would suggest. Oddly, the duke, the source of his fiery coloring, was as cold and calculating as a man could be. Would Adam barter any of his daughters to a man reputed to be a wife-killer?

He pushed the pointless question from his mind. His daughters could never marry.

"I have come to ask for your daughter's hand in marriage, Your Grace."

"You cannot have it!" Abermarle raged, moving a few steps toward Adam before recalling the last incident and halting.

"She has already given it," Adam bit out, unable to contain his irritation any longer. "I am here out of courtesy, Abermarle. Your sister is a woman grown and has no need of any man's permission to marry."

The younger man gaped, robbed of all argument.

For an instant, Adam felt sorry for him.

He wished he could talk to him man-to-man and offer him some reassurance. He obviously loved his sister too much to hand her over to somebody with Adam's reputation.

He dismissed his foolish impulse. Abermarle, like the rest of the *ton,* had made up his mind about Adam long ago; talking to him about anything would serve no purpose.

Adam stood and faced the Duke of Carlisle. "Lady Euphemia and I are in agreement on the matter and neither of us sees any point in delay. I shall make myself available to you any day this week to discuss particulars."

The duke nodded. "Very well, I shall send word to my man of business and let you know."

Adam nodded and strode to the door. He waved away the footman who waited outside the duke's study. "I can find my own way."

The wailing of the older woman reached his ears halfway down the hall. Adam stopped outside the door, his hand resting lightly on the handle. He grimaced as a piercing sob came through the heavy wood. Hadn't he endured enough emoting for one day?

"You bloody coward," Adam muttered under his breath. He began to turn the handle but paused as another earsplitting wail rent the air.

Bloody hell! It was nothing but a weeping female. He jerked open the door.

His wife-to-be sat calmly on the sofa, the sobbing woman beside her. She smiled at Adam and whispered something into her cousin's ear. Whatever she said caused the wailing to drop to a noisy snuffling.

Adam clasped his hands behind his back. "Would you care to ride in the park tomorrow?"

She smiled and her emerald eyes glinted at his obvious discomfort. "I would like that very much."

"I shall come early, so that we might avoid the usual crush. Perhaps three o'clock?"

"I will be ready, my lord."

Adam bowed. "Your servant." He strode from the room with unseemly haste, wishing to be far away before the older woman recommenced her caterwauling.

He snatched his hat and gloves from the servant who waited in the foyer without stopping. Outside, a throng of curious onlookers milled across the street from the duke's imposing mansion. Mostly they were from the lower orders, people who had come to catch a glimpse of Euphemia Marlington.

Adam paused at the top of the steps and pulled on his gloves while he surveyed the restless crowd. He estimated close to one hundred people milled on the opposite side of the street. No doubt one or two newspapermen mingled within the herd and he would read all about his visit tomorrow, if not later today.

He leapt into the phaeton and took the reins, imagining the scandal sheet headlines: *"Murdering Marquess to Wed Duke's Mysterious Daughter."*

Adam snorted and earned an odd look from his groom. He snapped the reins and the grays sprang forward, their eagerness to be away from Carlisle House nothing to his.

CHAPTER SEVEN

LaValle placed the frothy confection on Mia's head with all the pomp of an archbishop crowning a queen. Mia squirmed in her seat but let the woman enjoy herself. After all, fussing with Mia's clothing seemed to be the only thing that made the humorless Frenchwoman smile.

Mia was looking forward to this time alone with her husband-to-be. There were several important matters they needed to discuss and a short time to do it before their marriage.

The duke had summoned her to his study after the marquess's departure yesterday. In marked contrast to his attitude during her last visit to his masculine sanctum, her father's mood had been ebullient, almost festive.

"Congratulations on your good fortune, my dear." He'd briefly patted her on the shoulder to express his joy, his hands clasped behind his back as he beamed down at her. "Exley wishes to marry as soon as possible. Do you have any objections to your fiancé's desire for haste?"

The word *fiancé* had sent a shiver of excitement up her spine.

"The sooner we are wed, the better, Your Grace."

The duke had become positively beatific at her response, going so far as to triple her pin money; money she was already putting to good use, thanks to an idea that had begun forming in her head.

Mia had been aware for some time that her father's youngest footman would cast yearning — and decidedly carnal — glances her way whenever he thought she wasn't looking. She could turn that carnality to her advantage with only a little effort. He would be just the person to do the things she could not. Things like going to pawnbrokers, visiting port towns, and, eventually, booking passage on a ship. It wasn't possible to make definite plans until she knew what the marquess would do after they were married, but she could start recruiting the young footman to her cause now. Her first step would be to have him measured for a fine cloak to match his livery, an act which would single him out as her favorite and elevate his status.

Even with her maid's excessive fiddling, Mia was dressed and ready for her ride with the marquess a quarter of an hour early. She had to pass the open door to the small sitting room before she could reach the stairs. Rebecca was inside the room, working on one of her interminable stitching projects. Mia tiptoed past the doorway, not wishing to draw her attention; the last thing she needed when the marquess came to collect her was a sniveling woman clinging to her side.

She couldn't help laughing at the memory of Exley's face yesterday. His normally impassive features had been rigid with terror when confronted with her wailing cousin. Mia tucked that convenient information away. If all else failed to move him, she could always weep.

Two footmen — one the very man she'd just been contemplating — stood beside the arched opening to the entry hall. Mia eyed his muscular form and came to a halt inappropriately close to him. "I am waiting for the Marquess of Exley."

"Very good, my lady. Will you be waiting . . . er . . . here?" His voice cracked on the last word and a slight sheen of sweat formed at his temples as he endured her silent, smoldering stare.

"Come fetch me from the drawing room when he arrives."

The footman scrambled to reach the door before her. She smiled to herself as the door closed behind her. The young man would be easy to recruit.

The English servant situation was beyond comprehension to Mia. She doubted she would ever become accustomed to having handsome, virile young men within her reach.

The sultan had kept his wives and daughters in an impregnable fortress and surrounded them with men incapable of sexual thoughts or behavior. In England, the more prestigious a household was, the more physically appealing the servants were. This was particularly true of footmen — most of whom spent far more time with the lady of the house than her husband ever did.

Mia knew of at least two ladies of the *ton* who enjoyed more than the usual run of services from their handsome young servants. While that was not the kind of servicing Mia wanted from the strapping blond man, she was willing to dangle the promise of amorous relations or anything else to get what she needed.

She crossed the handsome inlaid wood

floor and went to the window that over-looked the front entrance to the house. The Duke of Carlisle's house was the largest on the square, occupying the greater portion of the south side of the street. The street was empty save for the occasional scurrying servant and a handful of ubiquitous gawkers who milled day and night, hoping to get a glimpse of her. The crowd was thin now, but would swell as the day passed into night.

Just like the gawkers, Mia could hardly get her fill of looking out windows. There had been no windows in the women's part of the sultan's palace and she'd often gone months without seeing anything other than the enclosed courtyards, private apartments, and high stone walls.

A light tapping sound made her turn. Her footman stood in the open doorway.

"The Marquess of Exley to see you, my lady." His voice was more modulated than it had been a few moments before. He stood stiffly beside the door, holding it wide open.

Mia treated him to the same deliberate smile as earlier, brushing against him as she exited. She looked away from the man's flushing face just in time to avoid colliding with the marquess, who was frozen in the act of coming toward her.

Mia cursed her stupidity and dropped into

the low curtsy that had pleased him the first time they'd met. She rose to find his arctic gaze fixed on her face.

Exley gave a slight bow. "Are you quite finished here?" He glanced from her to the footman, who looked as if he'd like to melt into the silk-covered walls or gleaming marble floor.

Rather than answer, Mia preceded him out the double doors and down the steps. She stopped in front of an excessively handsome equipage. The vehicle — Mia had no clue what it was called — was as sleek and elegant as its owner. It seemed almost precariously perched on big wheels, the stylish body a silver lacquer that complemented the two gray horses hitched to it.

The marquess assisted her into the high vehicle, the feel of his lean, powerful hands on her waist maddeningly brief. He hopped up beside her, took the ribbons from his groom, and settled himself in the seat.

"Wait for me here, Townshend," he ordered coolly. The servant had barely disembarked when he snapped the reins and the horses leapt forward.

"What a lovely carriage, my lord." Mia reached one hand up to secure her hat. La-Valle would suffer spasms if she lost the thing.

The marquess turned to face her, his pupils narrowed to pinpricks. "Tell me, my lady, do you plan to engage in open flirtation with my servants, as well?"

"Only the young handsome ones," Mia quipped.

Judging by the slight flaring of his nostrils, her attempt at levity had fallen flat.

Anger swirled around him like sand in a sirocco; Mia looked from his stern profile to his powerful, leather-clad hands as they tightened on the reins. Would he strike her, as the sultan had done on more than one occasion when she'd displeased him? He looked furious enough to do so. Mia had not believed him capable of deep emotions, certainly not jealousy. Or perhaps it was not jealousy, but a concern for appearances? In any case, she had been wrong in her assessment. At least a few emotions churned beneath the thick ice.

He kept his attention on the spirited pair, guiding them through the increasingly busy streets with a light touch. Something about the remoteness of his profile affected her. Her nature had always been far too playful and she should not have teased him.

"I am sorry, my lord. I have behaved badly. I am accustomed to dealing with eunuchs, you see. They require much pandering to manage. I often forget it is different here. It will not happen again." She laid a hand on his forearm as she looked up at him.

He glanced down with eyes as pale and hard as agates and she removed her hand and folded it in her lap before lowering her chin.

His voice, when it came, was like a blast of frosty air. "You aren't fooling me for an instant with your meek posturing."

Mia kept her head bowed to hide her smile. She was pleased he was intelligent enough to see through an act that had always fooled men like the sultan and her father. Of course, it would make deceiving him more difficult.

"You spoke plainly enough the night of the ball. I would ask that you continue in such a vein." He reined in the horses as they neared the massive gates to Hyde Park.

Mia decided it would be prudent to avoid toying with him, at least for the moment. "I, too, think it best if we continue to speak plainly."

He directed the carriage down a path that led to a less trafficked part of the park before speaking. "You mentioned eunuchs. They are not, I believe, a common fixture in most convents. It would please me to hear something of the past two decades of your life. The real story, this time."

"Are you concerned I am unable to behave with decorum, my lord? Perhaps you would like to reconsider your offer of marriage?" She bit her lip. Why did she feel the urge to taunt him so? He was not accustomed to it — that much was plain. But perhaps that was why she could not resist. His heated glare back at the house had been much more interesting than the bored expression he typically sported.

He slowed the carriage even more and turned to face her. "I have been accused of many things, but never of being a jilt, Lady Euphemia."

Again, she had to look down to hide her smile. His pride was certainly his tender underbelly.

They rode in silence and she composed her face into serious lines before looking up.

"As you no doubt guessed from the many inconsistencies in my story, I have never been to Malta. I lived outside of Oran, in the harem of Sultan Babba Hassan for seventeen years." Saying the words out loud was unexpectedly liberating.

His face registered no surprise.

"That does not shock you?"

"You will not find me easily shocked, my lady."

Mia didn't tell him she viewed such a statement as a personal challenge. She would save that for later. "Part of the story I told you was true. The ship was harried by corsairs, but they captured our vessel not far from Gibraltar."

"You were on the *Persephone*?"

Mia blinked. "How —"

"Such things are reported in the papers, my lady. I don't recall there being a passenger roster, but I do remember reading about it at the time. Please continue."

The fine hairs on her neck prickled; this man made it his business to know things. She swallowed her concern. Luckily for her, she'd made it hers to hide things.

"There were only a handful of English passengers aboard the ship, among them Hugh Redvers, Baron Ramsay — the same man who would eventually become the privateer One-Eyed Standish."

"Ah." Exley's chilly features thawed a little. "So that is your connection to him. I knew he was the one who brought you back to England. You have known Ramsay for many years, then."

"I wouldn't say I knew him. We were together for only a few days on the ship, until the corsairs docked at Oran to sell their captives." Mia realized her jaw had clenched and moved it from side to side. She would have believed this story was too old for her to feel such tension. Apparently, she had been wrong. "The corsairs raped and then decapitated my nurse the day they took the ship."

His body tensed beside her at the brutal words and she looked up. Their eyes locked, but he did not rush to offer pointless words of condolence.

"The corsairs never touched me. It did not fit with their plan, which was to give me to the sultan."

His brow furrowed. "But you are a duke's daughter. Why not ransom you? Surely they could have done so?"

"Ramsay argued the same thing with them, over and over, until they tied him to the mast and whipped him bloody." She could still see the big man if she closed her eyes. His broad back naked and streaming blood as an even bigger man delivered the twenty strokes the corsair captain, Faisal Barbarossa, had decreed.

"One whipping was not enough to stop Ramsay. He fought them again when we reached Oran, when the men put me into the carriage that would take me to the sultan. The last I saw of him — until I returned to England — he was being kicked and beaten by a dozen men."

Mia stared at the seams on her mint-green kid gloves but saw something else entirely. "I never forgot the big Englishman who took such risks on my behalf. I didn't learn that Ramsay survived the horrible beating until much later, when I heard of his escape from the sultan's prison."

Mia remembered the day clearly. Babba Hassan's fury at the escape had resulted in widespread beheadings. The sultan had been livid enough to offer a reward of gold equal to the weight of Ramsay's head.

"So, Ramsay escaped many years ago but only returned to England recently." There was more than a little curiosity in his cool voice.

"Yes, that is correct. I have no idea why Ramsay didn't return to England until now." She shrugged. "In any case, he and a dozen other slaves seized control of the very same ship that had captured us a few years earlier. He beheaded Faisal Barbarossa, rechristened the ship, and became One-Eyed Standish, the most feared British privateer in the Mediterranean. Even tucked away in the harem we heard of his exploits." She shook her head. "But my story has run ahead of itself. You asked why I was not ransomed?"

He nodded.

"The corsairs knew of the sultan's insatiable hunger for young girls."

The grooves that bracketed the marquess's mouth deepened and his hands tightened on the reins.

"They guessed he would find my red hair and green eyes an irresistible novelty. Some things were more valuable to them than money, and pleasing the sultan was one of them." She looked at the man who would soon be her husband. "The sultan was my only lover, my lord. I have never lain with another."

"There were no children from this union?" The words were clipped and his expression had become dogged. Was he regretting his desire for openness?

"There was a child — a son." Mia gritted her teeth and told the most difficult lie she'd yet spoken. "He died." She did not need to fake the pain that seized her as she ended her son's life, even if it was only in the mind of the man beside her.

Exley cut her a brief glance but said nothing.

"The sultan fathered no children during the last ten years of his life. He was unwell much of that time and could not participate in the act of conception without considerable effort." She was amused to see Exley's pale skin tint across the bridge of his fine nose.

Ah, even a jaded aristocrat could blush at such plain speaking.

"In any event, he showed little interest in taking me to his bed once I was beyond a certain age. He had many wives who were younger."

"What caused you to leave Oran?" he asked tightly.

"The sultan died and his son Assad seized control of his father's empire. Assad and I had had a misunderstanding years earlier and he held me in great dislike. I was lucky enough to escape the palace before he captured me. I hid in the souk, where I sold my jewels to live, and offered a substantial reward to the first person who delivered my message to Ramsay."

"And then Ramsay came to get you?"

Mia smiled up at him. "I swear you have been reading the scandal sheets, my lord."

Muscles flexed beneath his pale skin, making her hand twitch at the memory of touching the hard planes of his face. "It would have been impossible to get through the last few months without hearing at least a hundred stories about either you or Lord Ramsay," he said acidly.

"And some of those stories are so very, very naughty, my lord."

His nostrils flared. "I wouldn't know about those, *my lady.*" He shot her a look that sent heat surging through her body.

"Is that so?" she murmured, not waiting for an answer before continuing. "Ramsay could not come for me himself, but he sent his ship to collect me and bring me to East-bourne, his port of choice. He then accompanied me back to Burnewood Park."

Thinking of that journey — the last time she'd seen her son — made it difficult to breathe. Her vision became blurry and she stared down at her hands, blinking away tears.

The marquess broke the strained silence. "I will obtain a special license. Will ten days be sufficient time for you to prepare?"

Mia exhaled. She'd done it. She'd told the story without making any mistakes or rousing any suspicion. "Yes, my lord."

"My preference would be for an intimate ceremony."

She nodded. "Will you invite your sister and daughters, my lord?" When he didn't answer, she stole a look at him from beneath the brim of her hat. His features were set in characteristically harsh lines.

"No."

Mia tried to find some meaning in the single syllable but came up with nothing. She pushed her curiosity away — it did not serve her purpose. She would need to keep reminding herself that his children were not her affair. Nor was anything else in his life.

"You may, of course, invite as many people as you choose."

"Yes, my lord." Mia's guest list would be short. Other than family, the only person she knew in England was Baron Ramsay.

She'd seen Ramsay once or twice at London functions, but had never managed to speak with him in private. She had a sneaking suspicion the big peer wouldn't fall in with her escape plans, especially once she was married. Men had a tendency to stick together, even when they didn't know one another.

If he refused to help her, there were other men on his crew who might prove useful. His handsome first mate — a Frenchman named Martín Bouchard — came to mind. The amorous young man had made no secret of his interest in her. At least his interest in getting her into his bed. Mia would have succumbed to the man's advances if Jibril had not been on the ship.

Yes, Bouchard was definitely somebody she could turn to if necessary.

Mia would make it a point to find out from Ramsay when the Frenchman would be back in England. She could also press Ramsay for news of Jibril. The baron had given her son passage on his ship as well as money for supplies and weapons. The only thing he'd requested of Jibril was his word he would discontinue Babba Hassan's practice of dealing in slaves, a business her son already abhorred, being the son of a slave.

Mia realized the carriage had stopped and looked up. The marquess was staring. She smiled and a muscle jumped in her cheek. "I'm sorry, my lord, did you say something?"

"You were very far away and looked very pleased about something. Tell me, my lady, what were you thinking about to make you smile so?" His raptor-like stare belied his mild tone.

Nothing that would make you *smile,* Mia thought, bringing her twitching cheek under control. "I was wondering what we will do after the wedding."

His eyebrows shot up and his eyes lit with humor.

Heat flooded her face and she pressed her

hands to her cheeks. How was it this man had the power to make her blush?

"I meant *after* that, my lord. Where we will live?"

"Ah," he murmured, his expression mockingly crestfallen.

Mia found this small display of playfulness encouraging. "Will we stay in London or retire to your home in Hampshire?"

He made a soft clucking sound and the horses resumed their gentle pace. "Which would you prefer?"

"I should like to go to Exham Castle." Mia realized she was speaking the truth. Not just because of her escape plans, but because she was intrigued to meet the man's children, as well as the sister who was raising his daughters.

"We shall spend a few days in London after the ceremony and then remove to Exham. Will that please you?"

"Yes, my lord." She hesitated. "If you do not think me impertinent —"

He turned and gave her a cool look. "Yes?"

"Will you return to London immediately?"

"Would that please you?" he asked, his question a mocking echo.

"Of course not. It's just that I'm a bit curious."

He sighed. "Speak plainly, my lady."

"What is it that you do in London? I mean, if you do not attend *ton* functions and socialize?"

His face relaxed, as if she'd not asked the question he'd expected, or feared. He shrugged. "I attend my clubs, engage in a bit of fencing and shooting, and manage my various estates."

"And that is enough to occupy your time?"

His eyes narrowed, as if he suspected there was some other meaning lurking beneath her questions. "Estate management takes a good deal of time, if you are to do it correctly."

"Of course, my lord," she murmured, her tone placating. "So you have several estates?" *And are any of them closer to Eastbourne?*

"Yes."

"Have they been in your family long?"

"No, they have not."

This conversation reminded her of some she'd had with Jibril when he'd been young and had done something naughty, making her drag every small bit of information from him. Before she could come up with another question, he spoke.

"All but Exham and the London house are new properties which I have acquired."

"Acquired?"

Again he sighed. "To put it bluntly, I am skilled at cards. Most men, to their detriment, are not. When I encounter such men at a card table, it often results in the acquisition of houses and land. More property which, unfortunately, requires even more of my time and effort to manage." He raised one hand to suppress a yawn, as if speaking so many words had fatigued him.

Mia stared. What kind of man could take other men's homes with such cool detachment?

The marquess turned to her, as if he could hear her thoughts. Looking into his eyes at that moment was like standing on a ledge and looking down into thick, swirling fog. What did the mist obscure? A harmless step down or a bottomless pit?

Mia suddenly lost all desire to question him any further. In fact, she wondered if she should not leap from the moving carriage and begin running.

She faced forward, and they rode the remainder of the way home in silence.

Adam couldn't help noticing his future wife's look of relief when he refused her offer to come into Carlisle House for some refreshment. Who could blame her? He'd behaved like a jealous boor about a simple flirtation with the footman.

Hell, he'd even surprised himself.

Of course he'd done that a lot lately. Especially surprising had been his carriage ride to Carlisle House yesterday and his impulsive proposal.

He sighed. There was no point marveling over his actions now. What was done was done.

His jealous reaction today, however, was a different matter. He was not a jealous man. His first wife, Veronica, would have driven him mad within six months if he'd been the jealous sort. Lord knows the woman had never stopped trying. It had enraged her that he'd never said a word about her sexual escapades. Well, not until she brought her lovers into his house. Even then, it hadn't been jealousy he'd felt.

No, Adam couldn't recall ever having experienced the clawing sensation in his gut that had assailed him when he'd witnessed his betrothed's sensual smile at her handsome young footman. Even more unsettling was the haze of rage that had clouded his vision at the younger man's lusty appraisal of his fiancée.

But most disturbing was the vivid image of Euphemia Marlington's delicate, naked body pinned beneath the hulking footman, her head thrown back in ecstasy, green eyes reduced to sensual slits as the beefy blond man thrust himself into her, her body writhing with pleasure and her —

Adam jerked the reins with a clumsy spasm.

His ham-fisted handling of the ribbons startled his groom so badly, the man almost fell from his perch. "Your Lordship?" Thompson's eyes were round.

Adam didn't bother to explain. Besides, what could he say? That he was crippled with jealousy over a woman he'd known less than a week? He was stunned, ashamed, and terrified by the crude animal possession that had come out of nowhere, seized him by the scruff of the neck, and shaken him like a kitten.

The disturbing image of the footman and Mia again tried to slither into his head.

Mia! Just when did she become Mia, you dolt?

Adam gritted his teeth and shoved both the hectoring inner voice and snarling green-eyed monster into a corner of his mind and then locked them away.

He'd be damned if he would tolerate Veronica's brand of rampant whoring from *this* particular wife. If Euphemia Marlington wanted to rut like an animal, she could bloody well do so within the confines of his bedchamber. Or hers. Either way, Adam's body would be the only one she would be writhing beneath for the foreseeable future.

He gave a humorless crack of laughter, not caring who heard. Whatever scheme she was planning in her pretty little head — and he didn't doubt for a heartbeat she was up to something — it had better not involve Adam in the role of cuckold. He would not tolerate shaming from a third wife.

CHAPTER EIGHT

The informal wedding ceremony went smoothly. Even Cian behaved — after offering to spirit Mia away to freedom during the brief carriage ride to St. George's.

"It's your last chance, Mia. You merely need give me a sign and I'll have Cheyne turn the carriage."

"And where would you take me, Cian? Back to Carlisle House? To Burnewood Park?"

He'd leaned across to take her hands. "Ask Father to give you more time. There are other men . . . men who are less —"

She'd pulled away her hands. "Please do not speak ill of my betrothed, Cian."

He'd sat back at her sharp tone and Mia relented.

"Let us not argue, Brother. I have made my decision."

She'd not only made her decision, she'd then gone through with it; she was now the

Marchioness of Exley.

Mia glanced around the big room as it filled with guests, her head rather muddled after the whirlwind of the past ten days. The wedding had taken place just before noon and they'd returned to Carlisle House for a celebration feast. Small clusters of guests stood about the formal receiving room, conversing in low voices. The number of people gathered out in the street — and outside of St. George's — had been mob-like by comparison.

They were the most notorious couple in Britain.

The scandal sheet headlines shrieked, THE MURDEROUS MARQUESS TAKES THE DUKE OF CARLISLE'S MYSTERIOUS DAUGHTER TO WIFE!

Her new husband had taken it all in stride, flinging the sack of coins to the maddened crowd with the same cold contempt he showed everyone, peer or commoner.

The wedding had actually been far larger than she'd expected. Mia had had no hand in planning any of it. It had all been her cousin Rebecca's doing. After that first day, when her cousin had cried herself into a stupor, Rebecca had embraced the wedding with so much enthusiasm it might have been her own idea.

"He is, without a doubt, one of the most elegant men in the country, my dear," she'd told Mia in the confiding tone of one passing along a secret. "His personal wealth is enormous — even without the entailed properties."

Rebecca's sudden about-face amused Mia. "Are you privy to His Lordship's ledgers, Cousin?"

Her cousin's pale cheeks flared, the color making her appear young and pretty. "I am merely repeating what is well-known, that he possesses several magnificent estates."

Mia already knew that from their ride in the park — the only time they'd been alone in the days before the wedding. Exley had seemed determined to avoid spending time alone with her and she'd learned little else about him during the past week and a half. Anyone who might have told her about the marquess was hardly likely to gossip about him after their betrothal had been announced. The only person Mia knew well enough to ask about her mysterious husband was Baron Ramsay. She somehow doubted the privateer-turned-lord knew anything about the marquess as he'd hardly been back in England much longer than Mia.

As if her thoughts had summoned him,

Lord Ramsay entered the room and stopped to greet the duke. She still found it difficult to think of Lord Ramsay as anything other than One-Eyed Standish, a man whose exploits and sudden return to England had filled as many — if not more — scandal sheets than Mia.

More guests entered and the duke turned to welcome them, leaving Ramsay standing alone.

Mia leaned toward her cousin, who was clucking over some matter involving seating. "If you'll excuse me, Rebecca."

"Of course, my dear, of course."

Mia wasted no time.

"Lord Ramsay," she said, easing up beside him and giving him a flattering look from beneath her lashes. Flattery was not something she had to feign. Ramsay stood a good head taller than any other man in the room and he towered over Mia. His enormous body was well-formed and impeccably clad. And his face, although marred by the scar that ran across it and the patch that covered one eye, was almost obnoxiously attractive.

He bowed over her hand, an amiable smile on his handsome face. Mia opened her mouth to begin her campaign.

"Lady Exley," he said, putting emphasis on the two words. Mia looked closer and realized there was a hard glint in his solitary green eye. "I suspect you are about to embark on a tiresome subject we have already exhausted. Let us dispense with it now, so that we may enjoy the festivities. You are married. And even if you were not, I would not transport you back into that dangerous viper's nest." His unexpected offensive left her speechless.

His face softened as he surveyed her from his great height. "Jibril would have my head, Mia. Your son extracted a promise from me that I would not allow you back into danger," he added softly.

Mia's heart thrilled at the sound of her son's name — it had been so long since she'd spoken to anyone who even knew of his existence.

A small voice inside her insisted the baron's words were sensible, that Jibril, although young, was a well-respected leader of men who would not appreciate his mother's interference.

Mia suppressed the voice with all the ruthlessness she could not use on the man across from her. Her son was a boy who didn't know what was right for her, or himself, for that matter.

"What have you heard from him?" she asked.

"Very little, but enough to know he is realizing the futility of gaining control of his father's shrinking empire. Assad is beheading the family of anyone who shows the slightest inclination to support Jibril and that has had a cooling effect on his cause. I told him in my last message I would not throw good money after bad. I counseled him to come back to England. The Duke of Carlisle is a man of influence, Mia; he will take care of his grandson."

"As he has taken care of me?" she hissed, her resolve to deal sweetly with the towering baron dissolving at his arrogant words.

Ramsay's blond brows arched.

Mia scowled up at him. "You know Jibril can have no life here — *I* have no life here. I hate England." She fought to keep her voice down. "I wish with all my being I had never agreed to Jibril's demands and returned to this vile country." She swept the room with a hate-filled glare. "They will *never* accept me, Ramsay, and I was born here. How can you think they would accept my half-caste son?"

"You appear to have done well enough."

Mia followed Ramsay's gaze to her new husband. Even at his own wedding there was a gulf of empty space surrounding Exley, as though he were a lone British ship in enemy waters.

The aloof lord had invited no one to the ceremony save Viscount Danforth, who'd served as his only male attendant. Danforth was speaking to one of Mia's many cousins, so Exley was alone. He was watching Mia and Ramsay bicker. He met her eyes and cocked one brow, his lips curving into an amused, superior smile. The smile that made her want to do something shocking and wipe it from his face.

Mia groaned at the lustful thought and looked away from her husband's probing gaze. She stared up at the handsome giant beside her instead. "If I had a stick right now I would beat you with it."

Ramsay's booming laugh shook the very foundation of the house. Unlike his rich laughter, however, his eye was as hard as a faceted jewel. "Even such a dire threat as that will not make me change my mind."

Mia was too choked by frustration and rage to respond.

"You do Jibril a discourtesy by keeping his existence a secret. Your son is not so weak a man that scandal and gossip would overwhelm him." The baron gave a dismissive flick of his three-fingered hand. "He must forget his father's dying empire. The days of growing rich off slavery and piracy are at an end. Now that you are married and established, you could help him." His eye became shrewd and assessing. "Anyone who can navigate the shark-infested waters of the sultan's household — and flourish — would be a force to be reckoned with among the *ton.*"

Mia flushed at his unexpected praise.

His next words were not so flattering. "You are a fool if you haven't told Exley about the existence of Jibril and your desire to return to Oran. I agreed to keep the matter from the duke because I saw no point in making your homecoming any more difficult than it needed to be — especially since Jibril refused to do the wise thing and accompany you. However, I do not feel as sanguine hiding the truth from Exley. The man is your husband and it would behoove you to treat him with some respect and disclose your secret. If he were to ask me about you, I would feel compelled to tell the truth."

"It is not your secret to disclose," Mia hissed between clenched teeth.

Ramsay heaved an irritated sigh. "Do you imagine Exley will allow his wife to jaunter off into corsair-infested waters, Mia? The man is no fool and is possessed of a notoriously dangerous temper."

"Exley?" Mia looked at the unsmiling man across the room and gave an unladylike snort. "He is colder than a snake. I doubt you could rouse his temper — even if you could find it."

"I couldn't, but I'll wager *you* could, Mia."

Mia answered with a bitter laugh.

"Exley is not the sort to sit by and do nothing while you engage in intrigues. I've seen him shoot and fence, and I assure you, my lady, he is devilishly skilled at both. He has killed more than one man who has dared to make sport of him." Mia started at his words but Ramsay wasn't finished lecturing yet. "I should not try to deceive him were I you, madam." He paused, as if he wanted to say more on the subject, but then seemed to change his mind. "In any case, neither you nor Jibril will get my assistance retaking the sultan's crumbling empire. Nor will I transport you back into the middle of a desert war. Jibril is a man and must settle his own problems without his mother clucking over him like an overprotective hen. Your time would be better spent straightening out your affairs here."

Mia heard the steel beneath his words and bit back a scream. What did Ramsay know of her life? Who was he to say what was best for her or Jibril? Her head fairly jangled with rage but she took a deep breath and suppressed it. She needed the privateer. Right now he was her only connection to her son. It would be unwise to alienate him any further than necessary, no matter how unsympathetic he might appear to her cause.

She looked up and smiled. "I daresay you are correct. Let us not argue, my lord."

His single eye narrowed, as if he could see her devious thoughts.

"Has the *Batavia's Ghost* run into any trouble on her recent journeys?"

He stared.

It was Mia's turn to give an exaggerated sigh. "I only mention the matter because I've heard the French have increased their forays."

"She is out of the water and undergoing repairs in Eastbourne at the moment," he finally admitted.

"Is your crew enjoying this sojourn on English soil?"

His full lips compressed into a grim line. "Please, don't bring up such an irritating subject. Most of my crew has circled the globe dozens of times and one would think they'd know how to behave. Unfortunately, that is not the case. I seem to spend most of my time — and not a little of my coin —

rescuing them from either the authorities or armed, angry townsfolk. The sooner the ship is mended and off, the better it will be for all."

"Yes, I suppose most people have not often seen the likes of men like Two-Canoes or Martín Bouchard."

"Yes, Two-Canoes has managed to terrify the locals merely by existing. Martín is no longer disrupting either the townspeople or my household, as I have put him in charge of the *Ghost,* at least for the time being."

"Martín Bouchard is now captaining your ship?" Mia repeated, stunned.

Ramsay frowned at the excitement in her voice.

"So, he is a captain now," she said in a much calmer voice, even though inside she was leaping for joy at the news. There was no doubt in her mind that Martín Bouchard — for the right amount of money — would take Mia wherever she pleased. She bit her lip hard to keep from grinning.

Ramsay nodded slowly, his forehead deeply furrowed, as though he was working through something in his head.

"Why are you suddenly so interested in my ship and crew?" Ramsay asked, interrupting her private rejoicing.

Mia was spared from responding by the

approach of Lord Exley. Her husband, she mentally corrected.

"My lady, Lord Ramsay."

She had given up trying to look beyond his haughty façade. Maybe there was nothing behind it? Other than the brief show of passion when he'd proposed, and the equally brief flare of anger when Mia had flirted with her footman, she'd seen no sign of any other emotions. It was his wedding day and he'd shown no sign of caring one way or another that they were now man and wife. Did their marriage really matter so little to him? Mia knew the thought should please her — after all, the more distant he was, the better it was for her plans. Even so, the knowledge that he could be so cold left a chill in its wake.

Ramsay grinned at her husband, as though thrilled by the marquess's cold greeting. He held out a giant hand, a habit that was most certainly not English.

"I was just congratulating your lovely wife, Exley."

Her husband's elegant hand disappeared in Ramsay's enormous fist.

"I am the one you should congratulate," the marquess contradicted softly. Mia could see he didn't believe the baron. It didn't take a genius to see that her conversation with Ramsay had been heated. Well, heated on her side. Mia would need to behave with more circumspection around her husband in the future; his sharp eyes saw too much.

She placed her hand on his forearm. "I was just telling Lord Ramsay how eagerly I am looking forward to seeing Exham Castle."

The marquess laid a hand over hers, the almost imperceptible flush on his high, sharp cheekbones the only sign her possessive gesture had affected him.

Ramsay's gaze flickered back and forth, like an eager spectator at a play. "You cannot be leaving tonight for Hampshire?" He swept Mia's body with a lecherous look that caused Exley's hand to tighten around Mia's.

"We will spend our wedding night in town."

The words *wedding night* caused heat to creep up her neck. Once again her new husband had made her blush and feel like a girl, rather than a woman long past her prime. Mia beamed up at him and his eyes widened, as if he, too, had experienced something unexpected.

The baron looked from Mia to her new husband and snickered. Mia did not know Ramsay well, but she had quickly realized the big privateer had a mischievous streak a mile wide. He was clearly enjoying the awkward tension between her and Exley and looked eager to add to it. "My congratulations to you both. I wish you both very happy." He rocked back on his heels, his gleeful expression making him resemble a very large boy who was struggling to contain his amusement. "I understand you have children in Hampshire, Exley?"

"Yes, three daughters."

"Ah, daughters." Ramsay grinned for no apparent reason. "I daresay they will be thrilled with a new step-mama. Not to mention the prospect of a new sister or brother."

Mia's jaw dropped at his vulgar innuendo. Why the *obnoxious* —

The marquess ignored the other man's improper reference to pregnancy and looked from the towering baron to Mia, his pale eyes darkening, as if he were imagining putting her in such a condition.

Would she ever stop blushing? Mia looked away from her husband and caught the baron staring at her with a knowing smirk. She scowled up at him and shook her head.

Ramsay's booming laugh once again shook the room and Mia wondered if it was too late to kick him.

CHAPTER NINE

Adam settled his wife on the forward-facing seat and took the one across from her. He noticed, for the first time, faint smudges beneath her large green eyes. "You are tired, my lady?"

"A little. But I am relieved to have the ceremony over. I am looking forward to seeing your house." She gazed out the window into the darkening streets.

"It is your house, now, as well," he reminded her, admiring the graceful line of her neck.

"Yes, of course." She smiled and turned back to him, folding her hands in her lap. Her pale green gown was simple and becoming. It was modestly cut, displaying only the upper slopes of her small breasts. In the half-light she looked like a much younger woman, until the carriage passed beneath a lantern and illuminated her green eyes — eyes that usually sparkled with sinful, wicked things but now appeared tired and lackluster.

Adam cleared his throat. "I understand several of your servants have already settled in." He'd seen the hulking blond footman transporting boxes and portmanteaus into his house only this morning.

"Yes, my lord." Her compliant words matched her submissive look.

Adam was skilled at reading people's faces, part of what made him such an excellent card player. His new wife had several small, but telling looks. Like the one she had just given him. Whenever she widened her eyes and followed it with an innocent lowering of her gaze, he knew she was attempting to divert her listener away from something she wished to conceal. Was she trying to hide something about the footman?

"I have not brought many servants with me, my lord. LaValle, my maid, and Paley and Gamble, the footmen who served me at my father's house."

Adam remained silent, a tactic that rarely failed to bear results.

"I believe your butler has already found room for them."

"Hill is very efficient."

A long pause inserted itself.

"You keep quite a large staff at Exley House, my lord?"

"Yes." He was amused by her attempt to draw the conversation away from her handsome servant, but he would not aid her in the effort. He could see she waited for him to expand his one-word answer. When he didn't, she filled the brittle silence.

"Will that change now that we are going to the country?"

"All but a few of my servants will remain in London to keep the house prepared for my return." Adam would swear she was pleased by his words. That was interesting, not to mention somewhat humbling. So, she was eager for him to leave her at Exham and return to London. He supposed it was no less than he deserved.

Adam watched her silent profile, aware that he should be speaking to her, telling her about her new home, talking about the weather, anything but sitting here and brooding. He was behaving even more disobligingly than usual but he could not seem to stop himself. He knew the reason why, too, even though he'd spent the last ten days first denying it and then fighting it. He was obsessed by her — at least by the thought of bedding her — and it scared him. More than anything had scared him in a long,

long time.

He had hoped — foolishly, it now seemed — that time away from her before their wedding would help to cool his ardor. When that had not been enough to drive her from his thoughts, he'd gone to Susannah, a decision that had been ill-conceived, to say the least. The only thing to come out of that evening, other than a rather large gash on his forehead from the vase Susannah had hurled at him, was the realization their union was over.

He'd not planned to end his association with the tempestuous actress after he'd married. Why should he? The marriage he and his wife had planned was nothing more than a business arrangement. But kissing Susannah had been like eating sawdust and Adam knew it would be the same with any woman but one. At least until he'd bedded the green-eyed witch.

Adam studied the diminutive enigma seated across from him and was seized by a ferocious desire to lift her skirts and take her before they even reached Exley House. It was his legal right to do so. She was his, body and soul. And he was so bloody hard for her it was torture. He could pull her onto his lap and put an end to the quasi-erect state he'd been in for days.

His body ached with the primitive desire to possess her but his mind was appalled at the chaos of his emotions. He needed to rein in the rampaging lust, not to mention the ridiculous jealousy that assailed him like a hail of arrows every time another man even looked at her. He'd even wanted to hurt Ramsay when he'd seen how familiarly he'd treated Mia earlier. Adam frowned. And just what the hell had the two of them been talking about so intently?

And then there was that bloody footman. Adam bit back a groan. He was in danger of making himself mad about his wife's relationship — real or imagined — with her lummox of a footman.

Adam set his jaw. This interminable carriage ride would be the last time he permitted such mental disorder. He would bed the woman and they would leave for Exham in a few days. He would deposit her in the country, as she clearly wished for him to do, and visit her every four or five weeks until she was breeding. The sooner he got her with child, the sooner he could stay away from her and the unnerving effect she had on him and resume his quiet, predictable existence.

Mia gazed out the darkened window, her

mind on the man across from her. She was not accustomed to spending so much time with a man and certainly not with one who was so quiet and inscrutable.

The sultan had been simple in his wants if not always easy with his demands. She'd pleasured him or submitted to him and then returned to the comfort of the harem. Baba Hassan did not expect or desire conversation from a woman, quite the reverse. He had usually become displeased when faced with a garrulous woman.

Perhaps her new husband was the same. He seemed to have no wish to talk to her. She studied him through the gloom. His head was tipped back against the luxurious gray leather, his eyes closed, his sooty lashes fanned against his pale skin. Was he taking a nap? She seized the opportunity to look at him unobserved, beginning with the fine bones of his face. His lips were fuller at rest, made for kissing rather than sneering. Her breathing roughened as she recalled her single contact with them. His mouth had been so sweet, so firm, so . . .

She stopped and forced her eyes to resume their inspection. Who knew when she'd next get such a chance to stare at him?

His chest rose and fell gently and her body ached to explore the tantalizing expanse of his broad, sleek shoulders. She'd never touched a man in prime condition and she could not wait to slide her fingers beneath his coat and waistcoat and pull up his shirt to explore his skin.

Her eyelids became heavy, forcing her gaze down to the tantalizing gap between the bottom of his coat and the top of his snug breeches, the place where only a thin line of waistcoat was visible. That small slice of fabric taunted her — designed to draw a woman's eye to the front of a man's hips, forcing her to imagine what was above . . . and below.

She stared at the intriguing spot, her eyes drawn downward to the fall of his breeches. His muscular thighs were slightly spread, their chiseled hardness a sharp contrast to the soft leather seat that cushioned them. Something about the sight reminded her of the delicious chocolates she'd received from one of her suitors. She swallowed hard as she considered the similarities between the marquess's delectable body and a velvet-lined box of delicacies.

A slight cough caused her head to jerk up. Mia swallowed; her husband was looking at her from beneath hooded eyes. How long had he been watching?

"We are at Exley House."

The wheels of the carriage drew to a halt, an ironic counterpoint to Mia's racing pulse.

The door opened and the marquess kicked down the steps and exited. Once outside, he turned and said something to the two grooms, who'd leapt from the box. They moved to hold back the noisy horde who'd gathered around the carriage. It seemed she would have a collection of nosy onlookers at her new home, as well. Exley handed her down and Mia glanced toward the surging throng, many of whom had begun to yell bawdy suggestions.

The crowd here was louder and more raucous than the one that had held sway outside Carlisle House the first weeks after she'd returned. It would be impossible for her to execute any of her escape plans until she was in the country.

"Do you think they are dangerous, my lord?"

His cold gaze flickered over the mob, which was mostly comprised of men but also held a fair number of females — mainly women whose dress proclaimed their profession. Most of those gathered exhibited the exaggerated motions and overly loud voices of drunks.

"No, but you should never step out of the house alone, nor even just with your maid."

His lips twisted. "Always take your footman with you." He took her arm and led her up the steps to the imposing stone structure that was her new home.

Two rows of servants stood lined up in the large marble entry hall. The marquess approached the imposing older man at the head of the line and began the introductions.

"This is Hill, the man responsible for the smooth operation of the house."

"My lady." The older man bowed.

Mia smiled and nodded at him before moving to the forty odd servants who stood behind him, from Hill all the way down to the lowliest boot boy.

When she finished meeting the last of her new staff, Exley nodded to his dour housekeeper. "Mrs. Jenkins will show you to your chambers. There are a few matters that require my attention. I shall see you at dinner." He gave her a perfunctory bow and Mia watched him ascend the curving set of marble stairs that swept up the left side of the hall. He disappeared and she turned, trying not to feel alone as she stood among the crowd of strangers in her new home.

"If you would follow me, Lady Exley," Mrs. Jenkins asked, gesturing toward the other side of the hall, to the staircase that mirrored the one her husband had just taken.

Mia's chambers were on the third floor at the end of the hall.

The housekeeper opened one of the double doors, stood aside, and waited until Mia had entered.

The first things Mia saw were an enormous four-poster bed and her maid's pinched face. The haughty Frenchwoman was, for once, a welcome sight and Mia gave her an overly bright smile.

"Ah, LaValle. You are settling in, I see. Please have a bath sent up."

"Yes, my lady," LaValle murmured, her hard brown eyes dismissing the housekeeper as if she did not exist.

The older woman's flushed cheeks told Mia this was not the first time she'd endured the French dresser's scorn.

"Please have tea sent up as soon as my bath is prepared."

The older woman frowned, as if taking tea in one's bath was not done, but nodded and said, "Yes, my lady."

"That is all, Mrs. Jenkins."

The housekeeper left and Mia prowled through her new chambers. They were even more spacious than those she'd occupied at Carlisle House.

145

Mia examined the dressing room first. La-Valle had already hung most of her clothing and her shoes and other finery had been put away, making the room look as though it had been occupied for years. She stopped in front of a closed door: the door to her husband's chambers. She pressed her ear against the smoothly polished wood but could hear nothing. She twisted the handle. It was not locked. Mia released the knob and turned away. He'd said he had business. What manner of business would intrude on his wedding day? She shrugged. What did it matter? They were engaged in a marriage of name only, not cooing lovebirds. The fact that he'd already left her alone boded well for the future.

She inspected the rest of her new living quarters. An enormous copper tub took pride of place on a pedestal in the center of her bathing room. The tub looked large enough for several people and Mia shivered with anticipation. It was the first tub she'd seen in England that even remotely resembled the lavish bathing areas in the sultan's palace. The English did not view bathing as a leisure activity.

A collection of cut-glass bottles covered the vanity in front of a massive, wood-framed mirror. Mia took one and pulled the stopper: lavender, her favorite. She replaced the bottle and studied the rest of the room. The floor was an alabaster marble shot through with gray veins. If Mia were to stay here for long she would see that carpets were brought in to warm the beautiful, but cold-looking, floor. The walls were covered in ice blue silk, a color that was elegant but not particularly restful.

The bedchamber walls were a darker blue and a large four-poster bed with a damask canopy dominated the room. Plush rugs of silver, blue, and cream covered the polished wood floor. The only other furniture was a gilt settee and two spindly chairs clustered in front of a large, dormant fireplace. Mia briefly considered having a fire built. Summer in London was far colder than winter in Oran.

She was still wondering if a fire would make the room too hot for her new husband when LaValle returned, followed by a line of servants bearing steaming buckets.

Mia went to stand before the large mirror in her dressing room. "You may undress me."

The Frenchwoman hurriedly closed the doors that separated the rooms. The woman had a prudish mania when it came to Mia's naked person and thought her mistress's comfort with her own nudity disturbing.

LaValle worked in silence on the various buttons, tapes, and hooks that contributed to an Englishwoman's full battle armor. After years of wearing either nothing at all or a loose caftan, Mia found the restrictive clothing unbearable and wore only a dressing gown whenever possible.

LaValle removed her gown and draped it over the dress stand before she began unlacing the corset that was the misery of Mia's existence. She was almost boyishly skinny but she could not go without a corset. The only good she could see in the evil garment was that it pushed up her small breasts and made them look twice as large as they were, which was still not saying very much.

She exhaled a gusty sigh of relief when her maid removed the stiff garment and finally lifted off her chemise. Mia examined her naked body in the mirror as LaValle removed her slippers and stockings. She thrust out her small breasts and frowned at the result. What would her new husband think of her? She was no longer young, but her body was still firm and supple. She did not think the marquess favored young girls. He'd looked displeased when he'd heard how early she'd lost her maidenhead. Perhaps he found mature women desirable.

She caught LaValle's disapproving stare in the mirror. The woman was looking at the small emerald that nestled in Mia's navel, her lips pursed. This wasn't the first time Mia had noticed her servant's disapproval.

Piercing had been common among the sultan's people, who traced their history to a Kabyle tribe that had long ago migrated down from the Atlas Mountains to the sea. Most of Babba Hassan's guards had had pierced ears and many of the eunuchs and women pierced noses, navels, and even nipples.

She leaned closer to the mirror and peered at the side of her nose. Only the smallest of dimples was still visible. Mia had removed the nose stud she'd worn for years before leaving Oran. At first she'd done so because the sight of a large diamond stud in the souk would have been too tempting a target for thieves. She'd had to sell it later and had never replaced it because she knew English-women did not go about with piercings. The marquess would never know her nose had once borne a diamond stud.

Mia looked down past her disappointing breasts to her navel and the small gold ring set with a beautiful emerald. It was one of the first gifts she'd received from the sultan when he'd had her pierced. She fingered the gem and it glinted a rich green in the well-lighted dressing room. Should she remove the jewelry?

Judging by the Frenchwoman's reaction, perhaps it would be better.

She looked from the emerald to her servant's critical face. She would leave the piece of jewelry. If her husband did not like it, he could tell her himself.

Chapter Ten

Adam submitted to Sayer's ministrations in silence, the two men conducting the business of master and servant with their usual lack of conversation. Sayer was the only servant Adam had retained after the death of his first wife, Veronica. He'd either pensioned off or found new positions for the others. Especially those at Exham Castle, many of whom had witnessed far more than was comfortable for either Adam or his family. His daughters were already burdened with their father's reputation; the last thing they needed was to grow up with scandalous tales of their mother.

But Adam hadn't been able to part with Sayer, who'd been with him since Oxford. Not only was he an excellent valet, but his taciturn manner suited Adam to perfection. He would have been hard-pressed to recall the man's speaking more than ten full sentences in the past year. He was so in tune with Adam's tastes, it was no longer necessary for him to even enter a shop. Sayer took care of every aspect of his clothing except actually wearing the garments.

The last thing Adam would countenance was an emotional or high-strung servant — like his friend Danforth's valet, Creel, who was given to bouts of near-hysteria whenever his master came home with a wine-stained cravat or scuffed Hessian.

Adam considered his closest friend's reaction to the news of his impending nuptials while Sayer undressed him. The two had been sitting at their club, relaxing after a successful night at the tables.

"I have asked Euphemia Marlington to marry me and she has agreed. I would like you to attend me at our wedding ceremony."

Danforth had choked and spilled half a glass of port down the front of his erstwhile snowy white cravat. Adam had imagined he could hear the anguished screams of Danforth's valet as the crimson liquid discolored the fine linen.

"You're . . . I beg your pardon?" Danforth said, as uncaring of his ruined cravat as he was his valet's sanity. There was scarcely a night when Danforth did not return home looking as if he'd been rolled by highwaymen.

"I am betrothed to Lady Euphemia Marlington."

Danforth's deceptively angelic eyes had opened even wider than usual as he digested the news, a grin growing on his boyish face. "Well, congratulations, old man. A toast!" He'd mashed his glass so hard against Adam's he'd almost covered *him* with the remainder of its contents.

"She's a lovely woman, Exley." The younger man's warm, speculative look had caused Adam's hand to tighten around his glass. Part of his mind — the part not urging him to call out his friend — had been disgusted by his rampant jealousy.

Adam realized his mind had dragged him back to the same tedious topic: his obsession for his new wife.

"Fetch me a brandy, Sayer." He left his small clothes on the floor and headed toward his bathing chamber, where a steaming tub awaited. He dipped one foot into the almost scalding bathwater and flinched back. It took him several minutes before he could ease himself into the tub.

He believed baths were one of life's great indulgences and always had the servants heat the water beyond what was comfortable so he could soak longer. Once he was submerged in the steaming water, he lay against the sloped back and pondered his obsession. He was more upset that he was capable of *being* obsessed than he was at the subject of his obsession.

In effect, he was obsessed by the fact he was obsessed. *Christ.*

"Sayer!"

Sayer's head appeared around the corner. "Yes, my lord?"

"Are you distilling the brandy?"

"I've had to send for a new bottle." Sayer paused. "You finished the last one, my lord." His head disappeared.

Adam didn't need his valet's significant pause to remind him of how much alcohol he'd consumed lately. Especially today — his wedding day. He'd been drinking steadily since he'd retired to his study, where he was allegedly seeing to important business. Business comprised of pacing and trying to get his rampaging lust under some semblance of control. He needed to stop imagining his new wife without clothing before he made an even greater fool of himself.

Even more important, he needed to stop imagining that other men were imagining her without clothing. Just because Adam could not think of her in any other way did not mean the entire male populace was mentally undressing her. If he could not get his jealous impulses under control, his social calendar would be filled with early morning appointments on Hampstead Heath.

Lust and jealousy. Adam snorted, what a delightfully lowering combination. Would he complete his transformation to callow youth by sporting high collars, wasp-waisted coats, and festooning himself with fobs and seals?

Adam groaned as the object of his obsession flashed into his mind and he stiffened, all over. He scrubbed his offending appendage roughly, as if that would somehow scour away his bothersome thoughts.

His lust would abate after he got the bedding out of the way. That was the way it had been in the past when it came to his amours. Although perhaps he'd never been quite so consumed before. He dismissed the worry. By this time tomorrow he would be back to his normal self. He would make sure of it.

Adam closed his eyes at the soothing notion and relaxed. He'd almost drifted off when a horrible thought slammed into him. Water flooded over the side of the tub and fanned across the white marble floor as he struggled to sit up.

Good God. What if bedding her once only made his obsession worse?

■ ■ ■ ■

Mia's splendidly handsome husband was drunk. She glanced about the enormous formal dining room and repressed a sigh. Not that it mattered if he was unfit for conversation. The only way to talk would be to bellow over the monumental floral arrangement that dominated the center of the twenty-foot table. It was less an assortment of cut flowers and more an impenetrable hedge of vegetation that seemed to have sprouted from the table itself.

Eight footmen descended on the table to set out multiple courses that consisted of at least a half dozen offerings. Gamble was among the men waiting at the table, conspicuous in his ducal livery, a gold and green dragonfly buzzing among seven black and silver.

Mia glanced from the handsome young footman to her husband and found his eyes boring through her. He was paler than usual, the only color two slashes of crimson on his cheekbones, like cuts from a knife. He'd been watching her with a sullen intensity since the moment she entered the room and had, no doubt, noticed her examination of Gamble.

She leaned to the side and smiled around the carnivorous-looking floral display. "My rooms are quite lovely, my lord. Did you have them decorated recently?" she shouted.

He tipped back his head and drained fully half his glass of wine.

Mia's eyes widened. *Good Lord.*

"You must give your compliments to Hill. He is responsible for all of it. It was done two years ago, after the death of my mother." His voice was as cold and unemotional as ever. Perhaps he was not as intoxicated as she assumed. Or maybe food would halt the process.

He glanced down at his untouched plate and pushed it aside.

Or perhaps not.

"Have you only the one sibling, my lord?" Mia almost laughed after the question left her mouth. They were married and yet she had no idea how many brothers and sisters he had. What must their silent audience think of such an asinine conversation?

Judging by the contemptuous twist of his lips, her new husband was thinking something similar.

"Yes, my sister, Jessica. She is the younger by three years."

The footman hovering behind him refilled his glass. The marquess glanced down and his expressive brows hooked, as if he was surprised to discover his glass had required filling.

Mia wondered if he typically consumed such quantities of alcohol. The frown he gave his newly replenished glass suggested he was wondering the same thing.

"Your sister lives at Exham Castle?"

"Yes."

"With your daughters."

"Yes."

When it was clear they'd once again devolved to monosyllables, Mia gave her attention to her plate.

She ate.

He drank.

The clinking of cutlery filled the silence.

"Jessica and my eldest daughter, Catherine, assist the governess with Eva and Melissa." The dense hedge of greenery muffled his words. "Jessica is of a retiring disposition and does not often venture out into society. She has not come back to London since her only Season some years ago." His expression was a trifle dazed, as though he'd stunned himself with this veritable flood of information.

"Will Catherine make her come-out next Season?"

The marquess stared stonily at her, as if

Mia had asked whether his eldest daughter had plans to take up bear-baiting in Hyde Park. He took a drink and glared at the arrival of more dishes. "There are no such plans."

Why would such a man not want to give his daughter a Season? And why was she wondering about such a thing? His daughters were none of her concern. He was marrying her for an heir, not to present his daughters, something she would be woefully inexperienced at, in any case. She was marrying him to escape, and, if she was completely honest with herself, because she wished to have him as a lover. All her life she'd given sexual pleasure and never received it. Mia studied her attractive, drunk husband and wondered if that would continue to be the case.

She helped herself to a portion of trout before steering the conversation in a less contentious direction. "You mentioned on our ride in the park you enjoy card games. Which games do you prefer?"

The marquess scrutinized her for an almost insultingly long moment before answering.

"Yes, I have an affinity for cards."

Mia gave up waiting for more and cut another slice of fish. The food at her husband's table was superior to her father's, so the marquess obviously cared about such matters — even though he did not appear to be a great eater. She ate a piece of fish and took a sip of a particularly exquisite wine.

"Do you enjoy playing cards?"

Mia's head jerked up at the question; was that a slight slurring she detected?

"My brother taught me cribbage and piquet, both of which I enjoy, although I am not very skilled. I am used to chess and Zamma."

"Zamma?" He sounded interested for the first time that evening, perhaps even that day.

"Yes, it is played on a board with stones or beads. You may have heard it referred to as Hunt and Capture?"

"Hunt and Capture," he repeated, his lips curling into an odd smile. "No, I have not heard of it. I am partial to games. Perhaps you will teach me Zamma?" Mia was rendered speechless by this unprecedented display of . . . anything. As if determined to stupefy her with his garrulousness, he continued, "I enjoy chess with the right opponent. It is a demanding game; the requirement of seeing so many moves ahead is challenging. Many players become too attached to their pieces and are unable to sacrifice something important in order to lure their opponent into a fatal indiscretion. You say you enjoy the game?"

Mia knew he was not talking about chess. What had she done or said to give him the idea she was playing games with him? Whatever it was, she needed to stop doing it.

"I like chess very much, my lord."

"Are you a challenging opponent?"

"We must play and you may judge for yourself."

He signaled for the footman to remove his untouched plate and then turned to his refreshed glass, evidently finished with the conversation.

The meal was the longest of her life. Her husband's determined drinking mediated against conversation, as did the dozen or so servants milling between them. As the daughter of a duke, Mia was accustomed to formal dining. But even at Carlisle House they dined with less pomp when it was only family. His icy manner remained unchanged but she detected a slight sway to his posture. Was he a dipsomaniac or merely avoiding taking her to bed for some reason?

By the end of the meal she was exhausted and the marquess was beyond drunk, no matter how well he hid it. After the last dish was cleared, Mia debated the wisdom of leaving him to his port. But then she met his flat stare. He wanted her to leave.

Mia stood and the marquess stood with her, bracing himself with two hands on the dining table.

"I shall retire to my chambers, my lord." She refused to wait for him in the solitude of some cavernous sitting or drawing room. If he wanted her, he could come to her bed-chamber.

CHAPTER ELEVEN

Adam exhaled after the door closed, as if he'd been holding his breath for the past hour instead of pouring prodigious amounts of alcohol down his throat. The tray of port had somehow materialized in front of him. He motioned to the footmen flanking the door.

"You may finish clearing later."

Once the room was empty he slumped back in his chair and stared at the ceiling. The view above him was a baroque extravaganza, some forgotten artist's rendering of Velazquez's *Triumph of Bacchus.* The young god wore little more than a crown of grape leaves and a bemused frown, as though he'd been waylaid by rambunctious revelers rather than the other way around. Those who flanked him bore the inebriated leers of men who would have whopping headaches in the morning. Men like Adam.

He closed his eyes. "You bloody fool." The

words were more than a little slurred. The result of most of a bottle of brandy, Lord knew how much wine, and an almost empty stomach. And all of it had been for nothing.

The naked truth was that he was terrified of bedding his wife. Not of the act, of course. No, he was relentlessly hard for that. Not to mention disturbingly eager. Where would such an intense yearning lead? If he'd felt this way about Veronica, he certainly didn't recall it.

Not that it mattered how he felt. He doubted he could even find his wife's bed-chamber at this point, and he wouldn't be any good to her if he did. Besides, she had probably barred the door and wouldn't admit him after his behavior tonight.

He groaned. The entire day had been a disaster, and he was its architect. He'd wanted to establish his self-control in their marriage right from the start with distance and formality. Instead, he'd behaved like the selfish, cold, inhuman monster society believed him to be. Not to mention a disgusting drunk.

He must have been mad to marry again; were not *two* disastrous, infamous marriages enough? How, in God's name, would this one end?

Adam grabbed the glass of port and threw

it back in one swallow. It only made him feel sicker and he pushed away the bottle to resist any further temptation. Pushing his thoughts away wasn't quite as easy.

When was the last time he'd consumed so much alcohol? University? He lowered his head into his hands and squeezed his pounding temples. He'd not become a drunken sot the entire time he'd been married to Veronica. Not even after the horror of her death had he needed to suffocate his pain with drink. In fact, he'd felt no pain — or anything at all by the end of it.

He'd always assumed that was because Veronica had stolen away his ability to feel bit by bit — a little love here, some joy there — she'd even taken emotions like sadness, fear, and shame. Ultimately, she'd taken everything and left him riddled with holes. Empty gaps he'd filled with pride, contempt, and arrogance, until he'd become the man society thought he was: an inhuman monster who'd ruthlessly done away with two wives.

A bitter smile twitched at the thought of his second wife, who technically did not qualify for the title of wife. Poor, poor Sarah. While Veronica had done her best to capture his attention and drive him insane, Sarah had only wanted to escape his notice — and him. Adam filled his glass and lifted it in a silent toast to his unfortunate second wife and their very short-lived marriage. He tipped back the glass and then hurled it at the far wall. It exploded with a sharp *pop* and he blinked at the glittering shards on the floor. That had been foolish. Now he would need to drink from the bottle.

Sarah had come and gone quickly, her departure far more noticeable than her actual presence in his life. Veronica, on the other hand, had left none of his family unscathed. For all his wealth and power, Adam had been helpless to shield the people he loved any more than he'd been able to shield himself. Everyone had suffered because of his lack of judgment — his daughters most of all. Had he just committed the same offense again? Had he allowed desire for a woman to plunge his family into Hell?

Even in his drunken, self-pitying state he knew that was unfair. Euphemia Marlington had done nothing to inspire such fears. It was his own enfeebled character that seemed to be unraveling the more he saw of her. He owed her an apology.

Adam tried to read the time on the long-case clock that stood only a few feet away but couldn't focus. He fumbled for his watch. Even holding it two inches from his face, he couldn't read it. His face became hot with shame. He was too damn drunk to read his own watch and he'd abandoned his bride on her wedding night. His hand crept toward the port and this time he didn't stop it.

Mia woke with a start and sat bolt upright. She blinked and looked around, trying to recall where she was. As her vision became less blurry and her brain less sleep-addled she remembered she was in her new chambers at Exley House. It was her wedding night, the only one she'd ever had; Babba Hassan had not married his concubines.

She looked down at her now-rumpled clothing. She'd instructed LaValle to dress her in a lovely confection of pale green lace. What a waste. Mia dropped her head back onto the pillow. Evidently, Exley really was as bored as he appeared. The man had forgotten her existence before even bedding her. She told herself that was just as well. It was better that he never came near her at all. That way there would never be the slightest danger of a child.

Mia clasped her hands over her stomach and waited for that argument to become more persuasive. But the only thing that sank in was anger. How dare he neglect her like this, especially when she burned for him

— or at least his body?

She gave a growl of frustration. What a fool she was, lusting for a man who was so clearly damaged. But also so very, very intriguing.

Her bedside clock read almost three o'clock. Fueled by emotions she didn't want to examine, she rose and put on her dressing gown before stalking to the door that led to her husband's bedchamber. She tapped softly. The door jerked open and she gave a squeak of surprise.

Not her husband, but a servant, stood before her.

"Yes, my lady?" the reserved-looking man inquired.

"You are Lord Exley's valet?" It was a stupid question.

"Yes, my lady."

Mia refused to feel any embarrassment. She would leave that to her husband.

"Has Lord Exley left the house?"

"I believe he is still in the dining room, my lady."

"Does he sleep there often?" she snapped, annoyed by the man's aloofness, which was so similar to his employer's.

He coughed. "No, my lady."

She planted a hand on each hip. "Is it a de Courtney family tradition for grooms to spend their wedding nights in the dining room?"

The valet colored. "I do not believe so, my lady." He paused. "I'm afraid I cannot say why His Lordship is still in the dining room. He sent me away earlier and requested me not to disturb him."

"Come with me." Mia stormed past him, not bothering to see if he followed. She flew down two flights of cold marble stairs in her bare feet, marched past rooms she'd not yet been inside, and flung open the dining room door before the valet could reach it and open it for her.

The Marquess of Exley sat in the same seat he'd occupied at dinner. His head, instead of an untouched plate of food, rested on the table before him. Loud, sawing snores filled the room.

Mia let out a stream of crudities in three languages and the valet jolted beside her. "Fetch some help," she ordered.

The valet left and Mia went to her husband, noting the glitter of broken glass on the far side of the room. She brushed back the dark lock of hair that hung over his cheek. There was a rather large scratch on his forehead and she wondered how he'd hurt himself.

Rough bristles scratched her hand and she

smiled at the masculine friction.

"My lord?"

His eyes fluttered open, his expression sleepily confused as she stroked his face, feathering away the lines that radiated out from his drowsy eyes.

His lips curved. "Mia?"

Mia started. She couldn't have said which stunned her more, his unexpected use of her diminutive name or the sweet smile. Who was this man? He looked nothing like her condescending husband.

"Go back to sleep, my lord," she counseled, sliding her hand beneath his cravat and rubbing his neck. His muscles were hard and knotted, like rocks beneath the hot silk of his skin.

He muttered something unintelligible and his face went slack with pleasure, and, no doubt, alcohol. He closed his eyes and resumed snoring.

"My lady?"

Mia had been so intent, she hadn't noticed the valet's return. A large footman stood beside him.

"Please take him to his room." Mia stepped aside to let the men do their work.

Exley appeared slim, but he was solid muscle, sinew, and bone and the two men were gasping for breath by the time they took him up several flights of stairs and finally deposited him on his bed.

Mia dismissed the footman and turned to the valet. "What is your name?"

"Sayer, my lady."

"Sayer, strip His Lordship and put him in bed. Knock on my door when you are finished."

Twin streaks of color darkened the man's narrow, impassive face. "Ah, strip him? And dress him in his nightshirt?"

"No, leave him naked."

His entire face reddened. "Yes, my lady."

By the time he knocked on her door a short time later Mia had washed her face, pulled back her hair, and was waiting with the small bottle of lavender oil.

The marquess lay faceup on his enormous bed, the bedding pulled up to his chin. Mia smiled at the valet's efforts to protect his master's virtue.

"Good night, Sayer."

The valet hesitated a fraction of a second. "Good night, my lady."

Mia waited until the door closed before pulling back the blanket to her husband's waist, leaving the most intriguing part of him covered.

"Oh my," she muttered. This was going to be a true pleasure. She poured some oil into her hands and rubbed them together. First, she would study him at her leisure. It was unlikely she'd get another chance like this unless he drank to stupefaction every night. She shook that unpleasant thought away. He would not look so healthy if heavy drinking was a regular habit.

His jaw muscles were relaxed in sleep and his lips slightly parted. Mia traced a finger over them, her featherlight touch causing him to brush at his face with one hand and turn his head to the side.

His angular jaw and chin sprouted with his night beard, a striking black against the whiteness of his skin. Mia followed the beautifully chiseled jaw down to an elegant column of throat to sculpted shoulders. He was dusted with dark hair but not enough to hide the intriguing latticework of muscles that began at his chest and led to his narrow hips with a precision that was almost mathematical.

Her eyes lingered on his small, pink nipples and her sex tightened. Her mouth watered to suck his nipples until he writhed in ecstasy.

Instead, she pulled the covers back up to his chin.

Mia had hoped to give him a massage while he slept, not violate him without his consent. That was what it would be if she massaged him while her body thrummed with so much pent-up desire.

No, the massage would need to wait until some other time, if ever.

She picked up the bottle of oil, extinguished the candle, and left her husband's room through the connecting door. It appeared she would have to satisfy her body's almost constant state of arousal without her new husband's help.

Chapter Twelve

Somebody had driven a dagger into his skull; a large, dull, rusty dagger. Adam raised a hand to pull it out but found nothing other than his own pounding head. He opened his eyes and quickly shut them again. It was a miracle he didn't cry out.

He would just breathe for a while. An unusual, but not unpleasant, smell tickled his nostrils, something sharp, yet floral. Lavender? Adam braced himself and took another breath. Yes, it was lavender. He exhaled with great care but his head still ached. Right now, the slight fragrance was the only pleasant thing about his morning.

He was experimenting with various methods of squeezing his head in a vise constructed of thumb and fingers when he heard the sound of a door opening.

"Sayer?" he whispered.

"Good morning, my lord."

Adam gritted his teeth. "Ah . . . not so

loud, Sayer."

"I believe this may help, my lord." A glass was pressed into his hand. Without thinking, Adam raised it to his mouth, swallowed, and then choked.

"Good God, man," he wheezed, thrusting the mostly full glass away before doubling over. He didn't need to ask what was in it; he recalled it from the last time he'd tipped the barrel and made a fool of himself, his first year at Oxford.

Memories of yesterday and last night came crashing down, causing his skull to throb even harder. *Christ.* He grimaced at both his behavior and the burning sensation the drink had left in his throat. The memory of last night was far, far worse.

He held out his hand and Sayer placed the glass in it. He took a deep breath, placed the glass against his mouth, and tipped the rest of its contents down his throat. It took all his strength and gritting his teeth to keep from screaming as the noxious liquid made its way into his system.

It may have been many years since his last bout with Sayer's cure-all but the beverage had not gotten any better. The last time he'd asked Sayer what was in his concoction. He'd only recited charcoal, goat's milk, raw egg, and port before Adam had begged him to stop.

Adam gave his servant the empty glass and flopped onto his pillow, gasping. "Bath. Tea. Toast."

"Very good, my lord."

He heard Sayer give instructions to a servant who must have been hovering nearby for just that purpose.

"Sayer?"

"Yes, my lord?"

"What time did I . . . er . . . come to bed last night?"

"It was after two-thirty, my lord."

Adam hesitated. "*Did* I come to bed?"

"No, my lord."

"I see. Did you help me to bed, then?"

"Yes, my lord."

Adam spent some time considering this mortifying fact. He had just about decided to leave off examining the matter any further when Sayer spoke.

"Lady Exley had you brought to your room, my lord."

Adam's eyes flew open in surprise, and a moan tore out of his raw throat. He tried to close them again, but they seemed to be stuck open. He looked at his servant through eyes that were on fire. He couldn't focus on Sayer's face, but he recognized the slight reprimand in his voice and knew he deserved it.

After a long soak and several pots of strong black tea, Adam's body was much recovered. His pride, however, was sniveling and trying to hide in a dark corner. His conscience, which was both appalled and relentless, demanded he seek his wife *immediately.* And perhaps even apologize. Pride and conscience struggled while he bathed and poured tea down his throat, the battle ending in compromise.

Adam entered the sunny breakfast room only a half hour after his usual time. He stopped in the doorway and stared. His wife was sipping a steaming cup of coffee and leafing through the *Gazette.*

His copy of the *Gazette,* an affronted voice in his mind observed.

Adam banished the voice. "Good morning, my lady."

"Good morning, my lord." She smiled up at him, fresh as a new day. "I hope you do not mind that I am reading your paper."

Yes. Yes, I do bloody well mind.

"Of course not," he lied.

He went to the sideboard and began filling his plate with food as he considered her discountenancing presence. It was his experience that ladies didn't leave their rooms until after twelve. Veronica never had.

What was his wife doing eating breakfast in the breakfast room at a quarter after nine? He suddenly recalled she had not spent the better part of their wedding night quaffing the contents of his cellar. He closed his eyes as yet another wave of embarrassment engulfed him. The truth was she had every right to be in his breakfast room — *their* breakfast room — reading his paper.

He opened his eyes to find he'd heaped his plate with a stunning pile of food. He turned and went to the only other place that had been set, the seat across from her. Her eyes widened at the enormous heap of meat, eggs, and bread on his plate.

"Have you anything planned for your afternoon?" He asked the question as much to distract her attention from his plate as anything else.

"I'd thought I would visit Hatchards and purchase some books to take with me to Exham."

Adam chewed and swallowed before scalding his mouth with black coffee.

"Are you looking for anything in particular?" he lisped, the scorched flesh of his mouth numb.

"No, I'm merely looking for something

enjoyable and engaging." She crumbled the corner of a piece of toast before looking up. "I'm ashamed to admit it, but my English skills are rather rusty. There were not many books where I lived."

Adam was a dunce. Of course life in a harem would provide few opportunities to expand one's knowledge of literature. He forked more food into his burning mouth and glanced around the breakfast room. There were six footmen. The number seemed . . . excessive. Were there always this many?

It suddenly dawned on him that his servants' curiosity about his exotic new wife probably accounted for the increase in breakfast service. No doubt it would reach even greater heights after word of his late-night drunk made the rounds. Adam grimaced. He'd made her position here bloody awkward and he'd also made an ass of himself. The shame that had been hovering just out of sight descended on him like a flock of starving crows.

He put down his fork, no longer able to pretend he was hungry. He'd made a dreadful hash of things, beginning with taking a wife in the first place. That said, she was not Veronica and did not deserve to be treated as such.

Adam signaled for the servants to leave and waited until the door closed behind the last one before turning back to his wife. "I would like to apologize for last night."

She nodded. "Thank you, my lord."

He waited for her to inquire as to the source of his wretched behavior, but she seemed determined to show him mercy. "Our library here is quite extensive. Hill purchases a great number of new books each year, including novels. If you like, I could familiarize you with the way the library is organized after breakfast."

She gave him a smile he did not deserve. "I would like that very much. I'm afraid I've had very little time to read these past months and my father's library had very few works of fiction, in any case."

Adam nodded, unable to speak as the enormity of this woman's life for the past few months — hell — for the prior two decades, crashed down on him. She'd been torn from her family, raped at fourteen, and abandoned in a bloody harem for seventeen years. And when she was able to return, her father auctioned her to the highest bidder before less than a quarter of a year had passed. And Adam — the weak reed on which she was forced to lean — had spent the few hours they'd shared baiting her, ignoring her, or getting drunk.

"Would you care to go to the theater tonight?"

She paused, a piece of toast halfway to her mouth. She put it back down without taking a bite. "I should love to go to the theater." Her voice was even lower than usual.

Adam raised his cooling coffee to his mouth, wishing the cup were larger so that he might hide behind it. Her obvious pleasure at his small kindness gutted him. He'd been such a bloody cad.

He lowered his cup, spilling half in the saucer. "I've left it rather late, so don't get your hopes up," he said gruffly. He glanced at the pile of cooling food on his plate. "Shall I take you to the library and give you the general lay of the land before I set off?" He glanced at her plate. "After you've finished eating, of course."

"I am finished." She stood and smoothed the front of her gown, the action drawing his eyes to her body. She was again garbed in green, her frilled costume flattering to her small, feminine form.

"Do you ride?" The question escaped before his mind vetted it. It seemed he'd lost control of his mouth, along with everything else in his life.

"I've not ridden much since I was a child. My brother and I rode in Hyde Park several mornings a week these past months but I don't suppose it was greatly enjoyable for an experienced rider to accompany me."

Adam could read the truth without her speaking it. Nobody had done much of anything with her since she'd returned to England other than thrust her into the marriage mart.

He opened the breakfast room door for her, once again taken by how tiny she was. Her head barely reached his shoulder, and he was not a tall man. She turned back when he didn't immediately follow, her tilted green eyes putting him in mind of a cat.

Adam followed her up the curving staircase without speaking and opened the library door, motioning her into the large book-lined room.

"The books are organized by subject and then author." He realized the thousands of titles might be overwhelming to a person unused to so many books. "Perhaps if you told me what type of book you enjoy reading, I could help you select a few?"

"I would like something entertaining but not too difficult. As I mentioned, I didn't have access to English books until I returned."

"You read Arabic?"

"Yes, but most of the books that came into the — into my possession were in French."

Adam caught the hesitation. "There is no need to avoid mentioning your past around me. Indeed, I don't see why you can't tell the truth to whomever you please." He strode across the room to the section he wanted.

"You do not care if people know where I've been all these years?"

"Why should I?" he asked, scanning the shelves.

"My father was concerned the truth would destroy the family honor." Her voice came from somewhere behind him. "Aren't you worried, too?"

Adam smiled bitterly. "No, I am not worried you will destroy the family honor. So the duke knew the truth about your past, did he?"

"Some of it."

Adam turned to her. "How much?"

"He knew I lived in Babba Hassan's palace outside Oran. He never asked any questions about my life in the palace or . . . or whether I'd had any children."

The cowardly bastard. Adam turned back to the shelf, walking his fingers over the titles until he found the one he wanted. He plucked it from the shelf.

"This was a great favorite of mine when I was a boy and I've seen the girls reading it at home." He handed her the somewhat dog-eared book.

"*Gulliver's Travels?*" A small line formed between her auburn brows. "I may have read this when I was very young." Her brow cleared. "Yes . . . I recall, Yahoos! This is an excellent choice. Thank you, my lord." She reached out to touch his sleeve, as she'd done that day in the phaeton, but stopped herself.

Adam grimaced. They'd been married less than a day and he'd already managed to suppress her natural, affectionate nature. He reached out and took her hand. She wasn't wearing gloves and her skin was warm and soft, the bones delicate and fragile. He looked down into her flowerlike face but did not know what to say. Instead, he lifted her hand to his lips, allowing his mouth to linger. His entire body stiffened at the responsive curve of her lips.

"I will instruct Hill to pull a selection that I think you will enjoy and we shall take them with us. The library at Exham is larger than this but it contains fewer works of fiction." He released her hand and it fluttered back to her side like a pale butterfly.

Gratitude glowed from her face and overwhelmed him. And filled him with shame.

Adam turned away. "I had better be off if I'm to secure entertainment for this evening."

It is one night at the theater, he told himself a short time later, as he tooled the phaeton past an overloaded coach. It wasn't as if he was courting her. It certainly wasn't as if he believed that an evening spent in his company would make her happy.

It was none of those things. It was common decency. The fact was, for better or for worse, he'd made the woman his wife. It was time for him to cease behaving like a clod and make the very simple arrangement work.

It was his duty to bed her and get her with child as quickly as possible. She could not have the independence she craved until he'd performed his side of the bargain. Her part of the bargain was living free of him.

This was not like his marriage to Veronica. There was no love involved, no feelings at stake.

Adam would do well to remember that. This was not a real marriage; it was nothing more than a business agreement.

Chapter Thirteen

Mia settled onto the soft leather seat and studied her husband. He was immaculate in his evening garb, his expression less contemptuous than usual. He was looking at her, his eyes drifting across her gown. She'd had it made the week following their betrothal, when she no longer had to worry whether her father would approve.

Mia reveled in the variety of shades and luxurious fabrics that were available in London. She'd chosen to offset the antique gold satin bodice and underskirt with yards of flowing cream silk chiffon.

"You look stunning." His words startled her.

Mia couldn't see his face as the carriage had entered the relative darkness that reigned between the streetlamps.

"Thank you, my lord."

"There is a necklace and earrings among my mother's jewels that are much the same shade as your gown — I believe it is topaz. They are not particularly valuable, but they are pretty and were one of her favorite sets. I shall have Hill fetch them from the vault for you." His voice was detached, as if he were speaking of the weather rather than giving her his mother's possessions.

Mia's hand sought the necklace at her throat and she fingered the square green stone that had once belonged to her own mother. Unlike the Carlisle emeralds, which were the property of the dukedom, this necklace was Mia's. Her father had handed over all the jewels a few days before her wedding, counseling her to give them to Exley to keep in a vault.

She'd decided to sell her mother's jewels to finance her journey rather than use any money from the marquess. Especially after she'd learned that Exley had not asked for any part of her dowry but had instead been exceptionally generous with settlements, an action that had surprised her as much as it had the duke. No, she would not take money from him if she could help it.

"I'm afraid you'll find the theater a bit thin tonight." His observation pulled her away from her uncomfortable thoughts.

"I've never been to see a play before so I'm sure I won't be a harsh critic."

The carriage approached the next lantern and she could see his eyebrows arch. "Your father did not take you to the theater?"

"We did not have the time." Why bother telling him how much the duke hated to take her anywhere in public?

Her husband remained quiet and Mia's mind drifted back to her mother's jewels. Should she try to sell them in London? If she did so, it would have to be soon. The marquess had indicated they were leaving in only a few days. Mia had spent the ten days before her wedding wrapping Gamble around her finger but she was not yet at the point where she felt comfortable trusting him with such a job. Would the footman wonder why she was selling jewels and mention the fact to another servant? How long would it take for such information to make its way to Sayer and next —

"Would you care to go and see your family tomorrow?"

Mia blinked. What was this? More kindness? He'd been so kind today it made her head hurt. She hoped his behavior was not always so erratic.

He cleared his throat and she realized he was waiting for her answer. "My father will have left for Burnewood Park already, my lord. He will stay there a few weeks before removing to Bath. Cian is meeting friends in Scotland and my cousin Rebecca is joining my aunt Elizabeth and her girls in Brighton."

"Would you care to go to Bath? Or perhaps Brighton?"

Mia had no idea where Bath was located. She knew where Brighton was, but would such a crowded place be a good choice for her needs? "I will be guided by your taste in such matters. Do you generally go to either?"

The entire evening had consisted of stilted talk like the night before — but without the excessive drinking on her husband's part. What other kind of conversation could a person engage in with eighteen ears attending to every word?

"Bath is not my first choice for entertainment."

That statement certainly begged a question. "You prefer Brighton?"

They passed under a lamp and she saw his shrug. "I expect there will be a host of matters that require my attention at Exham. It has been some time since I've been home. We are not prohibitively far from Brighton if you should desire more lively entertainments."

Mia found the notion of Brighton depressing. "I collect the society in Brighton is much the same as London?"

"You find such a notion lacking in appeal?" His question exhibited a degree of perception that made Mia nervous.

"I'm sure I will learn to enjoy it in time." She was not sure of any such thing. The allure of life among the *ton* had already paled. Years spent among such people was not something she would have looked forward to even if she had planned to remain in England.

"What do *you* enjoy, my lady?"

Mia shook her head. "I'm afraid I do not know." The words were too pathetic to be left standing alone. "Merely surviving in the sultan's harem required most of my attention. I didn't have time for much else." She grimaced; that was hardly any better. The silence in the carriage was louder than the sounds from beyond the carriage window. She tried again. "I'm sure I will come to enjoy society more in time. Perhaps it will become more entertaining as I meet more people. It is not very interesting to engage in conversations when one isn't acquainted with the people under discussion."

He gave a mirthless laugh. "I counsel you against expecting your circle of friends to increase anytime soon."

His words were like a slap. "You think I am not . . ." Mia struggled to find words that would not betray her deep sense of injury at his comment. "You think I cannot earn the friendship of others?"

He leaned forward and took one of her hands, holding it while he smiled with genuine amusement. "My dear wife, you misunderstand. It is not your social skills I doubt. You are married to me, now. You have chosen to become the next victim of the Murdering Marquess." His pale eyes glinted, all traces of humor gone.

"The Murdering Marquess?" she repeated.

"Oh come," he mocked. "You cannot tell me you've not heard my charming sobriquet? I'll swear there were plenty wanting to tell you. Your brother, for one." His lips twisted into an unpleasant smile and Mia snatched her hand away, loath to touch someone who brimmed with such bile. He nodded his head as though she'd spoken out loud, his white teeth gleaming in the darkness. "If your surprise is genuine, then you may have reason for an annulment."

"It is you who have given me reason for an annulment, sir."

He chuckled. "Touché, my lady."

Mia's heart beat like a hummingbird's,

but she forced herself to hold his eyes. She would tolerate many things, but criticism of her family was not one of them. "I have not heard the name before and you do a great disservice to my brother if you believe he would repeat such scurrilous nonsense. It is true he did not wish me to marry you, but not for the reasons you may think."

"Oh? What were those?" he asked in a bored voice, staring out the window.

"My brother did not believe I should be forced into a loveless marriage merely to please my father."

"Mmm." The sound dripped cynicism and made her recall the gulf of empty space that surrounded him the few times she'd seen him in public. Nobody could be untouched by so much rejection. He was not immune, no matter how cold he appeared.

"Whatever my brother believed before we were wed hardly matters now, my lord. We are family and Cian is now your brother. I will not tolerate the speaking of such stupid nicknames by anyone, even you. When you disparage yourself, you disparage me."

The carriage stopped, but the marquess made no move to get out when the door opened.

Mia's heart became heavy in her chest and she suddenly felt tired. She had insulted him by speaking so harshly. It was the same as it had always been. She was opening her mouth to make the inevitable apology when he leaned forward and adjusted her gauzy shawl around her shoulders.

His hooded eyes flickered with something she couldn't read, but his lips twitched into a smile. He stepped out of the carriage and handed her down the steps.

Mia couldn't suppress the flare of triumph that surged in her breast. For just a moment there'd been a small crack in the high walls that surrounded him. It had sealed up quickly, but she'd seen something behind it before the gap closed and it had looked suspiciously like affection.

Adam did not have high expectations for the evening, at least not when it came to the quality of the entertainment.

The box he'd acquired belonged to Lord Jeffries, a member at one of the gaming clubs Adam frequented, one of the few card players who actually offered him a challenge. Jeffries was departing London the next day and had been pleased to offer Adam the use of the private box.

Adam had run into Danforth at White's and, on an impulse, invited him and his two lively sisters to join them. Like their brother, the women were of an open and pleasant disposition. They would not find the prospect of socializing with Adam or his wife beneath them.

Danforth had approached Adam one evening several years ago, after a late night at the tables. His open friendship and gregarious nature had gradually chipped away at Adam's reserve and before he knew it, the younger man had become a friend. The viscount's sisters soon completed Adam's very small circle. The two women had refused to be deterred by Adam's signature off-putting stare since the first night they'd met. They accepted him without question, as if their brother's approval was enough for them, and treated Adam like another brother, to be bullied and cossetted in equal amounts.

Danforth and his sisters were already in the box when they arrived.

"Thank God you are here, Exley. My sisters are savages and you must save me from them." Danforth rolled his eyes dramatically at the two thin women sitting across from him.

Livia, the smaller of the women, launched herself at Adam with her usual lack of decorum and caught him in a full embrace.

"Adam, darling, how naughty of you not

to invite us to your wedding. I have the perfect wedding hat." Livia turned to his wife before Adam could open his mouth. "And you must be Lady Exley. My goodness, you are so lovely," Livia exclaimed, releasing Adam to grasp the smaller woman by her upper arms and hold her at a distance while inspecting her.

To Adam's relief his wife looked amused rather than alarmed at the enthusiastic reception.

"You must call me Livia. We don't stand on ceremony," she added, before sweeping the smaller woman into an embrace.

His wife appeared to eagerly return the other woman's enveloping hug before meeting her friendly look with one of her own. "And you must call me Mia." Her face was flushed and her voice husky with pleasure.

Livia grinned. "Mia, this is Octavia. We have been most excited to meet you ever since Gaius told us about your betrothal to Adam."

Mia blinked at the unusual trio of names.

"Indeed, Livia, indeed." Octavia nodded her head vigorously, her enormous, feathered headdress swaying erratically. "We've been longing to meet you ever since we first read of your return to England."

"We should dearly love to hear the *real*

story about your years away."

Danforth raised a hand to his forehead and closed his eyes. *"Livia —"*

"But only if you feel comfortable talking about it, of course. We are souls of discretion, are we not, Livia?"

"Indeed we are, Octavia. None more so. Just consider how we kept to ourselves Gaius's unfortunate *tendre* for that young opera dancer his first year at Oxford. Can you recall the reams of appalling poetry he generated in her honor?" She laughed, ignoring her brother's scandalized squawk.

"Yes, especially the one in which he rhymed *sighs* with *thighs.*"

Adam shook his head at his friend's red, agonized face and turned to his wife. "You may as well divulge all you know now, Mia. They will extract your deepest secrets regardless."

She looked surprised and Adam wondered if the friendly invitation to use her pet name had not extended to him?

Livia smacked him on the arm with the oversize fan she clutched in one chartreuse-gloved hand. "Oh Adam, you would make her afraid of us."

"You don't need any help with that," her brother said *sotto voce.*

■ ■ ■ ■

Mia enjoyed the company even more than she enjoyed the play, which they hardly watched. Viscount Danforth and the two Miss Mantons were magnets for interesting people. Those who crowded the box were not content to merely watch the play, but insisted on interpreting and dissecting it.

Mia laughed until her sides ached at the acerbic observations coming from Livia and the supercilious blond poet who sat beside her. She could see by the number of quizzing glasses turned in their direction that they were drawing attention. Exley, who was seated beside Octavia, threw back his head and laughed more than once during the first half of the play. Gone was the bored, contemptuous sneer he habitually wore. His face, usually a mask of indifference, was relaxed and almost happy. She could not believe it was the same man. He submitted to the relentless teasing of Livia and Octavia with a good humor she never would have thought he possessed.

During the long break between the first and second half of the play even more friends of the Mantons' flooded into the box, none of them too shy to enjoy the champagne and wine that flowed freely. Mia found herself crowded into the back corner with Livia after they both had glasses.

Livia examined the small baize-covered table that was inexplicably in the corner of the box. "I'd heard Lady Jeffries was partial to cards during all but the arias."

Mia's eyebrows shot up. "Cards? During a play?"

"Oh come, my dear. Surely the behavior of our ill-bred pack of associates tonight has shown you one does not come to the theater to watch, but to *be* watched." She tapped Mia's arm with her fan and peered at her through her opera glass in mock demonstration.

Mia laughed.

"Octavia and I were *very* happy to learn Adam was to be married." Livia's expression became more serious. "He is a man desperately in need of a woman's touch. The right woman, of course." Her gray eyes became rather piercing as they roamed Mia's face. Mia was not sure what to say to such an odd statement, but luckily Livia needed no response. "His first wife, Veronica, was a monster, albeit an extremely lovely one. She came out the same year I did." She took a small sip of wine and gave a bitter laugh. "With Veronica around nobody looked at anyone else. Not that they would have looked at me without her, I assure you. I have never been able to claim more than a decent figure. But there was no one to compare to Veronica. It was most disheartening to see the men throwing themselves at her. This may sound like the benefit of hindsight, my dear, but I could see her for what she was even then." She shrugged. "But men will be men. Which is to say, they will be tragically stupid when it comes to a pretty face."

She glanced across the room. "I recall Adam from that time, too, although we were not acquainted back then. I still remember the first time I saw him." She opened her fan and plied it rapidly, as though the room had heated. "I had never seen such a handsome man in my life." She tapped Mia with her fan. "But you mustn't tell Gaius that. Octavia and I have convinced him that he is *quite* the handsomest man of our acquaintance.

"Adam could have had his pick that Season, but he had to have Veronica." Livia paused and they both looked across the room at the subject of their conversation. Adam was engaged in what looked like a lively argument with Danforth while two very attractive women watched, clearly rapt at such a display of male beauty. Mia experienced an odd feeling in her stomach as she watched her handsome husband captivate his audience. She turned away and encountered Livia's shrewd stare. The other woman wore a tiny smile on her expressive face and nodded, as if Mia had just answered a question to her satisfaction.

"There were tales of Veronica's appalling behavior long before Adam took steps. Most people wondered why he put up with her shocking conduct for as long as he did. She took up with a crowd that could never get enough of anything — spirits, gambling, racing . . . sex."

Mia started at the unusually plain speaking and Livia leaned forward, an odd gleam in her eyes.

"Adam finally caught her with two men, in their own house. He called them out, something that should have meant certain death for both of them. One of the men escaped town, choosing his life over his honor. The younger man met Adam. I am very glad to say Adam showed mercy." Livia noticed Mia's puzzled look. "My dear, surely you're aware your husband is one of the most accomplished blades in the entire country? Has nobody told you?"

Mia recalled something Ramsay had said

at their wedding — about her husband's skills with swords and pistols. She'd been too angry to consider the big privateer's words at the time.

"He could have easily killed both men, probably even if he'd fought them at the same time."

"I had no idea."

Livia gave her a sympathetic look. "You have been back in England only a few months, I think?"

Mia nodded, embarrassed by the other woman's pity. Even though the marriage was in name only, it did not make her happy to realize just how little she knew about her new husband.

Livia covered Mia's hand with her own. "You must be wretchedly lonely, my dear. I daresay your father is the reason you married so quickly." Her clear gray eyes had become hard, and she did not wait for a response. "And Adam, too, for all that he might have meant well marrying you. Men." She shook her head. The kindness in her eyes caused a sudden lump to form in Mia's throat.

"My sister and I have faced the obstacles unwed and unwanted women must endure and are determined to help our sisters whenever we can. Only an idiot couldn't see that you are a stranger in a strange land." Again she looked at Adam.

Mia followed her gaze. Exley was now the sole audience, rather than entertainer, of one of the women he'd been talking to earlier. The woman was standing too close for polite conversation, her elegantly gloved hand clutching his dark sleeve. She was speaking intently, undeterred by the look of scorching disdain he bent down on her, all trace of his earlier good humor gone.

Mia looked at the hand clutching his sleeve and felt the sharp claws of jealousy. Who was this woman taking liberties with her husband right in front of her?

"You care for him." Livia's statement slowed the jealous rage building within her but she still could not pull her eyes away from the riveting scene. Adam lifted the woman's hand from his arm, gently, but with a look that should have left the woman a smoking pile of rubble, and walked away.

The woman reached out a hand, as if she might stop him, but drew it back, her shoulders sinking as she stared after him. She looked around the room to see if anyone had been watching and her eyes met Mia's. Hatred flared openly on her face before she turned her back and moved to rejoin her friend.

"That woman is Lord Exley's lover?" Mia's voice was breathy, as though she'd been running. Where had such a possessive, visceral response come from? And about a man she hardly knew?

Livia sighed and squeezed Mia's hand. "Not anymore, which I believe is the source of her disagreement with him." The beautiful blonde was with a group of men, smiling with determined vivacity. "Adam met her at a dinner party at our house about six months ago. Susannah had her eyes on him, probably before she even met him. She is an actress, you know, and she did her best to convince him he could not live without her." She laughed and patted Mia's arm. "She is not a very good actress and I could see that he'd tired of her even before he met you."

Mia knew Livia's words were meant to soothe but they were slight balm. The woman was tall and voluptuous and Mia's slim body could not compare favorably. Somehow the knowledge that he'd tired of his mistress could not erase the mental picture that had formed in her head: that of the body she'd seen last night wrapped around the shapely blonde. This woman had made love to her husband; something Mia had not managed to do even though it was his sole reason for marrying her.

"Mia, my dear." Livia took her hands and held them, drawing Mia's eyes from the woman across the room. "I have seen how Adam looks at you. He never looked at Susannah St. Martin that way. She is no threat to you, my dear."

Mia appreciated the sentiment behind her words but Livia did not know her marriage to Adam was merely a business union.

Livia stood. "Oh look, Danforth and Exley are playing servant and dispensing more champagne. Let us go have some." She grabbed Mia's hand and pulled her toward the group.

Adam had a slightly questioning look as he refilled Mia's glass. "Has Livia been raking you over the coals?"

"Only a gentle raking, my lord."

"No bruises or abrasions?"

Livia broke in, "I never leave any trace of my interrogations. You should know that, Adam."

Octavia joined their group. "Is this our serious Lord Exley, actually smiling?"

"It's either laugh or cry where your sister is concerned, and I didn't want to cry in front of my new wife, at least not yet," he added drily.

Livia tapped him with her fan. "I cannot

bear to watch a grown man weep, Adam. Between you and Gaius, there is scarcely a dry cloth in the house some nights." She turned to Mia. "You must know that your husband and my brother aspire to become the greatest card sharps in the history of gaming?"

"Are they succeeding?"

"Gad no," Octavia answered. "I shudder to think how much they have lost to Livia and myself — hence all the manly weeping we must endure."

"They fear us," Livia added.

"Indeed, they refuse to bring us with them on their evening jaunts to the various hells they frequent." Octavia added in a stage whisper, "They are afraid we would show them up."

"Or get us killed," the marquess said, giving the women a pained look before turning to Mia. "They cheat at cards, my lady. Openly, incontestably, and shamelessly." His last words were drowned out by the women's loud denials.

The conversation devolved into an argument regarding the finer points of whist, a card game Mia did not know. The three friends tossed phrases like "schoolboy rules," and "Hoyle-obsessed harridans," back and forth at one another.

"Do you play cards, my lady?" Octavia drew her off to one side as Livia and the marquess bickered about their last game.

"My brother has been teaching me cribbage and piquet, but I am slow at learning the subtleties."

"And where you lived before, what did one do for amusement?"

Mia smiled at her not-very-subtle attempt to pry out the details of her past. Her first impulse was to spin the usual tale. But she looked at Octavia's kind face and realized she didn't want to begin a friendship with lies. Besides, Adam had said she should do as she pleased.

"I lived on the outskirts of a city called Oran, in the palace of a sultan who ruled that area. As to what we did for amusement?" Mia stopped. While it felt good to speak the truth, she wasn't sure how much of it she should share with a gently bred lady.

"Will you sit with me?" Octavia asked. "We have a little time before we must pretend to watch the remainder of this wretched play. Let us go away from Adam and Livia; they are liable to commence hair-pulling soon and it would be better to be at a safe distance."

Mia laughed at the mental picture her

words evoked and followed the older woman back to the same spot she'd occupied with Livia.

"I know I am bad, but I really must hear more about your life. You may take my word of silence to the bank." Octavia placed her hand solemnly over her heart.

"You asked what we did for amusement? We did not have to manage a household in the same way women do here. The sultan maintained factors for such matters. We spent our time with the palace children, playing games or teaching them; we had a rather large indoor garden in which we grew herbs and flowers; and there were those who wove or painted or played music. There were also those of us who could read and we would entertain the others whenever we had something to share. I spent much of my time gardening and painting." *And keeping my son alive.*

"When you say a 'sultan's palace,' do mean you lived in a seraglio?" Octavia's voice dropped to a whisper on the last word.

"Yes, it belonged to the Sultan Babba Hassan. There were more than sixty of us when he died and his son Assad seized control — which was why I had to leave. Most of the wives with children did not survive Assad's purge unless they escaped."

Mia realized what she'd said a moment too late.

"This Assad, why was he a danger to you if you had no children?"

Mia twisted her large emerald wedding ring as she carefully considered her words. "Even though I was part of Babba Hassan's household for almost seventeen years, I was still viewed as an outsider by many. When a new sultan takes power, it is only wise that he clear away any who might create trouble or cause others to question his power. Like his father before him, Assad was only acting in a manner designed to secure his power."

Octavia's eyes were almost comically round. "There has been much written of the Barbary corsairs these past ten years. It is shocking how many people they have abducted. I understand it is not unusual for them to —"

"I am so glad to finally meet you, Lady Exley," a low, sultry voice purred.

Mia looked up to find Susannah St. Martin smiling down at her, her full, shapely lips curved in a welcoming smile that didn't extend to her blue eyes, which were as hard as the sapphires she wore around her neck.

"Susannah." Octavia stood up and so did Mia. Even standing she had to look up at the Junoesque blonde woman. Would she always be the shortest person in any room?

"Octavia, my dear, I'm having such a wonderful time. I just wanted to meet the new bride." Susannah draped her plump arms around Octavia, who received her embrace rather woodenly.

"What a surprise to see you here tonight, Susannah." Octavia's normally warm smile was fixed.

The blonde woman did not appear to notice. "I am always at wit's end between shows." She spoke to Octavia but her eyes roamed up and down Mia's body. A look designed to convey her open disdain. "I have heard so much about you, Lady Exley." Her sly smile suggested most of it had been learned while naked in bed with Mia's husband. "I suppose you have not heard nearly as much about me?"

"No. Not much," Mia agreed. "But I do know you were once my husband's mistress." She spoke so softly the other woman's brow furrowed, as if she must have misheard. "I also know he is finished with you but too well-mannered to tell you in a way you will understand." The woman's smile had frozen into a rictus of surprise. "As you may have heard, I have been away from England for a very long time. I'm afraid I've picked up some rather savage habits and lack my husband's lovely manners." Mia allowed the built-up anger of the last few months to settle in her gaze. "If you approach me or my husband again, I will see to it that you are no longer able to conduct business — of any kind — in London, ever again." Mia held out her hand. "I understand you are an actress?"

The woman nodded, her mouth ajar.

"Consider this an opportunity to exhibit your talents. Smile, take my hand, and *act* as if you are finished congratulating me on my marriage. You will then approach your friend and *act* as though you have a headache and wish to leave."

Maybe the beautiful blonde saw something in Mia's eyes to back up her threat. Or maybe she believed a marchioness really did have the power to end her theater career. Either way, she smiled, dropped Mia a curtsy, and left.

Mia turned to Octavia, who stared for a long moment before laughing. "My dear Lady Exley, you will never know how much I enjoyed that." She took Mia's arm and squeezed it, her eyes shining with admiration. "Don't look now, but Adam is watching and appears more than a little concerned."

CHAPTER FOURTEEN

The ride back to Exley house was uneventful. Adam wondered if Mia might confront him about Susannah and then realized that was a ridiculous concern. Their marriage was a business arrangement; his wife would hardly be jealous of his ex-lover.

As it was, she'd been very pleasant, chatting about the people she'd met and the quality of the play, which Adam had found unusually poor. The night was still early when they arrived home. Far too early to drag his wife up to bed and roger her silly, no matter how much he might want to.

"Would you care to join me for a drink in the library?" he asked after they'd divested themselves of cloaks, hats, and gloves.

"That would be nice."

Adam crossed to the large silver tray that held an assortment of decanters. "Shall I ring for tea or do you prefer something a bit stronger?" He opened one of the decanters and recoiled at the sugary smell that assaulted his nostrils.

"I'll have whatever you are having — as long as it is not that." She moved away to look at the books on the nearest wall while he located a dry, pleasing Madeira and poured two glasses.

"I hope this will suit."

She took the glass and sipped, smiling at him before turning back to the shelves.

"I am enjoying *Gulliver's Travels.* I read several chapters this afternoon and recall quite a bit of it."

Her inadvertent confession as to how she'd spent her afternoon sent ripples of guilt through him. While he was off pursuing his own pleasure, his wife was living a lonely existence, isolated and friendless in her new home — this cold pile of stone.

"My brother has been teaching me piquet. Do you know it?" she asked, breaking into his thoughts.

Adam raised his glass to hide his smile. "I am familiar with piquet. Would you care for a rubber or two?"

"I should like to play very much. Although . . ." A small line formed between her brows.

"Yes?"

"I would prefer not to wager too much as

I am not a very good player."

It was only with a Herculean effort that Adam was able to keep a straight face. "We needn't wager at all, if you'd rather not."

"I believe wagering makes the play more interesting. Cian and I always played for penny stakes. Shall I go to my room and fetch my purse?"

"I shall trust you to honor your debts," he said, seriously.

Adam rang for a servant to fetch a pack of cards while two footmen set up a card table. He watched as Mia prowled the room, pausing near the chess table and running her finger over the delicate ivory pieces. "Would you prefer a game of chess to cards?" he asked.

"No, we can play chess some other time. I am eager to learn cards."

"The table is ready, my lord." The footman spoke before Adam could ask her why she was so interested in learning to play cards. Was it to play with him? He dismissed the foolish thought and picked up the deck of cards, breaking them open while she took her seat. He shuffled, his fingers working without any help from his distracted mind.

She stared with open delight at his hands and his smooth shuffling stuttered. A few cards escaped and fluttered to the floor and

Mia moved to pick them up but he put his hand on hers. "I'll get them, my lady."

Adam reassembled his wits while he collected the fallen cards. Was he so besotted that a sliver of admiration gave him a case of youthful jitters?

When he sat up he was in control.

He began to deal the cards. "A penny a point, is it?"

"Mmm."

She picked up her cards as they hit the table, studying them intently while chewing her lower lip. Adam forced himself to look at his own hand.

The first rubber showed him her mind was very keen, although her skills were only rudimentary. He offered gentle observations on her discards and was impressed when she incorporated his suggestions during the next hand, parlaying cards that were merely decent into a very close game. After Mia scored a repique against him in the third game, the play became competitive.

Adam had to remind himself more than once to curb his predatory instincts. Judging by the intensity of her stare and rapt concentration she, too, hated to lose.

Mia was still lamenting her last trade — a poor one — when the ormolu clock on the mantel chimed. They'd been playing for almost two hours and it seemed like only minutes. She bent over the tally sheet, which he'd insisted she keep to help her learn, brushing her chin with the quill as she added up the final damage. She frowned and handed him the sheet. "I owe you."

He barely glanced at the total as he scraped up the cards and returned them to their case, somehow managing to make even such a small movement appear elegant and enticing.

"Considering you only learned recently, you are quite a good player. Much better than many of the men I've had the misfortune to sit across from over the years."

Mia did not believe him. "I do not like to lose. Next time we should play chess. Perhaps we can wager on that, as well."

He looked amused. "You believe you will be luckier with chess?"

"Not luck, my lord, skill."

"Ah, the gauntlet has been thrown. I look forward to taking up the challenge. But not tonight, I think. I believe it is time to retire." His voice was mild but his eyes were dark and direct. "I will come to you in a half hour."

LaValle was awake when she entered her room, even though Mia had told her not to wait up.

"I shall wear the white lawn tonight."

LaValle took an inordinate amount of time undressing, dressing, and fussing with her clothing, until Mia began to fret. Would she still be half-clothed when her husband arrived? Why did that thought cause her so much anxiety? Was she worried he'd turn around and leave if she wasn't ready? Really, she'd become pathetic.

Her nightgown was simple but the matching dressing gown had a short, closely fitted bodice with a skirt made of yards and yards of diaphanous white fabric. It also had more buttons than a garment meant to be immediately removed should have.

LaValle was loosening her hair when the connecting door opened and the marquess entered. Mia met his gaze in the mirror. The now familiar heat flared in her stomach as he crossed the room toward her, clad only in a dark blue silk banyan.

He stopped behind her. "I will play hairdresser to Lady Exley, er . . . ?" He pulled his eyes away from Mia's reflection just long enough to glance at the Frenchwoman.

"LaValle, my lord." She dropped a deep curtsy.

Mia said, "You may go, LaValle. I will not need you again tonight."

The door closed and her husband set his glass on the dressing table and commenced to search out the pins in her hair, removing them one by one as he watched her face in the mirror.

The feel of his light, deft fingers on her scalp left trails of fire. When he'd unbound the last of the fiery red curls, he admired his work before lowering his hands to her shoulders.

"You are very lovely." His eyes remained fixed to hers, his face unsmiling.

Mia deliberately leaned back against him. The thin layers between them did nothing to hide his arousal. His eyelids fluttered and his hands tightened as he pulled her against his body. He glanced toward the branch of candles beside her dressing table.

"Do you want me to extinguish the candles?"

Mia shook her head. "I would like you to light more."

Humor glinted in his darkening eyes. She covered his hands with hers and brought them lower, shuddering as his fingers came to rest over her breasts. His stroked a finger lightly across one nipple and Mia inhaled sharply.

His hand came beneath her elbow and he raised her to her feet, his clever fingers quickly undoing the row of buttons LaValle had fastened only moments before. Mia tried not to think about how many women's garments he'd removed to become so skilled.

When he peeled back the robe, his eyes darkened as they rested on the tips of her breasts beneath the almost transparent fabric. He traced the outline of her body through the sheer shift as he watched their reflection in the mirror. He ran a finger down her belly, over her mound, his eyelids lowering and his heart thudding against her back.

Mia reached behind her while his hand teased and maddened and slid her own hand between the flaps of his robe. His entire body went rigid as she slowly ran her hand down his silky hardness, drinking in his reflection in the glass.

"Naughty," he said softly, one of his hands teasing the tip of her breast while the other slowly inched the fabric of her nightgown up her thighs.

She stroked back up his length but he pulled out of her grasp.

"No."

"But —"

Their eyes locked in the glass. "No."

He spoke with an arrogant assurance that

made her tighten with expectation. She dropped her hands to her sides. She would obey him . . . for the time being.

He lifted the hem above her waist and held the fabric bunched in one hand while his other slid over her hip into the springy red curls. Sensitive fingers surrounded her mound and imprisoned her, cupping her possessively while his middle finger stroked, stopping agonizingly short of her aching bud.

A slight, mocking smile flickered across his face. "You make me wish I had more hands." He stroked her again, this time giving the source of her pleasure an almost careless flick. Mia gasped and pushed her bottom against him.

A low, satisfied laugh vibrated against her back. "Part your thighs for me, darling."

The muscles in her legs twitched and jumped as she slid her feet apart.

He stroked her again, this time deeper. Mia jerked in his hands, her vision blurring with frustrated desire as his slick finger began to move in firm, languid circles. Her entire body stiffened with expectation as the pleasure built, tenuously at first and then —

And then he stopped.

She opened her eyes and met his in the glass.

His lips curved as he took in the flushed, mottled skin of her face. "I think you are wicked."

Mia blinked. *Wicked?* The insistent, relentless pulsing between her legs was making it impossible to think. She pushed against him and he moved away.

"*Are* you wicked?" His finger circled her lightly, suggestively, *maddeningly.*

Mia squeezed her eyes shut, fighting the urge to yell. What did he want from her?

"Are you?" he whispered, his breath hot on her ear.

She opened her eyes. His eyebrows were two black hooks and his smile was one she'd not seen before, teasing and devilish, making him resemble an evil satyr. His finger remained infuriatingly still.

"Yes," she rasped.

"Yes, what?"

She glared at his reflection. "Yes, Adam. I'm wicked."

His eyes darkened but his hand remained still.

"You thought to control me — to make me come in your hand, didn't you? Or against your sweet, naked bottom." He thrust against her to illustrate his point.

Her jaw dropped at his raw words.

He released her and stepped away, his ice blue eyes intent on her reflection.

"Remove your gown." All traces of the satyr had fled and he was every inch the cool aristocrat. She hesitated. How could he be so calm when she was ready to burst? It was annoying. It was humiliating. It was —

"Mia."

She huffed out a sharp breath and lifted the loose, flimsy fabric over her head, flinging it to one side.

His eyes flickered up and down her body, and then darted back to her navel. His lips parted. "What the devil?" He didn't wait for her to answer before dropping to his haunches. He lightly brushed the ring and small jewel with his index finger and glanced up. "Does it hurt?"

She smiled. "Not even a little."

His mouth pulled into a lopsided smile that robbed her lungs of air.

"I have never seen such a thing," he marveled, glancing from her eyes to her navel, a grin on his face. The awe in his tone told her there wasn't much he hadn't seen when it came to women's bodies.

He fingered the skin around her piercing in suggestive circles, appearing to have forgotten about her sex, even though it was mere inches from his face.

He stood, his eyes still on the small jewel. Judging by the movement beneath his robe he was not disgusted by her as LaValle was. She reached out and tugged on the sash that held his banyan closed. The robe parted to reveal a narrow strip of pale, hard body.

Her eyes settled on the part of him that was not pale.

"Oh." He shrugged and the robe fell to the floor.

They stood staring at one another, exploring each other's bodies with their eyes.

His penis rose from a tangle of black curls, the smooth head resting against his muscled abdomen. He was . . . perfection. She took a step toward him and reached out a hand to touch him. Before she could take a second step, he scooped her up and closed the short distance to the bed. His mouth crushed hers and he thrust into her without tender preamble. Mia opened beneath the onslaught and took him deeper, their tongues tangling while her hand found the part of him she wanted.

Again he moved away, shaking his head.

"Didn't we just talk about this?" He cocked one black brow at her. "It's my turn first."

"Your turn?"

"Mmm-hmm." He ran one finger down her jaw, his lips curved in a way that made her shiver. What she wouldn't give to know what he was thinking.

Just looking at her responsive body was causing Adam to unravel. What would being inside her do to him?

His eyes dropped to that intriguing ring in her navel. He wanted to tongue it and suck it. To catch it between his teeth and tug. To lick and probe her delicate dimple. To —

He reined in his rampant arousal. If he mounted her right now he would ride her hard and fast, taking his pleasure with no care for hers.

"Lie back," he said, giving her a gentle push.

She obeyed with a swift compliance at odds with her sensual half smile. She was a vixen. A mocking, teasing siren. She was danger in a dozen forms and Adam would only allow himself to touch her with one finger.

Only one finger. How could he lose control with only one finger?

He began at her brow, smoothing the graceful auburn wing that arched beneath his finger, almost losing himself in her brilliant green eyes. He lightly traced the blue vein that pulsed in her temple, moving over the slight down of her jaw toward the pulse at the base of her neck. His finger lingered in the soft depression and his lips curved at the quickening he felt. Her delicate nostrils flared at her body's betrayal of her need. Adam smiled and resumed his exploration.

He drifted over her lightly freckled breastbone to her breast, avoiding her already pebbled nipple and instead stroking the sensitive skin on the side of her breast. She thrust herself against his hand but he continued his downward journey without so much as a flick or a pinch. It was a Herculean struggle to force his resisting finger to move on. Every particle of his being wanted to linger, to torment each perfect breast, to take her in his mouth and suck her until she screamed. But his finger moved on, like a nomad rejecting the mirage of a desert oasis.

He sent the fortunate digit across her quivering stomach, circling and grazing the jewelry in her navel several times before inexorably continuing to his target.

His finger stopped above the damp curls that protected her sex and his hand shook as he captured her eyes and held them, pushing slowly but deliberately into the most private part of her. Her hips rose to meet him and she groaned and closed her eyes.

And that was all it took.

His fingers broke ranks and his hands rebelled, refusing to obey his brain any longer; his treacherous mouth joined the mutiny and hurried to claim a breast for itself. His tongue, lips, and teeth feasted on her body like a glutton in Dante's inferno while his fingers stroked into her silken heat, seeking the only thing that would ease his hunger.

When she began to come apart, he pushed a finger inside her to share in the pleasure he'd unleashed. She convulsed around him and he teased one last shudder from her before pushing her thighs farther apart and guiding himself to the entrance of her body.

He went only as deep as his aching head before stopping. A bead of sweat broke from his temple and trickled down his jaw as he stared down into her slitted green eyes. His control strained at its tether like a rabid dog on a leash. Once he began moving, there would be no finesse.

She smiled lazily, tilted her hips, and took him inside her.

"Ah, God." The words burst from him like a plea for mercy.

Any vestige of control disappeared, and his best intentions with it. He used her with a savagery he knew would shame him later but he was beyond caring. He thrust into her as if he could drive away the unwilling yearning she aroused in him. As if he could fuck his obsession into submission. His vision went black and his body exploded. He crushed her hips in a punishing grip and held her still as he filled her and claimed her.

Mine.

He exhaled raggedly and rolled over, not wanting to crush her. Her legs tangled with his and she turned with him, a girlish giggle breaking from her when they tumbled onto their sides, still connected at the hips, their faces inches from each other.

Adam looked into her flushed, joyous face and his heart beat a deafening tattoo in his ears.

She kissed his chest, closed her eyes, and snuggled into his arms, completely unaware of the damage she'd done — the damage she was still doing. She pulled his hips tighter with her slim but powerful legs and went on to destroy him.

"That was delicious, Adam. I am very happy you are so skilled at pleasuring women." He could only stare dumbly as his body throbbed at her words. She sighed again. "I have not climaxed with a man before." She inched closer, squirming and pushing at his chest like a cat kneading a pillow. "It is so much nicer than pleasuring oneself." The last words were distorted by a huge yawn.

Adam couldn't have said which stunned him more — that a woman of her obvious sensuality had never had an orgasm with a man, or her open admission of masturbation. Either way, he'd hardened again, still buried inside her. A distant part of his brain pointed out that was no mean feat for a man on the far side of thirty.

He smoothed back the tangle of copper curls to look at her face. She smiled drowsily but didn't open her eyes. Adam felt a terrible stiffening sensation, this time in the vicinity of his heart.

He dropped his head onto the bed and shook it from side to side. His body was exhausted but his mind spun with the implications of this evening. He was not going to be tired of bedding her tomorrow. Nor the day after. Or anytime soon.

He ground his palm between his eyes, trying to massage away the chaos in his head. Somewhere in the room a clock ticked, a steady counterpoint to the anger, frustration, and confusion that chased one another around inside his addled mind.

He yearned to pull the blankets up over them both and drift off to sleep, molding her delicious shape to his. Instead, he left the warmth of her body and bed and shrugged on his discarded robe before turning back to look at her. His new wife was lying atop the covers, naked and entirely desirable. His body and brain engaged in a brief, violent struggle and it took every last scrap of his shredded self-control not to slip off his robe and crawl back in beside her.

Instead, he covered her, extinguished the candles that still guttered in their sockets, and returned to his room.

Adam lay in the darkness in his massive bed and told himself this was where he belonged. The logical part of him, a part that seemed to be eroding fast, argued that sex with any woman — not to mention one as unrestrained and sensual as his wife — triggered unexpected sensations. It only followed that the more physically intense the experience, the more important it was to keep a proper distance.

That was the answer: distance. It also happened to be the one thing she'd asked for in this marriage of convenience.

CHAPTER FIFTEEN

Mia woke up to midmorning sun streaming across her bed. She knew without looking that she was alone. She lifted the blankets and glanced down at her body. She dropped the covers and grinned at the blue damask canopy over her bed. She was naked and deliciously sore, so it hadn't been a dream.

She wasn't surprised to wake up alone. A man like Exley would have clear lines drawn about such things. What had surprised her was last night. Not so much his lovemaking, which had been commanding yet generous, but the night itself. It had been delightful to observe his interaction with his friends and to play cards with him. He'd been . . . human.

But even at the peak of his pleasure last night, she'd sensed a reserve in him. It was as though his self-control was so much a part of him it could never slip. Mia sighed. She should be grateful for the distance he maintained. After all, it would make leaving him that much easier. And that, she reminded herself sternly, was the entire point of the marriage.

Memories of last night — of his dark eyes and near-feral expression at the moment of climax — assailed and aroused her. Her hand slid between her legs. She wanted him again — now. It was . . . frustrating. She snatched her hand away from her pulsing, nagging sex, and sat up. What was wrong with her? One tumble with a decent — well, superb, actually — lover and she was enthralled. What would she think after the next bedding? Would she be questioning her plans for escape?

She frowned. Last night wasn't about love; it was about business. Well, and maybe a little lust. The marquess wanted an heir, and he had taken steps to get what he wanted. The fact that he'd made the transaction a pleasure rather than a chore didn't alter the truth. He didn't want a wife or a lover or a friend. He wanted a child. She was a broodmare and it was her duty to breed. Period. He'd come to her, serviced her, and departed as soon as politely possible. She would do well to keep that in mind. Just because he was tender in bed, did not mean he was tender in general. He was pursuing his reason for marriage just as she would pursue hers when he dumped her at his country home.

The few hours he'd managed to sleep had been flooded with images of his new wife. None of the images had been the type to encourage peaceful slumber and Adam awoke feeling edgy, but also resolved. He thought about how close he'd been to carrying through on his schoolboy infatuation and sleeping in his wife's bed and shuddered. Well, his brain shuddered but his treacherous cock kept reminding him why waking in his wife's bed would be a much more rewarding experience than waking alone.

They'd barely spent any time at all together and she'd already invaded his hard-won peace of mind and caused havoc. Who knew what would happen if he were to indulge his obsession and enjoy her company as freely as he seemed to want? Of one thing he was certain: only rigid control would answer.

To that end, he commenced his morning with a freezing bath. Once he'd extinguished his insistent arousal, he sent word to saddle his newest hack. Phoebe was an unusual silvery gray mare with intriguing white spots scattered across her withers and flank. She was as eager as she was beautiful and the perfect companion for a bruising morning ride.

The park was almost deserted and Adam rode her like a demon. His mount was cursed with as much excess energy and tension as her master, and Adam returned to Exley House as lathered as the mare. Unfortunately, he was still brimming with mental energy, no matter how savagely he'd abused his body.

He snatched a quick breakfast while still in his top boots, bolting down a cup of coffee and ordering a pot for his room, just in case his new wife proved to be an equally early riser this morning as last and surprised him in the breakfast room.

After another bath — this one less icy than the first — he spent a few hours in his study, looking at the latest bills from the army of workers he'd employed to repair a massive and somewhat hideous building off Tavistock Street in the Strand. Adam had won the building from a man who'd had more luck making money speculating than he did keeping it at the card table.

Based on the latest report from the architect supervising the work, it should be ready for its new residents before the end of the year. After a brief meeting with Hill regarding his plans to remove to Exham, Adam ordered the phaeton brought round and went to look at the ongoing renovations in person. He killed an hour examining a cracked lead roof and rusted drains before going to his club.

At White's, he checked the betting books and found his wife's name almost conspicuously absent. He smiled. Mia was now off limits. At least to any man who wished to continue breathing.

He'd just finished reading the last of several newspapers and was contemplating calling on Danforth when the man himself wandered in.

Adam set aside his paper.

"Hullo, old man." Danforth signaled for a footman before dropping heavily in a chair. "Brandy and coffee. In that order."

Adam arched an eyebrow. Danforth's clothing was meticulous, indicating he'd just been prepared and released into the world by his valet, but his eyes were red-rimmed and watery.

"Hitting it a bit hard, Danforth?"

He grunted. "I went out last night after the play."

"Oh? And how was it?"

Again he grunted. The waiter arrived with

his drinks and he took the brandy with a shaking hand, tossed it back, hissed through his teeth, and frowned. "My sisters informed me this morning that I'm overripe for a repairing lease."

"You look like hell, Danforth. I'd advise you to heed them."

"And when have *you* ever heeded a woman, Exley?" Danforth asked, his expression uncharacteristically arch.

Adam ignored the question and led the discussion into safer areas. They argued over the last Peninsular clash, the Battle of Fuentes de Oñoro, which was still a heated topic for debate even weeks later.

Adam did his best to dampen the younger man's desire to purchase a commission and do his duty. "You must stay alive and succeed to the earldom, Danforth. You are the only real means of security and support for Octavia and Olivia."

His friend flushed at the mild rebuke. "Yes, yes, I know. It would be foolish and cruel to risk their future, but —"

Adam stood, tired of a subject that would do his young friend no good. "Join me for a session at Beaulaux's?"

Danforth scowled up at him, aware he was being rudely managed.

"Come, it'll be almost as fun trying to kill

me as it would killing Frenchies."

"More fun," Danforth muttered.

Beauleaux's was an elite fencing club where Adam spent a good part of each week. Danforth was not a member at the expensive club for the simple fact that he couldn't afford it. Adam was one of Jean Bealeax's most valuable customers and he brought the younger man as frequently as he could, contributing to a silent membership for Danforth, unbeknownst to the impoverished, but proud, viscount.

Adam first took his scheduled period with the great Beauleaux himself. It would be far better to expend some of his energy on a more worthy foe before beating on the enthusiastic, but less skilled, Danforth.

Adam and Beauleaux worked hard on each other for over an hour. A small crowd of regulars gathered to watch in the gallery that surrounded the larger of the fencing arenas. He could see by Beauleaux's satisfied smile at the end of their exhausting bout that the crowd was much more rewarding to him than the actual fencing. Adam suspected the business-savvy Frenchman allowed his touches, merely to keep him coming back and drawing more clientele in his wake.

"Gad, Exley." Danforth shook his head as

he approached. "Aren't you beat to death? Are you sure you want more?" He stood back and took a few swipes at the air, as if to convince Adam otherwise.

Adam barely suppressed a smile as he watched Danforth duel his imaginary foe. "Make sure your mask is secure," he cautioned the younger man, switching his foil to his left hand.

Danforth dropped his arm. "Well, that's good! Bloody wonderful, in fact." His usually mild-mannered face settled into mulish lines. "Are you quite sure you want to use your left hand? Perhaps you'd feel more comfortable using one of your feet?"

Adam closed his mask before grinning. "Come, come, time is wasting, stripling."

The two friends were actually well matched when Adam used his left hand. Danforth was able to get in several touches, even without Adam's complicity. After the fifth, and most painful, touch even Adam had had enough.

"Ha!" Danforth cried in triumph. "No doubt you will head back to the arms of your wife and drown your sorrows."

At his friend's words, Adam was glad he was still wearing his mask. The sensations that thundered through his body at the mere thought of Mia almost knocked him to his knees. For two hours he'd managed to avoid thinking about her and now he would have to resume the struggle.

He choked back a laugh. Perhaps he could stay at Bealeaux's from morning until night, sparring until such time as he could reasonably go home to a woman who'd made it a condition of their marriage that he leave her alone?

"I say, old man, are you all right?"

Adam realized he'd been standing and staring at nothing. He pulled off his mask, brushed his forearm over his damp forehead, and looked at the younger man.

"Are you commencing your rustication today, or would you care to join me for a spot of dinner and some entertainment?"

Chapter Sixteen

Hordes of servants milled about in the hall outside Adam's wife's chambers when he returned home after a singularly unprofitable night at the tables. Danforth had been sitting on a pile of winnings when Adam had finally decided it was best that he go home and lick his wounds.

It was just past midnight, and such an amount of activity seemed . . . unusual. Sayer met Adam at the door and wordlessly handed him a piece of paper.

"What is this?" Adam looked at the small envelope with nothing written on it.

Sayer held out a pair of spectacles without needing to be asked.

"It is from Lady Exley. Your wife, my lord," he added when Adam didn't answer.

Adam scowled and snatched the glasses from his servant's hand. "Thank you, Sayer. I know who my wife is." He tore open the seal and unfolded the single piece of paper.

My Lord Exley:

You are invited to an indoor alfresco party for two in my chambers.

Respectfully,
Your Wife

Adam pulled off the glasses and glanced at Sayer but his valet was carefully examining his feet. "Right *now?*"

"I believe so, sir."

"Do you think she wishes me to come as I am, or should I change into more suitable clothing and shave?" The question was only half-facetious.

"I could not say as to the first, my lord, but I've hot water waiting for you."

Adam sighed and handed Sayer the spectacles and invitation. "What does one wear to an evening alfresco party, Sayer?"

"I'm afraid that is beyond my experience, sir."

Adam snorted. "What good are you, Sayer?"

"That is not for me to say, my lord."

Freshly shaved and wearing slippers, a gray silk banyan, and a nightshirt — for the first time in years — he entered his wife's room. She was surrounded by chattering, bustling servants and wearing a gown of forest green silk that sheathed her delectable body like a second skin. Adam looked at the milling servants, frowning when he spotted the giant blond oaf.

Mia's eyes flickered between him and the footman.

"You may go now." She made shooing motions toward the door with both hands and servants, male and female, hurried from the room.

Heaps of cushions were scattered in front of the fireplace — where there was a bloody fire burning. A coffee table groaned with food.

"You've been busy," he noted.

She came toward him with her usual sinuous grace and took his hand. "Thank you for coming," she said, in all seriousness, pulling him toward the pile of pillows.

Adam gestured toward the fire with his free hand. "Are you cold?"

"Always." She frowned. "Is it too hot? Are you uncomfortable? Should I —"

"I'm fine."

She waded into the center of the cushions and gracefully lowered herself, pulling him down with her. Adam glanced down at the floor and grimaced.

"Please?" She cut him a look he could only call the "Irresistible Kitten Look."

Adam grunted and lowered himself gingerly onto a big cushion. "Very well, but it shall be on your head if I can't get up again."

She turned to the table. "Wine, my lord?"

Adam paused in the act of shoving several of the larger pillows between his back and a nearby chair. "Please." Whatever was going on, he might need a bit of fortification.

She poured two glasses and handed one to him. "Are you hungry?" She gestured to the formidable array of food.

Adam wasn't, but she seemed to have gone to a lot of effort. What the devil did the woman want? He'd stayed away from his own house all bloody day thinking to please her with his absence, and now this? He sighed. "Perhaps some bread and cheese." He sipped his wine as she filled a small plate and brought it toward him, somehow managing to look graceful on her knees.

She fussed with her own pile of pillows until she was satisfied and then reached out and took his foot in her hand. She removed first one slipper and then the next, her eyebrows raised as if in challenge. She motioned to the delicate chair he was leaning against.

"In the palace we rarely sat on furniture, and never any as uncomfortable as this." She sat with her small unshod feet crossed and resting against her calves. The last time Adam recalled sitting in such a position was when he had been a very young child. At seven and thirty he doubted he could manage it.

He sipped his wine and waited. This was her orchestra; he would let her conduct.

"I enjoyed yesterday evening very much, the company more than the play. The only part I did not enjoy was realizing everyone else knows so much more about you than I do." Her brow creased. "I can see what you are thinking. Please don't poker up. I think that is the correct saying?" She cut him an inquiring look.

"*Poker up* is one way of expressing it," he said wryly.

"Tsst!" She tossed her head with contempt.

"And that is certainly another way of expressing something, although I know not what." He took a piece of cheese.

She frowned, clearly in no mood to be distracted from her point. "I look a fool not knowing what everyone else does."

Adam took a large drink of wine, wondering what it was she thought *everyone* knew.

"You are not planning on drinking too much and losing consciousness?" She arched one russet brow but her green eyes sparkled with humor. "Not that I did not enjoy the time I spent with you the first time." She lowered her eyes and fiddled with the corner of an ice-blue velvet cushion.

"What time?"

A slow, sly smile spread across her face.

"My lady?" He used a tone that usually obtained instant results from both those who knew him and those who didn't. He could see by her growing smile his new wife was not a member of either of those groups.

"I will offer you a bargain."

"Bargain?" Adam repeated warily.

"Are you afraid to bargain with me?"

He stared at her.

She crossed her arms and stared back.

Adam cast his eyes ceilingward. "Fine. A bargain."

She gave him a smile that told him there'd never been any doubt in her mind he would yield. Adam had just been out-maneuvered, and the unusual feeling was not one he enjoyed.

"Bartering is the way of things in Oran. We will trade questions for answers. You will tell me what I want to know and I will tell you what I did to you on our wedding night. Or perhaps I could show you?" Her green eyes smoldered.

Adam ignored her attempt to distract him, even if his cock did not. He gave her a bored shrug. "I will answer one of your questions in exchange for three of my own."

"Three for two."

"Two for three."

"An even exchange."

He sighed and rolled his eyes. "Fine, an even exchange."

Her smile was triumphant and Adam realized she would have taken two for three. Minx.

"Shall we spit on our palms and shake hands?"

Adam grimaced. "What a revolting suggestion. Is that another custom from the sultan's palace?"

"No, that is what Cian and I did to seal a pact when we were children."

"Spit will not be necessary. I shall take you at your word." He held out his glass. She gave him a skeptical look and he scowled. "Don't tease yourself — I shan't lose consciousness again. Although it sounds as if you were able to find some sort of entertainment in the matter."

Rather than answer, she leaned back and subjected him to a thorough examination while she considered her line of attack. Her eyes glinted with clever, cunning plans and he suppressed a groan. Why had he agreed to this?

As usual she did the unexpected. "I have heard, twice now, that you are very skilled with a sword. I would like to watch you."

He took a sip of wine to hide his surprise — and his pleasure. What man didn't like feminine admiration?

"That was not a question," he pointed out.

She gave him the same look she'd given him the night of her ball, when he'd mentioned her notorious dance. He decided he would label this look the "Menacing Kitten Stare."

"Very well." He held up one hand in surrender. "Whom shall I call out, Lady Exley?"

She laughed, her eyes sparkling.

It was like being punched in the chest. But in a good way. *Christ.* He was a pitiful, pitiful man.

Still chuckling, she shook her head. "That will not be necessary. I should just like to see you spar? I think that is the term — spar?" Her eyes roamed his body in a manner that made him think of other forms of sparring.

He shifted on his cushion. "You wish to see me spar?"

She nodded.

"You couldn't go to Beauleaux's —"

"What is Beauleaux's?"

"It is where I go to practice."

"Why can't I go there?"

"It is not done, that is why." Adam braced himself for an argument but again she surprised him.

"Then spar here," she said, wisely choosing her battles. Any daughter of the Duke of Carlisle, a man with a punishing code of "what was and what was not done," had probably learned the futility of argument.

"Why is it so important that you watch me spar?"

"Is that one of your questions, my lord?"

It was Adam's turn to laugh.

"Never mind, I will answer it for free. Why is it odd that I would wish to watch my husband do something he does well and enjoys?"

Adam's stomach tightened at the word *husband.* Why were they wasting precious time with talk? He wanted to throw her back on these bloody cushions, strip that dress from her body, and —

"Well, my lord?" She was regarding him with that knowing look; the one that burnt away his carefully maintained veneer of ennui and detachment.

"What activities do you enjoy?" he finally asked.

"That is one of your questions?"

"Surely you could answer such a simple question for free?"

"Perhaps later." She crossed her arms. "You have not yet given me an answer."

"Very well, I will have Beauleaux send someone over and we will give you an exhibition match."

"When?"

"Would tomorrow be soon enough? Or should I send for him right now?"

"No, tomorrow will suffice."

Adam relaxed back against the cushion. But his little haggler wasn't done yet.

"Tell me about your gambling and the many properties you have taken from other men."

Adam gaped, and then shut his mouth. When was the last time anyone had surprised him so utterly and completely? It wasn't a sensation he wanted to get accustomed to.

"Bloody hell," he muttered.

She sat up straighter. "Bloody hell." She repeated the words, as if trying out the taste and feel of them on her tongue.

"Those words are not for you, my dear."

"You like to use them, my lord."

"Yes, well, I'm a man, so I am allowed." He flashed her a quick, unamused smile.

The look in her eyes was no longer playful.

Ah, the kitten has claws.

"Do your *man's* words mean you will not answer my question?"

The temperature in the room had become chilly, in spite of the fire. Adam realized he liked the soft, cuddly kitten far better.

"I'm happy to answer your question. I've acquired several small farms. One in Sussex, one in Lincolnshire, and one all the way up in Yorkshire. They are currently tenanted and operate without much oversight. There are two baronial halls, I suppose you would call them. One in Cumbria, leased for the long term. The other in Essex is a shell, uninhabited and uninhabitable at present. Two — no, three — full estates, all quite far north. Two are still occupied by members of the family under life-estate agreements. The third is undergoing renovations. I have a town house in Brighton, several buildings in the city, three of which are leased and the newest of which is nearing completion." He mentally counted to see if he had missed anything.

"For what purpose are you renovating these buildings?"

"Is this a third question?"

She rolled her eyes and made the hissing sound he was beginning to expect whenever she was irritated.

Adam almost grinned. "What is sauce for the goose, my dear."

She glanced at the table of food. "What does saucing the goose mean?"

"*What is sauce for the goose is sauce for the gander.* It means it is permissible for one person to behave a certain way if another person has already done so."

She smirked. "Well, bloody hell."

Adam threw his head back and laughed. "Touché."

Adam had been about to take a drink of wine when he noticed her staring. He lowered the glass. "Don't worry, I promised I wouldn't become intoxicated."

"No, it isn't that. It's . . ."

He cocked an eyebrow. "Yes?"

"It pleases me to see you laugh. It is . . . a rarity."

He frowned and stared into the glass as he swirled its contents. Was he really that much of a dour, miserable bastard?

"My third question," she said, interrupting his thoughts. "What are you going to do with the two buildings you are restoring?"

Piqued, repiqued, and capoted. Adam was

almost insulted by her lack of interest in his dangerous reputation. Perhaps a man with two dead wives was no match for seventeen years in a harem? But why did she care what he was doing with his properties? And how the devil did she manage to sense the subjects he preferred to keep private?

"My lord?"

"I don't think you really need an answer to your question. I can only suppose either Livia or Octavia has been talking out of school?"

She leaned back among her pile of cushions, her expression as innocent as a baby's. "Is that one of your questions, my lord?"

Adam had the distinct feeling he'd just been stage managed by an expert.

CHAPTER SEVENTEEN

Mia could see by his scowl that the cold, haughty, contemptuous Lord Exley didn't like revealing his acts of charity. Why would he be ashamed of providing a home for impoverished women and children? She recalled something Livia had told her at the theater.

"For whatever reason, my dear Mia, Adam insists on promoting his reputation as that of a hard, cold man who cares for nobody but himself."

Mia had several ideas as to why he would be eager to preserve such a reputation. Now she just had to chisel and chip her way through the thick wall of ice around him to find the truth.

"It is your turn to ask questions, my lord." She made herself comfortable among the cushions and took a sip of wine.

"Why were you arguing with Ramsay on our wedding day?" he asked, proving that he, too, could ask questions that disconcerted.

Mia resisted the urge to hiss. "We were merely discussing the situation in the Mediterranean. He can be very passionate when it comes to political issues." She told herself the answer wasn't completely a lie. After all, Jibril *was* part of the political situation in the Mediterranean.

"How odd. It seemed to me that you were the one who was passionate."

A telling heat began to creep up her neck. How was he able to *do* this to her?

Her husband watched her reddening face with his usual lack of expression, which only served to make her blush harder. He turned away and put his empty glass on the table. "Tell me what happened the other night — our wedding night."

She wasted no time wondering why he'd let the other matter rest. "It's easier to show you, my lord. Come to the bed."

His lips twisted but he stood, the motion athletic and easy, in spite of what he'd claimed earlier. He helped her to her feet and Mia led him to the bed.

She pulled at the sash on his robe and then frowned. He was wearing a nightshirt.

He looked down at her. "Am I to understand you valeted me the other night?"

"No, Sayer managed that for me." She slid the robe from his shoulders, unveiling him slowly, like a statue. She tossed the beautiful silk robe over a nearby chair and stood back to examine his sleepwear. Like all his garments, the cloth was superlative. It was obviously a summer garment, light and soft. Her husband was a sensualist. He was also quite aroused. She studied the tantalizing outline of his erection through fabric so fine she could see almost see the finer details.

She wrenched her gaze away and met his eyes, tingling at the raw hunger she saw. When she reached for his nightshirt, he grabbed her wrists, his hands like manacles.

"Are you toying with me, my lady?" His chest was rising and falling fast. "Are you, perhaps, being wicked again?"

The mere word brought a vivid flash of the prior night, of his relentless, torturous, glorious lovemaking.

"No, Adam."

His breathing roughened even more at her use of his Christian name. It aroused him. And it aroused her to say it. He released her wrists and she lifted his shirt. He raised his arms to accommodate her, but she was too short to lift it all the way over his head.

"My lord." The two words hung in the air between them.

"Yes?"

"Do I need to summon Sayer?"

He ducked his head, muttering something about the poor quality of help and she tugged the shirt off. Now there was only one thing between them. His eyes were half-closed as he watched her, watching him.

Mia felt an overpowering urge to bite him, to gorge as if he were some rare and tasty delicacy that was only in season for a brief time. Instead she reached out and placed her hands flat on his chest, dragging her nails over the muscular ridges of his torso while she pushed him toward the bed. When his thighs hit the mattress she hiked her skirts up to her hips and straddled him. He lay still beneath her, his erection pulsing against her sensitive, swollen cleft.

"Now then, I can begin," she said.

"Good God. You mean to tell me you are only now beginning?" He closed his eyes and dropped his head back on the bed.

Mia laughed and took the oil from her nightstand. She drizzled the cold liquid on his bare chest.

He gasped and looked up at her with hot, affronted eyes. "That was unkind."

"Mm," she agreed absently, working the oil over his chest, spreading it like a canvas she was preparing for paint. The slick marble of his skin was quickly hot beneath her fingers and his erection provided some much-needed friction as she rubbed and stroked and kneaded the glorious muscles of his torso.

"Hell and damnation," he murmured, his muscles jumping beneath her firm, probing fingers. "I slept through this?" He opened one eye a silvery crack.

"Well, I didn't actually get this far," she confessed.

"Yes, well I'm glad —" He broke off with a guttural moan as she applied pressure to a knot in one of his shoulders. "Good God!" He shuddered as she worked down the length of one of his arms. "How did you learn to do such a thing?"

"We practiced on one another in the harem."

The full body reaction her words evoked was more than a little amusing.

"We'll talk more about that later," he murmured. "When I'm actually able to talk."

"I'm afraid you are out of questions, my lord."

He muttered something that sounded like *duplicitous shrew* and she laughed, working his arms from his shoulders to his hands, drawing more moans of pleasure before she finally sat back.

"I am as limp as a wet rag."

"Not all of you," she said. "I am finished with your front. Now, you must flip over."

"Oh, is that what I must do?" he asked, opening his eyes and lacing his hands behind his head, the action making the muscles of his chest and arms tighten and stretch in a mesmerizing fashion. He watched her openly admiring looks with an arrogant smirk and thrust his hips against her to show the direction of his thoughts.

"But I am not finished," she protested.

He began to sit up, his eyes never leaving hers. "I shall finish you."

Before she could protest his hands latched on to her and he flipped her onto her back. She looked up at his triumphant face above her, his equally triumphant member pressed against her stomach, hard and hot through the fabric of her dress.

He eyed the green silk. "Hmm, what manner of sartorial torture do you have for me this evening?" He squinted down at the multitude of tiny buttons that ran down the front of her gown. "Hell."

She reached out to help and he brushed her hands away. "No."

In spite of his complaint, his fingers made short work of not only the buttons, but several clasps and ties.

He pulled open the front of her gown and his eyes burned.

"Mmm." He touched her with maddening softness, never coming anywhere near her aching nipples, his evil fingers tracing the outlines of her through the thin silk barrier of her chemise until she was ready to explode.

"Adam," she said through gritted teeth as his right hand ever so gently cupped her breast.

"Yes?" He released her and met her eyes with an innocent, inquiring look.

She glared, the relentless throbbing between her thighs robbing the situation of humor.

"You are in a hurry?"

"Yes," she gritted out.

"Let me see what I can do about that." Instead of coming into her, he pulled away and backed down the bed, his eyes never leaving hers as he pushed apart her knees.

Mia decided she would scream if he teased her even a second longer.

As if reading her mind he gave her one of his rare smiles and shoved her skirt around her waist. He glanced up.

"No drawers. How perceptive of you. Or did I mention my preference?" His husky voice made a lie of his light words. Strong, cool hands stroked the tops of her thighs and his eyes burned with pale blue fire as he watched himself slip a finger inside her.

"Tell me what you want."

She bucked against his hand. "Kiss me, Adam. Pleasure me with your mouth."

A vein in his temple pulsed at her words.

"As you wish." His eyes locked with hers as he lowered his mouth.

Mia shivered, rocked to the core by the soft heat of him and his clever teasing tongue.

"Oh, Adam." She tangled her hands in his hair, holding him while she moved against him. She'd been so close to her pleasure, it did not take him long to push her over the edge. She cried out as he brought on a succession of climaxes, each paroxysm more violent than the last. He held her hips firmly, covering her with gentle, probing kisses as he rode out the waves of bliss that wracked her body.

Mia drifted in a haze, barely aware that he'd moved until his face was above hers.

He came into her slowly and both of them made low sounds of satisfaction as he filled her. "My God, you feel good," he whispered, his cheek pressed against hers, his breath hot on her ear. "I need to take you."

She answered by tilting her hips to take him even deeper and then squeezing the length of him until he moaned.

"That was very naughty," he gasped, drawing almost all the way out of her and then stroking into her hard and fast. The power of his thrust drove her up the bed and he rode her so hard she barely had the breath to cry out when the first climax overtook her. She choked with a combination of laughter and sobbing as he refused to let up. Just when she thought she could not take one more wave of overwhelming sensation and pleasure, he drove himself deep inside and stiffened, holding her tightly as he climaxed, his black curls damp against his brow, his body rigid and slick with sweat.

"Bloody hell!" he moaned, just before he collapsed, still deep inside her.

Mia laughed weakly. "Bloody hell," she agreed, wishing he would stay where he was forever.

Adam awoke with a start, his eyes immediately assessing his surroundings, his brain lagging behind. He was still in his wife's bed. He turned his head slightly to get a better view of the clock that stood on the nightstand. He encountered the wide-open eyes of his wife instead.

"Good morning, Adam." She smiled at him through a wild tangle of red hair.

"Mm," Adam nodded, disconcerted. "What time is it?" As if that mattered.

"It is half six." She surprised him into a seated position with the information.

"I slept like a rock." Pale yellow light was filtering through the gap between the blue velvet drapes.

"Yes, like a rock," she agreed, looking down toward the sheet that lay between them, inadequately concealing his morning erection.

He gave her his best quelling look but she looked back at him, unquelled.

"I apologize, my lady." His voice was level and cold. "I had meant to return to my bed. I must have been more exhausted than I realized."

She took his wrist as he shoved back the blankets. "Don't go."

He searched his foggy brain for something better than the real reason — that he was a besotted, cowardly fool afraid of his wife. "You need your rest."

"I have rested enough." She stroked him above the sheet, one flame-colored brow cocked.

Good Lord, she couldn't mean . . . ?

She released his hand, pulled the sheet

up, and ducked beneath it.

She did.

Adam was not accustomed to women wanting to make love in the broad light of day. In general, most of the females he'd bedded had squawked in terror at the first sign of light, locking themselves in their dressing rooms and not coming out until they were impeccably coiffed and dressed.

Small hands snaked up his thighs and stopped at the juncture of his legs, expertly taking him in one hand while she insinuated herself between his legs, one hand reaching up and shoving gently against his chest. "Lie back." The order was muffled, but clear enough.

Adam fell back against the pillow. Maybe just this once? He couldn't think of a good reason to go. After all, he'd already slept in her bed. Why not — his body jolted as she began stroking, his hips moving of their own accord.

What harm could it do?

Her expert touch sent him into an almost dreamlike state. She skillfully massaged his aching testicles while she stroked, the combination of sensations clearing any residual rational thoughts from his head. And then the wet softness of her mouth closed over him.

A groan tore out of his throat and he had to fight the urge to fist his hands in her hair and ram himself into her. But she didn't need any assistance from him. She worked him ruthlessly, taking him deeper than he thought possible and bringing him all too quickly to the brink of a shattering orgasm before abruptly stopping. He stared at the canopy with unfocused eyes as a low, sensual laugh rippled from her wicked mouth through his taut body. And then she nipped the sensitive skin of his head and released him, crawling up his body until her head poked out from under the sheet. Adam lifted his head to look at her. She had an insufferably smug look on her face.

"You are so impatient," she gently chided him, the words a mockery of his own from last night. She wiggled around under the sheet until she'd adjusted herself to her satisfaction, straddling him and sitting up, looming over him.

"Now then, my lord. Have you been wicked?"

Adam groaned. This would kill him.

She lowered herself onto him — hard.

Adam gasped and his hands moved instinctively toward her hips, preparing to assist her.

"No," she said, shaking her head and raising her eyebrows. "It is my turn." Her tone brooked no argument.

Adam shrugged, compressed his lips into a bored frown, and laced his hands beneath his head. "As you wish."

The look of naked sensuality on her face was almost more arousing than her rhythmic grinding. He willed away his orgasm, not ready to give up the heady sight of her riding him. As her flush deepened one small hand crept between her thighs and found the place that gave her so much pleasure. Adam didn't think he'd ever been harder in his entire life as he watched her work herself while riding him.

Her other hand moved to her breast and stroked her erect nipples. Her back arched and her eyes closed and that was enough. He grabbed her hips and drove himself home.

She fixed him with an unfocused gaze as he pounded into her. "Come with me, Adam."

Her words were the last straw and he convulsed against her with the sheer force of his orgasm, yelling out God-knows-what as he spent himself.

She laughed with breathless delight as she gave in to her climax.

Adam stared up at her as if poleaxed. He

had never seen such a beautiful sight in his entire life. She was rosy and flushed, her glorious hair spiraling out in all directions. Her head fell back as if it were too heavy, her hands absently stroking her nipples before she dropped down beside him.

"Mm." She snaked an arm around his torso and buried her head in his side. "I'm hungry. Can we have breakfast in bed, Adam?"

Adam laughed weakly. "You seem to be nothing but a collection of hungers."

His hand found its way into her hair and he twisted a long curly strand around his finger, absently inspecting the result.

"Of course you may have breakfast in bed," he said, the fiery red curl coiled around his finger making his chest tighten.

"Will you stay with me, Adam? And perhaps bathe me?" The words were sleepy, yet eager. He stared at the red twist of hair, groping for the right words.

"Adam?"

"I will stay." Thank God she could not see his face.

She tightened her arm around him and sighed with contentment, snuggling closer. It took him a few minutes to realize she'd fallen asleep.

Adam listened to her soft, rhythmic

breathing and stared at the riot of hair spread across his body. It was like a living thing, like the strong, seeking tendrils of red seaweed, and it wove and wrapped itself around him. Its hold was inexorable and he was slipping beneath the waves, without even so much as a struggle.

Adam let Mia sleep while he took care of several issues that couldn't wait.

One of which was, of course, a fencing demonstration for his wife. After sending one footman to his fencing master, another with a draft for payment for the remainder of the work on the London building, and his groom to arrange the delivery of a new mare he'd purchased, Adam went back to his wife's chambers to see if she was awake.

The only difference in the room was that she'd turned onto her other side.

Adam moved a tangled mass of curls from her face. The twist of bedding was barely covering her breasts. He drank her in with the hot greedy gaze of a lecher. Hundreds of tiny freckles dotted the skin of her chest and shoulders. Her lips were slightly parted as she breathed slowly and heavily. In the light of day he could see the lines around her eyes and the somewhat deeper creases around her mouth — smile lines.

Longing, lust, and fear flickered through his mind like quickly moving images outside a carriage window. She was so joyous and happy to please and be pleased. The impulse to hold her at arm's length — a behavior he'd honed to near perfection — was strong. But now he'd enjoyed a taste of her warmth and he wanted more. And so had she, he told himself. It had been his wife who'd asked him to stay this morning. He hadn't forced his company on her; she had asked for it.

You fool.

Adam ran the tips of his fingers over her delicate brow, smoothing back stray tendrils of hair. He leaned close to breathe in the spicy scent of her hair.

She opened her eyes and a languorous smile crept across her face. "Mm. Good morning, Adam."

The sound of his name on her lips had the predictable effect on his groin.

"Did I fall asleep?"

"You proclaimed you were famished, told me I must wash you, and then dropped off to sleep." He sat back and gave her what he hoped was a cool smile rather than the lustful, rutting leer that threatened to overtake his face the longer he contemplated last night . . . and this morning.

"I understand how exhausted you may be after last night. And this morning." His lips twitched. "But I wanted to get you out of bed just long enough to give you something." He abruptly rose from the bed at the look of joy on her face, which threatened to unman him.

"A surprise?" She pushed back the covers, stretching and yawning, naked and unashamed.

Adam's eyes dropped to the small green gem resting in the swell of her belly. He had a powerful urge to drop before her right now and bury his face in the tangle of red hair. Was he demented to be dragging her out of bed?

"Is there anything amiss, my lord?" She stood only a few inches away, twisting her hair quickly into a rope and then winding it into a knot as she blinked up at him.

Adam prayed he wasn't gaping or drooling. "No, there is nothing amiss," he lied. Her obvious comfort with her nudity was intriguing, disturbing, and arousing, among other things.

She strode to her dressing table and took up a pair of pointed, smooth sticks, which she jammed into her hair at odd angles, keeping the heavy bun firmly at the back of her head. The clever trick distracted him and his eyes followed her as she moved toward the bellpull and then halted. "Shall I order breakfast and a bath or have you already done so?" she asked.

There was no hurry about introducing her to the mare.

"Both sound delightful." He watched her from beneath lowered lids, like some hole-and-corner pervert.

Mia pulled the bell and then poured herself a glass of water from the pitcher that sat on the console table. She was refilling the glass when the door swung open and one of the housemaids entered. The girl's jaw came unhinged and her eyes fixed on the naked backside of her mistress.

He lurched to his feet. "Come back in five minutes."

The door clicked shut almost before the words left his mouth.

Mia glanced behind her and then cut him a puzzled look. "What is it, my lord?" She absently scratched one of her shoulders, her forearm brushing the tips of her delicious breasts.

Adam felt as though he was falling from a great height.

"Have you changed your mind, Adam?" she asked, flopping down onto her bed and folding her legs into the same cross-legged position as last night. Except last night she'd not been naked.

Adam could not pull his eyes from the tiny bit of pink peeking from the tangle of red hair. He was rock-hard and unable to put even two sensible words together. The silence lengthened before he managed to pull his eyes away from her sex. He coughed and cleared his throat, hoping to God he didn't squeak like a rodent when he spoke.

"Perhaps you should put some clothing on when you call for a servant? It could have been one of the footmen who answered the bell."

Mia looked down, as if realizing she was naked, and then looked back at him, a slow, sensual smile spreading across her face before she laughed, the action causing her small breasts to shake enticingly.

Adam snatched up the robe she'd worn last night. "Put this on."

She shrugged into it. "I am accustomed to wearing fewer clothes."

"Yes, well, I am very fond of seeing you without any clothing but would prefer others were not allowed the same privilege." *Like that bloody footman.* A scorching wave of jealousy made one head hot with anger while the other throbbed to take her again, just to make sure she knew whom it was she belonged to.

Her knowing smile said she read him like a book. "Will you button me?" She came to stand close to him.

Adam fastened the small buttons, disgusted by the way his hands were shaking. "What would you like first, breakfast or bath?"

"Both. I would like to eat some breakfast while I soak with you."

"Mm-hm." It was the only sound he was capable of making as the clenching of his testicles almost doubled him over.

They lay in the enormous tub and Adam marveled that he'd never bathed with a lover. Mia, on the other hand, seemed as comfortable washing his body as she was her own. She scrubbed and soaped him with sensual efficiency. Her amusement at his constant erection was somewhat humiliating. She cocked one eyebrow as she studied the head of his penis above the water and met his eyes.

He shook his head. "No. Give me your foot." He soaped her toes, trying to keep to the parts of her body that would not cause him to shame himself by ejaculating.

She lay back as he rubbed her feet and legs and took a piece of toast from the tea tray that had been placed next to the enormous bathtub.

"This is heaven." Her eyes closed.

She was right. Adam was more relaxed this morning than he'd been in years — if ever. He was certainly more satisfied than he'd ever felt with his mistresses, whom he'd bedded and gifted but never exchanged intimacies with such as this.

"You'll probably need to wait for your exhibition match until tomorrow. At this rate I'll not have enough energy left to wield a fork."

Her eyes opened to mere slits. "That is a pitiful admission, my lord marquess. Perhaps you need a more rigorous sparring partner to train with?"

"Are you applying for that position?" He wondered yet again whether he could take her once more and still have time to introduce her to her gift.

"I may have some available time." She wrinkled her brow, as if mentally surveying a very crowded calendar.

Adam tugged on her foot and she slid forward. "Yes, yes, my lord! Of course I have space for just one more," she laughingly protested as her chin dipped below the water, one hand held high to keep her toast dry.

He released her and rose from the tub. Her toast-free hand shot out and grabbed him.

By God, she was fast!

Adam took her by the wrist and gently pried away her fingers, gritting his teeth.

"You can play with that later." He stepped away from her dangerous body and wrapped one of the large towels around his waist. "Dress for riding and meet me in the library in an hour." He delivered the order with a stern look.

"I have a brand-new habit. I must warn you, it is of my own design and will most likely cause a sensation," she called after him.

"I would expect nothing less."

CHAPTER EIGHTEEN

When Mia came down to the library — a whole fifteen minutes before the scheduled time — Adam could see she'd not exaggerated. Her riding habit was a bold black-and-white-striped affair. The stripes were full over her breasts and hips and narrowed at the waist, making her small figure appear a perfect hourglass.

The hat she wore was high-crowned with enormous white and black plumes on one side. The starkness of her black-and-white ensemble made her flame-colored hair and emerald green eyes even more stunning.

She stood before the desk and held her hands out to her sides, cocking one hip.

Adam surveyed her from head to toe before making a circular motion with his hand.

"Your father cannot have seen this," he said, admiring the view of her small, pert bottom.

She looked over her shoulder at him, her eyes twinkling. "The first batch of items I ordered he deemed much too unusual. He ordered them given away to some charity. I learned from that experience and allowed my cousin to influence the rest of my choices."

Adam winced. "Ah. The estimable — and weepy — Miss Devane." He paused. "She is not to accompany you to Exham as a companion?"

"I am afraid you shall not have that pleasure. I was happy to recommend her to my aunt Elizabeth, who is desperately in need of a companion due to her imminent lying-in. If I couldn't have found poor Rebecca a place, you would have found yourself saddled with her. Indeed, you might find her in our home again sometime. I'm afraid she has only a small annuity. Such women are terribly vulnerable and reliant on the kindness of relatives."

Adam didn't say what he was thinking: that he would gladly settle a fortune and a house on the woman in order to keep her far away. Instead he said, "That reminds me. We must talk about your pin money and the account I have set up for you. Unless your father spoke to you?"

"He told me a little." She gave him a look

he couldn't decipher.

Hill opened the door. "My lord, Townshend is bringing your gift around front."

"Very good, Hill." Adam stood, barely stopping himself from rubbing his hands together with excitement. He was worse than a young idiot on Christmas morning.

The mare he'd purchased for Mia was a superb animal, perfect for a rider with Mia's limited experience yet young enough to grow with her. She was black except for a blaze on her forehead and two white socks, one in front and one in back.

Townshend brought the horses around front just as he and Mia descended the steps.

"Adam!" She instinctively went toward the smaller black horse instead of the tall, smoky gray. "She's just gorgeous."

She stripped off her gloves and dropped them and her crop to the sidewalk in her haste to stroke the glossy black neck. She murmured foreign words into the curiously bent ear.

"What is her name?" she asked, her eyes still on the horse.

"Her name is Maven but you may change that if it does not suit. I was given to understand the word means 'one who understands.' " Adam collected her gloves and whip and handed them to Thompson before taking Mia lightly around the waist and lifting her into the saddle.

"Thank you, Adam," she said, suddenly shy.

Adam frowned and made a *harrumphing* sound, unable to come up with anything more sensible. Instead, he helped her with the long habit train and adjusted the stirrup. For once, the street was blessedly free of gawkers. Adam had hired several large men to patrol the block and encourage people to move along. It had served to diminish the carnival atmosphere that tended to develop wherever Mia went.

It was an unfashionable hour to ride and the park was thin. They were able to ride with almost no interruption, which suited Adam perfectly. He kept his attention on Mia, careful to make sure she was comfortable with their pace.

"You must have ridden a great deal as a child?" he asked, noticing her natural grace in the saddle. It was clear that she would quickly become comfortable again with only a little practice.

"Oh yes, too much, my mother said. In fact, my hoydenish obsession with horses and my inability to keep to my embroidery was a large part of why I was sent away to begin with."

"Are you telling me I have created a hoyden by giving you a horse, my lady?"

"Oh no, I already was one. You are only providing a hoyden with the proper accouterments." Her smile faded slightly. "My father is a great hunter and was desperate for a son. My mother had tried and failed thrice before they had me. I believe he was beginning to become resigned to me when Cian was born. But Cian was a very sickly child so His Grace made certain to prepare me for the hunt to cover his bets, I believe the saying is?" She cocked an eyebrow at him.

"That is one way of putting it. Is that something you picked up since your return to England?"

She shrugged, the gesture elegant and exotic when she did it. "I learned it on board the *Batavia's Ghost*. The men did almost nothing but gamble when they were not at their tasks. It was very amusing to watch and listen although my — my servant was very disgusted in my interest in their games." She gave him a vague smile, her face oddly flushed.

Now what was that about?

"When my brother grew stronger and it became clear my father would have the son he wanted, my mother decided she would have the daughter *she* wanted." She gave him a wry smile. "And she did not want a girl who rode horses all day and spent the remainder of her time in the stables following the grooms and coming in late for dinner smelling like a horse."

Adam could easily imagine her as a little girl: skinny, wild hair flying, mischievous green eyes.

"Your seat is very good," he said, deciding he would let the earlier hitch in conversation go unremarked. He was far too suspicious of every small thing.

"Thank you, my lord. Thank you also for Maven. Will we take her with us?"

"Yes, of course. Although it sounds as if you might need a couple of hunters to keep up with you in the country."

She gave a delighted laugh. "I would love to ride to hounds."

Adam basked like a lovestruck ninny in the warmth of her laughter.

"Tell me of Exham Castle and the country around it. What is it like?"

"The castle was commissioned to protect England against the incessant threat of French invasion. It overlooks the River Exe and the earliest parts date from the 1380s. We no longer have catapults and cannons, of course, but you can see the places where they were once anchored. The castle has hosted its share of famous guests over the years, among them Richard III, Henry VIII, Queen Elizabeth, and Charles II. During the Civil War the castle was held by Baron Robert de Courtney against the Roundheads for almost a year, until he was finally felled and the castle taken. But Robert's loyalty was not forgotten and Charles II granted the castle to his offspring, Adam de Courtney, and elevated the family with an earldom."

As Adam described the impressive de Courtney seat, he realized how much he was looking forward to going home. He missed both Exham and his family, no matter that each visit to his daughters was accompanied by so much anxiety.

He went on to describe the countryside, the small town of Exham, which had grown up to serve the castle, and the challenges of making a residence out of a military fortification. The ride passed quickly and they were back at Exley House before he knew it.

"What a chatterbox I am, my lady," he murmured.

"I believe it is the first time you have spoken without the application of hot irons, my lord." She looked at him with such open affection it took his breath away. Good God, she was adept at working her way under a man's skin. Or at least his.

"Have we plans for this evening, my lord?"

"I had not made any. What would you care to do?"

"I thought perhaps a quiet dinner at home."

Adam tried to ignore the rush of pleasure he felt at her words. "Very well. Perhaps afterward we can have that game of chess you threatened me with?"

"On one condition."

Adam met her dancing green eyes and shook his head. "You haggle like a fishwife, my lady. What, then, is your condition?"

"I would ask that we dine less formally?"

"Do you mean with fewer servants? Or perhaps you mean you prefer to dine naked?"

She laughed and cut him a wicked look as they approached the waiting groom. "You will find me more than amenable to both suggestions, my lord."

Adam was glad to dismount as his current condition was rapidly becoming unconducive to either comfort or his health. "You are being wicked, my lady," he murmured, loud enough only for her ears.

"I trust you will not forget my wickedness . . . *Adam.*"

Good Lord.

CHAPTER NINETEEN

Mia got her sparring match the next day.

When the owner of the fencing school, a Frenchman named Beauleaux, learned of the proposed match, nothing would do but for him to come to Exley House himself.

Viscount Danforth also attended the informal event. He'd learned of the match from Adam when the two had met at his club.

"I told Exley that wild horses would not keep me away, my lady," he told Mia when he arrived to witness the match.

Mia had quickly relaxed around the handsome young lord, who was easy-mannered and amusing. Danforth passed along several messages from his sisters, complete with intonation and actual wording, leaving her breathless with laughter by the time he was done.

The two of them amused each other while Adam and the fencing master donned their safety equipment and clothing, murmuring quietly to each other as they limbered up across the room.

They used the largest drawing room, which had an enormous set of wooden doors along one side that could be folded back, joining the room to the adjacent music room to make a nice-sized ballroom — or, in this case, fencing arena.

"Do you fence, my lord?" Mia asked Danforth after they had both stopped laughing at a message Livia sent.

"I try, but I am nothing to your husband. He is quite singular, as you will soon see. I believe even Beauleaux has his hands full with him. Of course, Beauleaux is now past his prime, but he was reckoned to be one of the best in the world in his youth."

"Adam practices quite a bit, I believe?"

"Yes, I think he enjoys it as much for the exercise as for the actual fencing. He has an enormous amount of energy." He looked at her. "But you probably know that far better than I, my lady."

She raised her brows at him and, to her amusement, he colored as darkly as the burgundy silk that covered the drawing room walls.

"Begging your pardon, my lady, that is to say," he stuttered. "I only meant you must know him best, as you are his wife."

"Oh, I doubt that," Mia said, watching as Adam lowered his fencing mask. Mia believed he was just as enigmatic-looking without the mask. "He is a private man."

"Yes, he is. I daresay he's always been that way, even before his disastrous first marriage."

Even this man knew more about Adam's marriages than Mia. The last day and a half had been filled with an entirely unexpected growing ease between her and Adam, although he'd still not volunteered anything about himself or his past wives. She'd had her chance when she'd bargained for answers. Of course, she was curious about his past, but she didn't want to be the one who broached a subject he could only find unpleasant. She would leave the timing of such disclosures to him.

Danforth leaned closer. "Exley does his best to cultivate a reputation as an uncaring hedonist but he has been remarkably helpful to my sisters. They are beginning a home for disadvantaged women, complete with a school to teach them new skills. Without his help — and money — the school would never have become reality. He is also converting one of his larger properties into a place where orphaned boys can learn a trade without the cruelty associated with so many apprenticeships. He spends a lot of his time on these projects and has become quite a force for reform, and his views are respected in Parliament. Luckily, the men who sit in Lords are not as condemning of his past as their wives and daughters."

"Your sisters told me about both projects. I am grateful as he would never talk about such things, at least not willingly."

"Give him time. He will open his budget with you, just as he has with me and my sisters." He grinned, exposing a charming dimple. "Exley will thrash me if he learns I've been talking out of school but I don't regret telling you." He looked across the room at his armed friend and frowned. "Even so, perhaps you should not tell him until you are well out of London."

She laughed at his mock-terrified expression.

His look turned serious. "If it were up to Exley, everyone would believe him to be the villain he is painted."

Mia had come to the same conclusion. Her husband was much more comfortable with censure than praise. Perhaps it was merely a matter of habit, or the result of enduring years of suspicious looks and snubs.

The match between the two men was exciting and invigorating. The energy they expended, and the grace and power with which they moved, was very like a lethal dance.

As far as Mia could tell, her husband was indeed a master of the art. He was as smooth and clever with his foil as his instructor. The number of touches they scored off each other was never off by more than one.

The exhibition lasted perhaps three-quarters of an hour, and by its conclusion the Frenchman was breathing so heavily Mia did not think he'd given ground to his wealthy student.

Adam's pale face was flushed when he removed his protective headgear. His damp hair and slick skin were mute evidence of the effort the match had required of him.

The men toweled off and removed their plastrons before coming to join Mia and Danforth. Beauleaux was persuaded to take a small glass of wine before returning to his studio, where he said the students would be lined up and waiting.

Danforth made his bow shortly afterward, reminding them he would see them later that evening at his sisters' dinner party.

Mia found herself alone with her uncharacteristically rumpled husband.

He stood. "I will go make myself more respectable. Shall we take a ride after I have washed and changed?"

Mia stared, unable to fathom how he could not see how aroused she'd become watching him. She took his arm and walked with him toward the door. "I have a better idea, my lord."

"Oh?" he asked, allowing himself to be led up the stairs.

Mia marched him toward his chambers, flinging open the door before Adam could reach the handle. Sayer stood inside the room, his arms filled with a stack of linen.

"You are not needed here, Sayer. I will valet His Lordship."

Mia turned to her silent, stupefied husband and pulled at his cravat, deftly removing it in one motion. She smiled up at Adam, who was shaking his head at her. He mouthed the word *naughty.*

"Have a bath made ready for His Lordship in an hour," Mia ordered.

"Very good, my lady," Sayer murmured, as if the mistress of the house came into her husband's chambers every day and acted as valet.

Adam ignored his servant, never taking his eyes from Mia.

She grabbed his coat as the door closed and roughly pulled it down, enjoying his shocked sputter of laughter as she yanked it off his arms and dropped it to the floor before moving to the buttons of his waistcoat.

"I believe you are trying to make me blush, my lady."

"I see no sign of a blush yet, my lord." But she would, before she was finished with him.

He braced his feet as she pulled off his waistcoat and flung it behind her.

His eyes flickered from the discarded garment back to her face. "You are perhaps the most careless valet I have ever seen," he said mildly.

Mia shoved him onto the bed before turning her back to him and straddling his booted leg, looking back over her shoulder. "Push," she ordered.

He bit his lower lip and shook with laughter, but brought his other foot up and gave her bottom a firm push. She dropped his boot and grabbed his other foot, taking the same position.

"While your valeting skills leave something to be desired, you are the most attractive bootjack I've ever used," he said, pushing against her buttock with his stockinged foot.

Mia tossed his other boot off to the side and then converged upon him, deftly unbuttoning his breeches and shoving him onto his back.

He lifted his hips and she yanked them off, pulling off each stocking while she was in the process. She hiked her skirts to her waist to climb on top of him but found herself on her back before she knew what had happened.

He stared down at her. "I'll take over from here, darling."

Mia pushed herself up onto her elbows and crawled backward. He lunged forward to grab her, but she was faster. But she had nowhere to go and the headboard cut off her retreat.

"You've reached the end of the road," he said, backing her up against the ornately carved wood. She bent close, rather than trying to get away, flicking her tongue over one of his nipples.

"Witch," he hissed, his eyes closing.

Her skilled tongue worked his nipples, alternating painful little nips with soothing sucking while his erection pulsed between them.

"You are so beautiful," she murmured, her sharp teeth catching him and pulling, the pain exquisite. "Ever since the day you kissed me at my father's house, I become wet whenever I think of making love to you."

Adam's brain severed its connection with the rest of his body. He slammed her against the headboard, tearing her gown in his haste to spread her legs. He slid his hands beneath her bottom and lifted her up, his fingers digging into her flesh as he impaled her.

She bit the side of his neck hard enough to make him cry out and he lifted her higher, positioning her for deeper penetration, grunting and straining as he drove into her. He crushed her breasts against him, his muscles screaming with effort, her legs tight around his hips as he slammed into her like a battering ram.

He heard an odd noise and realized it was Mia and that she was laughing with each brutal thrust.

She met his startled gaze with eyes that were fired with pleasure. "Oh Adam, forgive me," she gasped, "I am only laughing because I am so happy I cannot help it."

He couldn't resist a smile — in between gasping for air and thrusting. Her laughter was infectious and he found himself laughing at her sheer enjoyment, redoubling his efforts to bring her through to climax.

At the sound of her long, guttural moan,

he allowed himself the release he had been holding back. Every muscle in his body tensed as he spent himself inside her, his legs and arse suddenly wobbly and weak. He lowered her onto her back and then collapsed beside her with a groan, luxuriating in the loose-limbed feeling of exhaustion, the air growing cold on his sweat-slicked skin as he slowly came back to himself.

Mia felt him laugh beside her.

"What is it?"

"I pains me, but I'm afraid I will have to give Sayer the sack," her husband said, his voice still thick with passion.

Mia's giggle turned into a groan when he pulled his arm out from under her.

"Where are you going? I will bathe you." She propped herself up on her elbow.

Adam shook his head emphatically. "I would not survive it. Are you prepared to go to the dinner party without me? Are you ready to tell everyone that you have put a period to my existence after less than a week of marriage?"

"There will be no premature death. I'm not finished with you, yet, my lord. Once I have finished cleaning every part of you, I will turn you over to Sayer for dressing."

Needless to say, the bathing took significantly longer than anticipated.

When Mia entered her chambers almost two hours later, she found a new gown on her bed, a card in the bodice.

There was only one sentence, written in a surprisingly compact hand:

Come to my study after you've dressed.
A.

Mia ran her thumb over the note, charmed to think of him penning a missive to her, no matter how brief. The dress was gorgeous. More importantly, it was something he'd chosen just for her.

The underdress was emerald green silk, but only hints of the sheath were visible beneath layers of antique gold lace that floated over the skirt. It was high-waisted and the bodice fit her like a glove. It was devoid of any other adornment or frippery and was striking in its simplicity. Even La-Valle, whose superior French taste generally meant she turned her nose up at English fashions, looked impressed.

Mia rushed LaValle as she dressed her hair, eager to thank Adam for the spectacular garment. When she entered the study the look he gave her as he rose from behind the large desk was all she could have wanted.

His face was serious and unsmiling, as usual, but his magnificent eyes swept over her several times, taking in every detail.

"You look . . ." He stopped, shaking his head and finally shrugging his shoulders in defeat. "I don't have a word for how exquisite you look." His lips flexed into the slight smile that made her wish to be in bed with him again. Or even on the big leather couch across from his desk.

Mia dropped a deep curtsy at his praise. "Thank you so much, Adam. Your taste is divine."

"I still think you are missing something."

She looked down at her gloves and the front of her gown. "What?"

He walked back to his desk and took a large black velvet box from the top drawer.

Mia pursed her mouth and shook her head. "Oh Adam, I have nothing for you. You are making me feel terrible."

"Yes, you'd better work on that, Lady Exley." His mouth twisted mockingly as he placed the box in her hands. "Now, shut up and open your gift."

She stroked the smooth velvet for a moment as she considered his handsome face.

He met her eyes with his standard haughty look.

"Thank you." Her heart twisted in her chest at his cold expression. He thought to fool her, but Mia already knew it was a disguise he donned whenever his emotions rose too close to the surface.

"Don't thank me yet. You haven't opened the box." He folded his arms and leaned back against his desk, his pose one of indolence. "Perhaps it contains a live ferret? Or maybe a dead ferret?"

She couldn't help laughing.

"Hush and open it." His face was severe but his lips twitched.

The necklace and earrings in the box took away Mia's breath. She stared in disbelief at the enormous emeralds, set in a delicate filigree that looked like a golden spider's web. She glanced up, her mouth open.

Adam dropped his jaw and goggled and she laughed. His playfulness was more delightful than the beautiful gift in the box, but of course she could not tell him that. He took the box from her hands and turned her around, his hands warm and strong on the naked flesh of her arms.

A shiver of desire went through her as his fingers brushed her neck, removing her necklace and drawing the new one around her throat and fastening it. His hands smoothed and centered the jewelry before settling on her shoulders and giving her an almost imperceptible squeeze. He leaned down and kissed the side of her neck.

"You look good enough to eat," he murmured. "I will save room for dessert." The words were barely a whisper and his devilish hands were as light as feathers as he stroked her arms.

He turned her around in a businesslike manner and took her arm, gloved to past the elbow, and clasped the matching bracelet around her wrist, his hot eyes making a lie of his prosaic behavior.

"You must fasten your own earrings, darling. I'm afraid I'd be stabbing about uselessly."

Mia had lived for thirty-two years and never been anyone's darling. The casual endearment made blood surge loudly in her ears. She wanted to throw herself into his arms but instead she removed and replaced each earring, requiring no mirror. When she was finished she looked up at him, her insides molten at the memory of the word *darling* on his tongue. Her vision blurred with sudden tears and she stepped toward him and slid her arms around his waist.

"What's this?" he asked, his chest rumbling against her ear.

"Thank you, Adam." She pushed closer and smiled when she felt evidence of his desire for her. "Already, my lord?"

"It's been a long time," he whispered into her hair.

"Almost three hours."

She reached up and pulled his face down, impatient for the taste of him.

"You are the devil," he accused, catching her lower lip in his teeth and holding her for a long moment, his eyes hooded and hot.

Hill entered the room and then took a step backward.

"Ahem. I beg your pardon, my lord. The carriage has been brought around. As you ordered," he reminded, his stare like a rabbit's transfixed by a cobra.

"Thank you, Hill," Mia cut in, before Adam gave the poor man one of his frosty setdowns. The steward darted out of the room just like the hare he'd resembled.

Mia gave Adam one last squeeze through his breeches and straightened his crushed cravat.

"I suppose I should be grateful I didn't have you bent over the desk when Hill came in."

Mia chuckled. "I'm not." She stepped

back, her entire body thrumming with desire.

He caught her wrist and yanked her back.

"I shall be able to think of nothing else all night." The words were menacing but his eyes were dark with promise.

CHAPTER TWENTY

Mia gazed out the carriage window as she thought back on the events of the past two weeks, some of the happiest of her life. They'd delayed their departure from London several times over the prior weeks. Not only did the Mantons remain in town, but Adam toured Mia around the London sights when he learned nobody else had bothered to take the time.

He truly was a man transformed. Gone was the impassive, bored, or contemptuous marquess she'd married. Beneath that cool, cultivated façade was a lover who was playful, witty, and generous.

Mia reflected on the nights — and days — of passion with a pleasurable shiver. Adam de Courtney was turning out to be more fascinating than she ever could have imagined. She found that sharing her life with a man was like suddenly discovering dozens of new colors that you never even knew existed. And Mia was supposed to leave him.

She shivered.

"Are you chilled, my dear?" Adam asked, looking up from the book he was reading. He was sitting on the seat across from her, an ocean of cushions and rugs scattered between them.

"I am," she lied. "Won't you sit beside me? Only to keep me warm," she added quickly when he looked ready to scold.

"Only to keep you warm." He closed his book and shifted gracefully across to her side of the luxurious and well-sprung coach.

"Come here," he said, leaning back in the corner and beckoning her toward the space between his legs.

She pushed up close between his thighs and lay against his chest. He wrapped his arm around her, holding her lightly but firmly beneath her breasts while his legs gripped her more securely.

"Mm," she sighed, shifting and adjusting cushions under her legs and feet until she felt a deep laugh in his chest, his arm tightening around her as he leaned down to kiss the top of her head.

"You are just like the Mantons' cat."

"Their cat?"

"Yes, their cat. I believe they call the beast

Boadicea, which is not surprising for them, I suppose."

"How am I like a cat?" she persisted, pleased by the happy, relaxed note in his voice.

"The way you take a sensual pleasure in your surroundings and comfort. Although you're so small that maybe I should say you're like a kitten."

Mia sighed and snuggled closer. She was thoroughly enjoying the journey even though an unexpected summer storm made their post stops a wet, muddy business. She was eager to see her new home but she couldn't help treasuring the novelty of a long carriage ride with her husband.

The truth was, Mia was far from miserable with her life and that realization made her feel guilty. Every day she promised herself she'd begin taking steps toward making her escape. Yet every day ended with her no closer to selling her jewelry or sending a message to Bouchard.

Was her hesitation purely selfish or had Ramsay been correct in saying her presence in the middle of a violent struggle would not help Jibril's cause? Mia nibbled on the end of a curl that insisted on breaking free and tickling her nose. She might view Jibril as a boy, but men were fighting and dying because they wanted him as their leader. It had been her son who'd pleaded with her to go to England to begin with.

But wasn't that argument merely self-serving?

Mia didn't think so. Instead, she was beginning to see merit in Ramsay's suggestion she tell Adam the truth and bring Jibril to England. Adam had been a social outcast for years and had done well enough for himself; why could not Jibril do the same?

Mia released the strand of hair and frowned. She was not even sure anymore if she *could* leave her husband. Every day she became more certain she loved him; not that she had any experience in what love was supposed to feel like. Whatever she felt for him, she didn't want to live without it. She absently stroked her hand down his thigh.

"Mia," Adam warned.

"I won't, Adam, I promise." She stopped her stroking but smiled as she felt his stiffness against her back. In the middle of their last tussle in the carriage — earlier that day — the vehicle had become stuck in a deep rut. Adam had been forced to curtail his pleasure and had warned her against teasing him any further en route.

"I shan't let you work me into a lather and then be forced to muck around in a ditch with a bloody cockstand," he'd muttered.

Mia almost giggled as she recalled his irritation. He *had* been at attention.

It had taken all five men to budge the large vehicle. By the time Adam reentered the carriage he'd been wet and muddied almost to the tops of his boots. Mia stroked the soft buckskin of his breeches at the memory. Why was it she found him even more arousing covered in mud and disheveled? His hand closed over hers, steadying the stroking gesture she'd unconsciously resumed.

Mia closed her eyes. It had been only two weeks. Surely she could consider the matter for a little longer before making any decisions? Perhaps she might even tell him the truth?

"We are here, my lady," Adam told his gently snoring wife.

"Mm?" She pushed herself up off his chest, where she'd spent the last two hours of the journey sleeping like a cat, curled up in his lap. "Already?"

"Yes, already," he agreed drily. Adam raised the shade higher as the carriage rolled beneath the exterior castle wall into the large cobbled courtyard. It was past dusk but the drive was well-lighted with torches burning in the ancient holders.

The structure was a fine example of a walled castle, built to protect the early coastline from invaders. The river that had used to run in front of it had spread into a sluggish estuary, and the outlet had been abandoned as other, deeper water ports developed.

Over the years Exham Castle had seen many changes. The moat, of course, no longer held water and wooden spikes but was only visible as a slight indentation, now filled with grasses and wildflowers.

Adam had spent a good deal of time and money reconstructing those parts of the old wall that had crumbled. The rock he'd used had been quarried from the same sites as the original and painstakingly milled to fit the gaps. He'd been pleased by the result, a façade that looked almost uniform. It was not the most comfortable place to live but he always felt a rush of pride when he beheld it for the first time after a long absence.

Jessica was standing in front of the rather barbaric main entrance, where more torches burned in massive medieval holders, much as they must have done hundreds of years ago.

Adam shoved through the myriad of pillows his wife required in every situation and opened the door to the carriage, leaping out before the steps had been placed. He stretched and yawned as one of the footmen unfolded the steps. Adam reached for Mia's hand and grinned at the expression on her face, which was wondrous as she took in the castle behind him.

"It is so magnificent and imposing." She didn't bother looking where she was stepping but luckily, he was close enough to catch her, whispering in her ear as he lowered her to the ground.

"You must be more careful, my dear. We don't want my detractors saying I murdered you the very day you arrived."

She looked so startled he laughed.

"Welcome home, Adam. I'm sorry I don't have everyone here to greet you, but we believed you had been delayed when you didn't show up earlier."

Adam turned to greet his sister. "We ran into some rather wet weather both days, I'm afraid. Sorry to have left you guessing." He took Jessica's hands and smiled down at her. "You are looking well, Sister."

She flushed, discomposed by his unusual gesture of affection. A small, nervous smile spasmed across her narrow, pale face and

Adam realized how changed he must appear. Well, for better or worse, he *was* changed.

"Jessica, this is your new sister — Mia."

"I have been so looking forward to meeting you, Jessica. I've never had a sister." Mia reached toward his sister as if to embrace her, but stopped when the other woman flinched back.

Mia had not even a speck of English reserve. She liked nothing better than to be in physical contact with other people. Adam's family rarely touched. He supposed that would all change now.

"I'm pleased to meet you," Jessica murmured, her natural shyness making her appear haughty, almost unfriendly. She had the same dark hair and pale skin as Adam but had inherited their father' gray eyes, along with his almost crippling reserve.

Mia's exuberant manner shifted subtly and became gentler. Adam realized it was the same way she'd handled him those first few days of his marriage, before he'd crumbled like a biscuit dipped in hot tea.

"Come," he said, his emotions making him brisk. "It's chilly out here and we've been on the road for hours. Is there a fire in the book room?"

"Yes, of course, and Bailey has prepared

tea. I thought you might be hungry."

"I'm dying for tea," Mia said, companionably taking Jessica's arm and walking with her. "I'm afraid our late arrival must be putting you out. Do you keep early hours in the country?"

"Yes, we do. I suppose you will find things rather quiet after London . . ." Jessica trailed off, clearly unsure of what to do with his new wife. She turned and looked at Adam, who followed them. "The girls are in bed, of course. I am sure they are not sleeping. I cannot seem to get Eva to stop reading under her blankets, no matter how dangerous I tell her it is."

Adam suspected his headstrong daughter was becoming more than a match for her quiet, retiring aunt.

Mia stripped off her gloves and gave Adam a saucy wink. "I'm afraid I was the same when I was a girl, Jessica. My mother quite despaired of me. Of course, Adam won't let me read under the covers now," she confided, drawing a startled gasp from his sister.

Adam tried to frown but couldn't.

Mia gave one of her wide-eyed looks — an expression he imagined her using frequently to get her way with the sultan.

"Oh, I'm sorry, Jessica. Was that shocking? Adam despairs of my ever being fit for decent company."

Jessica tittered nervously at such playful conversation.

Mia waited until Jessica had turned away and poked out her tongue at Adam.

He mouthed the word *wicked* and became instantly hard at his wife's sultry smile. He should be ashamed of behaving like a schoolboy but he'd given up trying to resist Mia and her high spirits. Besides, what was the point?

The book room was Adam's favorite room in the castle. It took up the base of one of the four turrets. The ceiling was rather low, giving the room a cozy feeling, and the circular walls were lined with books from floor to ceiling.

The fireplace could roast an entire ox but now it held only fire. It blazed like a furnace, the oddly curved back throwing heat better than any other fireplace in the castle. It might be summer but the castle was always cold.

"It's lovely," Mia said, absently handing her reticule and gloves to Adam, who smiled wryly at his sister's face — shocked to see her brother acting as his wife's footman and enjoying it.

The tea tray arrived and Jessica moved toward it and then hesitated.

"Oh please, will you pour?" Mia asked, giving Jessica a pleading smile. "I know I should, but I'm so frightfully clumsy about such things," said his wife, one of the most sinuously graceful women Adam had ever met.

"Certainly." The gentle flush that spread across Jessica's cheeks was the only sign Mia's invitation had pleased her. Adam's heart, which he'd forgotten existed until a few weeks ago, swelled. Mia was unfailingly thoughtful and kind, and it pleased him more than he could believe that she was making such an effort to reassure Jessica that her place was secure.

"I am surprised to find the weather so clear here," Adam said. "It rained almost the entire way." He shook his head at Jessica's offer of tea and poured himself a brandy instead.

"It must be moving north, we were covered for some days with a gray blanket of clouds. The rain was so heavy Eva and Melissa were teasing poor Miss Banks almost mad. Neither had been riding for almost a week. You know how they can become."

Adam's heart stuttered and then sped up. "She is able to keep them in hand, I trust?"

he asked in a voice that was sharper than he wished.

"Oh yes, Adam." Tea sloshed over the rim of the cup she was pouring. She shot a quick glance at Mia, who was standing in front of the fireplace, gaping up at the mantel, which arched a good foot above her head.

Small tendrils of alarm grew in his stomach and spread through his body, just as they always did when he came home. He watched Mia as she moved around the room, inspecting the many items of interest. Just looking at her made him . . . happy?

"And Catherine, how is she?" Adam asked, the maelstrom of emotions leaving him rather breathless and dazed.

"She is well. Very well, in fact," Jessica assured him, seeming eager to dispel the cloud that had already formed. "Tea, my lady?" Jessica glanced toward where Mia was standing.

"Oh, yes. Thank you! But please, won't you call me Mia?"

"Yes, of course . . . Mia. And you must call me Jessica." Jessica's smile was somewhat tremulous.

Adam had never noticed before just how fragile his sister appeared. A spasm of guilt joined his other emotions as he realized how little assistance she'd received from him since their mother had died.

Mia settled in the corner of a large sofa and looked expectantly at Adam. He couldn't resist the smile that curved her lips as he sat next to her and she fitted herself to his side. She was the most physical person he had ever known. Even Danforth's sisters, who constantly ruffled and smacked and embraced those close to them, were not as tactile as Mia.

With him, in particular, she was not only tactile but unconsciously sensual. When they were alone she was never far from him, preferring to sit on a cushion next to his chair if he was working at his desk, rather than on a chair farther away. He had become accustomed to her unusual habits in a remarkably short time, finding her casual and comfortable manners a welcome relief to his more formal ones.

"Townshend will be along tomorrow, I expect," he said, taking a sip of brandy and reaching for one of the small sandwiches. He handed it to Mia, who consumed it in two bites. He looked up to find his sister viewing their interaction with slack-jawed amazement and his face tightened into the mask that had been his defense for almost a decade.

"This is perfect, Jessica. Thank you," Mia

said, finishing another small sandwich and smiling at his sister over the rim of her tea, unaware of the currents of shock eddying through the room.

Jessica nodded, dazed.

Adam suddenly realized he didn't care if he appeared to be the fatuously happy idiot he was. He smiled at Jessica, shocking her even more.

"Have you set up the Olive Rooms, Jess?"

"Yes, I think you will like them much better than your old room. Both fireplaces burn without smoking, which is more than I can say for that appalling stack in your old chambers." She sounded more normal as she warmed to her favorite topic: the castle.

Adam had not moved to the master suite after his father's death, but the big group of interconnected rooms was the only one that would suit a married couple. The chambers were attached to an unusually large bathing chamber, which Adam hazarded was one of his ancestor's attempts to mimic the old Roman baths occasionally found in the area. He believed Mia would enjoy it very much.

They spoke of castle matters while Mia consumed a shocking amount of food and several cups of tea, finally suppressing a giant yawn, her eyes sleepy.

"I take it you are ready to retire?"

"Yes, I'm afraid I'm dead on my feet," Mia said, giving Jessica an apologetic smile.

Jessica stood. "Let me show you to your rooms."

Adam, of course, knew the way, but he didn't stop her. He knew how much she enjoyed showing the castle to people for the first time. Mia, especially, was an enthusiastic audience, cooing and remarking in all the right ways.

When Adam opened the door to his father's old rooms he was stunned.

"Do you like it?" Jessica asked nervously.

"Very much. You must have worked quickly to have effected such a grand change in such a short time." He smiled at her. "You have truly outdone yourself, Jess — it is quite magnificent."

Jessica flushed with pleasure.

"But I'm not sure we can call it the Olive Rooms any longer. Where in the world did you find it all?" The room's harsh stone walls were relieved by four enormous mullioned windows, a later addition to the castle. Tapestries and heavy drapes in gray and rose velvet softened the rather heavy room. Enormous furniture, built to fit the scale of the room, had been re-covered in plush velvets, the chairs and sofas overstuffed and softened to make up for their massive size.

"It's lovely," Mia said, reaching out to stroke the velvet arm of a sofa. Jessica couldn't have chosen any better for his wife. The large cushions and ottomans scattered about were the kind of thing she loved. He wondered how his sister had guessed with such accuracy. He hadn't given her much time, barely a month. The transformation was quite impressive.

Bedchambers sat off to either side of the giant sitting room, each with massive armoires as there were no traditional dressing rooms. Sayer and LaValle were already busy in their respective domains, hanging and organizing and fussing with the first round of their baggage.

After making sure they had everything they needed, Jessica bid them good night and left them together in the joint sitting area.

"It's absolutely magnificent, Adam." Mia leaned against him and wrapped her arm around his waist as she surveyed the room.

Adam took her chin and tipped her small face upward. "Yes," he said, "it is."

She laughed and buried her face in his coat. "Oh don't, I must look a fright. I was burrowed into you like a forest creature in the carriage."

"Yes, you do look a fright." She hit him and buried her face deeper. "Luckily, I have just the thing. Come with me." He took her hand and led her through his room, where he nodded his dismissal to Sayer, who left the remaining luggage and quietly took himself off to his usual room.

Adam opened the heavy arched door that led off his bedchamber, which Jessica had not shown during her brief tour.

"Close your eyes." Mia complied and he led her inside. "You may open them."

She gasped, her eyes wide as she looked about the room. She walked toward the square sunken tub that occupied one entire corner of the room. "Oh, Adam." She looked up at him before leaning down to dip her finger in the water. "It's hot! But how is that?" She stared at him as if he were a magician.

"It is no work of mine. An ancestor built it, using water that is heated naturally deep underground. He took his cue from the Romans, who had this kind of bath wherever such geology existed. I thought you might like it."

She laid her hands against his chest, looking up at him in a way that did disconcerting things to his stomach. "Will you bathe with me, my lord?"

He released into his gaze all the hunger and lust he had been controlling since their truncated lovemaking earlier in the day. Her face flushed and her lids lowered as he pushed against her, forcing her to take a step back, and then another as he relentlessly advanced on her, not stopping until he'd pinned her against the hard stone wall of the bathing chamber.

"Unbutton me," he told her, his voice harsh with need. Her deft hands worked fast to free him.

He pulled up the skirt of her traveling costume, his hand moving to what he knew would be waiting for him. She wore no drawers. He shook with desire as he delved into her curls and found the part of her that transformed her into something that was his alone.

Adam was not the only one who'd found the long carriage ride protracted foreplay. She was wet and ready and he was far too impatient to employ his usual teasing methods. While she was still shuddering with pleasure he grasped her bottom, lifted her against the wall, and slid into her, holding very still once he was seated. He braced himself, his feet spread shoulder-width apart, gaining control of himself. She moved restlessly above him, her hips grinding, wanting more.

He pulled back to look at her. Her eyes were hooded, her mouth slack and willful.

"So greedy." He snuggled her tighter to his body as he worked himself deeper. "You've hardly finished one orgasm and you already want another. You'll not come again until you've earned it," he whispered, punctuating his words with a quick thrust of his hips.

She gasped.

"Did you enjoy teasing me today, my lady? I think you did," he mused, again thrusting hard and quick, wanting her to know he was in complete control of her pleasure. "It amused you to think of me sitting behind you, hard with need for you. You enjoyed making me suffer."

Thrust.

She whimpered, her lips parting as her breathing grew rougher.

Thrust.

"What was that, my dear? I couldn't hear you?" He was almost mad with the effort of holding back.

Thrust.

Another whimper.

Thrust.

"You'll have to speak up, my lady,"

Thrust.

"Please."

"I beg your pardon, darling?"

Thrust.

"Please, Adam, more." Her voice was barely a sigh.

Thrust.

"More? More what, my little tormenting devil? I should like to hear you beg."

Thrust.

"Please, Adam, please make me come." The last word was almost a sob and it was like a match to a powder keg.

When his climax came it stunned him. Wave after wave of pleasure pounded him. He was a piece of helpless flotsam, battered and carried along on the relentless flow until he was wrecked and spent, cast up on passion's shore.

His legs shook and he wrapped one arm under Mia's bottom, yanked up his fallen breeches with the other, and brought her to the long wooden bench where he gently lowered her before dropping down beside her.

Mia nuzzled beside him, lifting his arm and draping it over her shoulders as she burrowed into his side.

"Thank you, Adam. That was quite nice," she purred, a smile in her voice as she stifled a giant yawn.

He barely had enough energy left for a weak laugh. "You will be the death of me."

Adam was to remember those words many times during the coming weeks.

Not even when he'd been five and twenty and married to Veronica — who'd been more sexually voracious than most men — had he engaged in so frequent, enjoyable, or exhausting amours. But whereas Veronica had been bent on seeking pleasure, Mia was bent on giving it. Adam could not get enough of his new wife and the feeling was mutual.

He smiled to himself as he left the gun room and mounted the stairs up to the main level of the house, thinking about their lovemaking that morning — which had made him late for his meeting with Kearns, his steward.

It had pained him to leave her in bed. Her tangled hair and swollen lips erotic proof he'd used her hard, but the invitation in her eyes telling him she was ready for more.

Adam had never had a lover so eager or generous — or so openly joyous. She had no qualms about approaching him anytime or anywhere. He thought back to their last game of chess, which had ended — once again — with her supremely trouncing him.

He had been forced to retaliate by bending her over the large desk in the library.

He could no longer see a chessboard without getting an erection.

She was so skilled at arousing him, he should have been embarrassed. Like a trained dog, he knew that whenever the words *my lord* came out of her wicked mouth she was either imagining their last coupling or planning the next. He paused in the hallway to adjust himself, meeting the startled eyes of one of his footmen as he did so.

None of the servants could be unaware of what was taking place in their master's chamber every night and morning. And in several other parts of the castle and grounds any other time of day. Adam didn't care.

He entered the smaller of the castle's two sitting rooms, pausing for a moment to take in the scene before him: three dark heads, one sandy-blond, and a flame-red one bent over something on the table. Jessica, Catherine, Eva, Melissa, and Mia were so enraptured by whatever they were looking at, they didn't notice his entrance.

Adam cleared his throat.

Five pairs of eyes swept up toward him.

"Papa, look what Mia brought." His eldest daughter gestured to the item of interest.

Adam walked to the table and tilted his head. It was a fashion magazine, apparently in French.

"Hmm." He looked at his wife with raised brows. "Do you have connections that run the Channel for you, my lady?"

Mia smiled but didn't answer.

"Mia says we may have new frocks, Papa," Eva said.

Adam eyed the dress she was currently wearing, a disaster, and felt a pained expression forming as he studied his middle child. Eva was, as always, an utter mess. She flushed under his critical examination, the mulish expression he knew so well forming on her face.

Mia caught his eye and gave a minute shake of her head.

Adam sighed and clamped his mouth shut. Mia didn't need to speak; he could see the plea in her face and he'd heard all her arguments before. As recently as two days ago, in fact, when she'd come to his study to plead Eva's case after a particularly unhappy clash between Adam and his daughter that morning in the stables.

Adam had been thrilled by her sudden appearance in his study and the interruption of his bill paying — until he'd learned the topic she had come to pursue yet again.

"You must not chide Eva so, Adam. She is a little careless of her apparel and she is perhaps sometimes a bit of a hoyden . . ."

Adam had cast down his quill and pushed aside his ledger, looking up at his wife as she stood before him, pleading his daughter's case so passionately.

The fight in question had arisen when Adam agreed to take Mia and the girls riding. When he and Mia arrived at the stables, they found two of the three girls neatly and attractively dressed and waiting. Eva, on the other hand, had arrived for the ride late and in a wrinkled and too-large habit, one of her sister Catherine's castoffs, he surmised, her hair loose and wild, no hat, and filthy gloves with one finger protruding.

Whether his children liked it or not, they knew Adam despised unpunctual behavior and did not tolerate a slovenly appearance. He sent her back to the house, telling her she could arrive on time and properly dressed in the future, or not ride.

What had ensued had been the kind of scene that turned Adam's blood cold. By the time Eva stormed back to the house, he'd been emotionally drained — and frightened.

The subsequent ride had been subdued. Catherine and Melissa, both generally well-behaved and pleasant girls, had barely spoken a word. Even Mia's irrepressible good humor had not been able to lighten the atmosphere.

Mia had come to him later, after talking with Eva, who was refusing to leave her room in protest.

"She won't come out of her room, Adam," Mia said, as if the matter were Adam's doing.

"That is an excellent place for her," he said coolly.

Mia was not put off by his words or demeanor. Indeed, Adam noticed, with no small alarm, Mia no longer appeared repressed by his disapproving looks or tone. Instead, she responded to his cold contempt by wedging her body between him and his desk.

He sighed and leaned back in the chair. Undaunted, she moved closer, pushing apart his legs and standing in between his thighs, smiling down at him.

Like the well-trained dog he'd become, he began to respond.

"She is a very sensitive girl, Adam. More so than Cat or Mel." She'd been here less than a month and already had pet names for the girls. And the girls absolutely loved it, and her.

"I was so much like her as a young girl."

Adam's eyes ran up and down his immaculately dressed wife and he snorted. She ignored him.

"I was, darling," she insisted, wiggling between his thighs in a most intriguing manner, guaranteed to attach his interest. His hands drifted toward her hips, as if they had minds of their own. He was only vaguely aware of her words as he stroked her slim body through her plain but enchanting morning dress.

"Don't you think? Adam?"

"I beg your pardon?" He reluctantly dragged his eyes away from her body and looked up at her inquiring face.

"You aren't listening to me."

"Of course I'm listening to you, but it's very distracting to crane my neck. Here, sit, my love." He pulled her down onto one leg, flexing his thigh against her small, tight bottom, bouncing her slightly up and down, smiling at the charming picture she made.

"Adam," she said, her tone meant to be threatening.

"Yes?" he asked absently, unable to resist cupping her small breast as he dandled her on his knee.

"You must listen first, and then you can

play with me." She grabbed his hand and held it.

He gave an exaggerated sigh and crossed his arms. "Speak, you redheaded harpy."

She nodded happily. "Eva tries very hard to please you. She adores you, Adam. Can you not look beyond her torn and muddy frocks and see the girl who lives for your approval? She's a spanking rider, very good with horses, and she knows every inch of your land as well as you do. If she were a son you would think her famous, wouldn't you?"

Adam was startled by her insight. She was right. Eva would make the perfect son. Well, apart from her appalling emotional outbursts. But Mia didn't know about those and what they might mean. Coward that he was, Adam was not ready to tackle that subject.

"You may be right, Mia, but she is *not* a man and cannot expect to be treated as one. You do her no favors if you encourage her in her belief that she can carry on as if she were my son."

Mia was already shaking her head halfway through his sentence. "I am not arguing that you should treat her as a boy and she does not want such treatment in any case. I am asking that you are more forgiving of her failures as a girl. She is messy and often disheveled, but she will grow past that. Please, can you not try to let some of her failings pass? Try for a short while; if things between you do not improve, you can always revert to your old ways."

Adam had studied her for a long moment. Could she possibly be as perfect as she seemed? He looked into her clear green eyes, seeking any sign of deception or guile, and found none. But would he be able to see deception even if it were there? He was so bloody besotted, he was all but blind.

He pushed the question aside for another time and considered her request. It was practical and kind. It behooved him as a parent to rise above the childish urge to fratch with his own daughter.

"I shall implement your advice. I thank you for having such a care for my children. I know it cannot be easy for you to inherit three nearly grown girls."

She shook her head at his words. "Pooh!"

"Pooh?" He cocked an eyebrow at this new addition to her vocabulary, undoubtedly the gift of one of his daughters. "And where did you learn the term 'spanking'? I'll wager from the girl under discussion. If you use that term in polite society you *will* get a spanking," he promised.

She ignored the threat. "Now," she said, getting up off his lap and looking down on him, "I have something I would like to show you, my lord."

Adam's stomach lurched with joy at the two small words.

"I think you might find it interesting," she continued, standing on her toes and putting her bottom on his desk, dangling her feet as she slowly inched up the hem of her gown.

"Oh?" Adam asked faintly, unwilling to trust his voice any further than that.

"Yes." She nodded. "I found it this morning when I was getting dressed and I immediately thought of you."

Adam's eyes followed the rising hem, holding his breath as she slowly pulled the skirt over her knees and then all the way back to her hips.

As usual, she was not wearing any drawers.

"Ah," he said, his voice choked. "I think I may have seen something like that once before." He'd lowered a hand on each of her knees and gently pushed.

"Perhaps you need a closer look to be certain, my lord?" She slid her hips closer to the edge of the desk — to him.

"Adam. Adam?"

At the sound of his name, Adam shoved

the erotic memory into the increasingly overcrowded corner of his brain where he stored such treasures.

Mia had come to stand before him, an amused look on her face, her glance flickering down to his bulging buckskins, which she was strategically hiding from the curious faces behind her.

"We were speaking of frocks, Adam."

He frowned, looking past his wife's shoulder and then back. "We were?" He cleared his throat. "Yes, I mean we were. Speaking of frocks. What an excellent idea. I suppose that means a trip. Will Brighton satisfy you? Or need we take an armed frigate to Paris?" He tried to sound resigned to his fate, but actually found the idea of a trip to Brighton appealing.

The room erupted in female chatter and Adam hastened to escape as the women returned their attention to the magazine on the table. Just as he closed the door he caught his wife's eye and she gave him a smile of pure joy that rocked him to his core.

It had been a long time since Adam had placed his happiness so fully in the keeping of another person. The realization of what he'd done sent a ripple of anxiety through the otherwise pleasurable wave he'd been riding. He'd learned long ago that happiness was a two-sided coin — and the other side was pain.

CHAPTER TWENTY-ONE

While many women — especially step-mamas — would have found the company of three girls for six hours in an enclosed carriage torture, Mia found their company both delightful and liberating. After months spent with adults in London, whose notions of propriety and decorum never matched hers, it was a relief to be with three people who admired, rather than despised, her temperament and manners. The same could not be said for their disapproving governess, Miss Temple, who thankfully rode in the second carriage.

Mia had tried to persuade Jessica to join them on a trip that promised to be pleasure-filled and of not too long a duration, but her sister-in-law — generally so retiring on most subjects — had adamantly refused to join the party.

"It might be selfish, but I would rather enjoy some time to myself," Jessica had admitted before giving Mia one of her rare smiles. "But I have no qualms about sending you off with a long shopping list."

The three girls were more than a handful and Jessica had given selflessly to them. Her new daughters were sweet and unspoiled girls. Even Eva, whose high spirits might have been viewed by outsiders to be a sign of overindulgence, was thoughtful and kind to both her sisters and the people on Adam's estate.

They sat crowded in the seat across from her, bickering about some book Catherine had brought to entertain them on the journey. Two jet-black heads and one sandy-blond.

Mia had guessed almost immediately that Melissa could not be Adam's child. Unlike her two older sisters, whose delicate bone structure and dark hair were the very image of their father's, Melissa was fair and plump, her button nose, full mouth, and brown eyes demonstrating no sign of the marquess, her aunt, or any of her sisters.

To give Adam his due, he dealt equally with all three of his daughters. That was to say, equally distant. Mia could not understand why he held his children at such a remove. Beneath his façade of cool disdain was a loving and generous man. It had taken

Mia a shockingly short time to discover the real man beneath the thick façade. But, try as she might, she could not expand the circle of warm affection the two of them shared to include his children.

She simply could not understand his remote attitude toward his daughters. Her love of Jibril was such an overpowering emotion, she could no more hold him at arm's length than she could survive without breathing. She knew Adam loved his daughters, even the one who was not his own blood. She'd seen the affection in his eyes in those brief moments when his guard lowered and he allowed his love for them to show. But those moments were always short, and seemed to be followed immediately by an expression she could only describe as dread.

She had tried to probe the matter a few times, but his face had become shuttered, as closed and hard as it had been the first weeks of their acquaintance. Mia had recoiled like a coward, terrified the intervening weeks of loving and passionate companionship had been nothing but a vivid product of her imagination.

She shuddered at the strength of her emotions. She could no longer hide from the truth. For the first time in her adult life, she was in love; in love with her husband.

He rode beside the carriage, acting as outrider, his elegant form in no way diminished by the mist that covered his black curls and handsome caped coat. He glanced toward the carriage and saw her watching. His mouth curved slowly into a smile that caused her entire body to thrum. As if he knew what effect he had on her, he turned to face the road, his attractive profile smug.

Mia realized that Eva was gazing fixedly out the window, her eyes raw with yearning as they followed the man who rode so close at hand, but was always beyond her reach. Watching the mute suffering on her face, Mia resolved to get to the bottom of the marquess's reserve. The next time she broached the matter with Adam, she would not let the threat of ruining their growing intimacy turn her from her purpose.

Adam was in his study, staring blankly at the bills and letters that cluttered his desk, once again marveling at his sudden good fortune.

He'd been pleasantly surprised by the Brighton house when they'd arrived two weeks earlier. He'd not stayed in Brighton, or visited the house, since the year before Veronica's death. After she died Adam had arranged to have the entire house stripped and redecorated; her taste in décor had been as repugnant to him as her taste in entertainment.

The rooms, once draped in dark reds, were now hung in blues and greens with touches of warm brown or gold, the combinations making the rooms feel light and comfortable.

The chambers he shared with Mia were much smaller than those at either the castle or Exley House. It mattered little, as she refused to sleep alone and he no longer wanted to go to bed without her.

He smiled to think of his once impeccable bedchamber, now strewn with all the signs of Mia's occupation: the omnipresent cushions, rugs, articles of her clothing and footwear discarded on a whim.

To Adam's surprise, Sayer seemed quite satisfied with the new arrangement. Although Adam had almost suffered a stroke the first time Mia wandered half-naked into his dressing room while Sayer was clothing him.

She had no qualms about interrupting his dressing, offering suggestions or observations and generally upsetting what had been a quiet, predictable routine of long standing.

He'd been stunned when he'd caught a glimpse of his normally staid valet's face in the mirror during one such session. For the first time in Adam's memory Sayer's face wore a smile at some outrageous suggestion his wife had tossed over her shoulder before Adam sent her back to her room to finish dressing. He'd heard her laughter as the door closed, a single slipper left behind in the middle of his room as proof of her presence.

Adam never would have believed it, but he loved the myriad invasions. He supposed it was the natural result of the life she had led. It appeared her existence had been a communal one in which she spent most of her time in the sultan's palace naked with a hundred women and children. As a result, her need for privacy was almost nonexistent.

The only area in which Adam drew the line was with his intimate business, firmly requesting her to leave one small screened portion of his rooms off limits. She'd smiled at his request, as if it were eccentric.

She regarded her own intimate habits as anything but, shocking him to near stupefaction with her casual approach to her body as well as his.

It was because of their unusual level of intimacy that he noticed Mia's sudden illness. While she might look dainty and frail, Adam had learned she had an iron constitution.

She ate more than any other woman of his acquaintance and never seemed to lack for energy. The only area in which she showed any laziness at all was in her unwillingness to leave the bed if he was still in it. As long as he was beside her, she was contented to lounge and sleep. He had learned to rise while she was still sleeping, take care of any pressing or necessary matters, and then slip back into bed without her ever knowing he'd left.

Adam had woken early several mornings before, intending to complete some letters about work on the London property. He'd immediately noticed she was not in bed.

He went to their shared sitting room and then her room. He didn't see her at first and was turning to leave when he heard a retching noise. He found her on the far side of the bed, naked, of course, sitting cross-legged on the floor with a basin in her lap.

He dropped into a crouch beside her. "Darling, are you ill?"

She'd laughed weakly and then retched again.

Adam located the water pitcher and a cloth and knelt beside her on the floor, pushing back the spirals of red hair that had come loose from the casual knot she favored. Using a damp cloth he wiped the sweat from her brow and neck. She collapsed back against the bed with a heavy sigh.

"Why don't you let me put you in bed? I'll tuck you in and send for the doctor." He stroked the side of her wan face as he looked into her eyes, noting the small wrinkles of pain at the corners.

She took his hand and brought it to her lips, kissing the tips of his fingers and meeting his eyes with a tired smile. "I don't need the doctor, Adam." She pressed his hand against her face, where the skin was hot to the touch.

"Nonsense, Mia, you must have caught the influenza. He will at least give you something to soothe your stomach and allow you to get some sleep."

"I don't have the influenza, Adam. There is no cure for what I have."

Terror stabbed at his heart and stopped his breathing. "What do you mean?" His voice was cold, almost hostile.

"Sleeping powders won't help me. I'll just have to wait nine months."

He was stunned, his mind counting the weeks since they'd married.

"Darling," he finally said, unable to come up with anything more intelligent. His eyes dropped to her bare stomach, its gentle swell unchanged. His fingers went to the belly ring he found so arousing and he stroked her, meeting her eyes.

"Don't worry, Adam." A wicked smile flickered across her lips. "This doesn't mean we need to stop trying."

He had laughed immoderately, his brain flooding with relief at her reaction, so very different from Veronica's when she'd learned she was breeding.

Adam's hands tightened on the wooden arms of his chair at the memory of Veronica's rage. He'd worried around the clock when she'd been pregnant with both Eva and Melissa, terrified she would do something to harm her unborn children.

He would not have those worries this time. Mia's face glowed with the knowledge she carried a child. In spite of an inability to keep food down, she looked happier than ever.

Adam had ordered every delicacy from the kitchen that he could think of that morning, hoping something would soothe her stomach. Part of him knew he was acting ridiculously, but another part refused to listen, not caring how foolish he might appear. He'd been overjoyed to learn that what pleased her most was simply the feel of his hands on her.

"Mm, yes, stroke my stomach," she'd murmured, making contented sounds as he rubbed her flat belly. "I am feeling better already," she promised, her face indeed looking less taut and pale.

In the days that followed he could not stop marveling that she not only allowed his touch, but sought it. Veronica had hidden herself from him as though she were obscene.

Mia, on the other hand, seemed even more determined to spend all their time naked, speculating about what he would think of her when she was big and round. Laughing and teasing him when she saw he was more aroused by her than before, something he'd not believed possible.

It was as if he'd been transported into some brighter, more intense version of his life. He was torn by emotions he'd not known he possessed, sensations he'd believed to have dried up and blown away long ago. Adam couldn't bear to leave her for even a day, feeling as if he were missing part of himself.

He'd made two simple promises when he'd asked for her hand in marriage — one to her and one to himself — and he'd broken them both. He'd fallen in love with a woman who'd told him in plain English that she never wanted to live with her husband.

What the devil was he supposed to do now?

What the devil was she supposed to do now?

She was pregnant.

Mia took a sip of tea, hoping it would calm her churning stomach, if not her churning mind. Would Adam return to London now that she was breeding? Was the source of so much joy — the fact she was carrying his baby — also the death knell for the happy, wonderful life they'd been living?

Well, one thing was certain. She could not go off to Oran while carrying his child. She winced away from the relief and happiness she felt at finally making the decision. Was she really so shallow, so ephemeral, she could rejoice in abandoning her son?

She'd wrestled with the argument until she wanted to scream. In the end, she told herself it didn't matter how she felt about her decision to stay — at least until she had the baby — it was the only decision she could make. That did not mean she couldn't send her son money.

The door opened and Gamble stepped into the room.

"You wished to see me, my lady?" The blond man's attitude toward her had become surlier as the weeks passed. He was long past the point of believing she intended to share anything with him, let alone her favors. She'd given him expensive gifts and generous vails — far more than she gave any of the other servants — but he was not appeased.

Mia smiled, wanting to set him at ease before she sent him on her errand. "It occurs to me you might be missing London, Gamble? Would you care to go back for a few days?"

He squinted and his mouth opened. Nothing came out.

"I'm not displeased with you, Gamble. I just thought you might be a little homesick. This is your first time away from London, isn't it?"

He colored, whether in embarrassment or pleasure, Mia could not have guessed. "Yes, my lady. I'm London born and bred."

He sounded so proud Mia smiled. "I need you to take a package to Eastbourne. After that, you could go to Exley House and spend a week before returning to Brighton.

Would you like that?"

This time he was definitely flushing with pleasure. "Yes, my lady."

"Good." She stood and went to her desk. She paused, as if just remembering something. "And Gamble?"

"Yes, my lady?" He came closer, his eyebrows raised in question, but his mind clearly on the holiday ahead.

"This is a private matter." She opened the desk drawer and extracted twenty pounds, which she held out to him. His eyes widened and his hand hesitated. "Take it. You will need it for traveling money. Whatever is left is yours. Consider it a token of my appreciation."

He locked eyes with her, his expression not one a good servant would show his mistress. "Very good, my lady."

Mia wondered if it had been wise to give him so much. Well, it was too late now. She opened the lower drawer on the desk and extracted the slim but heavy packet. It contained her mother's jewels, all except a few pieces. She'd never gotten around to selling them, but Bouchard would know what to do.

She looked up at him, considering his formfitting livery. "There is a direction on the packet. The man in question might not be around when you arrive, but the owner of the Pig and Whistle will know what to do. I want you to leave today. Take whatever method of travel is most expeditious. You may take your time on the return journey, if you'd rather. Here —" She held up the parcel. "I don't want you to walk out of here with this in your hand, Gamble. Is there any way you can tuck it into your coat?"

He looked too befuddled by the twenty pounds she'd given him to find her request odd. He pulled out his lapel and undid a couple buttons. Mia stood on tiptoe and shoved the packet into the opening he made. She pushed it down harder, making sure it was secure, and then fastened the buttons. "It's hardly noticeable," she said, smoothing her hand over the front of his broad chest. "I want you to keep —"

"Mia?" It was Adam's voice.

She froze, her hands clutching at Gamble's lapels to steady herself as disbelief, anger, and terror swirled inside her. How was it she had not heard him enter? *How?*

Mia realized she would be hidden from the doorway by the big footman's body and closed her eyes, wanting to stay where she was, to hide. Maybe if she remained quiet Adam would simply turn around and go away. But then she opened her eyes and realized he was standing a few feet away, his face a mask of cold fury as he looked at her hands, which rested on Gamble's chest.

Mia released her servant's coat and nodded. "You may go, Gamble."

Adam didn't move a muscle as the big footman eased past him and quietly closed the door.

She smiled brightly. "Were you looking for me, darling?"

Right away, Mia knew she had made a mistake; an enormous mistake.

His eyelids dropped and he gave her a smile that made her shiver. "I was, my dear."

"Adam, I —"

"I'm terribly sorry to interrupt whatever you were doing," he said, his tone clipped, emotionless, and businesslike. "I came to tell you the dressmaker has arrived." He gave her an abrupt bow. "Now, if you'll excuse me."

"Adam, please —"

He turned back to her as fast as an adder. "I meant to tell you that I will be returning to London on Tuesday. I would leave sooner, but I promised the girls to take them to the theater."

She reached out to touch him and he stopped her with a look that was pure venom.

"You have honored your part of the bargain, madam, and must be eager and grateful that I can now honor mine."

The room spun around her at the cold loathing in his voice. The door clicked shut and she felt behind her for something to hold on to as the floor tilted beneath her feet.

Oh God. What had she done?

CHAPTER TWENTY-TWO

Mia absently listened to the conversation of the girls and the occasional remark Miss Temple directed — generally at Eva and usually to ask her to stop doing something or other. Mia couldn't help thinking the governess's constant harping was a large part of why Eva was so awkward and uncomfortable. She was tempted to send the woman back to the house on some pretext and would have done so if she could only summon up an excuse. But her brain would do nothing to help her.

It had been five wretched days since Adam had caught her with Gamble. She'd returned from the sitting room that day to find the connecting door to his room locked. Oh, she could have made a scene or entered through the hallway door, but to what end?

She had tried to bluff her way out of a bad situation and had only made it worse. And he would be leaving tomorrow. She probably wouldn't see him for nine months, if then. She needed to *do* something or *say* something and she needed to do it quickly.

"May we, Mia?" Catherine asked, breaking into Mia's thoughts.

"I'm sorry, darling, what did you ask?"

Catherine smiled shyly at the endearment. "Could we look at some gloves afterwards, if you are planning to allow me to attend Lady Hammersmith's rout, that is." She blushed as she gently reminded Mia of the engagement with Lady Hammersmith's granddaughter Amanda, a girl her age who'd quickly become her special friend.

Mia squeezed her arm. "Of course you should have some proper gloves. We will go after Eva has finished choosing her last two fabrics."

The carriage came to a stop and Mia looked out the window directly into a pair of unforgettable eyes set in a very handsome face.

Martín Bouchard. And he was standing outside the shop they were going to visit, staring boldly at Mia. As stunned as she was, Mia was aware enough to shake her head, the slight movement halting him in his tracks. He gave one of his amused sneers and sank back against the stone façade, crossing his arms over his broad chest and assuming the attitude of a man forced to wait.

"Mia, did you see that man staring so rudely?" Catherine asked, drawing close to Mia, as if to offer protection against the stranger.

"No, dear, was someone staring?"

Eva laughed loudly and Miss Temple shushed her. But the irrepressible girl continued, undaunted by her governess's severe look. "I believe he was coming toward you with the intention of speaking to you. Do you know him? He looked as if he knew you." Her blue eyes were sly as she studied Mia's face.

Mia smiled coolly at her mischievous face, which so resembled Adam's in features, if not expression. "I'm sure I wouldn't have forgotten such a face. Come, let us not dally." She hustled them out of the carriage and into the dressmaker's shop, brushing past him.

"Excuse me, sir," she murmured.

"The park," he said in a loud whisper.

Mia glanced at the girls. They were too excited to get into the dress shop to notice anything else. Miss Temple, who was just behind her, did not comment on her un-usual encounter but gave Mia a speculative look as she walked past.

The quarter of an hour she had to wait before making her escape was agonizing. Even then, she wondered if she were leaving too soon after Martín's disruptive appearance. But she had to take the risk; she was terrified he would wander off and she'd never find him. Or worse: he'd show up at the house. She grimaced at the thought of Adam's reaction to the virile, arrogant captain on his doorstep.

"I have something of a headache, Miss Temple. I believe I will take a chair and go back to the house."

Mia dealt with the usual questions and concerns with polite demurs and smiles. Inside she was screaming. She was almost frantic by the time she was able to convince them she wouldn't take the carriage and instead climbed into the chair that had been hailed by the dressmaker's boy.

She had no idea what park Bouchard meant; the only parklike place she could think of was a square they'd driven past on their way to the dress shop.

Mia saw his broad shoulders and golden head from the far side of the street. She stopped the chair and paid the sturdy men the entire price for the journey.

She restrained herself from running to meet him, but still made the short journey with unseemly haste, her eyes sweeping the streets as she approached the bench where he sat. It was not private, but it would have to do. A wicked smile spread across his lips as he saw her flushed and anxious face. She seated herself and turned expectantly, annoyed by his arrogant expression. Had she made a mistake trusting him?

"Madame," he greeted her, moving closer. *Too* close. She inched away from him and frowned to communicate her disapproval. It was pointless; he merely smiled.

"Why are you here, Bouchard?"

"So uncivil," he answered in French.

She stared at him, waiting.

He smirked, amused by her irritation. "I met your man at Eastbourne. I tried to pay the big English idiot you sent to bring word to you, but he would not come back." He raked her body with eyes the color of very old gold. "What have you done to your servant, *madame*?" Mia flushed at the man's impertinent innuendoes. He shrugged at her narrow-eyed stare. "I take it the jewels you sent were not a gift for me?"

"Didn't you read my note?"

He waved a dismissive hand. "My ship is having repairs and I decided to come see you myself."

Mia snorted. What an arrogant fool. "You

mean Ramsay's ship is being repaired." *Drat! More delays.*

"No, I mean my ship."

"You no longer captain for Ramsay?"

"No. I now captain my own ship, the *Golden Scythe.*" Bouchard seemed to double in size, his expression beyond smug.

"The *Golden Scythe,*" she repeated dumbly.

He smirked. *"Oui."*

Mia had heard of the ship before — many times, in fact. It had once been part of the loose fleet of corsairs who served the sultan. If Bouchard had seized the ship that meant her stepson Assad's hold on his father's empire must be slipping. Did that mean Jibril was gaining support?

She looked at Bouchard. "So you have a ship of your own now. Good. You will be able to take the packet I sent you and deliver it to my son. How long will your ship be under repair?"

"She is almost ready."

Mia bit back a scream. "Then why are you wasting time coming here?" Her eyes narrowed. "If you think to bed me, Bouchard, you are —" He raised a hand, no longer smiling. Dread and terror flooded her as she saw the pity in his hard eyes. She grabbed his arm. "What? What is it? Why are you here?" Her high-pitched words drew the attention of a passing nanny carrying a baby and Mia swallowed down her hysteria. "Why have you come?" she repeated.

"I came because I thought to deliver the news myself."

"Good God, Bouchard! What news?"

"Your son, he has been taken by Assad." He looked away from her face and down at his hands, not so comfortable any longer.

"Oh my God," she whispered. "Is he . . . ?"

"He is alive. He will remain so unless he does something foolish. Assad is demanding ransom."

Mia almost wept with relief. If Assad wanted money that meant Jibril was safe.

"How much?"

Bouchard gave another shrug. "He knows you are the rich daughter of a duke —"

"How much, Bouchard?"

"Twenty-five thousand pounds."

Good God. Mia's mind raced round and round like a fly trapped in a bottle. How in the world could she get such an amount quickly?

One thing was certain: she could never ask Adam. At least not now. She might have asked him a week ago, before he'd become a stranger to her. She had been on the verge of telling him about Jibril several times since that horrible day. But confessing that she'd only married him with the intention of leaving him would hardly make their current situation any better. How could she convince him that she'd changed and did not want to leave him? Especially since the bungling mess she'd made of her meeting with Gamble.

"I still have the jewels you sent me." He broke into her anguished thoughts, the concerned expression resting awkwardly on his face, as if he had little experience with the emotion. "I gave them only a short look, but it is perhaps ten thousand."

She nodded, not trusting herself to speak, her mind calculating the amount she might get from the rest of her jewels if she could sell them. Several of the items Adam had given her were of immense value. She cringed at what she would tell him when he found out, but pushed the thought away. She would have to confess everything — but only after she had done the deed and sent Martín on his way.

"I have more jewels I could give to you. It will be a very close thing." Her eyes flickered sightlessly at the greenery around them.

Martín gave her a long look before sighing noisily and releasing a stream of curse words, shaking his head with a look of self-loathing. "*Ça suffit!* Keep your jewels. I will loan you the money. For interest, of course," he added in English, his expression hard.

Mia almost smiled at the obvious torture it caused him to make the generous offer, but she was too close to crying. "Thank you, Martín! Thank you." She took his hands. "You know I will honor my debt."

He hesitated, his lips oddly twisted. "There is one more thing."

Mia's skin crawled at the look in his eyes. "What?"

"Assad says he will only take the money from you."

"But —"

"It is madness, my lady," Martín said, "I only tell you this because I do not feel right keeping anything back. But there is no way you can make this journey. Even if you did, you know that if Assad has you both, he will kill you both. That is the only reason he wants the money from your hands. You know this is true." His unusual eyes were deadly certain. *"Se venger."*

Revenge.

Mia fought the paralyzing horror flooding her. Oh God, how was this possible? It was her fault. She should have forced Jibril to come with her. Or tricked him, or hit him over the head and dragged him to England against his will, anything rather than let him return to a half brother who was mad with hate and envy.

"Where are you staying? I will meet you there tonight."

He lifted his hands. "My lady," he began, using the protesting tone she knew too well. Once again a man was going to tell her what she had to do.

"Martín!" Her voice rose. "You must have known that I would come when you told me? You must have. Do not waste precious time with argument. I will meet you tonight. Now, where are you staying?"

Bouchard regarded her as if she were a dangerous animal in need of careful handling. *"Madame."* He paused, his expression one of agony. He scrubbed his big square hand through his sun-bleached hair, making a mess of his careful coif. He gave her a pleading look. "If I take you into the waters of the Mediterranean, you know that Ramsay will cut off my testicles. You *know* this is true. I like my testicles, my lady. They are close friends to me." He stared hard, his worry unfeigned.

Mia stared right back.

She may as well have been trying to stare down the weather or the tide. "What would you have me do?" she asked, her voice hoarse with the effort of not screaming.

"I will take you to Ramsay. He can help you decide what you must do. He understands the way these men think better than any of us, he always has. He and Delacroix are the only people to have escaped the sultan's palace still alive."

"I escaped the palace," Mia protested. "I lived most of my life there. I know of a secret way inside. I can get us back in just as easily as Ramsay can."

"Can you get into the slave quarters? Do you even know where they are? Where do you think they are holding Jibril? Inside of Assad's harem with his women?"

Mia's heart dropped at the truth of his words. She had no clue as to where the slave quarters were. She'd lived in the palace for seventeen years and never even saw most of the massive structure where the sultan's people lived and worked.

"My lady," he said levelly, taking her hands in his and holding them tight. "You must go to Ramsay. He will do everything he can to make sure no harm comes to your son. You know that is the only way."

"I can't go to London, Bouchard. We don't have the time!"

"Ramsay is not in London. He is in Eastbourne, at his family's country house. It will not be out of our way at all."

"He is at Lessing Hall?"

Bouchard nodded.

She chewed her lip but then shook her head. "I can't go there — he has family there, they will find out about this and my husband will learn where I am before I can even leave the country."

"Ramsay is alone, the rest of the family are in London." Bouchard's eyes flickered nervously. "I cannot say why, but there is nobody at Lessing Hall save for the baron."

Mia didn't care why Ramsay was by himself. She stared into Martín's eyes, which had shifted from arrogant to earnest. If this man — a man with a fierce reputation of his own — counseled Ramsay's guidance, she could not dismiss his suggestion without due consideration. She had to go to Eastbourne to get on Bouchard's ship, so talking to Ramsay would not take her out of her way. Still, it was almost more than she could bear to bring her problems to Ramsay. He would fight her with every weapon at his disposal. Chief of those weapons would be exposing her plans to Adam. And she knew, beyond any doubt, Adam would not risk his unborn child on such a journey.

But what other choice did she have?

"You will not help me otherwise?"

He shook his head.

"Be ready to leave tonight."

Mia left Martín in the small park, a thousand thoughts running through her head as she made her way home. The pain in her chest as she made plans to sneak off almost dropped her to her knees.

She loved Adam, but she loved Jibril, too. It was not a contest as to which she loved more; she would go into the same situation to save either of them. Adam had the power to stop her. If he did, and if anything happened to Jibril, Mia knew she would never forgive her husband. She could not risk that, even though it meant risking the life within her, which she knew meant so much to him.

She would have to act fast. She'd have no trouble feigning sickness and avoiding the play tonight — she *was* sick, sick with grief.

Before Mia knew it, she was climbing the steps to the town house. She handed her cloak to the waiting footman before stripping off her gloves and checking her reflection in the large mirror. Her face gave no sign that her entire life had just collapsed.

"Is Lord Exley in?"

"He went out a little while ago, my lady. Shall I check with Batson and see where His Lordship was bound?"

Mia almost wept with relief. She wouldn't need to run the risk of facing him. Yet. For the first time in days she was grateful he was avoiding her.

"No, that won't be necessary."

LaValle was busy with something in her dressing room when Mia entered her chambers.

"My lady?" The Frenchwoman frowned. "Are you unwell?"

Mia lifted a hand to her forehead. "My head aches dreadfully. Perhaps you could prepare me a posset like the one you gave me at my father's house?"

"*Bien sûr,* madam! But I will have to check with the kitchen. I am perhaps missing something to make a proper dose," she mused, her mind already on her task.

"Yes, well, you go and find what you need," Mia urged.

"Shouldn't I help you undress, so you may go to bed?"

"I'd rather you make the drink for me."

LaValle nodded and departed without another word. Mia wanted nothing more than to crawl into her bed and sleep until the nightmare was over, but she needed to pack her bag before LaValle returned.

It took her longer than she would have liked to find a bag small enough for her to carry. It only had room for one change of clothing and some essentials. She would wear several layers of clothing on her person when she left this evening.

Leaving — how was she to leave the house without being seen? She bit her lip — there were hours yet to come up with something. In the meantime, she needed to write a letter to Adam. She could not simply leave without a word and abandon him to even more horrid speculation.

She shivered at the thought of his face when he found out she'd gone. She could leave him a letter, but she could not tell him the truth. If he suspected even for a moment that she was leaving for the Mediterranean, he would know to look for her in Eastbourne, at the house of Lord Ramsay.

She sat at the small writing desk in her sitting room and stared at the blank sheet of paper, wondering what she could say that would keep her safe yet not completely destroy the man she'd come to love. Should she lie to him? Tell him the truth? What could she say that would be kind but not give away her destination? What could she say that would not make him feel betrayed and hate her?

What could she say?

The clock ticked loudly, its even cadence

nagging and implacable: *Time to go, time to go, time to go,* it said.

Time to go.

She bent her head to the empty parchment and began to fill it. . . .

CHAPTER TWENTY-THREE

Mia lay in bed with a cool cloth on her forehead as her husband frowned down at her, concern clouding his beautiful eyes. Even though she knew it was only concern for the baby inside her, she still treasured the look. She memorized every detail of his face so she could feed her soul with the memory in the weeks to come.

"Are you certain I shouldn't send for the doctor?" he asked again.

"No, it will go away with rest." Deceiving him was truly making her ill.

"I'm sorry I will miss the play, Adam. The girls have been looking forward to this evening and planning their outfits for days."

He regarded her from beneath lowered lids. "I shall pass along your regrets," he said coolly, turning away.

"Adam —"

"Yes?"

Mia swallowed. She would wreck things if

she wasn't careful. "I just wanted you to know that you have become very important to me." It wasn't what she'd meant to say, but it was the best she could manage with such deception in her heart.

He stared at her for a long moment, his eyes so heavily shuttered he looked like a stranger. Mia searched for any clue that he might still feel something for her, but could not see past his beautiful face.

LaValle bustled into the room and placed yet another glass on her nightstand. "I beg your pardon, Lord Exley. This is something Mrs. Harper sent for you, my lady." LaValle sniffed, her dismissive tone indicating her feelings on the matter before she turned away to fuss with something on the dresser, completely unaware of what she had just interrupted.

Adam's mouth smiled but the expression never reached his eyes. "Get some rest, my lady."

Mia watched his elegant form disappear. He knew. He didn't know what he knew, but he knew something was wrong. It was a good thing she wouldn't need to see him again before she left. She was one step away from throwing herself on his mercy.

Adam closed the door to his wife's bedroom

and then stared at it, as if the wood might tell him what was causing alarm bells to sound in his head.

Her words had stupefied him. What the devil did that mean — he'd become important to her? If he was so bloody important, what had she been doing with her hand in the damned footman's coat? And if what she'd been doing was so bloody innocent, then why had she not explained herself?

The last four and a half days had been the worst in almost a decade. The fact that he'd known this would end badly since the beginning only made matters worse. How could he ever have forgotten the painful, crushing, and humiliating lesson he had learned — that love led to disillusionment at best and betrayal at worst? Christ! The woman hadn't even waited until the child was born before seeking comfort in another man's arms. Adam didn't even want to contemplate the idea that the child might not be his.

Was it just something about Adam that drove women away? Did he do or say something that repelled them? And how could he have been so stupid as to believe her? He was beyond furious with himself. He was —

"Papa?" The word was so soft he almost didn't hear it. He turned. The vision he encountered took his breath away: Eva, dressed in a cloud of strawberry-colored muslin, her masses of black curly hair tamed into ringlets. Adam stared. He'd always thought she was the very image of Veronica, but he'd been wrong. She resembled his mother, her heart-shaped face and dark blue eyes those of a stunning beauty.

A red flush spread across her high cheekbones — cheekbones like his own, he noticed — as she waited for his reaction.

He smiled and took her hand. "You look beautiful, darling."

"Thank you, Papa." She smiled, making her beauty complete.

"Papa?" Catherine and Melissa appeared behind Eva, their smiles hesitant and sweet.

"My goodness," Adam murmured, something in his chest making it difficult to say more.

"Mia helped us choose the colors," Melissa said, wearing a pale yellow gown that made her sandy hair and freckled face golden.

Adam looked at his youngest daughter, a child he knew was not his, and cupped her rounded chin. "You're as pretty as a buttercup. And you look so grown up." He turned to Catherine. "And you — you *are* grown up. White suits you," he added, an odd, proud pang shooting through him. Eva and Catherine had inherited his and Veronica's dark hair and eye color. They would be beauties like their mother.

Adam could only hope blue eyes and sable hair were the only things they'd inherited.

Adam enjoyed the evening far more than he'd thought he would. It wasn't the production itself he enjoyed, but the pleasure his daughters took in the performance. They shared lemonade in their private box with Lady Hammersmith's granddaughter and several other young women of their acquaintance. Bringing Eva and Melissa — who were still in the schoolroom — would be viewed as odd, but Mia had argued it could not hurt them to be out in public a little and Adam thought she'd been correct. He was so charmed by their obvious delight in the event, he was sorry Mia had missed it, even though her presence in the box would have made things more awkward. At least for him.

Not only his butler, Batson, but also Sayer and his wife's maid were in the foyer when they arrived home, as if they'd been waiting for him. He met Sayer's eyes and saw the usually unflappable man was, for lack of a better word, flapped.

Cold fingers of dread crept down his spine.

"Wait for me in the study," Adam told Sayer and LaValle.

It seemed to take ages before his daughters were finished thanking him, bidding him good night, giving their love to Mia, and finally trundling sleepily to their beds.

Gesturing to Batson to follow, he strode into the study and found the two servants standing nervously in front of the large desk.

"What is it, Sayer?"

"My lord," his valet began, darting a nervous look at the Frenchwoman. "Er, Mademoiselle LaValle found a letter bearing your name when she went to check on Lady Exley earlier. She, well —" He gave the maid a look of appeal, which she ignored. "Well, Lady Exley seems to be gone, my lord." Sayer held out one of Mia's embossed, sealed sheets of stationery.

Adam sat down before he fell down. He looked at the missive in his hands, almost too terrified to open it.

It was all happening again, like some bloody nightmare that wouldn't stop.

"Sit," he said to the three servants looming around his desk.

His wife's handwriting was girlish and

free-flowing, the hand of a woman who'd not had much to write about most of her adult life. The pages were spotted and spattered with blots of ink and water spots.

Adam,

I am more sorry than you can ever know for what I am about to do. I cannot make these words any more palatable: I am leaving you because I can see no other way. I cannot tell you why I am leaving or where I am going. You would stop me if I told you and I cannot let that happen.

I am not leaving you because I want to. I am leaving because I must.

I will come back when I have finished what I need to do. I know you will be anxious for the child I am carrying and worried about harm to your heir. Please know I will take all possible care of our unborn child.

I hope you will be able to forgive me for what I am doing, but I will understand if you cannot find it in your heart to do so.

Your wife,
Mia

Adam reread the letter several times,

certain he must have missed something, some essential piece of information that may have been lost in his quick, frenzied reading.

He looked at his servants. His confusion must have been plain on his face. Batson, whose presence had yet to be explained, finally spoke.

"My lord, what I am about to say is, well, not something I would wish to say." His dignified butler was pale and shaken.

"What is it, Batson?" How was he able to sound so calm when inside he was flying to pieces?

"This afternoon, when I sent Carlson on an errand, he saw Lady Exley in rather, erm, well, heated conversation with a . . . person."

"A person?"

"Yes, my lord, a male person."

Adam frowned, heat creeping up his neck. "Very well. My wife was talking to a man — what of it?"

Batson swallowed. "They seemed to be discussing something very . . . passionately, my lord. Now, it was wrong of Carlson, but he lingered, getting closer to, er, well to put it plainly my lord, he got close enough to eavesdrop on Lady Exley and the young man." Again Batson paused.

"Bloody hell, man, get to the damned

point!" Adam startled both himself and everyone else in the room. So much for calm and controlled.

"Carlson said they only spoke some of the conversation in English. He said the man sounded like a Frenchie when he spoke English. He said Lady Exley spoke both French and some other language. Something very foreign-like. Carlson didn't get most of it, but he heard the word 'ransom.' "

Adam could only stare.

"He couldn't make heads nor tails of who was being ransomed, my lord." Batson's voice was filled with regret. "I'm sure it was garbled, but he said it sounded like Her Ladyship was worried about someone called . . . Gabriel."

"Gabriel?"

Batson nodded. "Yes, my lord, Gabriel. Or something like that."

Adam glanced at the letter in his hand. There was certainly no mention of any Gabriel in it. "Was that all Carlson heard?"

Batson's pale cheeks became as red as two apples.

"Batson, if you do not tell me absolutely everything this very instant, I shall send you packing." Adam's quiet words seemed to frighten his servant even more than his emotional outburst had.

"He heard them make plans to meet tonight. At the Black Swan, my lord."

Bloody hell. The Black Swan was the most unsavory inn in Brighton. It had been raided dozens of times by excisemen. The inn had been — before the raids — perhaps one of the best-known meeting places for free-traders, its underground cellars notoriously labyrinthine storage places for smuggled goods.

"Fetch Carlson."

Adam turned back to the other servants after the butler left. "Do either of you have anything to add to this tale?"

"Only that she 'as taken some small number of 'er tings, my lord," the Frenchwoman said, her narrow face pinched with disapproval, as if Mia's departure were somehow Adam's fault.

"You may go." She rose and left the room with obvious reluctance.

Adam flung himself back in his chair and looked at Sayer. "After we speak to Carlson and get a description of this man, you will go to the Black Swan and find out when they left and where they have gone."

Sayer nodded, his expression as unreadable as ever. Adam couldn't help wondering what the man was thinking. His master had yet a third wife who couldn't wait to get away from him. He shook his head. *God Almighty, wait until the scandal sheets got hold of this!*

Carlson entered the room like a man approaching the gallows.

"You have nothing to fear, Carlson. I merely want you to describe the man you saw talking with Lady Exley. Please do so thoroughly, but with all haste. Time is of the essence."

The handsome young footman took a deep breath. "He was youngish, perhaps five and twenty. He spoke like a Frenchie but he didn't really look like a Frenchie. He was —" Carlson struggled to find the correct words. "He was a big fellow, my lord. He looked like he'd been in the sun a lot. His hair was brown but had been bleached by the sun. He had real strange eyes. Demon yellow," he added, looking embarrassed by his words. "That is, they were very unusual, my lord." He stopped, looking at Adam to judge his reaction.

Adam nodded at him curtly. "Go on."

"He was dressed like Quality, not like you would have expected, him kind of looking rough."

"Rough?" Adam interrupted.

"Yes, my lord," Carlson agreed, frowning at the effort of describing the man. "His hands were big and he had shoulders like an ox. Even from where I stood I could see he weren't no stranger to hard work. Beggin' your pardon, my lord," Carlson said, flushing for some reason Adam could not discern.

Adam raised his brows. "Is that all?"

Carlson thought a moment. "Yes, my lord."

Adam dismissed him and turned to Sayer. "I have a few matters to take care of before I change. Pack lightly and quickly and then saddle Breaker for you and Max for me. I shall meet you at the Black Swan and we can depart from there." He paused. "I don't know who this man is, but she knows very few people in this country. I am fairly certain of her destination and only need some small bit of confirmation." His words surprised a flicker of emotion from Sayer but Adam saw no need to enlighten him just yet.

Sayer left and Adam took a ring of keys from its hiding place behind the clock and unlocked the small gun cabinet that stood against the far wall of his study. The cabinet held only a few items as most of the weapons he owned were in the gun room at Exham. He took out a highly polished wooden box containing dueling pistols and his short sword before relocking the cabinet and making his way to his rooms.

As he changed into his riding clothes he ran through the half dozen things he would need to mention to Batson before his departure, not the least of which was an explanation for his daughters about his and Mia's sudden departure.

Adam shrugged on his coat and felt something in the breast pocket. He pulled out a single green glove — a small woman's glove. The sight of his wife's lost or forgotten item, one of the many things that had cluttered his life before he'd purged her from his space — if not his mind — five days ago, brought a smile to his face. And then he recalled what she'd done. Without thinking, he brought it to his face. The faint scent of her lingered in the soft leather and almost doubled him over. He stared at the small article of clothing in his hand.

"I'm going to find you, my lady," he told the glove, drawing strength from the sound of his own voice. "And when I do . . ." He stopped. What would he do? Could anything she said or did make any difference to how he felt at this point — enraged, destroyed, and abandoned, again?

Adam shrugged away the questions, tucked the glove inside his waistcoat, and snatched up his own gloves. He could demand answers to those questions once he got his hands on her.

CHAPTER TWENTY-FOUR

Mia marveled at the difference a carriage could make to a journey. She longed for the luxury of Adam's coach, where she had lounged in comfort against piles of cushions and her husband's muscular, protective body.

The post-chaise Bouchard had engaged was fast, and she told herself that that was all that mattered. She tried to banish yearning thoughts of her husband from her mind and concentrate on the journey before her. Not the least of which was the struggle she anticipated having with Baron Ramsay.

Very little moonlight shone through the grimy carriage window. Martín had not had an easy time convincing the post company to make a journey on such a dark night. Money had finally won the argument and he'd paid three times the usual rate.

Mia had the carriage to herself as Bouchard had insisted on riding ahead of the postilions to ensure there were no unanticipated obstacles in the road. The road still showed signs of the recent heavy rains, but not enough to impede their progress in any serious way. Mia could only assume he meant thieves or robbers.

Mia couldn't imagine that any highwayman would be stupid enough to meddle with Martín. In addition to the pair of loaded pistols he kept in a holster that fit across his saddle, he also had a wicked-looking sword at his hip. All three weapons were beautiful and ornate, as were their tooled leather carriers. Martín himself was rather beautiful and ornate on his enormous blood bay horse, his elegantly tailored riding outfit as well made as anything her husband owned.

Mia had been shocked by the quality and fit of his clothing. Having only ever seen him aboard Baron Ramsay's ship, she had not realized he possessed the wealth and taste necessary to turn himself out in such a fashion. She supposed he must have made a fortune during his association with Ramsay, who had seized almost as many corsair vessels as the corsairs themselves.

Mia couldn't recall very much of her journey from Oran to Eastbourne. She'd been too relieved by Jibril's agreement to accompany her back to England to think of much else. One of the few details of the trip that had stayed with her, however, was Martín Bouchard.

He'd made his interest in Mia apparent her very first day on the *Batavia's Ghost.*

She'd found his open, lustful admiration more than a little thrilling after years with the sultan, a man who had considered any female over thirteen a crone. She'd soon begun staring at him when she wasn't even aware of doing it. Watching as he'd strutted about the ship, stripped down to only an old leather vest and worn buckskin breeches that covered his body like a coat of paint.

While his raw sensuality had woken long dormant urges in her body, it had driven Jibril almost to the brink of insanity.

"That man is a swine and I forbid you to have anything to do with him, Mother. In the future you will cover yourself before coming on deck."

Jibril knew it was not the tradition of English women to cover their faces and bodies. But the Berber side of him — that part that approved the manner in which the sultan had sequestered and protected his women — could not bear to see men gawking at his mother.

Bouchard had come up to Mia after Jibril

had stormed off one day, disgusted with her refusal to don her hijab.

"Your son guards you like a dog guards a bone," the Frenchman had said in heavily accented English, his smile mocking.

Mia had assessed him from top to bottom before meeting his astonishing gold eyes.

"There are many hungry dogs on this ship. Perhaps he is wise to do so."

He'd laughed but he'd not denied her words. And Mia could tell there were few dogs as hungry as Martín Bouchard.

Mia had only avoided his bed on the journey because she'd known what it would do to her son to see his mother fraternizing with a man he'd viewed as a servant. While Mia liked to think she'd had the lion's share in forming Jibril's character, the sultan had left his imprint on their son.

And now Bouchard was the captain of his own vessel — the *Golden Scythe* — a corsair ship that had terrorized the waters of the Mediterranean for decades. Bouchard was no longer a ship's mate but a wealthy, independent man. That, added to his looks and arrogance, made him a force of nature.

The short time she'd spent in the private dining room of the Black Swan had shown her his effect on both men and women alike. The serving wenches at the dirty, rough inn had been lined up to please the exotic, wealthy man. The way his eyes had roamed and raked their bodies had convinced Mia he'd already worked his way through the most attractive of the staff in the short time he'd spent at the inn.

The hostile attitude of the men at the posting company had demonstrated the effect of his looks, attitude, and money on the male population. Mia could not blame the men; she had never seen a man behave so contemptuously toward others. Even Adam, who had no compunction about using his haughty stare on a duke, had never displayed such wholesale disregard of everyone in his orbit. If Adam ever happened upon the Black Swan, which was unlikely, he would have no difficulty getting information about the arrogant Frenchman from the stunned staff of that shady establishment.

Mia smiled in spite of herself at Bouchard's obnoxious, swaggering behavior. In his mind, if not in reality, he undressed every woman he encountered and thrashed every man. He was sensuality and violence personified. She had to admit he was more blatantly attractive than her husband, but she was no longer tempted by him — a development Bouchard found highly annoying.

Mia had put him in a surly, pouting mood after she was forced to make it plain that she had no intention of becoming his bed partner. Or, as the case had been, stable partner, which was where they'd been standing when he'd made his first overture, describing to her with smug assurance how he could pleasure her in multiple ways before their carriage was even made ready. Mia didn't doubt it.

She sighed as she leaned her head back against her seat. She'd given her heart to her husband, a man who most likely didn't want it. The thought of lying with another man — even one as attractive as Martín Bouchard — held no interest for her. His molten eyes, which she had once thought so mesmerizing, offered no comparison to the icy blue pair that heated with searing passion when Adam looked at her.

The Frenchman's ridiculously lush and shapely lips did not for a moment challenge her preference for Adam's thinner, yet somehow more sensuous pair, with their enigmatic ability to shift from cruel to amused in the blink of an eye. She had no desire to spend her time with any other man. No other man's inner workings seemed as interesting, unknowable, or intriguing as his.

Mia was infatuated by her husband.

Rather than find that admission repugnant or terrifying, she surrendered to the knowledge with joy and relief. She had waited a long time to find love and had never really believed or expected it would happen. Now that she'd found it, she could not regret it. Even if he never took her back after this, even if he only remained her husband for the sake of an heir, she would not regret the depth of feeling she felt for him.

The only other person she cared more for was her son. He was also the only person for whom she would have left Adam. Mia had no room in her mind to entertain regret about her decision just now. She had the sick suspicion she'd have the rest of her life to live with the effects of today's actions.

Mia wouldn't have believed she could sleep in the miserable chaise, but when the carriage came to a halt, she realized she must have slept for several hours. The outlines of Baron Ramsay's ancestral home were barely visible in the predawn light. The only other time she'd been to Lessing Hall had been in the middle of the night and she had been too upset to notice anything about her surroundings.

Martín's face appeared in the carriage

window, the dark smudges beneath his unnerving eyes showing the toll the ride in virtual darkness had taken.

"Stay here while I send word to the baron."

Mia was in the process of rearranging her disordered hair and frock when the door opened again and Martín put down the stairs and held out his hand for her. His expression was thunderous and Mia wondered what had happened in the short interval to make him so furious.

The answer to her question was apparent when she reached the door and encountered the stiff mien of a man who could only be the butler.

"Lady Exley?"

"Yes. I am Lady Exley."

The butler hesitated, considering the best approach as he regarded a woman who might be the daughter of a duke and a marchioness in her own right. He turned to Martín, looking at him much as a man would look at a pile of malodorous refuse he had almost stepped in.

Martín threw his hands in the air. "*Voyons!* You have seen her. Now go get the baron!"

He snatched up Mia's hand, pushed past the horrified butler, and led her through the enormous foyer, up a flight of stairs, and down a long hallway, pausing at a console table and taking the small candelabrum that sat on it. He opened the door and gently pushed her inside before closing the door behind them.

"Sit." He gestured to a chair and placed the candelabrum on a long table behind the sofa across from it. He lighted several other candles before going to a small table, where the clinking of glass told her he was pouring a drink. He threw back the contents and then poured another.

"Brandy?" he asked after the second glass went the way of the first, as if he was only now realizing the rudeness of quaffing a beverage without offering some to her.

"Yes, perhaps a very small amount." She would probably need more than that.

He grunted and busied himself with the decanter before unceremoniously handing her the glass and flinging himself onto the couch across from her, his beautiful riding clothes wrinkled and filthy from the long night. He sipped his drink and regarded her with a suspicious gaze, a distinctly un-friendly gleam in his eyes.

"It looks as if they know of you here," she said.

He snorted rudely and took a drink. "That fool butler. I would thrash him if he were not at death's door already."

"Do you stay here often?" Now that he was no longer trying to seduce her with every word and glance, she found his arrogance boyishly endearing. Jibril often behaved in such a high-handed manner.

"Not if I can help it." He finished his drink and put it down with a thump before dragging the back of his hand across his lips. Lips that were compressed in an expression of annoyance rather than their habitual sensual pout.

Mia laughed and drew a venomous look.

The door flew open and bounced off the wall.

Mia and Martín both sprang to their feet.

"My lord, I am —" the younger man began.

"What in the bloody hell are you doing here?" Ramsay yelled, his single green eye on Mia. She felt, rather than saw, Martín release a sigh as he realized he was not the focus of the other man's ire.

Mia refused to let Ramsay intimidate her, no matter how intimidating he was. She placed her fists on her hips. "Assad has taken Jibril."

Ramsay stopped a foot away from her, his hands lifted, as if he'd been on the point of picking her up, carrying her back to the carriage, and stuffing her in it.

He turned to Bouchard.

The erstwhile arrogant captain shrugged and commenced to examine his boots.

"Where is Exley?" His gaze flickered across the room, as if Mia might have hidden him somewhere.

"He does not know I am here."

He let out a wordless bellow and shoved one big hand through his sleep-mussed hair, which already stood out at odd angles. "You came here *without* him? Are you insane? The man will probably shoot me *and* run his sword through me when he finds out you're here."

"Did you not hear me?" Mia demanded, rage boiling up inside her and driving her voice up at least two octaves.

"Yes," he yelled back. "I heard you, Mia. Your son has been taken by his brother. They are engaged in a bloody war! What the devil did you expect to happen? I told the young hothead he should stay, but he would not listen." He stared down at her with a murderous look on his face. "Just as *you* did not listen when I told you to confess to Exley." He threw his big hands in the air. "What a surprise! Like mother, like son."

Of all the arrogant, obnoxious, odious — Mia reached up and poked him hard in the chest with her finger. "Listen to me you . . . you . . ." Mia stamped her foot, too furious to even think straight. "You beefhead!"

Ramsay's mouth formed a stunned O of surprise that would have been humorous under other circumstances but only irritated her now.

"I didn't want to come here — to speak to you or listen to your orders — but Bouchard made me. So, will you let me tell you what has happened instead of roaring like an enraged bull? Will you just *shut up* and listen to me for once?" Mia's last words echoed through the big room like shots from a pistol.

Ramsay's mouth made a snapping sound when it shut. Martín, on the other hand, looked as if his jaw would graze the floor. His eyes bulged as they flickered from Mia to his former captain, a man feared by some of the worst killers and rogues on the planet. The silence in the room was brittle, broken only by the sound of Ramsay's grinding teeth. Years seemed to pass before he nodded abruptly and gestured to the settee behind her. "Sit and tell me how you have come to be here." He dropped into the chair across from her.

Mia's legs shook like blancmange as she resumed her seat and related the events of the last twelve hours. Once she had finished she added, "I have only come to you because Martín insisted. He argued, rightfully, that you are one of the few people to have escaped the sultan's slave quarters, which is probably where they are holding Jibril. Martín believes you could give me information that would help to smuggle Jibril out. He does not think Assad will release Jibril even if I bring the money."

The baron's eye narrowed as he looked at Martín. Whatever Martín saw in his face made him flush and drop his eyes under the bigger man's gaze.

Ramsay heaved a sigh and rubbed the scar that ran from his temple to his jaw. It was the same injury that had taken his eye and was a souvenir from Sultan Babba Hassan — the father of the man Mia was asking him to help. The irony was not lost on her.

"Martín should have come to me before he told you of this, Mia. But he's right. The only reason Assad would ask you to deliver the ransom is to take revenge. And you know it."

Mia nodded. "Yes, he has always believed I convinced the sultan to order his mother's death. It is not true. I never spoke to Babba Hassan in favor of her death, but I did nothing to discourage him, either."

"I am pleased to hear it," Ramsay said. "Assad's mother was a monster and terrified any slaves who worked in the palace."

"I do not dispute she was an evil woman, Ramsay. But the manner of her death did not serve her son. The sultan never trusted Assad after what his mother did. The manner of her death left Assad ashamed and angry — and it raised my own son to favored status at his expense."

He waved his hand. "That is water over the dam." His expression shifted from irritated to businesslike. "Martín is correct in that we will have to steal Jibril away from the palace."

"We? Surely *you* will not go? You have only just returned to England."

"Yes, *I* will go." Ramsay scowled, although the expression seemed more directed at himself than Mia. "No matter how bloody inconvenient it is, no matter that she will flay the skin from my back," he added under his breath. "But *you*? You" — he pointed a big finger at Mia — "will be of absolutely no assistance. In fact, the only thing your presence will serve to do is make an easy target for Assad. So, if you —"

Loud voices came from beyond the door.

Ramsay lunged to his feet. "What the devil is it now?" he demanded of nobody in particular before striding toward the door and wrenching it open. Mia tried to peer around him but his huge body blocked the view into the hallway.

"Ah, Ramsay. Just the man I was looking for."

Mia jumped to her feet at the sound of Adam's voice.

"Now, I am past the point of asking nicely, Ramsay. Where. Is. My. Wife?" The hiss of a sword leaving its scabbard punctuated his demand.

CHAPTER TWENTY-FIVE

Adam had to glare up a good six inches to meet Baron Ramsay's eye. He'd not intended to draw his sword, but the protracted interaction with Ramsay's butler had frayed his already tenuous grip on his temper. He stood rigidly before the much larger man, his sword drawn but still at his side.

The baron lifted his hands and took a step back into the room. "I have no sword and would not fight you if I did." He smiled wryly. "I am not eager to leave this life just yet."

Adam re-sheathed his weapon and stalked past him into the room. He cast a quick look at his wife to assure himself she was unharmed before his gaze settled on the man who'd abducted her.

"You." He strode toward the smirking, handsome face.

Before he could reach the arrogant-looking bastard — who'd scrambled to his feet and actually taken a step *toward* Adam — a hand like a vise landed on his shoulder and a second one closed around his forearm as it moved to the hilt of his sword.

"Now, now Exley," Ramsay said, his tone pacific as he held Adam in an unbreakable grip. "I cannot let you kill Martín. You see, that is a pleasure I am reserving for myself. Perhaps you should ask your wife why she is here. I think she has several matters to discuss with you."

The baron turned him to face Mia before releasing him. "Make yourselves comfortable. Martín and I will adjourn to the library." The baron cut the younger man a grim look. "I have a few things to say to him. When you are finished here, you can join us and we can discuss the problem like level-headed adults."

Adam stared at his wife's bowed head while the others left the room. Once the door had closed he went to the large picture window and leaned one hand against it, looking out at the breaking dawn.

"Adam?"

He steeled himself and turned. Mia was looking up at him with eyes etched by fatigue and worry.

"Please —" She gestured to the small sofa. "Won't you sit? I would like to tell you everything."

Adam was shaking with fury born of an almost heart-stopping fear. Fear that he wouldn't find her in time, fear that she might be hurt, fear that she would never return, fear that she might — God forbid — die. He clenched his jaw and sat.

She laid a hand on his forearm. "I have wanted to tell you the truth since almost the beginning, but I was afraid you would hate me when you learned how I deceived you." She looked up at him, her eyes searching and desperate.

Adam crossed his arms, the action pulling his arm from her grip. "Go on."

"I was so unhappy when we first met. The weeks I spent in England were hellish. My father was cold and controlling and I quickly understood that he wished I'd never come back. It took only days before I wished the same thing — that I had gone anywhere else in the world except here. Somewhere I could live without being a public spectacle or the latest *on-dit* for people who despised me." She swallowed so hard he could hear it. "I have to confess that I entered our marriage with every intention of running away as soon as you left me at Exham and returned to London."

Each breath Adam took was a struggle, as

though some invisible force was crushing and squeezing his chest. He could not stop staring at her. She'd chosen him not in spite of his background, but *because of it:* she had wanted a man with a proven inability to keep a wife and she had found the perfect, pathetic fool.

Again she took his arm. "My plan was to return to the Mediterranean, where I could rejoin my son."

His jaw dropped. "Your son?"

"Yes, I lied when I told you he'd died. I decided to keep his existence a secret after I returned to England. I could see any mention of a child born to a man who'd not been my husband would make an even more disastrous situation worse, not to mention give my father the idea I might one day want to escape."

Her son? *That* was what she had been hiding?

"My son was his father's true heir. Although Jibril — that is Arabic for Gabriel," she said, fierce pride blazing across her face — "although he was not his father's eldest, he was his most favored. His older brother Assad refused to step aside for him when the sultan died. For more than half a year they have fought for possession of their father's wealth, power, and people. And now

Assad has captured Jibril and is holding him for ransom. If I do not bring him the money" — she passed a hand over her face, as if to wipe the horrible thought away — "Assad will kill him." She grasped his arm with both hands. "Don't you see now? Why I had to leave you?"

Adam pulled away, too furious and confused to want her touch. "Why didn't you come to *me* when you learned of your son's abduction? Why did you turn to that . . . that —" He gestured angrily toward the chair where the arrogant bastard had sat, grinning at Adam, smirking at the fact that he — and not Adam — had been the one Mia had turned to. The pain and rejection he heard in his own voice only made him more irate.

Her mouth trembled, "I wanted to — so badly. But I was afraid. You see, I need to go to him, Adam. I must go to Oran."

"What?"

"Assad wants me to bring him the ransom."

"You want to go to Africa?" His voice was unnaturally high.

She nodded.

"Have you gone bloody *mad*?" He stood and glared down at her. "Absolutely not. I will send Ramsay's man with the money. I will pay him for the use of his ship, his crew — whatever is necessary. The only place you're going, ma'am, is back to Exham."

She clutched at his arm. "*I* must go. Assad wants the money only from *my* hand."

Adam felt like he was a player in some bizarre farce. It was a struggle not to grab her and shake her until her teeth rattled.

"I don't care what he wants, Mia. Any plans you've made for leaving English soil are out of the question. The sooner you accept it, the better it will be for everyone."

She sank to her knees beside him. "Adam, if you forbid me to go to my son and anything happens to him, I will never forgive you. Do you understand what that will do to us?" Tears ran from her red-rimmed eyes — eyes already swollen from crying.

"You mean other than what you've already done to us?" His words were like the crack of a whip. He pulled away from her, sickened by her begging and how it made him feel — brutal and heartless. And scared.

"Let me explain, Adam, about Gamble. That was all a misunderstanding."

Adam pulled her to her feet and motioned to the settee. "Sit." He turned and paced the room. "Go ahead. Tell me about the misunderstanding."

"It was true that I led him to believe I

would grant him my favors."

Adam snorted. He couldn't look at her. He wanted to throw things, to break things. Something substantial. His eyes lit on a large marble in the corner, a representation of Fortuna. He gave a bitter laugh. How bloody appropriate, yet another duplicitous, scheming woman.

"Adam, I only did it because I —"

He swung around. "I don't care *why* you did it, Mia. You brought a servant into my house — under my roof — with the promise that he would become your lover?"

She nodded, her face creased in misery.

"How far did it go?"

"Nothing! We did nothing. He was getting angry because I would not lie with him. I decided to get him out of the house for a time, until I could think what I would do about my son. I gave him my mother's jewels to take to Eastbourne. I wanted Bouchard to sell them and give the money to Jibril. That was what I was doing the day you came into the room and caught us. It was true I had unbuttoned his coat and waistcoat, but it was only so I could put the packet inside and make certain it was not too bulky and that nobody could see it if . . ." She trailed off, shaking her head. "It sounds ridiculous, doesn't it?" Her voice was barely a whisper.

It did, but Adam believed her. Nobody — certainly not a woman of her intelligence — would make up such a story. But the truth was that she'd brought a man into his house intending to sleep with him, to offer her body in exchange for his help. That was bad enough, but then she'd kept him around, even after their feelings had changed and they'd realized — he stopped. *Their* feelings had changed? No, *his* feelings had changed. He still had no idea what she felt about him — if anything. Who was to —

"Adam." She'd come to stand beside him again, her small hands grabbing his arm. "You must let me go to him, Adam, you must. If I do not and he is hurt, I will hate you forever."

Adam looked at her tearstained face and felt the force of her words. He remembered the hopeless rage he'd experienced — still experienced — when he realized there was nothing he could do to save his own children. If there was a way to save his daughters from their uncertain futures and if any person — man or woman, stood in his way — he would kill them.

He closed his eyes. Africa? How could he allow it? It would be like cutting off his arm and sending it to the Mediterranean. No, it would be worse. He could learn to live without his arm. He was not sure he could live without Mia, no matter how angry and hurt and battered he felt. He might never be able to forgive her, but that didn't mean he would ever let her get away from him.

"Adam?"

He glared down at her, at this woman who'd shredded his heart as easily as a piece of paper. Her expression was one of mute misery and crushing anxiety.

He held out his arm. "Come, let us rejoin the others."

Mia was too terrified to ask what decision her husband had made. The butler waited for them outside the sitting room door.

"This way if you please, my lord, my lady."

They found the other two waiting for them in the library. Ramsay came forward when they entered the room.

Adam stared up at him. "I am going to choose to believe you would not have allowed my wife to make a journey of this magnitude without first consulting me."

Mia hid a smile as her rapier-slim husband challenged the towering man.

Ramsay nodded. "You are absolutely correct, Exley. I had not entertained such a thought even for an instant. No matter how big a bully your wife is." He smiled amiably and motioned to the tray of food and empty seats.

Adam ignored him, released Mia, and approached Martín.

Mia's breath caught in her throat as the insouciant Bouchard rose to his feet. The two men were almost of equal height, she realized, but the Frenchman was bulky and broad beside Adam's sleek elegance.

"Lady Exley tells me you brought her the information regarding her son."

Martín smirked.

"For that, I thank you. But if you go against me or around me in any way, on any matter concerning my wife, I will not be so sanguine the next time." His hand rested close to the rapier he still wore.

For a long, horrible moment Mia thought Martín would press the issue. But, whether it was because he did not really care, did not feel like fighting, or did not want to incur Ramsay's ire, he shrugged and the tension broke.

Adam sat on the settee beside Mia but looked at the baron.

"So, when do we leave?"

They discussed matters until Mia, Adam, and Martín could hardly stay awake. Much of what they would do would depend on the situation they would find in Oran when they arrived.

"In any case," Ramsay said when he noticed the amount of yawning among the three, "we can't decide everything right now. You might as well get some sleep as there is nothing else you can do today. The earliest we can depart will be tomorrow, and we will need a bit of luck for that." His lips twisted into a mocking smile. "I had a rather important engagement in London and will need to send word to postpone things before I leave. You will have to give me the afternoon to see to matters and we can meet to discuss everything at dinner."

Lessing Hall, the seat of the Davenport earldom, was considered one of England's most impressive country seats and it was easy to see why. The ancient house dated from the Saxon period but had been expanded upon in the centuries that followed.

The mistress of the house, Lord Ramsay's aunt — the current Countess Davenport — was away in London with her twin sons but her housekeeper, Mrs. Faring, had lovely and spacious chambers ready and waiting for them.

Adam had brought Sayer with him and the two disappeared into his bedchambers while Mrs. Faring showed Mia to an adjoining room, where a maid waited.

"I've taken the liberty of having Bessie wait on you, my lady, as you've brought no maid with you. Please don't hesitate to let me know if you need anything."

"Thank you, Mrs. Faring."

The housekeeper departed and Mia waited until Bessie finished undressing her and took her clothing somewhere to be cleaned before opening the connecting door to Adam's room. The bathing chamber held the largest copper tub she had ever seen. Standing beside it, with a towel in his hand, was her husband. Something moved at the corner of her vision and she saw Sayer, his arms full of clothing. He saw her and left the room without saying a word.

It hurt more than she could have believed that Adam would take his bath without her; he knew how much she loved bathing with him.

He was angry and she had no idea how to find her way back to the intimacy they'd shared before her lies had divided them. Had she broken the fragile bond that had grown between them? Had she found love after all these years only to ruin it?

Mia must have made a sound because he lifted his head and looked at her.

She went toward him and held out her hand, not asking, but taking the towel he was using to dry himself. His eyes were like disks of glass as he watched her rub the water from his body. He returned her smile with an impassive stare.

"This is quite the largest bathing tub I've seen."

"Ramsay is a large man and his uncle and grandfather were the same." He lifted his arm so she could dry beneath it.

It seemed to Mia that no matter how often she saw her husband naked, she could not keep her heart from leaping into her mouth. When she looked up into his eyes she saw that his eyebrows were two black slashes on his pale brow and she flushed under his direct stare, ashamed at how she'd forced him to chase her and fight his way into another man's house. She'd treated him badly and exposed him to yet more ridicule — no different from his other wives, it seemed.

"I am ashamed at how I treated you, Adam."

He gave her the same cold look he'd given her the night they met. The night he'd come alone to her father's house, one man in a crowd of hundreds who would not even acknowledge him. "Can you forgive me?"

He leaned down until their faces were almost touching. This close she could see the white and blue shards of his eyes. The muscles in his jaws tightened and Mia could feel his anger — his pain. She did not know what to do or what words to say to bring back the warmth.

"Is my forgiveness so important to you?"

Her heart pounded as she considered his cold, mocking words. She could think of nothing that would express how she felt, how her heart had broken to leave him. She took his hand and lifted it to her mouth, kissing his palm.

"What can I do to apologize, my lord?"

He shrugged lazily, the muscles of his chest and shoulders contracting in a way that made her want to lick every inch of him. "I daresay you'll think of something."

He watched through narrowed eyes as she sank to her knees before him.

His pose was arrogant, his hands on his hips. The sight of calluses on his thumb and forefinger — mute evidence of his hours spent fencing — was unbearably erotic. She looked at his face and saw the faint, dismissive smile she'd not seen since the early days of their marriage — he'd once again donned his mask. The only sign he was not bored hung between them. Mia looked from his cool gaze to his erection and brought her mouth to the level of his hips. She leaned closer and flicked him with her tongue, pleased by the violent shudder that tore through his body.

No, not bored.

She ran her tongue the length of the pulsing vein, an action that ripped a gasp from him.

"Good God." The words were harsh and utterly lacking in contempt.

Mia smiled and took him in her mouth.

Adam wove his fingers into her coppery hair as she took him deep, working him with a relentless skill that brought him to the point of climax far quicker than he wanted.

Her kneeling form was the very embodiment of feminine submission and contrition. But Adam could not forget how easily she'd made love to him while she'd kept another man dangling in his very own house, no matter how skillfully she employed her mouth. He stepped away from her and she looked up, no doubt annoyed he'd interrupted her masterful performance.

"Get up." He took her upper arms and lifted her. Her lips were swollen and slick from their tender labor and the sight made him burn. He looked into the huge pupils

of her green eyes and the desire he felt —
no, the *love* he felt — robbed him of breath.

And so did the hate.

Hatred for the power she had over him,
the power to take his happiness and sanity
away, the power to give him either pleasure
or pain as she chose; hatred for the thousand
ways in which she now held him in the palm
of her hand.

"Turn around and put your hands on the
wall."

She complied without speaking. He
trapped her hands with his and pulled her
arms taut, roughly shoving apart her legs
before stepping between her thighs. He
entered her with a thrust so violent he lifted
her off her feet. She moaned and pushed
back against him and the last vestiges of his
sanity burned away.

"You will *never* leave me again," he gritted the words into the back of her fiery head
as he filled her. "Do you hear me?" He
slammed into her. "You are *mine*," he said
from between jaws clenched so hard it hurt.
She arched against him in answer.

"If I ever catch you with another man, I
will kill him while I make you watch. And
then I will punish you." He thrust savagely
to illustrate his point. He rode her without
any finesse, tenderness, or care for her

pleasure, the only thought in his mind the need to brand, dominate, and possess.

His climax was violent and all-consuming. It turned his body inside out, the brief escape from everything except pleasure a gift unlike any other. But all too soon he came back, collapsing against her and vaguely aware of her contractions subsiding around him.

God, how he loved her.

The realization gave him no pleasure and was like a cold fist around his heart.

The thought of his seed filling her caused him to burn with a primitive satisfaction but it reminded him his child was already growing within her. It was like having ice water dashed over his head.

Adam turned her from the wall with as little tenderness as he'd placed her there.

"I have not harmed you? I have not harmed the child?" His coldly abrupt words could barely squeeze past the lump lodged in his throat.

She shook her head, her green eyes languid and sleepy, her skin still mottled with passion.

He turned away, snatched a towel off the pile, and walked to the door.

"Adam?" The word was breathless.

"What?" He stopped to wrap the towel

around his waist but he didn't turn around.

"Are we going to sleep in your room or mine?"

"Both," he said, slamming the door behind him.

CHAPTER TWENTY-SIX

The two ships were bustling with activity when they boarded them the next day.

Ramsay had already tried to give Adam and Mia his cabin but it was clear there would be no place large enough to comfortably hold the baron if they accepted his offer.

Adam thanked him, saying a smaller cabin would suffice. Ramsay stared intently at Martín until he heaved an exaggerated sigh and flung his hands in the air.

"Take my cabin, my lord."

Adam opened his mouth but Mia intervened before he could reject the offer.

She knew her husband would much rather travel on Ramsay's ship, but she'd already made the journey once and knew the discomfort of small cabins.

"Thank you, Captain Bouchard, we should be very pleased to accept your kind offer."

Bouchard's hostile eye roll was more rewarding than the slap she'd wanted to administer the day before. "Follow me," he said abruptly, turning on his heel and striding ahead of them, not waiting to see if they were behind him.

The *Golden Scythe* had been one of the sultan's finest ships for years and Mia knew it must have infuriated Assad to lose it to a privateer so soon after his father's death. The sultanate relied heavily on its ships, both to engage in legitimate trading as well as the lucrative and highly illegal slave trade. It did not bode well for Assad's crumbling empire that he was unable to maintain control of his small fleet.

The *Scythe* was smaller than Ramsay's *Ghost* but impressively armed and as clean and polished as the finest carriage in Hyde Park. Mia could see by the way the sailors greeted their captain they held him in high regard. Indeed, Bouchard became a different man when he boarded the ship, his movements sharper and more purposeful. He almost appeared . . . mature.

He led them belowdecks to his cabin and Mia stared in wonder when he opened the door. She'd stayed in Ramsay's cabin on the *Ghost* and it had been larger than usual, altered to fit the man's size. But Bouchard's cabin? It was like . . .

"Good Lord, it is just like a brothel," her husband muttered. Mia bit back a laugh, and then frowned, wondering how her husband knew of such things. She would ask him later, if he ever relented toward her.

"Thank you, Captain," Mia said, when it was clear Adam would say nothing good. "It is quite . . . luxurious." And it was. The bed took up half the room and was piled high with velvet and silk bedding, the dark wood and brass polished to a blinding shine. One wall, the wardrobe, she supposed, bore large mirrors, a silent but vocal testament to Bouchard's staggering vanity.

The captain grunted and flung open the wardrobe doors. "I have made the room for your cloth." He paused. "Cloths, clothe." He finally gave up, shaking his head in disgust, his tongue unable to accommodate the English combination of *t* and *h.*

Mia thought his English was much improved even in the short time since she'd last seen him, and the mistakes he made were rather charming, not that she would ever tell him so.

"Thank you, Captain."

He nodded abruptly. "I leave you now."

Adam turned to his luggage once the

Frenchman had gone, his expression perplexed.

"I shall put away our clothing," Mia said. Like the aristocrat he was, Adam had not done without servants in quite some time, if ever. He nodded and Mia could feel the tension coiled inside him as he paced about the small space. He'd not forgiven her. Oh, he answered her questions and discussed the details of their trip readily enough, but there was a distance between them that had not existed since the early days of their marriage. Mia had no idea how to cross it. She'd tried to sway him with her lovemaking, but he'd slept alone last night and she'd not had the courage to force her way into his bed. He was very, very angry and hurt. Mia could not blame him for either feeling. It was her job to bridge the distance between them.

She took a step toward him and it felt symbolic. "Will you keep me company for a stroll on deck?"

Adam looked down into his wife's pleading eyes, fully aware he was acting childishly. He'd managed to discard the anger he'd felt regarding her lies, but her abandonment was another matter entirely. He still couldn't forgive her for looking to another man in her time of trouble. Maybe he never would.

He resumed his pacing without answering her, coming to a halt in front of the built-in bookshelf above the desk.

"Our captain likes to read," Adam murmured, browsing the small selection of books.

"He also likes to play chess." Mia gestured to a handsome box and board that sat beside the bed.

Adam snorted. "Let us hope he has cards, as well."

A month of getting thrashed at chess by his wife would be enough to rattle even the most sanguine man, and Adam was far from that. Especially not since he now had his own lies to hide.

"I will not allow my wife to leave that ship, Ramsay. If I had my way, she'd not be on it in the first place," he'd told the baron last night after Mia had finally gone to bed — but not before she'd cast him enough suggestive, longing looks to melt stone.

"I understand and I would not like to be in your position. I'm sorry I agreed that she should go with us, but I would hate to go all that way and not have her on hand if we can't find the boy as easily as we think. Or if Assad demands to see her before he produces him."

Adam had lowered the glass of port he'd just raised to his mouth. "Please tell me you aren't planning to use my wife to bait a hook, Ramsay."

The baron waved Adam's glare away with his brawny three-fingered hand. "No, of course I'm not. However, if Assad believes she is there, he may trot the boy out and make things a lot easier. Besides, I don't fancy your chances of keeping her from going, not if you ever want her to speak to you again."

Adam grunted, knowing the big man was correct. He wished her displeasure did not matter to him, but there was no denying it did — even though he was currently too furious to speak to her.

"I will draw the line at her stepping foot on shore. I want her far away from those docks when you and I go to find her son."

Ramsay grinned. "You and I?"

Adam knew Ramsay was no fool, for all he enjoyed playing the jester. If he did not believe Adam would contribute anything, he would have no qualms about leaving him on board the ship, just as Adam had no qualms about leaving Mia.

"You cannot think to leave me behind. I will be valuable when it comes to fighting in close quarters and dispatching men without

413

a pistol. I'm assuming we will want to keep our presence quiet if we need to get close to the palace."

"I'm hoping there will *be* no dispatching," Ramsay pointed out.

Adam nodded, willing to be amenable, as long as it served his interests. "As am I. However, *praemonitus, praemunitus.*"

Ramsay laughed. "I take your point and I would certainly rather be forearmed in this situation." He looked at the liquid in his glass, his usually amused face pensive as he considered the matter. "Assad will expect me to bring her back, so he'll think she's on the *Ghost.* That means we should keep her on the *Scythe.* We could always move her to the *Scythe* before we reach Oran, but I can't help thinking that would make her suspicious. It would be better if you commenced your trip on Martín's ship. He will protect her when you're not there, Exley," he added, after noting Adam's skeptical expression. "Since he will not be coming with us, he will be the best we have to offer."

Adam bristled at the notion of spending weeks at sea with the obnoxious Frenchman and then leaving Mia alone with the arrogant lothario.

He allowed the fine brandy to warm him as he considered the man's words.

"Bouchard is that good?"

"Bouchard is who I would want to guard my own wife, if I had one." He gave one of his booming laughs. "Well, perhaps not when it came to her virtue."

Adam flicked Ramsay a look of contempt. "I am not concerned about that," he lied, a hateful wave of jealousy cresting all the way to his eyeballs when he thought of the younger man even *looking* at his wife.

Adam thought back on that conversation now, for the hundredth time wondering if he'd been foolish to allow her to come. He did not feel good about deceiving her, but there wasn't any other choice. What did it matter if she was angry at being left? Would it be better that she was dead than angry?

He closed the book he was holding, annoyed at the way his thoughts chased one another around and around and yielded nothing new or productive. He sat down at the small table and watched his wife as she worked. He thought about the secret she'd kept from him, and how it had angered him. And then he thought about the secret he was keeping from her, and how much worse it was, how much more irreparable.

She caught him watching and gave him a loving look, not faltering under his scowl — a scowl that was born of guilt and fear rather than anger this time.

His stomach lurched sickly with the secret he could neither swallow nor seem to disclose.

Life aboard the *Scythe* quickly settled into a routine.

They woke not long after first light, as it became impossible to sleep with the sounds of activity. After a leisurely breakfast in their cabin they went on deck, foul or fair, to take some exercise.

Silence fell each time they came on deck. The crew, unused to having either women or haughty English peers aboard, couldn't help staring. Luckily, both Adam and Mia were well accustomed to being stared at and paid the men no mind.

When the heat of the day drove them back below deck they would read or play games to pass the time. While they'd not made love since beginning their journey, Adam seemed to unwind a little toward her with each day. Besides, it was enough for Mia that they slept together each night, the close confines of the cabin making any other arrangement uncomfortable, if not impossible.

Toward the end of the first week, when they were engaged in a game of chess and Mia was trying not to win too quickly,

Captain Bouchard knocked on their cabin.

He'd kept his distance for the first few days, but it was difficult to avoid one another in such small spaces. Mia frequently saw him eating with his chief mates in the small room that served as a medical bay, dining room, and meeting area.

"We are going to have a bit of weather in a few hours. Not too bad, I hope, but perhaps a little rough." The young captain spoke in his native French. He looked at the board between them and smirked at Mia, as if it amused him to think of a woman playing chess. "You play, eh?"

"Yes, would you care for a game, Captain?"

Adam shook his head, no doubt picturing the two of them bobbing behind the boat after she beat the mercurial captain.

Bouchard paused, his eyes sliding to Adam. Mia poked her husband under the table with her foot.

He sighed and answered in French, a language with which the captain was obviously more comfortable. "My wife is almost finished with me, Bouchard. I would be glad for a rest."

Captain Bouchard looked pleased by the offer and Mia realized he probably didn't have many other opponents on his ship.

Mia wrapped up the game, glad she no longer had to consider inventive ways not to beat her husband. Bouchard rang for a bottle of wine and took Adam's seat.

Mia held out closed fists with a pawn in each. Bouchard drew white and an almost childlike look of glee spread across his face, which he made no effort to hide. Captain Bouchard liked to win. She wondered if it would be politic to give him at least the first game. She was considering the matter when she looked up and saw Adam watching her over the top of a book, a glass of wine beside him on the desk. She swiveled her eyes to Bouchard and lifted her eyebrows. Adam shrugged, his resigned expression saying he'd washed his hands of the matter.

Coward, Mia mouthed. She turned to Bouchard's handsome, conceited face and decided she would enjoy thrashing him.

The game went much as she expected. Bouchard was not a bad player, but he thought no more than a few moves ahead. Also, he was too attached to his pieces to sacrifice any to further his cause. She chased him around the board a bit, not wanting to end it too quickly. By the time she had him in checkmate, she could see it would have been wiser to let him win. He seemed to have grown to twice his size and made no effort to hide his fury. For a moment she thought he might fling the board and pieces across the cabin.

As if sensing the incipient violence, Adam came to stand beside her.

"You are in good company, Bouchard. I have never beaten her. I should have warned you." He looked down at Mia, his eyes glinting with dark humor. "Why don't you let us have a game, my lady?"

Bouchard looked so enraged Mia thought he might decline Adam's offer. But he seemed to think better of it, no doubt believing his manly pride would suffer if he demurred.

The game between the two men was far better matched. The protracted slaughter finally ended in a draw after nothing but kings and pawns were left on the board.

When they finished Bouchard leaned back in his chair, his expression far less disgruntled than it had been an hour earlier.

"That was close, eh, my lord?" He cut Adam an arrogant smirk as the latter put the pieces back in their box.

Adam cocked an eyebrow but made no comment.

"Ramsay tell me you like to play card," he said, his broken English drawing a faint smile from her husband.

"I do," he admitted, replacing the box and board on their stand. "Unfortunately, I did not bring any with me."

Bouchard dismissed his words with a lazy wave. "I 'ave lots. What do you play?"

Adam took a seat beside Mia. "What do *you* play, Captain?"

"Piquet, *vingt et un,* lots of udders. Shall we 'ave a game?"

Mia gave her husband a look much like the one he'd given her earlier, but he ignored it.

"I'd welcome a game, Captain."

Bouchard smiled and switched to his native tongue, as if the conversation were too important to have in English. "Let us play in the boardroom. Perhaps my mate Beauville will join us."

"Are you coming, my dear?" It was the first time he'd used an endearment with her since she'd left Brighton.

"I think I will take a nap. You go and enjoy yourself, but not too much?"

Amusement flashed in his pale, predatory eyes.

The wild tossing of the ship woke her and Mia peered at the small clock: it was nearly midnight. Her stomach roiled and her neck was kinked from the odd angle at which she'd been sleeping. She needed fresh air, and quickly.

She sat up too fast and her head spun and throbbed. She forced herself to move more slowly, her stomach creeping inexorably toward her mouth as she fastened her cloak around her and inched toward the door, holding on to walls and furniture as she went. She paused outside the door, glancing toward the end of the corridor, where the wardroom door stood open. The low rumble of male voices told her they were still playing cards. She would not disturb Adam.

Mia wrestled opened the door to the deck and encountered the opening scene from *The Tempest.* She considered returning to her cabin but the fresh air — as violent as it might be — was already beginning to scour away the nausea that had threatened to overcome her below.

She pulled the door shut and wrapped her cloak tighter before creeping toward one of the crates they frequently sat on whenever they came on deck. Wind and rain and salty sea spray whipped her face and the ship tipped wildly to one side just as she reached the first wooden crate. She scrambled for the crate and barely grasped the rough, splintered edge before her feet began to slide out from under her.

Her fingers burned as she struggled to hold on and drag herself upright. The boat crested another swell and then hit the trough, slamming her to her knees. Sharp pain shot from her knees to her hips.

This had been a dreadful idea.

She'd just pulled herself close enough to get a better grasp when the ship listed almost on its side and a sheet of cold water slapped her like a huge, frigid hand. She flinched away and lost her grip on the crate. Time slowed to a crawl as she slid toward the railing, her feet and hands scrabbling to find purchase on the wet, slippery wood of the deck.

A hand closed around her upper arm, the grip hard enough to make her cry out.

"What the bloody hell do you think you are doing?" Her husband's voice cut through the wind and rain as he jerked her toward the yellow glow of the stairwell. His arm slid around her and pulled her tight to his side as they staggered to safety. Bouchard appeared in the opening and took her other arm while Adam pushed her toward him and grabbed the doors, which were flapping like wings, trying to break free. He slammed the doors shut and turned to face her. The silence that followed seemed louder than the raging storm.

Bouchard released her as soon as the door closed.

"Are you mad at me, Adam?" she asked, stupidly.

Mia had thought Adam had been angry that day he'd caught her flirting with Gamble. And then she'd thought he was even angrier when he'd tracked her down to Ramsay's house that morning.

She'd been wrong. His eyes burned like fire opals in his red face and his black brows were drawn into a flat line. Mia flinched back and would have fallen had Bouchard not been right behind her and steadied her with his hands.

Adam froze and the color drained from his face like sand from an hourglass. His eyes flickered from Bouchard to Mia and back and his features settled into their normal, unreadable lines.

He politely offered Mia his arm. "Thank you for your help, Captain."

Bouchard shot back down the narrow corridor like an arrow from a bow.

Adam didn't speak until they were inside the cabin.

"Remove your clothes; they are soaked." His voice was colder than the water that had drenched her.

Mia fumbled with her cloak, her hands

shaking so badly she could not manipulate the simple closure.

He stepped closer. "I will do it."

She dropped her hands to her sides as his strong, dexterous fingers opened and removed first her cloak and then her gown, not stopping until she was stripped to her chemise, which was still dry. He pulled one of the blankets from the bed and wrapped it around her before tucking her into the remaining bedding.

He turned at the sound of a light knock on the door. "Enter," he called out.

Bouchard himself stood in the doorway, holding a small tray with a brown Betty and two cups.

Adam took the tray. "Thank you, Captain."

Bouchard met Mia's eyes over Adam's shoulder, as if to make sure she was unharmed.

"Good night, Captain Bouchard." The chill in Adam's voice served to cut the temperature in the small cabin by half. He hooked his foot around the door and pushed it shut without waiting for an answer. He lowered the tray to the small dining table with a clatter and spun around.

"He thinks I will beat you." He shoved one hand ruthlessly through his hair, as if that might serve to hold his emotions in check. His eyes blazed. He flung a hand toward the corridor, his lips thinned to fine, pale lines on his taut face. "*You* believed I would strike you out there."

Mia swallowed.

"When have I ever given you cause to expect such a thing?" He dropped into a chair and let his head fall back against the polished wood wall.

Mia struggled to emerge from the veritable cocoon he'd built around her, holding the bedding in one hand as she went toward him. He looked up at the touch of her hand, his beautiful eyes agonized.

"You should be in bed," he muttered.

She pulled the bedding around her and sat in his lap. He remained rigid for a moment before his arms came up to cradle her. She sighed and leaned against his chest, almost weeping when his chin came to rest on top of her head.

"Adam?"

"Yes?" His hand moved to tuck a loose curl behind her ear.

"I'm sorry. I don't think you would ever hurt me. It was just . . ."

"You've been struck before?"

She nodded, burrowing closer as his arms tightened. "The sultan would often become

425

irritable and strike the first thing — or person — at hand." She felt him shake his head and looked up. "It's all right, Adam. He never hurt me badly."

He took her chin in his hand, his eyes unusually bright. "How could any man ever hit you? It would be like striking a flower or a . . . kitten."

She smiled at the comparison. "A flower. That is one of the nicest compliments I've ever received."

His lips twisted, but it wasn't a smile. "I would never hurt you, Mia."

"I know that. You were scared and that made you angry. I've often felt the same way with Jibril. You saved my life out there, Adam."

He turned away. "Bouchard has brought us a feast." His lips curved. "I'm not happy for the reason, but I can't say I didn't enjoy having him wait on us like a housemaid."

Mia grinned and shifted over to the bench to prepare their tea. "I'm sure he will regret it tomorrow."

He snorted. "I'm sure he's regretting it already."

They sipped their tea and ate thick slabs of bread, butter, and jam. Mia was exhausted from both her experience on deck and below. She was also suddenly curious.

"Adam?"

He finished chewing his bread and washed it down with some tea. "Yes?"

"Will you tell me something of your other marriages?"

His eyes widened comically. "Now? You wish to hear about my infamous marriages now? After weeks of being married?"

She nodded.

"You are an unusual woman, Mia Exley."

A sense of warmth and well-being flooded her at the sound of her married name. "The reason I never asked you before is that I never believed you killed your wives, Adam."

"Oh, how can you be so certain?"

"I could tell even that first night."

"How is that?"

"You never looked ashamed or worried, only annoyed — at the stupidity of those who would believe such a thing. You are not the kind of man who hurts women, children, or anyone weaker than yourself."

"I appreciate your blind faith."

She cupped his jaw. "Please, tell me what happened."

He sat back in his chair and sighed. "Why not? I suppose I should work in chronological order. I was nineteen when I first saw Veronica. She was —" He stopped and shook his head at whatever he saw in his head. "Well, she was unlike anything I'd ever seen."

Jealousy for his dead wife rose in her throat like choking bile. The look on his face as he peered into his past was rapt. What dangerous box of secrets had she pried open?

"If I'd not been a young idiot, sick with calf-love, I would have taken note of what a devil she was. She tormented me and every other man who vied for her hand until matters reached a fever pitch, culminating in a challenge to the first of three men I would call out because of her."

"Three?"

"I didn't kill him, but he would never use his arm again." His lips twisted with disgust. "I was a fool, almost blind with joy when she consented to marry me."

Mia reached for her cup, her hand shaking so badly she left it in its saucer. He'd been in love with Veronica.

Adam was lost in his memories. "Veronica was a creature of pure passion, completely lacking the coldly rational outlook that had been drummed into me from birth. At first I was charmed by the differences between us. But I became less enamored of her tempestuous nature after Catherine was born." He frowned into his teacup.

"Why? What happened then?"

He inhaled deeply before looking up, his gaze flat. "Veronica became even wilder after she realized she'd not given birth to a son. She wanted nothing more than to leave the child in the country and remove to London." He shrugged. "I indulged her wishes until she became pregnant with Eva. Those were perhaps the longest nine months of both our lives. She was . . . devastated when she realized she'd had a second daughter. I kept her at Exham as long as possible, staying with her in the country even though she began to hate me — and my mother and sister, not to mention her daughters." He looked at her and this time Mia knew he was seeing her.

"I kept her at Exham, hoping she would overcome her unreasoning hatred of her own daughters. I didn't touch her." His razor-sharp cheekbones were stained a dark red. "I was afraid to get her with child." He shook his head. "How can a woman hate her own baby?"

Mia realized it was a serious question. "I saw it happen in the harem. Sometimes a woman would just neglect her child. Sometimes" — she grimaced — "sometimes mothers tried to hurt them. I don't know what it is, but it must be a horrible, horrible feeling."

"When I suggested we stay in the country and miss another Season she became insane. She attacked me with her hands. I tried to reason with her — to calm her — but she broke and ran from me like a madwoman.

"When she failed to return home by dark, I went to the stables to saddle a horse and go find her." His lips curled bitterly. "I found her in a stall mounted on one of my grooms. She laughed in my face and mocked me."

Mia reached for his hand. "Oh, Adam."

"I knew I had to let her go to London — to get her away from my family." He turned his hand palm up and clasped her fingers hard. "From the moment we arrived in London she immersed herself in an almost violent whirl of gaiety. It was easy to ignore her sexual liaisons and orgies as we moved in different circles by then. I was too relieved to be shed of her to care what she did, as long as she did it away from me.

"At the end of that Season she went to Brighton and I went home." He squeezed her hand, his face sick with guilt. "I was a coward and glad to be away from her. To be honest, I would have been happy never to see her again. As it was, I didn't see her for almost two years. I spent the time at Exham with my mother, sister, and the girls. There were days I could almost forget she existed." He pulled his hand away and pushed himself out of his chair. "I'm afraid I need something a little stronger than tea, my dear."

He sat down again with a glass of brandy. "I couldn't stay in the country forever and had to go to London on business. I was shocked at the changes in Veronica — physical and emotional. She was —" He took a drink. "Well, she looked haggard and worn to the bone. We rarely saw each other and she never slept at Exley House. I'd been in town a few weeks when something woke me at perhaps three or four in the morning. I noticed a light beneath Veronica's door. I could hear the sound of voices — male voices — along with my wife's."

Mia briefly closed her eyes. When she opened them she saw he'd drained his glass and was staring blindly at the wall.

"I can still remember what I felt in that instant and it wasn't jealousy. I'd known of her lovers for years." He laughed. "Hell, I'd been relieved. No, what I felt that night was hatred."

That same emotion glowed in his face as he spoke of the long-ago event. In that moment she could have believed him capable of anything, even murder.

"I hated what she'd done to me, to our children, to our *life*. And now she seemed determined to sully one of the few places that remained sacred to me. My own house. I didn't bother knocking." The smile he gave her was feral. "I found Veronica in bed with not one, but two men. I'd heard both men's names before but wasn't acquainted with either. One was the middle son of an impoverished baron who'd been part of Veronica's court when I first met her. The other was a mere boy — the son of an obscure country squire. Naturally, the two men were horrified. But not Veronica. At first she was furious. How she raged at me when I kicked out her lovers." He laughed and shook his head. "Even at the time I found the men's expressions amusing. I told them my second would attend them and then opened the door. They scrambled out of my house, tripping over each other to get away, clothes and shoes bundled in their arms as they scurried into the night. All the while Veronica screamed."

The humor drained from his face. "Veronica refused to go back to Exham. I don't want to talk about what I had to do to get her there. She was unbearable when we reached home. She was also pregnant."

Mia met his cold stare. She knew now that

he was always at his most emotional when his expression was inhumanly cool and impassive.

"She was inconsolable after she gave birth to Melissa. I engaged a nurse this time, but the woman could not be awake every hour of the day." He shrugged, the lines around his eyes and mouth deeper and more distinct. "She escaped and went to the west turret. It was a miserable night, so it's hard to say if she had an accident or jumped. Either way, she died. There was no question of my having murdered her as I was asleep in my bed at the time. One of the footmen had seen Veronica leave the room and followed her."

"Then how is it that everyone in London believed you killed her?" she demanded.

"People don't require proof to believe anything, darling. They believe what they want to believe. They knew we'd hated each other for years and they made up their own, more interesting story."

"Tell me about the duel."

Adam gave a genuine laugh this time. "Oh, the older man took off to the Continent. The younger man showed up, so frightened he soiled his breeches. I gave him a bit of a thrashing and sent him home with nothing worse than a few bruises."

"See, you cannot even hurt a man who deserves it."

"Oh, he didn't deserve either Veronica or me. He was just a boy."

Mia didn't agree with his assessment, but let the matter lie.

He tipped his head to one side and smiled. "Actually, it feels rather good to tell the story to another person."

"You've never told any of this to anyone?"

"Who the devil would I tell it to?"

"I don't know — perhaps your second wife?"

"I doubt I exchanged above a hundred words with the girl. Poor, poor Sarah." He shook his head. "My second marriage was a mistake only I can claim."

"What rubbish! She spoke the words, did she not?"

"Yes, she did. But she had no choice in the matter."

"How is that?"

To her surprise, he colored. "I beat her father in a card game — took everything he had. When I went to inspect my winnings I found Sarah there, living alone in a house with a couple of old servants who'd been too loyal to leave her."

Mia gasped.

"It seems she'd been living that way for

some time. She had no money, no family — her father had disappeared not long after our card game — and no place to go."

"So you married her?"

Adam nodded. "So I married her."

"But what . . ."

"What happened? Well, it turned out Sarah wasn't as alone as I'd believed. In fact, she was already pregnant when we wed."

Mia shook her head. "Oh, Adam."

"You seem to be saying that a lot tonight, my dear."

"You found out and divorced her?"

"Oh, not at all." He laughed at the shock he saw on her face. "I was perfectly willing to accept the brat as my own — why not? If she'd had a son, he'd be my heir and that would have been a relief. I'll tell you another secret, my love — I never consummated my second marriage."

Mia blinked.

"Sarah was such a frightened thing I never could manage to get past her terrified eyes and quivering lip. It must have been a month into our marriage when she fainted dead away while my mother and Jessica were receiving guests. It was my mother who told me she was with child. I was still trying to come up with a way to confront

435

her on the subject that wouldn't kill her with fright when she disappeared."

"Oh, Adam, no!"

He chuckled. "Oh, Mia, yes. It seems she decided to contact the father of her unborn child, a curate from the vicarage where she'd lived, and let him know of her condition. The young man had apparently decided to drown his sorrows in missionary work after she'd married me and was on the verge of departing to some godforsaken place. He finally came up to scratch and took Sarah with him."

"How did you learn all this?" she asked in wonder.

"I hired a man to investigate her disappearance. It took him almost three years to trace them from Liverpool to some wretched village in India."

Mia tried to image it — what her husband must have felt when his third wife had run from him. She swallowed her shame, vowing to show him how much she loved him to make up for his hideous past.

"What did she say when your man found her?"

"Nothing." His mouth was grim.

"Nothing?"

"She was already dead, both she and the curate. Apparently, they'd arrived in the midst of a cholera outbreak. For the second time I found myself a widower."

She went to him then, leaving her blanket behind and crawling into his lap.

"Are you sorry for me, my lady?"

She nodded, too shaken to speak.

"You should be worried about yourself — after all, wives of mine don't fare well, even if I don't have an actual hand in killing them."

She sniffed, holding him even tighter. "Adam?"

She felt his lips against her hair. "Mmm?"

"I love you."

His body froze against hers, his breath warm on her scalp.

"I should have told you that a long time ago. I think I've loved you from the night you took me to the theater and I saw you with your friends."

He remained silent.

"Loving you should have made my life easier, but all I could think was how you'd married me only for an heir and that my love would be the last thing you would want. Mostly, though, I didn't think of it at all, instead delaying my plans for escape to live in the moment. I'm so sorry."

"Shhh," he murmured into her hair, stroking her back as he held her.

Tears rolled down her face. "I just want our marriage to go back to the way we were before Brighton."

"We can't go back, Mia." He pulled away from her and looked down, brushing the tears from her face with his thumbs and smiling. "Besides, I think we should go forward and make our marriage even better."

CHAPTER TWENTY-SEVEN

The storm lasted for two long days but the weather for the rest of their journey proved smooth — both inside the ship and out. Adam would never have believed it, but he was enjoying himself hugely. In some ways it was almost a wedding trip, albeit with a shipload of strange men along for company. The trip would have been completely free of worries had his wife not been headed toward a man who wanted to kill her.

He and Mia made love and talked as they'd never done before, even during those first heady days of their marriage. She told him of life in the sultan's palace and how she'd decided early on that she would not be angry or self-pitying, but work to make a better life for her son. He told her of his childhood, his life at school, and the years he'd spent alone after his last marriage.

After that first week they'd taken to sharing their evening meal with Bouchard and then playing cribbage or a three-handed game the Frenchman knew called nines.

If someone had told him two weeks ago that he and Bouchard — a man he'd immediately wanted to kill — would enjoy each other's company, he would have thought they were mad.

As much as Adam enjoyed the afternoons and evenings lounging, he was accustomed to physical activity and long days without any way to exercise his body would have been hellish. The second week on board he'd found a spot where he was in nobody's way and woke just before dawn to practice fencing on the foredeck.

One of the sailors must have passed word along to their captain because Adam arrived the next morning to find Bouchard waiting for him, sword in hand.

"Captain, what a . . . surprise," Adam said, giving the younger man the chilling look he'd found so useful at the card table. He might like Bouchard, but he'd be damned before he ever showed it. The man was the most arrogant, obnoxious, and mercurial human Adam had ever met. There was no point in stroking his ego by demonstrating anything that might be misconstrued as admiration.

"I 'ear you are up 'ere stabbing de air, my

lord. I tink maybe you would enjoy stabbing me more, eh?"

Bouchard's smirk made Adam's hand twitch. Which made him look at his blade.

"I do not spar with real blades. The last thing I need is to kill you and have your crew toss me to the fishes."

Bouchard thought this was hilarious. "Yes, the last ting I need is to kill *you* and 'ave . . . *have,*" he corrected, "your wife toss me to the fishes."

They both had a laugh at that.

"It's a pity we don't have any practice blades." Adam thought for a moment and then had an idea. "We have killed more than one bottle of wine between us — are there any corks around? It would do for mine." He looked at the narrow point of his sword. Yes, one cork should blunt the end. They would need to make sure to test it frequently.

He looked at Bouchard's sabre. "I think perhaps yours may require a few."

The Frenchman nodded.

While Bouchard went to procure corks Adam stripped off his waistcoat and shirt and began the stretches Beauleaux insisted on before sparring.

He was midway through his final set when the younger man returned. He watched

Adam until he finished and then handed him a couple corks.

"What is dat you do?" Bouchard asked, carefully slicing the first of the corks he'd brought with the sharp blade.

"Stretching exercises." Adam pierced the cork with the end of his short sword and watched Bouchard. He'd brought a bucket of corks and was putting several down the blade. Probably a wise idea.

"Stretching exercises?" He said the last two words as if they were new to him. Which they probably were. The man's English was good — indeed he seemed to be improving every day — but he still missed many words.

"It is so you do not hurt yourself — your body." He saw Bouchard's smirk, and smiled. "You can laugh now. Just wait until you are my age. You will wish you'd treated your body better."

The Frenchman thought that was funny. " 'Ow old are you?" he asked, fitting the last cork onto the sabre.

"Older than you."

Bouchard found Adam's attempted set-down even more amusing.

"So, we are ready, old man? Or you need more *stretching exercises*?"

Adam ignored his taunting and took his position, *"En garde!"*

The next hour was one of the most grueling of Adam's entire life. Not even at Eton, where the goal of fencing practice had been to either behead or thrash one's mates as savagely as possible, had he ever fought the likes of Bouchard.

The Frenchman had learned his skills while using them and his was not the style of gentlemen's sons all over Europe. As a result, nothing Bouchard did was predictable or followed any particular style or school. If Adam wasn't aware every second, he ended up defending to within an inch of his life. Bouchard thrived on chaos: it didn't matter what Adam did; the man was ready to engage.

By the third morning they had a small audience, not to mention Ramsay, whose *Ghost* was running alongside the *Scythe* that day. The two ships came close enough for the baron to yell brief messages back and forth. The thrust of Ramsay's messages was to make certain the two men weren't trying to kill each other.

Every day they became a little more evenly matched, until it was almost impossible for either of them to score a touch.

This morning was their last bout. Adam bowed to the younger man once they'd finished, and they shook hands.

"You move good for an old man."

Adam snorted. "And you do all right for an undisciplined savage."

They laughed and parted ways. Adam entered the cabin to find Mia awake and eating breakfast. He dropped a kiss on her head before moving off to the bed to remove his sweaty clothing.

"What are you doing awake so early?" he asked.

"I woke up and you were not here. I decided it was not worth staying in bed." She took a bite of toast loaded with preserves and smiled.

"I should have stayed sleeping. I daresay I'll have bruises on every square inch of my body soon." He turned to look at his left side in the mirror, where several dark red marks joined their blue and black brethren.

His wife made an impolite noise. "I wish you would not fight with him. You will hurt him and then he will throw us overboard."

Adam smiled at his wife's somewhat regular refrain on the issue of Bouchard and the probable outcome of any interaction with him.

"It is too good an opportunity to pass up. He is quite skilled in his way. I will be able to teach Beauleaux a thing or two after this." Well, if he did not return to England

444

in a pine box.

He didn't tell Mia that in addition to playing cards and fencing with the man he'd also spoken to him about the danger they would face in Oran. The men they were going to try to fool were a group of hardened killers and rogues who were bent on vengeance for the man they served. The danger would be significant.

Adam had already spoken to Bouchard about Mia and his intention to leave her on board the *Scythe* while he and Ramsay went to the palace.

"She will not like it that you have lied to her, Exley," Bouchard said in French as he picked up his discarded shirt and wiped the sweat from his face after one of their morning bouts.

Adam pulled the cork off his sword and re-sheathed it. He would sharpen it after their last sparring match.

"She doesn't need to like it. It's bad enough that she will be so close to a man who wants her dead. Tell me again what you will do after I join Ramsay."

Bouchard pulled on his shirt and sat on one of the crates that held spare sails and equipment. He stuck with his native language for the conversation. "I will split off before we are in sight of the port and anchor off to the east of Quora's Bluff. If Assad has some tricks planned for the *Ghost* at the port, you and Ramsay will have to backtrack and come to the *Scythe,* instead.

"The journey won't take long, perhaps an hour or so from the palace on foot, but you might have company behind you." He shrugged. "Let us hope Assad does not have bigger plans or other ships patrolling the area with surprises. He may already know we are coming, or he may not. He does not have the impressive network his father did. I do not think he will want to risk too much destruction. He needs money to buy more ships, not a war to sink the few he has. He wants the ransom and your wife — but he wants the money more. He will forget about Lady Exley if the situation turns into too much trouble."

Adam tried to find his words reassuring, but couldn't.

The Frenchman scratched at his shoulder and sighed, as if forcing himself to say something he didn't want to. "You must tell her she is to stay here, my lord. I will keep her safe, but you must be the one to tell her it was your decision. She has already spoken several times of what she is planning when she reaches the palace." He fingered the ornate designs on the pommel of his sabre before returning it to its sheath and looking up at Adam. He no longer used a series of corks for their sparring. Instead one of his men had made a leather blade cover.

Adam knew the younger man was right. As much as he'd like to avoid the confrontation and simply leave, it was not this man's duty to give explanations to his wife.

Adam looked at her now as she ate breakfast and planned for tomorrow. She was eating and watching him clean himself in the basin of hot water. She, at least, was thoroughly enjoying this enforced lack of personal privacy. Adam had to admit he did not mind as much as he'd believed he would.

He wrung out the cloth and wiped down his chest and stomach. Her eyes consumed his body and made him hard, just as they always did. She dropped her unfinished toast onto the plate and daintily brushed crumbs off her fingers. She stood before him and pulled the sash. The dressing gown slid to the floor, exposing her naked body. Her stomach had only a gentle curve, a slight sign of the life that was growing inside her. But there was a pronounced lushness to her that worked on him like a miracle tonic, and he dropped the wet cloth and pulled her into his arms, her skin warm and dry against his. Her hands went to the front of his breeches, her nimble fingers stripping him in moments while he nuzzled her neck, jaw, ear, inhaling the sweet scent of her.

"I love you, Adam," she murmured into his chest, her mouth closing on a nipple, her clever tongue drawing a ragged hiss from him.

Adam could only hope she still felt the same way about him when he told her he would allow her no part in saving her son.

CHAPTER TWENTY-EIGHT

The night before they reached Oran, Adam and Mia dined alone, hopefully for the last time — at least on this journey. If all went well, Jibril would be with them for the return trip.

As much as she yearned for the return of her son, Mia had enjoyed her time shipboard with Adam. They'd become comfortable with each other in a way that was inevitable in such close quarters. Every day he seemed to become more natural around her. He didn't even look like the same man. It wasn't only his skin — which had become surprisingly dark during their weeks at sea, making his eyes appear even more striking — but he seemed to have grown younger. Mia attributed this to Captain Bouchard. The two men bickered like boys, constantly wrangling about cards, horses, pistols, swordplay, the weather, and probably women when Mia was not around. She'd

never seen Adam so open, even with Danforth. She wondered if this was what he'd been like before his marriage and the subsequent social censure.

Tonight was their last night before incredible danger, and she resolved to make every second together count.

"I would like to show you some of the clothing I brought with me. I have several robes, one of them Jibril's, which should fit you. They will be useful to conceal us." She watched as he cleared aside everything other than their glasses. "I think there might be some other things you could use as well."

He piled their dinner crockery on the tray and shoved it to the side of the table before giving her one of the slight smiles she found so infuriatingly sensual.

He patted his thigh. "Come and sit."

She lowered herself onto his lap, proof of his desire hard beneath her. But first she wanted to talk about the next day.

"Adam, I have some things you should wear. We can make a turban for you and perhaps see if Bouchard has a djellaba if Jibril's doesn't fit. You cannot wear your own clothing, which will set you apart."

His hands had begun working up her legs, the route to what he was seeking unfettered as she wore a caftan with nothing beneath

it. Mia tried to think, but it was becoming more difficult the higher his distracting hands came to the top of her thighs.

"Adam . . ." she began, and then stopped when he pushed apart her legs, his skillful fingers quickly finding the part of her that would stop all thought.

His breath was hot on her ear. "We can talk of clothing after. Right now I need to touch you. Spread for me, darling." She shuddered at the erotic command and opened to him, lying back in his arms, her body limp but exquisitely sensitive as he stroked her toward climax.

Her pleasure was the most intoxicating sight in the world to him. Her small, warm body was pliant in his arms. Adam could not get enough of her sweet face and the sensual satisfaction on it. He lifted her caftan over her head and dropped it, his eyes on the small ring in her navel. He knew it had been another man's way of marking his possession, but it was part of her and he loved it.

He slid his hand from the wetness between her thighs to the intriguing jewel, stroking around it in a way that made her squirm and rub her tight little bottom over his cock. Her breasts were sheened with sweat and her tight pink nipples beckoned. She writhed under his mouth as he nipped and sucked, cupping a breast in each hand.

"Unbutton me, Mia." His voice was husky against her taut bud.

She opened his breeches and grabbed him. Colorful blasts exploded behind his eyelids and rendered him speechless as she took him into her body in one long, hard slide.

He held her hips loosely as she rode him, looking down to where their bodies were joined. She knew what he wanted and pulled all the way off him before lowering herself, allowing him the breathtaking view of his shaft disappearing into her body. He thrust with all his might and she cried out, her hands gripping his shoulders while she convulsed around him.

His orgasm left him blind and he shuddered and pulled her against his heaving chest, stilling her body while his heart pounded so hard he thought it might explode.

Afterward they lay in bed, stripped of their clothing. Mia stroked his stomach because she could not get enough of the tight weave of muscles that separated his slim hips from his sculpted chest and shoulders.

He groaned. "I need some time to recover,

my lady. I am an old man, according to Bouchard."

"How unlike you to fish for compliments, my lord. Perhaps I should show you just how quickly you can recover?"

His body shook with laughter, but his hand moved down to arrest hers. "Stay, my love. I will need energy for what I must do tomorrow."

His words sobered her immediately.

She propped herself up on her elbow and looked down at him. "Are we finally to talk about tomorrow? You have avoided it for weeks."

He opened his eyes, and as she looked into their frozen blue depths, she knew what he would say.

"Ramsay is coming for me tonight and we will go to the port on the *Ghost*. You will stay on this ship, and Bouchard will anchor off Quora's Bluff, not Ramsay. You will remain on the ship until I return."

Even though she'd expected the words, they still robbed her of breath. He'd planned all this without her. *They'd* planned all this. She sat up, almost dizzy, struggling with the urge to fight and forcing herself to stay calm. No man would listen to an irate or emotional woman.

She looked down at him and opened her mouth.

He placed one long, callused finger over her lips. "Don't argue with me, Mia. You will do as I say. Do you understand? This is not a matter for negotiation and you are sorely mistaken if you think I will change my mind." His jaw tightened and the look he shot her was full of deep-seated anger. "I *gravely* regret allowing you to come on this voyage. That decision went against everything I knew to be wise. I will not act against my better judgment again."

Mia flung herself off the bed, too angry to be near him, but unable to look away.

His face softened. "There is nothing you could do to help. Believe me when I say you would only be in our way, you would only cause me to worry."

His quiet words were more infuriating than his harsh command had been. "You are like the sultan! Like my father! Like *every* man I've ever known!" she shouted, no longer bothering to maintain a façade of calm.

He pushed himself up. "That is an unfair accusation, Mia. I have already allowed you far more latitude than most husbands would." He swung his legs over the bed, his expression angry and affronted.

Mia didn't care; she wanted to hurt him.

"You *allow* me? Who are you to treat me like I am your slave?"

"Not like a slave — like a *wife. My* wife. I am your husband and that is the way of things."

"How much you must like that! I am lower even than your servants, who at least can leave your employ if they come to hate you." Her chest was rising and falling fast, yet she could not get enough air.

He would leave her here alone and if something bad happened, she would be the last person to know. And she would be powerless to help. Just as she'd been for years.

He picked his breeches off the floor, where they'd fallen in the midst of their passion.

"Tell yourself whatever you must, my lady. You will still obey me. You will do so even if I have to leave you here in leg irons." His voice was quiet but his movements were jerky.

She looked in his arctic eyes and sneered. "I am no better than a broodmare to you. As long as I submit to you, spread my legs, and bear your children like some ignorant sow, you will treat me well. The moment I wish to think for myself, I see what happens."

"You are becoming hysterical. I am only concerned for your safety."

The slight control that remained to her snapped at the word *hysterical.* "I am not becoming anything! You are *driving* me to hysteria! Is this how you drove one wife to kill herself and another to run to away?"

He'd been pulling his shirt over his head, and time froze as the garment floated down onto his shoulders. Mia closed her eyes, hoping the moment would go on forever, but she knew it wouldn't. She would have to face the consequences of her horrible words.

She opened her eyes and found a stranger in front of her. She took a step back at the hard look on his face.

The only sounds in the cabin were her labored breathing and Adam's quiet movements as he completed his dressing.

"Adam —"

He raised one hand, palm out. "No, you listen to me. I have tolerated enough from you on this matter. You will remain in this cabin until we depart for England. Bouchard has my leave to lock you in here if you disobey." He buttoned his waistcoat with deliberate movements and yanked his coat from the chair where it had been draped. He shoved back his hair, still damp from their lovemaking, and took his sword belt from the closet before going to the cabin door.

She rushed to him. "Adam, please!" She took his arm in both hands and he froze.

"Unhand me, madam." His quiet voice was like a razor.

She dropped her hands and he left without looking back, the door clicking softly shut behind him.

Adam was pitifully grateful nobody was up and about when he reached the deck. He couldn't imagine their argument had gone unnoticed, at least not Mia's half of it.

He went to the foredeck and sat on one of the storage boxes.

"Bloody hell," he muttered, resting his elbows on his thighs before dropping his head into his hands. That had not gone well. Her words had hurt, but it had been her heartbroken face that had almost undone him. She had believed he was angry with her, and he'd decided in that instant to use her belief and just go — it was easier to end it that way. She would never agree with his decision, and he would never change his mind.

"That bad, eh?" a voice behind him asked in French.

Adam jolted and looked up to see Bouchard standing beside him.

"You move like a damned cat."

Bouchard smiled and handed him a slim cigar.

"These come from a small plantation on Hispaniola. It is the only plantation that employs workers, not slaves."

Adam paused and then took it. What was the point in sitting here and reliving the disturbing confrontation with Mia? He might as well smoke.

The two men stood by the railing and looked at the distant shore.

"Ramsay will meet us soon."

Adam nodded. Both ships kept birds that were used to exchange messages when flags or yelling weren't an option. He took a puff of the cigar and contemplated the burning tip before slowly exhaling. "What do you think the chances are of Ramsay's plan working?"

"It depends on whether the old entrance to the slave quarters was ever found and if Assad is keeping the boy where we think."

Adam snorted. *If, if, if.* "Does that seem likely after almost twenty years?"

"I've heard of no other escapes from the sultan's palace."

It seemed like a lot to take on faith, but

Adam had no other ideas. "You will leave a boat waiting on shore for us just in case this all goes badly?"

"Oui."

"What if you don't hear anything from the *Ghost*?"

"If I hear nothing by dark, I will go to Gibraltar and wait."

Adam eyed the other man closely. Something about his words didn't quite ring true.

"You won't try to rescue anyone — Ramsay or his men? You'll leave immediately and take my wife to Gibraltar."

"Nom d'un chien!" The Frenchman turned to glare at him. "I already say I will, eh?" he snapped in broken English.

Adam nodded. "I don't doubt your word. It's just that my wife can be rather . . . insistent."

Adam let the other man's temper cool while he ran the rest of Ramsay's plan through his head for the thousandth time. The baron had tried to prepare for all eventualities. If Adam and Ramsay didn't return, the *Ghost* would get away from Oran and wait in the shallows a half-day's journey to the west. The ship would wait there in case something prevented the landing party from reaching the *Scythe* after they left the sultan's palace. Adam tried not to think

459

about that, even though he had taken time to memorize the hand-drawn map Ramsay had sent with the note.

If he somehow lost contact with Ramsay, he did not fancy his chances of finding his way across miles of foreign countryside, where he didn't speak the language and would stand out like a sore thumb.

He drew deeply on the cigar before blowing out a billowing cloud. "Ramsay must have friends here if he is so confident of acquiring supplies."

"Ramsay has friends everywhere."

"They will not disclose his plans to Assad's men?" Adam could believe Ramsay would have friends, but so must the young sultan.

"No. He is a hero to many. Also, he is very good at disguising himself."

Adam had a hard time believing Ramsay could disguise his six and a half feet anywhere, but he let the matter lie. "You know his crew well?"

Bouchard nodded, blowing a circle of smoke, and then blowing another inside it. Adam was impressed. "Yes, most of them were on the *Ghost* with me. They are good men, especially Delacroix, his captain."

"You've met Lady Exley's son, as well?" Adam couldn't help wondering what he could expect from the son of a sultan, a young man accustomed to receiving absolute obedience from his father's subjects.

Bouchard smirked. "Yes. He is . . . arrogant."

Coming from Bouchard this was quite a declaration.

"He fights for his father's empire but I think he knows that way of life is over. Even under the old sultan there were many changes. Slaving isn't so easy anymore. Jibril is smart enough to know that." He shrugged. "I think maybe half a year of fighting will make him more amenable to going to England." He flicked away the butt of his cigar and turned to Adam. "What kind of life would he have in England? He is like me, eh? A half-caste."

Adam studied the younger man, giving his question the consideration it deserved. Bouchard was certainly unusual-looking. Even with his fair hair and light eyes one would never mistake him for an Englishman. If Mia's son were similarly exotic, there would be no hiding his background and he would need to be a strong man to endure the endless snubs.

Adam tossed away what remained of his cigar. "It won't be easy. He may view desert warfare with fondness after his first Season in London."

Bouchard laughed. "Ramsay is like a nagging old mother to get me to go to London. He says I must take a wife who will like my money and civilize me. He likes to" — he paused, his hand churning the air as he searched for the correct idiom — "stir the kettle?"

"Stir the pot. Yes, I can well believe that. Ramsay has an odd sense of humor."

"Ah, milord, he is a constant tormentor and far too big a brute to thrash. I am glad he is on his own ship. No doubt he has driven Delacroix to the end of his rope." He laughed at something he did not bother to share and turned to Adam. "Take my cabin tonight. I will keep watch and come get you when it is time to go."

Adam nodded, grateful the man didn't pry. He wouldn't sleep; he would write the letter he should have written to his wife before he ever married her.

CHAPTER TWENTY-NINE

Mia was not surprised when Bouchard stopped her at the top of the stairs.

"Ah, Lady Exley." He stood in the middle of the narrow stairway, his arms crossed, blocking the way out with his big body. "What can I do for you?"

"I wish to speak to my husband."

Bouchard moved closer, forcing her to back down the stairs until they were at the bottom, their bodies almost touching in the narrow hallway. His behavior told her Adam had left; he would never behave so familiarly while her husband was on board.

"We will talk down 'ere, eh?"

"When did he leave?"

"Just a while ago, my lady. 'E said to give you dis." He handed her several sheets of folded paper.

She snatched them out of his hand and saw there was no seal. "You did not read them?"

He smiled, an odd twist to his lips. "No, I did not read them. Now, if you would go back to your cabin?" Mia allowed him to herd her down the hallway. He opened the door to his cabin and waited until she went inside. "I will 'ave food sent to you in an hour if that is *convenable*?"

Mia gave him a look she'd seen Adam use to intimidate those around him.

It didn't work. Bouchard just smiled and shut the door in her face. She heard the scrape of a key in the lock and grabbed the handle, but the door was already locked.

"Bouchard?" There was no answer. "Bouchard!" She pounded on the door. "You bastard!" She swore like a fishwife and beat the door until her palm stung. She collapsed against the door and slid down, only recalling the note in her hand as she landed roughly on the floor. It was crumpled. She straightened the two sheets and opened them, recognizing her husband's neat, compact hand.

Darling:

I'm sorry to leave you after such a terrible row. I am sorry to leave you, ever.

I can't regret my decision to make sure you had at least this much protection. You are my wife, and it is both my duty and my honor to keep you safe. As much as you wish to protect your son, I wish to protect you. Bouchard will take care of you if Assad presents us with any surprises, something both he and Ramsay have warned me about.

Stay in your cabin, darling. There is no point in risking you and our child. You know Assad will kill you if he gets the opportunity. Please don't make my decision meaningless.

I've left you one of my pistols. It is loaded and it is inside the wardrobe. Point it away from you and pull the trigger if you have need of it. I hope it does not come to that.

Try not to shoot Bouchard with it, even though he is provoking.

If all goes well, we will bring your son to you in only a few hours. If not, well, know that I love you, even though I have never spoken the words. Maybe that will cause you to feel kindly toward me after you read what follows.

I should have told you this long ago — certainly before we married — but I told myself I couldn't share the information for my daughters' sakes. It is, after all, their secret and they do not deserve that it be shared without the certainty it would be held sacred.

But somehow, after I came to know and love you, it was even more difficult to tell you. I will not beat about the bush any longer. The truth is my first wife was not only reckless, she was mad.

It wasn't until after her death that I learned the truth. Her only sibling, a brother named Dennis, came to the funeral and told me about his sister. He had been out of the country when we married and returned far too late to tell me the truth about her past and their family history. He apologized for not telling me after we'd married, but I cannot find it in me to blame the man. He told me their grandmother had killed herself when their own mother was just a child and that she had been mad for years before she took her life.

Dennis and his mother escaped the taint, but Veronica showed her madness from a young age.

You must see now why I can't allow my daughters to go into society, to take spouses, to have children and spread this stain to another generation. At the same time, what if they are like their uncle or grandmother and have avoided madness? It is a situation which has, I'm ashamed to say, driven me to avoid my own children.

Eva, especially, reminds me of her mother. Her passionate outbursts, sudden rages, and violent attachments are far too like Veronica's.

I wish I could tell you I have devised some solution, but I have not. And now I have brought you into the midst of potential tragedy, and you have formed attachments to all three girls. Three attachments that might one day yield heartache.

I deeply apologize, Mia, for not telling you sooner — for not telling you face-to-face.

That first night, as you grilled me at your father's dinner table, you recognized my cowardice regarding my daughters and attributed it to male arrogance. The truth is, I was a bad husband out of ignorance and I've been an even worse father out of fear. I've stayed away not because I don't love my daughters, but because I love them too much. When I am with them, I find myself watching, and watching, and watching. Ever watchful for signs of madness. Childish tantrums make my blood run cold — girlish arguments cause me to hold my breath in terror. This was not what my children needed — to be observed with the calculating eye of a jailor. What they needed was you, Mia. You and your friendship and love. You showed me how selfish I've been to allow my fear to paralyze me. More importantly, you showed my daughters what it is like to have a mother figure who loves them.

In a way, you gave my daughters back to me. In the weeks since we returned to Exham I have felt a joy in their presence I haven't experienced since that day Dennis shared the secret of their heritage.

I hope to repay you the only way I can — by giving you back your son.

Yours always,
Adam

Mia stared, stunned at the horror he'd borne alone. The thought of her beloved Jibril carrying something in him that could one day turn him mad was beyond bearing. To never know, to never be sure — how could a person live with the constant threat, the dread?

As she recalled the awful things she'd flung at him before he'd left, hot tears of shame burned her face. She wept for what she had said to him but she cried even more because she might never have a chance to apologize.

It was late in the afternoon when the *Ghost* dropped anchor. They'd hardly been there an hour before Ramsay began getting messages hinting Assad was planning something that appeared to require a great many men.

"It's possible Assad may attack us in the harbor — even tonight. We must act quickly and hope to be gone from here before he can carry out whatever it is he has planned."

The enormous baron was all but unrecognizable in his disguise. His hair, normally an almost guinea gold, was a greasy brown. He wore a ragged turban and capacious cloak the locals called a djellaba. He had a crutch and when he crouched over in his limping walk he seemed no larger than most men. He'd also removed his distinctive eye patch. Adam tried not to stare as he looked into Ramsay's mismatched eyes. The cut that had robbed his eye of sight had sliced from his forehead to his jaw, leaving a remarkably clean wound beneath his patch. The eye hardly appeared damaged except for the clearly bisected iris, which had turned a dull greenish gray.

"Should your captain take the ship farther

out after we go? We could always meet them elsewhere if you fear a trap," Adam suggested.

Ramsay shook his head. "We need the distraction. If Assad is watching the *Ghost,* he won't be paying too much attention to the palace or looking elsewhere — like Quora's Bluff. Fontine will be in charge. He is Delacroix's first mate and knows well enough what to do if he becomes overwhelmed. I have also sent messages to several other ships that are at anchor. We have friends nearby if we need them."

He handed Adam an old cloth bag. "Here, put these on. The quicker you do, the sooner we can be gone. Delacroix has already left for the Bluff and taken his men with him. They will locate the entrance and see to any clearing it might need. If it can't be cleared? We will then have a look at Assad's front door."

Adam pulled out a white and red cloth, which Ramsay showed him how to wind and wrap. He also had a loose, dirty white shirt and a djellaba similar to Ramsay's. When he was dressed, the bigger man had him rub ashes on his hands and face.

"Here is a piece of rope. Use it to secure your sword to your leg. As soon as we are off the pier you can scuff the polish from your boots. Until then try to stoop, keep your eyes on the ground, and be humble." The baron's lips twitched. "Try not to think like an English marquess. Think like . . ."

Adam snatched the piece of rope from his hands. "Thank you, Ramsay. I bloody well know how to think." He buckled his sword beneath the robe and secured it to his thigh. When he was done he looked up. "I am ready."

They headed west once they left the docks. Ramsay stopped a half dozen times to make sure they weren't being followed. They took the small, winding alleys through the district known as Hai Imam El-Houari. Above their heads, perched on a rocky promontory, was the massive fort that loomed over the city, watchful and menacing.

"Fort Santa Cruz is a plum that has been passed between many hands," Ramsay whispered, lurching beside him in the slow, painful walk he'd affected. "Beneath it are caverns running to the other two forts, as well as to the far west of the city. I have never been in them, but they are said to be extensive. I can't help feeling the tunnel at Quora's Bluff is somehow part of the same system." He stopped speaking when they came to a bottleneck in the narrow road, where a man with three camels was impeding a rustic wagon, pulled by a giant ox.

Ramsay yelled something very rude-sounding in Arabic, his big hand waving the crutch as he spoke. The man with the camels yelled something back, but grudgingly moved the animals aside. Adam followed a grumbling Ramsay through the small opening.

When they passed beyond the clutch of people, Ramsay again turned to him.

"Once we get into the slave quarters, Delacroix and I will separate as he knows the pens as well as I do. We will search our sections and then meet back at the Bluff afterward. If we get split up and one of us does not make it back by the appointed time, leave. Do not wait, do not come looking. We will either have left some other way, or you won't be able to help. Do you understand me, Exley? You will have to make sure Delacroix obeys you. He holds me in some affection." Ramsay gave a low chuckle.

Adam didn't bother asking how he was supposed to strong-arm a group of hardened privateers into doing anything they did not wish to do. He would deal with that eventuality if it happened.

Once they cleared the populated part of

the city, they were able to move faster on the hard-packed dirt road that led into the countryside. The odd stone houses that had been packed side by side dwindled to individual buildings, and then to the occasional hut.

"We leave the road here." Ramsay led him down a steep embankment and into a gully that looked like a dry riverbed. They followed the riverbed for perhaps a quarter of an hour before Ramsay cut west toward a small grove of trees.

"Here we are." He gestured to the right and Adam peered through the gloom. They were not fifty feet from the base of an impressive cliff face. "Quora's Bluff," Ramsay said.

Adam glanced around. "Are your men late?"

Ramsay whistled and men materialized from rock, sand, and scrub. He greeted his crew with the same forearm handshake Adam had seen many times in the past weeks. One of the men was Delacroix, Ramsay's captain. The Frenchman was squat, thick, heavily scarred, and looked every bit as roguish and disreputable as his employer.

"You found it?" Ramsay asked.

The Frenchman led them toward the cliff face. "*Oui,* Captain. It took a bit of digging.

I don't think it has been used in years." He shrugged. "Maybe not since we left."

A clump of scrubby trees were growing beside the big outcrop of rock and when Delacroix pushed apart some of the lower branches Adam could see a rude plank door sitting beside a rectangular hole cut into the stone face of the cliff.

Ramsay peered into the blackness of the cave and nodded. "Good. Let's hope Assad knows nothing of it." Ramsay took off his heavy robe and turban and tossed them onto the ground beside the trees. Adam did the same, and Delacroix handed them both torches. Ramsay took the lead.

The tunnel was so low the baron had to crouch almost double. Even Adam, just shy of six feet, had to walk in an uncomfortable slouch. Although the tunnel was cramped, it was remarkably cool compared to the muggy warm air of the harbor. Three times they came to a split, and three times Ramsay took the right-hand tunnel.

"Where do the others lead?" Adam asked Delacroix, who was behind him.

"Two of them were caved in and the third had a locked door. The guard we bought the information from only knew of the tunnels, not where they led. We were lucky to find the exit at the bluff. Even so, it took us a good six hours of digging to free the old door." Adam could hear the traces of long-ago anxiety in the other man's voice.

"Why did you agree to come back here today?" Adam asked, truly curious as to why this man would risk death for the son of the man who'd made him a slave.

"The Captain asked me." His words were simple, but Adam saw the complex emotions that lay beneath them. Bouchard had been correct; Ramsay commanded impressive loyalties.

The man in front of him stopped and turned to Adam.

"We are at the door to the first cell," he whispered. "Ramsay says it is one of the larger ones and there will be many slaves inside. Extinguish your torch and take my belt."

Adam nodded and snuffed the flame in the sandy floor of the tunnel. He hooked the fingers of his left hand through the other man's belt and lowered his right to his sword.

Even in the dark Adam could tell when they entered the cell. The heat in the room and the odor of dozens of unwashed bodies was almost overwhelming.

Adam felt something under his boot — a hand? — and stepped back.

He could hear Ramsay's voice a few feet away, the Arabic words low and soothing. Whatever he said must have been convincing because the only answering noises were a few soft words in return. He heard the sound of a flint being struck and a torch flared to life.

He blinked and opened his eyes to a sight that would stay with him until the day he died. Dozens of bodies lay around the room, some on pallets, but most on the uneven rock floor. A single waste bucket overflowed in one corner, bodies curled around it. The smell of excrement and despair made his eyes water. Most of the men were only sparsely clothed and many had scars, some still new and bleeding.

Ramsay spoke to a man stooped with either age or suffering or both. The people in the room, all men or boys, seemed remarkably wide awake. When Ramsay finished speaking, they rose almost as one body and moved toward the tunnel back to Quora's Bluff.

"What did he tell them?" Adam asked the man who'd been in front of him.

"He told them they are free, to disappear into the desert and not into town."

Adam relit his torch from Ramsay's and then handed it to a boy of about twelve.

The boy took the torch wordlessly, his eyes burning with desperate hope.

They waited until the room was empty and Ramsay turned to Adam.

"The old man told me Jibril was being held in a cell by himself. It is near the entrance to the slave quarters and two men always stand outside the door. The slaves pass it every day on the way to the outdoor pens. He says Assad was in the palace earlier today but he believes the guard presence is lighter than usual around the palace. Once we approach the cell, we will need to work quickly and quietly or they will alert whatever guards are left. Here is where your skills with the blade will be useful, Exley. You and I will go get the boy and Delacroix will go and release all the others."

Adam had not known freeing slaves was part of the plan but after seeing the hell in this single room he could not disagree. Delacroix and Ramsay shook hands and the Frenchman turned away, his lethal-looking helpers following close behind him.

Ramsay turned to him and grinned. "Are you ready to have some fun?"

CHAPTER THIRTY

The fetid smell of the cells grew less pungent as they approached the main entrance to the slave quarters. Ramsay put his hand on Adam's shoulder as they neared a corner, motioning to let him know the cell was to the right.

They rounded the corner and found two guards outside, just as the slaves had warned. One of the men was slumped in a chair, asleep. The other man had his shoe off and was doing something with his foot. Adam was beside him, his blade on the man's throat, before the guard could utter a peep. He looked up and Adam shook his head, placing a finger to his lips and pressing the blade closer.

The guard saw Ramsay and muttered something low in Arabic, his eyes becoming as big as cannonballs. Ramsay grabbed him, yanked the cloth from around his head, and stuffed a wad of it into the stunned man's open mouth. He looped it around his neck and then to the back of his body, where he used it to bind his hands.

Adam whacked the sleeping guard at the base of his bowed head with the pommel of his rapier. The man grunted and slid to the floor. A battered pistol sat on the bench and Adam checked to see if it was loaded and then tucked it in his waistband.

"Nicely done, Exley." Ramsay crouched beside his victim and searched for keys, finding a large ring on the one who was still conscious.

Adam tried key after key until one turned the heavy tumbler. The room beyond the door was perhaps six feet wide by ten feet long. There was only one occupant and he was lying on the floor, face to the wall. He muttered something in Arabic but did not turn. Adam could see his bare arms were striped with dried blood and welts.

"You'll have to speak English if you expect me to understand you," Adam said, raising the lantern and taking a step toward the silent figure.

A low laugh came from the pile of rags.

"Did my mother send you?" It was the voice of an English gentleman and Adam smiled. Mia had obviously schooled her son well.

"How did you guess?" Adam asked. "Now, can you get up? If I don't get you back to her, there is no point in my going back, either." He crouched down and put the lantern he'd taken from the guards on the floor beside the man.

Jibril rolled over and Adam winced when he saw his bruised and bloody face. A pair of familiar green eyes looked up at him but the face was darker and the eyes were separated by a beak that would have done a Roman senator proud. Jibril Marlington had his grandfather Carlisle's nose.

His green eyes flickered to the door, to where Ramsay stood with the unresisting guard.

"Well met, Ramsay! I see you are still allowing my mother to push you about."

Ramsay laughed. "I will remind you of those words later, you young rogue."

Jibril rolled onto his knees and began to struggle to his feet. Adam put a hand under his shoulder and lifted. For his height the boy was dangerously thin.

"Will you be able to walk?"

He grinned. "I'll bloody well be able to run, if it means leaving this cell."

Adam left Jibril outside the door and dragged the other guard into the cell by the feet. He pulled off his sandals and tossed them to Jibril.

They'd just locked the cell door when the sound of boots on stone came from outside the squat building. A group of guards came skidding around the corner and Adam grabbed Jibril's arm and dragged him back the way they'd come.

The guards yelled and the crack of a pistol deafened them in the stone hallway, chips of rock flying around them as they ran through the maze of corridors. Just as they turned into the hall that led to the big cell, voices came from the opposite end of the hall. There was a loud yell and the sound of feet running. Adam raised the pistol he'd taken from the guard and prepared to take aim.

Ramsay laid his hand on Adam's arm. "Lower the gun, Exley. That was Delacroix yelling."

Just then a torch flared to life in the gloom. It was Delacroix, with at least twenty-five men behind him. Adam raised his pistol again and then realized the men behind him were freed slaves rather than guards. Delacroix grinned when he saw Ramsay and motioned for the men behind him to halt.

The guards who'd been behind Adam, Jibril, and Ramsay fired blindly from behind a corner, clearly uninterested in coming out into the open.

"Only the east block of cells remains," Delacroix said. "Assad's men are returning double-time from town." He jerked a thumb at the two men closest to him. "These men were heading toward the road when they saw them and came back to warn us." The slaves were looking from man to man and following the English conversation with expressions of utter confusion.

"Was Assad with them?"

"Nobody has seen him."

Another shot ricocheted around the corner, this one hitting the ceiling overhead and throwing chips of stone down like rain.

Ramsay turned to Adam. "I need to get to the last block of cells, and it's obviously too hot in the harbor." He gestured with his chin to the frightened guards. "Delacroix will handle them and cover us. Do you remember where the *Scythe* will be waiting?"

"I've memorized the map. We will meet you back there."

"If we are not there in three hours, leave. Good luck, Exley." He held out his arm in the traditional way of his men.

Adam returned the sailor's greeting and turned to his stepson.

"Are you ready to leave?"

Jibril smiled, looking very like his mother. "I thought you'd never ask."

Adam put him in front with the lantern. "I'll keep an eye behind us."

When they reached the cell that led to the caves, Jibril headed straight for the tunnel.

"You take only lefts to get back to the exit," Adam told him, following close behind.

"I've been in these tunnels dozens of times in the last year. We used them to spy on my brother. You know where we are going?"

"Yes, we'll leave through Quora's Bluff and then I can lead us to a place where a boat should be waiting. Your mother is offshore, on Bouchard's ship."

Jibril stopped so suddenly, Adam ran into him. The boy turned and squinted at Adam.

"You brought my mother *here*?" he demanded in a menacing voice.

Adam gave the boy a withering look. "If you believe anyone could stop your mother from coming to get you, you are not as wise as I'd hoped."

"Who are you to speak so casually of my mother?"

Adam sighed. "I am her husband. Now, get moving. We can have this family discussion once we reach the safety of our ship."

Jibril gave him a look Adam had seen once or twice on Mia's face. He did, however, turn around and head down the tunnel.

They'd just taken the second left when they heard voices ahead. Arab voices. They stopped and Jibril held up his hand, tilting his head to listen. He mumbled something in Arabic and then turned to Adam.

"It is Assad's men. It sounds like they caught some of the escaped slaves and followed them back to the caves. We will have to go back."

"What?"

"It is the only way."

"What about the other tunnels? You said you've been using them for months?"

"One is closed off by rock and the other leads to the fort — you will find Turks waiting at the end of it."

Adam cursed quietly.

"Come!" Jibril shoved past him and headed back the way they'd come.

"Where are you going?" Adam hissed.

"I know a place we can hide between the courtyard and the apartments. We should be safe if we can make our way there."

"Safe until what?"

"Until I get us out."

Adam sighed but held his tongue. He followed Jibril through the same area they'd just left, the cells and halls now eerily quiet. They went down the corridor Delacroix had emerged from earlier, Jibril leading him all the way to the end, where a smallish cell stood, the door open.

Jibril stepped inside and Adam saw the cell led to another larger room.

"Stay in here and wait."

"What the hell am I waiting for?" Adam demanded.

"I'm going to leave you here while I go and search for some clothing — we'll be able to move about more easily if we have guard uniforms."

Adam thought about arguing and then realized the younger man was not only less conspicuous, even with his red hair, but he also knew his way around.

"Take the lantern," he said. "I don't need it."

The boy nodded and bolted for the door. "I will be back soon."

Adam gazed into the sudden darkness. He bloody well hoped so.

CHAPTER THIRTY-ONE

Mia sat on the bed, the gun beside her, loaded and ready to fire. She'd also found a short sword and wicked-looking knife in Bouchard's wardrobe and those lay within easy reach. Most importantly, she'd found a key to the cabin door. A second key Bouchard had forgotten, hidden inside a wooden box that held various trinkets.

Adam had left without the bag of ransom money, yet another little detail he and Ramsay had kept from her. They'd never planned to deliver it.

Men.

Mia bit back her pointless anger and thought about what she would do next.

It was late, very late. Adam and Ramsay should have been in the harbor hours ago. There had been plenty of time to reach the palace and get back to the *Ghost* or back here if they couldn't approach the harbor after escaping with Jibril.

Yet the ship still remained silent and motionless. They were anchored surprisingly close to the golden sands and high cliff walls that hid the sultan's palace. The *Golden Scythe*'s draft was such that she could go into remarkably shallow water with no trouble.

Mia had been staring at the dark outline of the shore, wondering what she should do, when a light flickered. It was a rowboat. She watched it come closer, until the sickness in her stomach almost doubled her over. Only one man sat in the boat.

She took the loaded gun and knife and tucked them under her djellaba. With a turban around her head, she could pass for a young boy in the dark — if a person wasn't looking too closely. If she was careful, nobody would see her at all.

She slid the key into the lock and prayed while she turned. The *click* seemed deafening, but nothing happened so she opened the door. The corridor outside the cabin was empty. She padded toward the stairs on the wool slippers she'd brought with her. Even before she reached the top of the stairs she could hear the murmur of voices and see the soft glow of a lantern.

She peeked over the top step. There was only a half moon, but it was bright and low in the sky. Bouchard stood some feet away as he and his second mate talked to the man from the rowboat. The three men were crouched over something — a map, probably. She waited until they'd leaned down to look closer before scurrying across the deck toward the stern, to where the rowboat was tied. She crouched behind a trio of barrels and took a quick look over the side. A hemp ladder led to the small rowboat below.

"Show me again on the map where you think they went, Jacques," Bouchard asked.

"Ramsay and Delacroix split from Jibril and the other Englishman here, and they distracted Assad's men while Jibril took the tunnel. Ramsay sent me to the meeting place. He told me to come to you no matter who else showed up and tell you they found the boy. He believed Assad himself was at the harbor. We could hear the sound of cannon even at the palace. He, Delacroix, and about thirty others were going to join them."

"What others? He only took a few of his crew with him."

"Some of the slaves he freed. They took weapons from the guards they captured and followed him."

Bouchard snorted. "Trust Ramsay to start a bloody rebellion." He paused. "I gather you met nobody at the beach? Did you see the entrance at Quora's Bluff?"

"Somebody caved it in. It had to have been Assad's men and they must have got there before Jibril and the Englishman escaped if they never made it back here."

Mia gasped and the men looked around.

"What was that?" Bouchard demanded. Nobody spoke for a long, agonizing moment. Bouchard continued: "If they didn't leave through Quora's Bluff, then where did they go?"

"I don't know. I never went down the other tunnels. We just followed Ramsay to the slave pens."

"Ramsay said there were multiple tunnels off the main one that led to the slave quarters. They must still be in one of those." Beauville pointed to something on the map. "They might have accessed any of them if they found the exit closed."

"Or they could be trapped in the palace itself." Bouchard turned back to Ramsay's man. "I've never even been in the palace. Is it possible they are still in there, Jacques?"

"I'm sorry, Captain, but I only saw the tunnel and the slave quarters."

"Maybe they doubled back from the tunnel and followed behind you?"

"I hope not," Jacques said. "I saw yet another group of Assad's men were headed back from the harbor, remember?" He paused. "It did not seem as if the slave area was connected to the rest of the palace — but could it be?"

"I believe it is," Beauville said. "This corridor looks as though it might join the barracks to the kitchen. The kitchen is connected to the family portion. Surely somebody like Jibril, who grew up there, would know of ways to make it across the palace? I can't see one on the map, but there must be a way out of the kitchens? An entrance for delivering supplies and removing waste from the palace, if nothing else?"

Mia could have told them the kitchen door was unlocked twice a day to remove waste and replenish supplies. The door had two massive metal bars with locks that were as big as her head, one on the inside and one on the outside. Only by a concerted effort could it be opened. The palace had been specifically constructed by the sultan's ancestors to keep family in and intruders out.

Besides, if Adam and Jibril had gotten out, they would have come to the beach. They were either still in the palace or they had been captured before they could reach the boat.

"How bad was the cave-in, Jacques?"

Bouchard was asking. "Could we move enough debris to get into the tunnel?"

"It looked bad from the outside."

Bouchard cursed. "We don't have time for this. Ramsay and Exley wanted the woman gone from here if they were not at the meeting place. We need to leave — soon."

"Yes, that was the last thing Ramsay said. He said you were to do as planned and go west and wait."

Mia had heard enough. Jibril knew both the area and the palace like the back of his hand. She'd told him of the passage that led from the harem — the way she had escaped Assad during the purge.

Unfortunately, he would need help from the outside to unlock the door. Mia had bribed one of the eunuchs to open the door when she'd escaped. Even if Jibril could find his way into the passage, there would be nobody to let them out.

She backed to where the ladder was tied and peered over the side. She could not carry the heavy bag containing the ransom and climb down at the same time. Mia glanced at the arguing men. They would hear it if she dropped the bag, but what choice did she have? Besides, by the time they lowered another boat, she would be halfway to shore. She slid her legs over the side, stepped down a rung, and dropped the bag into the boat below. It hit with a loud thump.

"What was that?" Bouchard yelled.

Mia had almost reached the bottom when the men looked over the side.

Precious seconds ticked past as she fumbled with the knot that kept the boat secured. The rope ladder jerked, telling her a man was on his way down. She finally managed to free the boat and shoved away from the ship as hard as she could before grabbing the oars.

A light flared briefly above her and then disappeared. Mia rowed with all the strength she could muster. She almost wept with relief as the small boat shot away from the ship. She pulled and pulled, ignoring the muffled shouts and splashing sounds that told her another boat had been lowered into the water. She pulled on the oars and glanced over her shoulder.

No matter how fast she rowed, the shore seemed to get farther away with every stroke.

Adam couldn't have dozed for more than a few minutes before he heard men's voices. He knew there was no place to hide — he'd seen as much before Jibril left. He felt his way in the darkness along the wall, until he reached the opening that led to the smaller, outside cell.

The voices came closer: Arabic. He held his sword lightly in his left hand, the pistol in the right. He would take at least a few with him.

The footsteps stopped just outside the small outer cell.

"We know you are in there. Give us Jibril and we will let you go." The French accent was so atrocious it took Adam a minute to translate.

"Come in here and take him if you want him," he yelled back in the same language.

His words detonated an explosion of Arabic. Adam supposed nobody wanted to be the first to step inside. He waited, straining his ears, in case they decided to come without light. His eyes were probably more acclimated to the darkness, so he'd have a minor edge. How long that would last depended on how many of them there were.

The bickering stopped and a burning torch flew through the doorway. It bounced off the stone floor and sent sparks flying in all directions before rolling to a halt beside the opposite wall, still burning.

So much for the advantage of darkness.

The first man came stumbling in right

after the torch, as if somebody had cata-
pulted him.

Adam discharged the pistol and the ball
hit his assailant dead center. The impact
and surprise knocked him back, right into
the man behind him. Their bodies tangled
and Adam lunged forward and pierced the
second attacker through the left side of his
chest. The man tripped over the first man's
body and fell hard onto the sword, dragging
Adam down as he went.

Adam barely kept his feet, dropping into a
crouch while trying to yank the sword free
from the other man's chest.

Yet another aggressor flew through the
door, hurtling over Adam and the two
bodies. Adam yanked on the sword and
wrenched it free, but not before a trail of
fire swept across his back, from shoulder to
hip. He rolled to the side just as his opponent swung again, moving his arm in a
wildly sweeping arc, his scimitar flashing
through the flickering light.

Adam jumped to his feet and raised his
blood-slicked blade in time to stop the killing blow but the impact knocked him back
against the wall. The man had no particular
skill, but he was built like an ox. Adam led
him in a dance across the floor, his arm
almost numb from repelling the repeated

blows from the much heavier sword. He needed to strike now or soon he would not be able.

He ignored the searing pain down his back and launched an attack that would have made Beauleaux proud. His sudden aggression surprised the man, who'd assumed — correctly — that Adam was exhausted, and had drawn back his arm in yet another huge, lazy arc, preparing for the kill. But he'd forgotten about the bodies behind him and stumbled.

Adam's blade made a squelching noise as it swept across the man's throat.

The man's scimitar clattered to the stone floor and he gave a gurgling wail and took yet another step onto the fallen body before crashing to the ground. Adam backed away, his lungs heaving like a bellows as he wiped the blood-slicked pommel of his sword.

He looked around in the dying torchlight. He was the last man standing. Outside, in the smaller cell and hallway, there was the sound of fighting.

An English voice came from the direction of the corridor. "I brought you some help, Stepfather!"

"It's about bloody time," Adam called back, sagging against the cool stone wall and listening to the sound of fighting.

Once he'd caught his breath, he inhaled deeply and then picked his way over fallen bodies and inched closer to see what was happening. It looked as though Jibril had brought at least a dozen men with him. The corridor was too crowded for anything other than hacking and slashing and there was no need for Adam to join them as Jibril's men made short work of the remaining guards.

He massaged his sword arm as he watched. The last guard had hardly hit the floor when the victors began to slap one another on the back in the self-congratulatory manner of very young men. It was a moment before Jibril recalled Adam's existence and came toward him, swathed in a gray wool djellaba with a red-and-black-checked turban on his head. He carried a large leather bag at his side.

"My men came down the main road from town, with a big group of Assad's men right behind them. They are fighting as we speak, at the main entrance."

"Is your half brother with them?" Adam asked, wincing as he pushed off from the wall.

"Are you injured?" The boy looked around at the three corpses and his auburn eyebrows rose. "You fought well, Stepfather."

"Assad, where is he?" Adam repeated.

God forbid the lunatic somehow found the *Scythe* before Bouchard took Mia to a safe distance.

"Still down at the port. My men say it is a madhouse there and several other ships and crews are now involved. Ramsay's ship is blowing holes in any vessel Assad was stupid enough to leave in the harbor." Jibril's eyes widened when he saw the bloody smear on the wall behind him. He went behind Adam. "A very nasty cut. You are more than a little lucky, eh, Stepfather?"

"I wouldn't mind being luckier."

Jibril lifted the lantern and looked closer. "One half is deep. I think we must give you a few stitches to stop it bleeding. Here —" He thrust a leather sack forward. "I found this food near the dead man who used to own this uniform. You can eat while I clean the cut and close it."

"Close it with what?"

"My men always have a small kit with them for such matters."

"I don't suppose they keep any brandy in that kit?" Adam asked as he pulled his shirt over his head. "Bloody hell," he hissed.

Jibril laughed. "No brandy. No tea and crumpets, either. There is water in the skin — give it to me first. I will cleanse the wound and you can fortify yourself with the rest."

The following quarter hour was one Adam would not care to repeat. By the time Jibril had finished the stitching Adam didn't think he'd be able to move.

"Here, chew on this." The boy shoved something into his hand.

"What is it?" Adam studied the small gray pellet in his palm.

"It will make you feel better."

"Yes, but what will it do for my sword arm?"

"Forget your sword arm. You have me to protect you now, Stepfather."

Adam snorted and dropped the pellet into his pocket. He might need it later.

After a quick exchange with Jibril, the rebels hurried off down the corridor, leaving only one man behind.

"This is Muhammed. The others have gone to join the fighting at the slave gate," Jibril said before turning back to the other man and asking him in French, "What did you find, my friend?"

"You are in no shape to fight," Muhammed said in heavily accented French, his mouth tight as he took in his leader's skeletal features. "Either are you," he said to Adam. "We will take care of Assad's men;

you must find someplace to wait. I'm sure you have many hiding places in the family apartments?"

Jibril nodded.

"I will go with you in case you find trouble. I already told the men that any guards they didn't kill they should send on a mad camel hunt to Al Mahbes."

The two young men laughed heartily at some private joke.

"Gentlemen?" Adam reminded them.

Jibril nodded. "Are you ready?"

"Tell me again why we're going into the heart of the palace?"

"To find the escape route my mother used."

"Why don't we just follow your friends?"

"Muhammed is right. Neither of us is in any shape for fighting."

Adam sighed. "And you know where your mother's escape tunnel is?"

Jibril grimaced. "I believe I can find it." Adam stared and the younger man shrugged. "I'm pretty sure I can find it."

"What happens if you can't?" he asked icily.

"We fight our way out?"

Christ.

"I am jesting, Stepfather. If we can't find it, we will go and find the others and take our chances. Does that suit you?"

Adam rotated his arm and winced at the stinging pain. He could fight, but he didn't know how well. He might be wounded, but Mia's son was weak and thin from weeks of harsh treatment and in no condition to fight.

"Very well."

Jibril thrust a wad of cloth toward him. "Put on this guard uniform."

Adam took a gray robe that had a large bloody hole in the front. He cocked an eyebrow at Jibril, who shrugged.

Once he was dressed with a turban wrapped around his head, Muhammed took the lead, followed by Jibril, and Adam at the rear.

They found the guard quarters empty of everyone other than a few frightened women and children.

"Won't they tell?" Adam whispered.

Jibril shrugged. "Maybe, maybe not. What other choice do we have? Besides, all they are seeing are three men in guard uniforms."

Once they'd left the series of connected barracks, Muhammed led them down a long dark hall without doors. There would be nowhere to hide if anyone came from the other direction.

"Just how far is this bloody bolt-hole of yours?" Adam hissed.

"Not far. We just need to get into the main storage room in the kitchens. Those connect to the women's side of the palace."

"The harem?" Adam tried to keep his voice expressionless but he must have missed the mark.

Jibril snorted. "You English are all the same."

"What the devil is that supposed to mean?"

"You think we are savages because of our way of life, our customs."

Adam opened his mouth to deny it and then paused. He *did* think it savage to have more than one spouse. At least at the same time. Even so, he had been perfectly willing to entertain the notion of keeping a mistress when he married Mia. Did that make him a hypocrite? Not that keeping a mistress was anything like keeping dozens — even hundreds — of women for one man's pleasure. Before he could come up with an answer Muhammed turned around.

"There is a small hole from which to watch. They are bringing through barrels right now. We will wait." He turned back to the spy hole.

The moments ticked past and the only thing he could hear was the sound of men breathing.

"You left my mother on a ship with Bouchard?"

"What the devil are you getting at, boy?"

"The man is a dog. What do you suppose I mean?"

Muhammed said something in Arabic and Jibril translated. "There is no time to argue. We are going in."

Adam bit back several choice responses. "We can continue this conversation later, Stepson."

"I look forward to it, Stepfather."

Adam gritted his teeth. Now was not the time to take the younger man to task for his insolent chiding. There would be plenty of time on board Bouchard's ship — or, God forbid — once the boy was living under his damned roof.

The door opened onto an even narrower corridor and they turned to the left. At the end was a scarred wooden door.

"This. is it," Jibril whispered over his shoulder, opening the door. The room beyond was dark and smelled of exotic spices that made Adam's mouth water. The only light streamed through the cracks beneath another door at the far end of the pantry. A door that must connect to the kitchen beyond.

Muhammed stopped and turned. "You

must take it from here, my brother."

Jibril nodded and pushed past him. "Follow me, Stepfather."

CHAPTER THIRTY-TWO

Mia thought her heart would explode. Who would have believed rowing such a small boat would be so agonizing? Even more agonizing was the sound of men gaining on her.

She was almost jolted off the seat when the boat struck the sandy bottom. She staggered over the side, dropping into knee-deep water and clutching her bag in one hand and shoes in the other.

Bouchard's boat was no more than twenty feet away.

Mia found a burst of energy and ran through the shallow water, not bothering to secure the boat. She made it almost to the stunted trees clustered at the cliff base before an arm snaked around her waist and pulled her to a sudden stop.

"What the hell do you think you are you doing?" Bouchard gasped, releasing her just long enough to grab her wrist and then doubling over and struggling to catch his breath.

Mia tried to shake off his hand but it was like trying to shake off her own arm.

"I'm saving my husband and son."

"You're going to get yourself killed."

"I *know* the palace — better than any of them. I escaped from the harem, the most highly guarded part of the palace. If my son and husband are trapped inside, I am their best hope for freedom."

Bouchard's yellow-gold eyes were narrow and hostile. He didn't say a word before pulling her back toward the shore, where two of his men had caught the other rowboat and secured it.

Mia fished the knife from her bag and poked him in the hand, hard enough to draw blood.

"Merde!" he swore, snatching his hand away. He gave her a reproachful glare, shaking his hand. "Do you think you will stop me by threatening me with that knife?"

Mia positioned the knife over her stomach. "No, but I think you will not want to face either my husband or Ramsay if I am dead."

His jaw dropped in a way that would have made her laugh if she were not so desperate.

"You wouldn't."

He was right, she wouldn't. But she couldn't let him see that.

"How badly do you want to find out?" she asked grimly.

His eyes stared blankly through her, as though he were imagining the aftermath of her act. As if he were imagining explaining things to Ramsay. His face hardened and his full lips thinned until they were as narrow as the blade of her knife.

"I hope to God you know what you are doing."

So do I, she thought.

The journey from the beach to the palace had been almost suspiciously easy. Nowhere along the way did they encounter any sign of fighting or men — either Assad's or any others.

Bouchard said they must be all engaged in the fight by the wharf. Even from this far away, the sound of cannon fire had been audible. It was clear the French captain was more than a little agitated by the sound and nervous for his mentor, Ramsay.

They were at the back garden wall. Mia was glad Bouchard had listened to her and sent Beauville back to the ship, leaving Jacques with their boat. The passageway was narrow and they would need to move fast once they were inside. If Jibril was trapped in the palace, she was pretty sure of where he would go.

Mia turned to Bouchard. "The stone we are looking for has five ankhs carved in it. We must push the stone to release the latch." They were outside the part of the palace where each of the sultan's wives had her private quarters.

Mia pressed hard on a series of stones and a gritty noise interrupted her thoughts.

"I think this might be it." The sound of stone grinding on stone disturbed the near darkness until she saw the gap.

"Don't open it all the way. We will need to get past the door."

He grunted and pushed. The gap grew wider.

"I will go first." She pushed past him before he could argue.

The passage was tight and dusty and her nose twitched. Behind her, Bouchard sneezed.

"Shhhhh!"

"Do you think I sneeze for my own pleasure?" he hissed.

Mia ignored him, feeling the wall on her right for the small indent that heralded the opening.

"It's here," she whispered, keeping her

507

fingers on the almost unnoticeable dimple in the stone wall. She heard the sound of a hand rubbing over stone and then felt Bouchard's large warm hand.

"Now what?"

"Push."

She pushed with him and for a moment it seemed the heavy slab of stone would not budge. When it finally did, it made the low-pitched grinding noise she remembered.

Bouchard swore and stopped. "We'll wake the whole damn palace!"

"No, we won't. This entrance is near the shared pools. Nobody will be here so late at night. Push."

The door swung easier once it passed over the flagstone and met the polished floor. Mia peeked around the edge into the open courtyard. Only one dim lantern glowed in the walled bathing area and there wasn't a soul around.

Bouchard followed her into the big open space and glanced around.

"So this is what a harem looks like, eh? I imagined it differently."

Mia had a pretty good idea of what he'd imagined.

"We need to keep going. If Jibril is in the palace, he will have gone to our old quarters. There are several excellent hiding places built into the walls."

"What if there is somebody *else* living in your old quarters?" he whispered.

Before Mia could answer, the sound of footsteps came from the direction of the kitchens.

Mia grabbed Bouchard and dragged him into the nearest hallway. She peered around the corner and saw silent shapes flickering into the courtyard. It wasn't until they reached the large bathing pool, which was directly below the light, that Mia saw who it was.

"Jibril!"

Bouchard reached out to cover her mouth but she was already bounding across the courtyard. Jibril grunted when she slammed into his arms.

"Mother?" He sounded stunned. And maybe a little angry. Mia kissed his cheek and his nose.

"Where is your stepfather?" she asked before Jibril could begin scolding her.

A voice she knew and loved came from somewhere behind her son.

"I'm right where I'm supposed to be, darling. What about you?"

"Perhaps we could have this family reunion later?" Bouchard whispered angrily.

"Bouchard?" It was Adam again, and he

sounded furious. "What the bloody damned blasted hell could you be thinking to bring her here?"

Bouchard made a sound of pure, frustrated rage.

"It's not his fault, Adam, I —"

"Not now, Mia," Adam said, coming to stand beside her. "I'll discuss this with you and Bouchard later. Right now we need to get the hell out of here."

Adam was entertaining himself with thoughts of how he would thrash Bouchard when they passed out of the narrow corridor into the open air.

"This is where I leave you, brother," Muhammed said.

"Where will you go?" Jibril's voice sounded hollow, as if he were tempted to go with him.

"We have made a most excellent deal with the Turks. They need an armed escort when they go to collect their next pay caravan." The man's smile faded. "Go with them, Jibril. There is no future here. Assad is master, but of a dying empire."

Jibril nodded with obvious reluctance and said something in Arabic before turning away.

"Thank you for everything you've done

for my son," Mia added, dropping a kiss on Muhammed's cheek.

He bowed low, and disappeared into the night.

"Come," Bouchard said, pushing past them. "I told Beauville only to wait until an hour before dusk."

"What?" Mia demanded, hurrying after him. "Why? You didn't tell me that."

"Did you think I would risk the lives of *all* my men for you?" The Frenchman threw the words over his shoulder. Adam could see the man was frazzled and more than a little worried. He could only imagine what Mia had been up to in his absence.

"How far to the ship?" Adam asked, hoping to head off a squabble between the mercurial captain and his dictatorial wife.

"It is less than an hour and most of it easy walking," Mia assured him, sliding her hand around his waist. He winced and she jerked her hand away. "What is wrong? Are you hurt?"

"It's nothing."

"But what happened? Should we stop so I can —"

"Darling."

"All right, Adam." She paused. "Is not Jibril wonderful?"

Adam snorted. "He is certainly something else."

Mia frowned.

"Mia, we can't stop to talk, my love," he urged. "We can speak of everything when we are safe on the ship. I'd hate to go through all this and find no ship at the end of it," he muttered almost to himself.

For a while, everyone walked in silence, the only sounds those of heavy breathing as they stumbled over rocks and shrubs in the near darkness.

Ahead of her Bouchard and Jibril were engaged in a conversation that was becoming increasingly heated.

"I'm assuming my stepfather *paid* you to do a job — a simple job?" Jibril's voice sliced through the darkness.

"Shhhh!" Mia hissed.

Bouchard muttered something Mia couldn't quite hear. She prayed they would make it to the boat before the arrogant young men began to fight in earnest.

Each step became a struggle and she realized they must be close to the shore because the path had become increasingly sandy. Ahead, the men's voices rose again. She had to take three steps to every one of theirs in order to catch up.

"Jibril!" she whispered.

"What do you mean you don't know?" Jibril demanded, as if he hadn't heard her.

"Just what I said, princeling. They will *leave.*"

"And what other plans did you have to get my mother out of here?"

"I had *no* plans!" Bouchard snapped, his voice rising.

"And you think that —"

"Jibril!" Mia caught her son's arm. "You are shouting, both of you."

"You should have heard what your precious mother threatened to do," Bouchard said, not bothering to lower his voice.

"Oh, and what —"

The sound of a lot of swords being drawn from scabbards cut off whatever else he was going to say.

CHAPTER THIRTY-THREE

Adam grabbed Mia around the waist, pushing her behind him, and away from the sound of men and weapons.

"Hello, Jibril — what a surprise to find you here," a voice called out in passable French.

"Assad!" Mia gasped behind him, struggling in Adam's grip to get around him.

Adam grimaced at the pain in his back as he held tightly to her arm.

"Stay behind me, Mia," he ordered in a low voice.

"I brought the ransom, just as you said. There is no need for more fighting, Assad," Mia called out.

Adam cursed.

A light flared and a torch came to life, revealing the soldiers who had been hiding in a small clearing off to one side of the path. The man holding the torch was smiling grimly. A dozen armed men stood around him and more torches appeared, until it was almost as bright as day.

"Hello, Stepmother, how nice to see you again," the smiling man said in French, his coffee brown eyes flickering between the members of their small group. "And who have you brought with you? From the description, I can only imagine this is the famous whoremonger Martín Bouchard." He gave a mocking bow. "What an honor to have you in my kingdom, Bouchard. Have you come to return my ship to me?"

The privateer said something in Arabic that made the other man's eyes narrow.

"That was uncalled for, but not entirely unexpected," Assad replied in French.

Adam could only assume Assad was avoiding Arabic because he didn't want his own men to understand what was being said. Was that because many of them might be loyal to Jibril?

"I will deal with you shortly, Captain," Assad said before turning to Adam. "You, I don't know."

"I'm the man whose wife you threatened." Adam shoved Mia back toward Jibril and took a step toward the wall of armed men. "It's easy to make threats when you've a dozen soldiers at your back," he said, using the most insulting tone he could find.

"Won't you fight me like a man? Or do you need your men to fight your battles for you?"

Assad's face shifted and his confident veneer slipped, revealing hatred mixed with fear.

"An English duel, eh? Like English gentlemen." He gave a shout of laughter. "I have read of such things. Unfortunately, I do not have time to play such games. I believe I will let my men kill all of you, beginning with you. Your whore of a wife can watch." He said something in Arabic and the men began to move toward them.

"I say!" a deep voice called from the darkness beyond Assad's men. "Did somebody forget to invite me to the party?"

The sound of weapons being drawn was like the crashing of waves on the beach. Ramsay stepped into the light, dozens of heads bobbing in the dimness behind him.

Adam had never been so happy to see anyone in his life.

"I thought you would be long gone by now, Exley," the grinning giant said, his gaze flickering over Assad's frozen, gaping men like a fox eyeing a henhouse.

"Well, one thing led to another, and . . ." Adam shrugged.

Ramsay noticed Mia and sighed. "Yes, I

see the way it is." He looked from Assad to Adam. "I also see I've interrupted something here." He strode toward one of Assad's men and removed the sword from his hand before shouting something in Arabic. The guards all clambered backward and Ramsay tossed the sword to Assad. "Best get on with it," he said to the younger man, nodding his head toward where Adam stood.

Assad gave Ramsay a look of pure loathing as he pulled off his heavy wool djellaba and tossed it to one of his men. He hefted the scimitar in his hand, took a few steps toward Adam, and dropped into a crouch.

Adam unsheathed his sword and Assad lunged forward before it was even free. The younger man was fast, but his eyes gave him away before he'd even moved. Adam stepped neatly to the side and Assad charged past, stumbling into a pair of large sandstone boulders that fringed the side of the path. He turned and roared, sounding so much like an angry bull Adam almost laughed.

This time, Assad approached more slowly, swinging his arm in broad, killing sweeps, like a man harvesting wheat. Adam's rapier would be very little defense against such a heavy, lethal weapon, and the younger, bulkier, man had at least three stone on him. He was ponderous and predictable — but he was also uninjured.

Adam backed away, feeling the ground behind him carefully so as not to be surprised by rocks or debris. Assad maintained the inexorable scythe-like motion. Adam's only chance was to get in under Assad's arm, but to do that he'd need to come within reach of the scimitar. His foot encountered something hard and he realized he must be close to the rock face that bordered the north edge of the path.

An evil-sounding chuckle bubbled from his opponent. "Nowhere else for you to run."

Adam smiled. "Now you just need to come and get me." His taunt was like a match to a fuse and the other man bolted toward him.

If Assad had continued his sweeping motions, Adam wouldn't have had a chance, but instead he drew his wicked blade up as if to cleave him in two. Adam dropped to his haunches and flicked the tip of his rapier up to the junction of the other man's thighs.

Assad made a high chirping noise and froze with the scimitar raised high over his head as the point of Adam's sword sliced through the fabric of his loose trousers.

"Drop it or I'll make you a eunuch."

The scimitar clattered to the rocks that lined the path.

Adam rose slowly, his back screaming with the effort and the stitches stinging like fiery nettles. But not for a second did he take his sword from the other man's crotch. He glanced to where he'd last seen Mia. She was still there, with Bouchard and Jibril shielding her.

Off to the other side he heard the sound of clapping.

"Bravo!" Ramsay called, chuckling while he applauded. "Very neatly — and quickly — done."

Adam ignored him. "Do you have the money, Bouchard?" he called out.

The Frenchman lifted the heavy canvas bag.

"Throw the bag toward his men," Adam ordered, not taking his eyes from the furious man at the point of his sword. The bag landed with a soft *thud*. "There is twenty-five thousand pounds of my money in that bag, Assad. That, plus your *jewels*" — he exerted a little pressure with his rapier and Assad winced — "should be enough to pay for the damage we caused here today. Are we agreed?"

Assad stared at him with hate-filled eyes. "You promise to take the two of them" —

Assad gestured with a toss of his head toward Mia and Jibril — "and never come back?"

Adam smiled. "That is my plan."

"Then we have a deal."

"Take her back to the ship," he told Bouchard. "I'll be along in a moment."

"No, Adam! I won't —" Her words were cut off, most likely by her son's hand over her mouth, and Adam watched from the corner of his eye as they disappeared down the path, through the stunted trees.

"One last thing, Assad. My wife told me this, and I believe her. You have been led astray by lies. It wasn't Mia who informed on your mother and demanded her death of the sultan. Take the money and forget about Mia and her son. Don't be foolish and dog our heels all the way back to England." Adam lowered his sword from the other man's genitals and took a step back.

Assad's eyes flashed in the light from the torch and his face twisted into a sneer. "If you are not gone by the time I've finished counting the money in the bag, I will kill you. I don't care how many men Ramsay has behind him." He turned his back before he'd even finished speaking.

Mia fought Jibril with all the strength in her

body, but her son held her almost immobile as Bouchard pushed the small boat off the sand and into the water.

"Why can't we wait for Adam?" she demanded. "What are they doing back there?"

"I don't know what my stepfather is doing, Mother. But I agree with his decision to get you out of there. Now, stop squirming or you will hurt yourself," Jibril said, his voice hoarse with the effort of holding her. Mia could feel his chest heaving and her heart hurt at how skinny he'd become. But his arms were like unbreakable chains around her.

"I will never forgive you if you put me in that boat and leave him, Jibril. Never!"

"We are not leaving him. Besides, he would kill me if I didn't follow his orders, and believe it or not, Mother, I'm far more afraid of him than you." Jibril lifted her easily but Mia extended her feet and kicked, ensuring that putting her into the small craft would take considerably more effort.

"Dammit! Will you help me, Bouchard?" Jibril cursed as one of Mia's flailing feet caught him somewhere soft.

"What? Can't you handle one small woman?" Bouchard taunted, wading through knee-deep water as he spoke and plucking her bodily from her son. His hand came close enough to Mia's mouth for her to catch it between her teeth.

The Frenchman screamed.

A cool voice cut through Bouchard's cursing. "I do wish you'd stop manhandling my wife, Bouchard."

CHAPTER THIRTY-FOUR

Neither Ramsay nor Bouchard wanted to linger in the waters around Oran and they set a grueling pace to reach the British-controlled city of Gibraltar.

The atmosphere on the *Scythe* was tense and alert and not conducive to rest. It was clear there would be no relaxing until they were well out of Assad's reach.

Adam was more than a little concerned for Mia, who looked ready to collapse from the stress and strain of the prior weeks.

"Won't you get some sleep, darling?" They'd just eaten a hot meal and were alone in Bouchard's cabin. Jibril had shuffled off to the small medical bay, where he'd collapsed in his cot and commenced to snore. Adam had finally convinced Mia to rest on the bed and he was sitting beside her.

She looked up, dark smudges beneath her green eyes. "I can't, Adam. I'm afraid I'll wake up and it will all have been a dream.

You and Jibril will still be gone, and I'll be trapped in this cabin."

He brushed a stray curl off her brow. "I'm sorry I had to leave you."

She gave him a tremulous smile. "I'm so sorry for the horrid things I said."

"Shhhh, darling."

She grabbed his hand and brought it to her mouth. "No, it was dreadful. *I* was dreadful."

"Yes, you were."

She gave a tired gurgle of laughter and closed her eyes.

"Adam?" she said a few minutes later, just when he'd hoped she'd fallen asleep.

"Mmm?"

"Why did you let Assad live?"

He'd wondered the same thing himself. Should he have killed the man? It would certainly have opened the way to leaving Jibril in charge. But in charge of what? Adam could not believe it would make either Mia or Jibril happy if the boy had stayed in Oran.

"For two reasons," he finally said. "One, whatever he has done, Assad is Jibril's brother."

Mia squeezed his hand and smiled. "What is the other reason?"

He shrugged. "If I killed him, Jibril would

have stayed. You would have hated that."

"Oh, Adam." Tears leaked from the corners of her eyes.

He leaned down to kiss them away. "Why are you crying now, you little termagant?"

"You are so good to me."

"I know," he agreed.

She chuckled. "How can I ever repay you for all you've done for me and my son?"

"He is our son now, Mia."

Her smile illuminated the cabin and her grip tightened on his hands. "Just like your daughters are also mine. I grieve for what you've suffered, Adam, but I am here to help shoulder your worries now."

Adam took a deep breath, trying to ease the tightening that occurred in his chest whenever this subject arose. "I am glad you know my secret, Mia. Now you understand why the girls can never marry."

"No, Adam, I don't understand."

He blinked. "I beg your pardon?"

"This is not a decision you can make for them, Adam. It is one they must make for themselves."

"But —"

"It is a terrible burden they will bear, Adam. But they are not without hope."

Her words angered, rather than soothed. "How can you say that?"

"Veronica was ill but her brother was not; neither was her mother. The girls are not Veronica, Adam. They have a chance, a good one, of escaping the taint and living normal lives."

Adam gaped at her, stunned speechless by the simple sense of her words.

What a fool he'd been! All these years he'd thought only of what might be — never what might *not* be. Adam had always believed sequestering his daughters at Exham had been the best decision for them — for their happiness. Now he realized it had only been the safest choice. Mia was correct: they had a chance and he must let them take it, no matter how much he hated and feared the thought of them being exposed to public ridicule and cruelty.

"They must be told, Adam. Catherine is old enough now to be given such a responsibility, and soon Eva will be, too. This is not your secret, Adam, it is theirs. Each of them must decide how they will manage the information and whom they will share it with. Just as you have with me."

Her words sent fear arrowing through him. "But what will happen if they fall in love? If they wish to marry? If people know of their secret, they will be ostracized and rejected. You and I know that is a terrible existence, Mia."

"That is true, Adam, but we both know it is an easier burden to bear when you have somebody you love to share it."

Adam stared down at her, overwhelmed by the truth of her words and astounded by his amazing good fortune. "Is it possible you are correct, my love?"

"Of course I am."

He chuckled. "What did I ever do to deserve you, Mia?"

She smiled, and this time there was a distinctly wicked gleam in her eyes. "I don't know. But I think you should make an effort to show some gratitude." Her small hand slid from beneath the covers into his lap.

Adam threw back his head and laughed. "Is that all you ever think about?"

She smiled and began unbuttoning his breeches. "Yes."

He lowered his mouth over hers. "Me too."

EPILOGUE

London, five years later

Jibril tossed the reins to the waiting groom and swung down from his horse. The front door to Exley House flew open and Eva came galloping down the stairs.

"Gabriel! You're finally home!"

He laughed. "Are you trying to knock me down, Evil?" He gave his half sister a rough hug to go along with the nickname.

"Don't call me that." The muffled reply came from his now ruined cravat but lacked any real heat. He held her at arm's length.

"What's wrong?" he asked, his chest tensing when he saw her tear-stained face.

"Mama and Papa are insisting on this dreadful ball."

He sighed. "Come along. Let's talk about this somewhere other than the front steps. You know how your father is." Jibril — or Gabriel as he was now accustomed to being called — liked his stepfather well enough,

528

but knew what a stickler he could be.

"Make them let me go home, Gabe," she wailed as they entered the foyer.

"Hello, Hill." Gabriel handed the butler his hat and gloves.

"Welcome home, Master Gabriel."

"Is my mother here?"

"I believe she is in the nursery. Will you be staying long, sir?"

Gabriel grinned. "That depends on His Lordship."

"Will Drake be joining you?"

"Yes, he's coming with the rest of my things later today."

Gabriel's dour valet had not been pleased by his employer's latest stunt, which had resulted in him being sent down. But Gabriel was relieved. At almost twenty-three, he was older than all of his friends at Oxford except Viscount Byer, who at twenty-six would probably never leave school.

He was tired of books, papers, and studies. Now that he'd been banished from school for good, there was no way his mother could insist he return. He could only hope neither Lord Exley nor his grandfather would exert any influence to get the powers that be at Oxford to relent.

"Tell my mother I'll be in the blue sitting room," he told Hill. "Come on, Brat." He grabbed Eva's arm and pulled her up the stairs.

Gabriel pushed her toward a chair and dropped down across from her. "Where's Mel?"

"She's gone to visit Lady Moira. I was invited but didn't want to go." Eva twisted a thick strand of glossy black hair around her finger, the action mute testimony to how the rest of her hair had come loose. She looked like she'd been beaten by high winds.

Gabriel sighed. "Now tell me, why don't you want a Season?"

Her pink dress had a tear at the hem and one of her shoes was stained with something that looked like horseshit, and probably was. Gabriel's younger stepsister always made his heart ache. Even though they shared no blood, he felt very close to her. Growing up in Babba Hassan's palace had meant he was raised with dozens of half siblings. Thanks to Assad, those half brothers and sisters were now lost to him.

It had been a relief to come to England and find three sisters waiting for him. Catherine had been a little older than he and too eager for her Season to have much time for a younger, foreign stepbrother. Melissa had been little more than a child, but Eva had been only two years younger and had behaved more like a boy than a girl. She'd also thought her new stepbrother was magnificent. Of course, she was unaware of how badly he'd botched everything in Oran, almost getting his mother and stepfather killed, while managing to lose control of his father's empire in the process. No, Eva thought he was wonderful.

"I hate it." Her quiet words yanked him from his reverie.

"Hate what?"

"All of it. The clothes, the dancing, the pointless chatter."

He smiled. "You won't once the young men start flocking."

She scowled.

"What?"

"They won't come flocking." She held out her arms. "Look at me, Gabe."

He frowned. "So you're a bit . . ."

"Not a bit, a lot. I'm a bloody mess."

Gabe wasn't shocked by her swearing. In fact, he'd been the one to teach her how to swear in two other languages.

"Just a small mess," he joked.

But she didn't smile. Instead she dropped her head against the chair back.

"Mama is so kind, but there is only so much she can do. She can help me choose attractive garments, but she can't *wear* my

531

clothes for me." She looked at him. "And then there is Father."

"He probably can't wear your clothes, either."

She threw a cushion at him, clearly annoyed by his attempts to cheer her out of her unhappy state. "I am a constant source of disappointment to him, and it will only get worse if I am forced to make a spectacle of myself in front of the entire *ton.*"

Gabriel grimaced. He knew what she meant. The Marquess of Exley was one of the most inscrutable, coldest, and haughtiest men he'd ever met. Oh, he liked the man well enough, but he feared him almost as much as he respected him.

Although Exley was shorter and slighter than Gabriel, he possessed an air of menace that caused even men like Baron Ramsay to treat him with careful respect. The Marquess of Exley was a very, very dangerous man. Obviously, he would not skewer his daughter with his rapier, but he *did* have a rapier-like wit that was almost as lethal. And his eyes. Gabe shuddered; the man's eyes cut worse than his short sword.

Not only that, but he was also inhumanly well turned out. He even made Gabriel feel like a mess, and Gabriel put a lot of time and effort into his daily toilet. Unlike Eva.

While Gabriel had never heard the marquess say anything to his messy, clumsy daughter, he knew he could do as much damage with an eyebrow as most men could do with a whip.

"What do you want to do, Eva? You've already managed to weasel out of having a Season longer than any other young lady I know."

She shrugged, miserably twisting her hands in her skirt, wrinkling the delicate muslin beyond repair. Gabriel opened his mouth and then closed it. What good would telling her to stop be?

The door to the sitting room opened and his mother swept in like a small, colorful storm.

"Jibril, darling, you're home early!" She was the only one to still call him by his real name.

He stood and received her enthusiastic embrace and then submitted to her raptor-like exam.

"You are thin," she declared. She turned to Eva. "Don't you think he is thin?"

"He appears to have lost a few pounds," his wretched sister agreed, smirking at him when his mother commenced clucking. "Maybe even a stone."

Gabriel looked over his tiny mother's head

and mouthed, *You shall pay for that.* He extricated himself from his mother's grasp. "I'm fine, Mama. You look blooming, as usual."

His mother dropped a small hand to her rounded stomach and smiled smugly, the fine lines around her eyes the only proof that she was closer to forty than thirty.

"I am well."

Gabriel knew well enough not to ask if this was going to be her final child. The last time he'd opened his mouth she'd volunteered the unwanted information that she would continue her favorite activity with her husband as long as she was able. She'd dropped this piece of conversational artillery at the breakfast table.

The marquess had only lowered the paper a fraction of an inch, his eyes narrowing in their sinister fashion, as if Gabriel might be stupid enough to pursue such a repulsive topic.

"And how are Anna and Beatrix and George?" he inquired.

"Your little sisters are doing well. They were both delighted to hear you were coming home."

Gabriel raised his eyebrows. The twins were not yet five and the heir was hardly two; just how excited could they be?

His mother ignored the skeptical look and dropped down on the chaise longue, propping her head on her hand and smiling from Eva to him.

"Did I interrupt something interesting?"

"No," Eva said hastily.

Lady Exley lowered her lashes and Gabriel shook his head. Eva had lived with his mother almost five years and still didn't know how to handle her insatiably curious nature.

"We were speaking of Eva's Season." He ignored Eva's scandalized look.

"That's odd," Eva said, her eyes narrowing with grim satisfaction. "I thought we were talking about the fact you'd just been sent down from school."

His mother gasped. "Oh, Jibril! What have you done now?"

Gabriel dropped his head back and closed his eyes. He would kill Eva.

"Still," his mother said in a musing tone, "I suppose this is as good a time as any for you to have returned home."

Gabriel opened his eyes and lowered his head. "What do you mean, Mother?"

She smiled, her green eyes sparkling. "Why, you will be the perfect person to escort Eva about this Season."

Gabriel let out an agonized groan but the

sound was drowned out by the delighted laughter of his evil mother and stepsister.

AUTHOR'S NOTE

To write historical fiction is to walk a fine line: How much history? How much fiction? I have stayed true to major historical events and mores but I have allowed my imagination some freedom in minor matters.

There was no Beauleaux's fencing salon in London, at least not as far as I know. However, there were similar salons and gentlemen were still engaging in swordplay during the early nineteenth century as a form of exercise and a sign of status.

I have my characters drinking champagne, which may or may not have been available to them, depending on what source of information one uses. Would they have drunk, eaten, or played cards in a theater box? There is ample evidence that all kinds of "non-theater" activity went on in private boxes.

Barbary corsairs really did kidnap hundreds of thousands of people — some estimates run well over a million — between the sixteenth and early nineteenth centuries. The United States Navy was, in large part, formed to combat the threat of the Barbary pirates. While some of these pirates were lone operators, many corsairs were in league with the coastal rulers of North Africa, some of whom were corsairs themselves. These men relied on both the steady supply of slaves and the ransom money they received for captives — like the author Cervantes, who was held for five years before his family could buy his freedom.

My sultan is fictional, as is his palace outside of Oran and the caves that run beneath the city. The Topkapı Palace in Istanbul, Turkey, is the inspiration for Sultan Babba Hassan's seraglio/palace.

ABOUT THE AUTHOR

Minerva Spencer was born in Saskatoon, Saskatchewan. She has lived in Canada, the US, Europe, Africa, and Mexico. After receiving her M.A. in Latin American History from The University of Houston she taught American History for five years before going to law school. She was a prosecutor and labor lawyer before purchasing a bed and breakfast in Taos, NM, where she lives with her husband and dozens of rescue animals.

The employees of Thorndike Press hope you have enjoyed this Large Print book. All our Thorndike, Wheeler, and Kennebec Large Print titles are designed for easy reading, and all our books are made to last. Other Thorndike Press Large Print books are available at your library, through selected bookstores, or directly from us.

For information about titles, please call:
(800) 223-1244

or visit our website at:
gale.com/thorndike

To share your comments, please write:
Publisher
Thorndike Press
10 Water St., Suite 310
Waterville, ME 04901